PLATEA S·PETRI

S·Catcrina

Cesis

CARAVAGGIO

CARAVAGGIO

a novel by

ROBERT PAYNE

LITTLE, BROWN AND COMPANY · BOSTON · TORONTO

*Published simultaneously in Canada
by Little, Brown & Company (Canada) Limited*

PRINTED IN THE UNITED STATES OF AMERICA

CARAVAGGIO

A Letter to the Cardinal

To the most illustrious Lord Francesco Maria del Monte, most holy Servant of God and of the Holy Father and of the Grand Duke of Tuscany, Cardinal and Alchemist, formerly my bedfellow, from the poor painter Michelangelo Merisi da Caravaggio, now in hiding in Naples from the cutthroats of the Grand Master of the Order of the Knights of Malta and with a warrant for murder hanging over his head, Greetings:

WHEN you asked me, Illustrissimo, to tell you the story of my life so that in future ages people would know what manner of man I was, I said: "Where should I begin?" and you answered: "Begin as the Bible begins, at the beginning," and then I said: "I was blind in the womb where my beginnings are," and I remember you laughed, throwing back your head until your silver beard rippled like streams of frost, and you said: "Begin with your first paintings, if it pleases you," and then I said: "Why should I celebrate my teachers, for they smell of the dungpit?" and you answered: "Begin wherever you please, my son, so long as you begin, and speak only the truth in Christ's name."

So I have spoken the truth, knowing that I have hurt myself

[3]

more frequently than I have hurt others, and that nothing is gained in this world or the next by dissimulation. But even now, though many years have passed since you gave me the order to write my life, I do not know where my beginnings are. Shall I begin in the poor town of Caravaggio whence I sprung, and paint you a picture of its dying walls and the lake where my father took me on Sundays for no reason that I recall except that he hated the town and wanted to get away from it; or should I tell you how with grappling irons we fished my father's body out of the lake, blue and bloated as it was, on a day when the church bells were ringing for the feast of St. Catherine; or should I tell you of that day, shortly after my father's death, when I saw an apple tree in the flaming sun and a voice spoke out of the tree, saying: "Take and eat, for I am the bread and the wine." Where does a man begin — in the womb or in the light?

True, I was only thirteen when I heard an apple tree speaking, and a boy of thirteen cannot be hanged for blasphemy, no more than he can be hanged for stealing apples. I remember that day when the apple tree shone in a sunset of sheets of emerald and sulphur yellow flames, and for the first time I saw the colors of the universe pouring out of the heavens; and I took the colors of the world and hugged them to my breast. They say Prometheus stole fire from heaven, but I would be happier if he stole only the colors of fire, leaving God to warm himself by the original flames. I know that sulphur catches fire and lime burns: from the columns built by the ancient Romans comes the lime in which we are buried and melted away. Our ending is certain, but our beginnings are more remote and insubstantial, and who shall speak of their certainty? Did I spring into the world out of a flaming lake or from an emerald sky? And if I wander backwards in time, shall I find myself again, a dark stranger coming toward me along the road to Caravaggio, where I was born?

I believe, Illustrissimo, you intended to lift a weight from my shoulders when, speaking gently, robed in scarlet silk, wearing a blinding crucifix encrusted with rubies, you ordered me to write about myself, yet the truth is that the burden crushes me under its weight, and wherever I turn I see myself as a stranger. I see my hand, the canvas and the paint; I see my models, the room where I live, the bed where I lie down at night, and these I know; but beyond these there is more darkness than light. God knows, I have painted myself often enough to know what shape I have in the mirror, but shall I trust the face I see in the mirror? I, too, would like to know who walks through my paintings.

This morning, here in Naples, talking with Fra Bartolomeo, who helps me to live because I am hiding in his house, and who acts as my occasional model and otherwise assists to my comforts, I heard myself saying: "Shall my hand ever know what it is painting?" "Surely your hand knows," Fra Bartolomeo answered, "for how else shall the paint reach the canvas?" I thought: "This is brilliantly spoken, but the closed hand conceals and the open hand reveals too much, and God knows which of the two speaks the truth." "And besides," Fra Bartolomeo went on, "the hand is the servant of the mind, and the mind is the servant of God, and there is no doubt at all that your hand is divinely appointed by God for His own purposes."

I said brutally: "With that same hand I have murdered," and he answered: "So you have, my son, and God has chastised you so that you live in poverty and fear for your life, but nevertheless God has manifested Himself in your hand, for how otherwise could you have painted so many divine paintings? So be calm, and know that God is in you. Continue to serve Him, and all will be well."

When I am painting, Fra Bartolomeo sometimes hovers over me with a bemused expression. He does not so much look at the painting as at my hand, at the tip of the brush, at the palette. Sometimes, when I have accomplished a more than usually daring design or when I have suddenly brought a face to life by quickly painting in the eyes, there comes from him a scarcely audible whistling sound, almost a cry of astonishment, and I confess this pleases me. He is an old man, very bent, with wisps of lank white hair reaching to his shoulders, his face so wrinkled that sometimes his smile vanishes among the wrinkles. He has appointed himself my guardian and protector, and watches over me with a devotion which troubles me. "God needs you," he says. "You must live a long life, Michelangelo."

Sometimes I wonder whether God intended me to live at all, but more often I wonder whether there are many hours left to me. I dare not appear any longer in the streets except at night, and then only when I have taken all precautions. There is a price on my head; the agents of the Grand Master of the Order of the Knights of Malta are after me; they have found one hiding place after another, and in the end they will find this one. They are not blind, and they know what they are looking for. They have said: "You cannot escape — even if you hide under the skirts of the Pope in Rome, we shall seek you out." They found me in Syracuse and Messina, and no doubt they will find me in Naples. Meanwhile for a little while longer the Church protects me, as it has done ever since the blessed day when I entered your service: but neither the Church nor God himself can protect me from determined men. A few more days or weeks, and it will be all over.

So I tell myself when I am alone in Fra Bartolomeo's house with only the old servant Maddalena to attend me. It is strange that she should be called Maddalena, for there was once another Maddalena who was made by God to be painted and who died before I had even begun to paint her as she deserved to be painted, but this old servant is so crabbed and gnarled with age that she has barely the strength to lift a pan to the fire, and Fra Bartolomeo keeps her for the same reason that he keeps stray cats. I, who was accustomed to living among youths, am given over to the old. It is like a foretaste of death.

"Read the Psalms and the New Testament, pray and worship God," Fra Bartolomeo tells me. "Surely in one lifetime there is no need for anything else."

"And my paintings?" I ask him.

"Your paintings are prayers," he answers, and then he smiles and glances at the pictures hanging on the wall — the four I painted in the last two months, and the two others which I am painting now.

But for me it is not so simple to believe that my paintings are prayers. Even now, after all these years, I do not know what my paintings are. I seem to myself to be a man wandering through a vanished house searching for a stairway. The ghosts come quick and fast — the ghosts of Maddalena, of the boy Giovanni Battista degli Angeli, and of Ranuccio Tomassoni — and when I question them they make no reply. Who are they? Did I ever know them? I see them as clearly as I see my own hands, but they always appear to me as they appeared in my paintings, and I, too, have vanished into my paintings, so that I see myself only as I painted myself, a dark face hanging in space while Salome clutches at my hair. Am I anything else but the face which appears in my paintings?

God knows, Illustrissimo, I have tried to find myself, searching my heart for some clue or other, but at the end of the journey I am aware only of my darkness and insignificance. Therefore God made me dark, with dark eyebrows, dark eyes, deep-sunken, and dark hair. My beard is black and bristling, and my complexion, too, is dark. If I met myself in a dark alleyway, I would flee in terror. I am a man obsessed with darkness, death, and despair.

[7]

There is scarcely a moment of the day when I am not aware that I have the appearance of a man who has been cursed, and I am never surprised when people make the sign against the evil eye in my presence. My face haunts me in its ugliness. Sometimes, far from commiserating with myself, I wonder that so many have shown affection for me and that so many commissions have passed through my hands.

My hands, too, baffle me: they are not the hands of a painter. The fingers are covered with fine black hairs, but are otherwise not to be distinguished from the hands of a laborer. On my left hand there is a great purple welt where I burned myself when climbing down a rope from the prison of Sant' Angelo. There are scars on all the knuckles. The hollows of my palms are cracked and leathery, discolored by a thousand pigments, so that each hand, when I lay it open before me, resembles a five-fingered rainbow of livid colors. To know a painter one should study his hands, not his face, but these hands of mine have always been strangers to me.

Yet with my swarthy skin and livid hands, coal-black eyes and bristling beard, I am not so far beyond my own knowledge that I do not recognize something God-given in me. I am not wholly the slave of my fears and desires. I am not only this mask of ugliness. I have never needed to sign a painting: the world knows me, or at least that small part of the world which is concerned with great art. The name of Michelangelo Merisi da Caravaggio will live on through the ages, and men will forget the black-visaged, tormented man while honoring his name. And there is some comfort in the knowledge that even if they kill me, I shall not wholly perish. It is small comfort, but it is better than none.

Only a moment ago, when Maddalena entered the room to bring me some syrup against the cold, and found me writing, she threw up her poor hands in horror.

"What are you doing?" she exclaimed, as though she had found me performing some strange and terrible act. "Holy Mother, what has come over you?"

I pointed to the paper and the ink.

"I am writing," I said. "What is there strange about writing?" She shook her head sadly.

"You should be painting," she said. "The clerks can write, but who can paint like you? God has given you this gift, and therefore you should be painting every moment of the day."

"No, Maddalena," I said, "not every moment of the day, for an artist must rest from his labors. Besides, my lord Cardinal del Monte once ordered me to write an account of my life, and I have delayed too long. I must know who I am before my time comes."

She laughed at this, showing her toothless gums, and throwing up her gnarled and wrinkled hands.

"You want to know who you are?" she cackled. "Holy Mother, how old are you that you have to know who you are? Next you will be asking yourself where you come from and where you are going. I'll have to tell that to Fra Bartolomeo when he comes home!"

She went on cackling for a while, wiping her hands on her skirts.

"It's all mystery," I said. "Mystery and darkness. A man can be toppled over by the mystery of being a man and by the darkness all round him. One comes out of a human grave and enters an earthly one, and if you ask yourself why, or how, or whence, there's no answer to be found anywhere!"

"Then you don't believe in the words of the blessed Lord?" she said sharply.

"Yes, I believe," I said, "but believing is not enough."

Poor Maddalena could make nothing of this. She had her arms akimbo by this time, and she was staring at me as though she had

[9]

never set eyes on me before. On her leathery face there passed expressions of revulsion, horror, disbelief, and finally acquiescence. She smiled timidly, threw up her hands again, crossed herself, and said: "The syrup will do you good. You won't talk such nonsense when you've drunk it." Then she was gone, closing the door softly behind her.

I heard her tripping down the stairs, to the clacking sound of her rosaries, and I confess I was relieved by her absence. I could make nothing of her. There was not one little corner of her mind where I could penetrate. I could not imagine her young. God knows what cordials and herbs she had poured into the syrup, or what cadaverous mysteries were enclosed in her evil-smelling skirts.

Still, I was grateful to her, and sometimes when I was painting her — for she was the best of models — I found myself envying her serenity, her composure, her faith which was as unchanging as the Pole star. She had been born, she told me, on a farm at Sorrento, being the seventh of fourteen children, of whom five died in infancy. At the age of fifteen she had married a ship's chandler, who shortly after the marriage deserted her. There were no children of this marriage, and she never married again. She had spent her life as a servant of many priests, quietly and dutifully performing whatever rites are demanded of servants, rarely complaining. It never occurred to her that she was leading a life of intolerable emptiness and despair. On the contrary, she believed she was leading a life of great richness. Once she said: "To place flowers on the altar — there is no greater blessing than this!"

Perhaps she is right. Perhaps, after all, even the greatest of artists can do no more than place flowers on the altar.

I confess I was in a better frame of mind when I had drunk the syrup. Food can allay fear, and a full belly is sometimes a powerful antidote to nightmares. I heard the wind thudding on the wooden windows, and the sounds of the creaking house no longer frightened me.

The truth is, of course, that I was once more in my element. Those hours of darkness have always comforted me. Night, and a gutting candle, are my familiars, as anyone should know who has looked at my paintings. I revel in the darkest dark and the brightest bright, and there is nothing brighter than a face seen in candlelight. My paintings, such as they are, have been composed at night or in dark cellars by the light of oil lamps: in this way I have hoped to achieve a depth, a luminous intensity, which were otherwise lacking. I have denuded the human figure of all that is adventitious, abrupt and commonplace. I have restored to men the richness of their colors.

Out of the darkness the creatures of my imagination come winging more brilliantly lit than they are ever seen in the diffused calm of daylight. I threw the light where I pleased: on face or shoulder or knee, and in this way I established my mastery over the model. They say a master must first draw an outline, but I never made a charcoal drawing on canvas. Instead I painted what I saw, or what the light saw. I was myself the enclosing darkness and the candle flame.

I have told myself often enough that this is the only truth worth knowing about me, and all the rest is insignificant. I am not like other painters: I have carved out my own road, and God knows whether others will have the courage to follow me along these dangerous paths. I wanted to see the world as it is, not the cloudy world devised by theologians, nor the sweet-tempered world of our habitual painters who will depict a murder as decorously as they depict lovers in each other's arms. When I paint St. Sebastian, he writhes under the arrows; and when I paint an Entombment of Christ, I paint a dead body, livid and mottled. I am not ashamed of the world as it is, or of suffering, or of blood. Men die horribly. Must I, as a painter, make them die sweetly?

It is because men are surrounded with depth upon depth of darkness that they glow most brilliantly. So I have made the darkness my accomplice. I belong to the world of bats and the creeping things that come out of the night, and by the same token I am an initiate of Vespers and the midnight Mass, not of Matins. I am happiest when evening falls; and if God should ask me to choose between the sun and the moon, I would assuredly ask for the sun to be put out so long as the moon should be permitted to reign. Then I remember that the moon is sacred to the Virgin, and all my perplexities begin.

You said once, Illustrissimo, that in all your life you had never seen a man who walked so surefootedly in the dark. There even came a time when it pleased you that I should live in your cellar; and you said you slept well at night in the knowledge that someone at least was awake in the Palazzo Madama. So you said, and I believed you. But that surefootedness was sometimes feigned. I did not always know whether I would step on dry land or into the abyss. Those who make the darkness their accomplice must travel lightly, with only a little baggage.

I snatch these hours from painting not to explain or defend myself, for I am beyond explaining or defending, but because you said that even the least of men conceal within themselves great riches if we could but find the key to open the treasure chest. My treasure is my painting; these writings are no more than an inventory; and you will know me better if you read this with my paintings in mind.

Soon Fra Bartolomeo will climb up the stairs to bid me goodnight. We shall kneel beside the altar, which is this table, and I shall repeat after him the prayers against the evil that comes out of the night and the other prayers demanding pardon and succor. Then we shall talk for a while, and he will tell me if he has seen any strangers pausing outside this house on a narrow street. Then I shall paint into the night by the light of a candle. I have only Maddalena and the priest for models now, but sometimes a working woman leaves her baby with Maddalena. In this way I paint Joseph, St. Anne, the shepherds and the kings, Mary mother of Salome, and the ancients of Israel as they gaze upon the Child; and if I am asked to paint a head of John the Baptist I have only to look in a mirror. There was a time when I could find more models in the streets of Rome than I could paint in a lifetime. I filled my studio with the most handsome young men and the most beautiful women of Rome. They were mine to do my bidding. I stripped off their clothes, and painted them naked, or dressed them in whatever finery I pleased; and it was always my greatest pleasure to paint the glow of young flesh. Now I paint my own ravaged face, livid as death.

You said once, Illustrissimo: "All that you have done, all you will ever do, must be for the glory of God." And I answered: "Is there no glory in men?" And then you smiled and said: "The glory of men is a portion of the glory of God."

So I have always painted for the glory of men, knowing that in their own way they reflect the face of God, and even the least of us possess immortal souls. God in His mercy protects even murderers, and no doubt he will protect me for a little while longer. I have no fear of death, for I have seen too many men die. What I fear above everything else is that I should die before my work is finished, before I have painted all the paintings which God entrusted to my care. If God grants me three or four more years of life, then I shall leave a treasure which will make men proud of my birthplace; for only now am I beginning to learn how to put a brush to the canvas.

Once when I was complaining of the difficulty of painting, you said: "Have patience, my son," and I said: "I have patience enough for all eternity, but patience will not help me now. What I need is God's grace." And you said: "That will come, if you have patience." But now my patience is wearing thin. Only when I am painting am I aware that God is looking over my shoulder.

I am not one of those who put their heads meekly on the block. I shall die fighting. A sword lies on my bed, there is a dagger beneath my pillow, and a rapier always within reach. There is a coil of rope beside the window which will enable me to descend quickly into the garden. I am not altogether unprotected, for all my life I have been accustomed to danger and I know what has to be done when death comes running, to put him off the scent. I shall give a good account of myself.

So I wait, on these long nights, for the sound of the assassins' footsteps on the stairs.

The Frosts of Winter

YESTERDAY, my lord, there was a sudden scare, like the ringing of a fire bell. Suddenly this small house, so calm and quiet in its backwater, seemed to be lifted up in a frenzy of excitement and fear, and I remember that while the fear gripped us all the objects in the house seemed to change color. There were yellows and blues I have never seen before; a pink cupboard turned white; the cross which hangs above my bed, a gift of Maddalena, once silver, seemed to turn the color of coral. And when I spoke of these changing colors to Maddalena and Fra Bartolomeo, they both remarked that they had seen these changing colors and had not dared to remark on them. If you are ever afraid, Illustrissimo, look carefully at colors.

It began in the morning, perhaps an hour after Fra Bartolomeo went out on his daily rounds, for every morning he absents himself from the house, visits the hospitals, and conducts his business, since he spends only a few hours every day in the oratory. He left the house with one of my paintings, a head of John the Baptist on a golden salver, hoping to sell it. The painting was rolled up, and Maddalena had wrapped it in some black cloth. It was not a large painting, and as he carried it under his arm, it was not likely to attract any attention. Nor was Fra Bartolomeo himself likely to attract attention, for as he says himself, he can wander like a shadow through the streets of Naples without anyone seeing him, because he is small and walks quickly and keeps to the shade. About an hour after he had gone there was a crash of thunder and some of the tiles from our old house were ripped loose, falling into the garden and smashing into a hundred pieces. Maddalena was terrified out of her wits and came running upstairs. She thought the assassins had come for me, but I told her that nothing special had happened, for it is not unusual to hear thunder in Naples even when the sky is perfectly clear, and no doubt the thunder had dislodged the tiles. I tried to comfort her, but she was shivering with fear.

"My poor Maddalena," I said, "you mustn't tremble so. There is always going to be some thunder from time to time."

"No, it is a sign," she said. "God speaks in signs. I swear there was a flash of lightning and it struck the roof above your bed. It was a thunderbolt, Michelangelo, and as sure as I am alive, God was warning you!"

"Warning me against what?"

"Against living here. You are not safe any longer, Michelangelo. That I know, and God help me for saying so."

Then for the first time I cursed the day I met this old woman with her broken gums and her spider's web of wrinkles on her face.

She was shivering and trembling and locking and unlocking her hands, and it was then, while I was wondering whether she would serve as the model of an old woman looking at the Beheading of John the Baptist, that I saw the colors change. Even the color of the air seemed to change. Fear had taken possession of the house.

I could not explain what was happening, and even now I cannot be certain there is any explanation. I remember looking at my paintbrush: it seemed to be bent. There was a canvas on the table on which I had sketched out a head of Christ crowned with thorns, and it seemed to me that a hot flame was burning underneath the painting, which was visibly shriveling before my eyes and the paint was cracking and forming little black blisters, and everything in the room was changing direction and color. I suppose a man on a sinking ship has much the same feeling. I threw my arms round Maddalena and we clung together as though the Day of Judgment had come.

About half an hour later we heard Fra Bartolomeo coming up the road, and he too was unrecognizable. His face was white and drawn, the color of mutton fat, and he was limping with excitement and breathlessness, as he motioned me to follow him into the small cubbyhole which serves as his study. He closed the door behind him and said: "Well, Michelangelo, while you were painting quietly, I have been through the fires of Hell —"

There were little white beads of sweat on his forehead, and he let them wander down his cheeks without brushing them away. He went to a cupboard and poured some wine. His hands were shaking violently, and some of the wine splashed on his ragged beard.

"I think I saw the devil incarnate walking the streets of Naples," he said at last, and went on to describe how he was walking near the port when a man wearing a Spanish cape darted out of the shadows and accosted him, forcing him closer to the wall, taking him by the shoulders and whispering urgently, not in Neapolitan but in some other dialect. He wore one of those Spanish capes which conceal the face, and Fra Bartolomeo had no clear image of his features. "Whether he was the devil or not I do not know, but he smelled like the devil," Fra Bartolomeo said. "He laid his hand on the painting which was rolled up under my arm, and he would have taken it if I had not called out to some passersby. Soon there was a crowd gathered around us, and all the time this man, this stranger, was trying to get this painting from me. I remember the church bells struck ten o'clock while he was still grappling with me."

Fra Bartolomeo went on to recount how he had appealed to the people around him to protect an old priest who had done no harm to anyone, and in the usual fashion the crowd divided into two separate parts, some taking the part of the priest, some of the man in the Spanish cape, and soon they were all shouting and bickering, and it was so large a crowd that it must have seemed that the business of the port would come to a standstill. What was surprising was that the painting was still rolled up in its black cloth; no one had seen it, no one had the faintest idea what was in it.

"As you know, Michelangelo, there is nothing more merciless than a crowd. They all become judges, advocates, prosecutors, torturers. Everyone must take a part and show himself to be knowledgeable. This is street justice, and a man may suffer penalties from his street judges as merciless as those he suffers in a court of law. Somehow the man in the Spanish cape had convinced them I had stolen something from him, and there was nothing to be done but to show them that I was carrying a perfectly harmless religious painting. So I showed it to them, hoping that would be the end of the matter, for there is nothing unusual in a priest carrying a painting. Then someone shouted: "Who painted it?" and before I could think up some suitable lie, another voice shouted: "It was painted by Michelangelo da Caravaggio — only he could have painted it!" That may be testimony to your fame, my son, but I felt such fear in my bones that I wished the earth would open out under me!

"All the time the man in the Spanish cape was watching me, hovering very close to me. I could not see his face, but I felt he was mocking me. Once he snatched the painting out of my hands, and only God gave me strength to snatch it back again. Then someone from the crowd asked me how I came into possession of the painting, and what I was going to do with it, and whether it was my intention to hang it in a church, and what church, and whether I knew the painter, and how did it come about that I was walking along the street with a rolled-up painting, and I had to answer all these questions although I was nearly dumb with terror. My knees were shaking, and I knew the man in the Spanish cape was watching me closely, observing every movement I made, and waiting for the moment when he could snatch the painting and run off with it. The crowd saved your painting, for they hemmed us in very close, and I had to show it to everyone, holding it up above my head.

"Oh, there's no doubt they liked your painting, Michelangelo, and they would have gone on gazing at it all morning and all afternoon. They admired the beauty of John the Baptist's face and the little lake of blood in which it swims. They like blood. They like death, for they know it so well. They commented on the way you painted the lank hair and the pinched nostrils and the glint of the teeth, and I thought I would have to spend the rest of my life telling lies about the painter. I told them it was not by Michelangelo da Caravaggio, but by one of his followers. God will forgive me for my lies.

"At last a carriage passed, scattering the crowd, and I was able to slip away, followed of course by the man in the Spanish cape. I shook him off at last, and then went to the shop of Ambrogio di Sanctis, who paid me for the painting, not without a good deal of bargaining. He says he has a client in Padua who may buy it from him, but I have a strange feeling that it will eventually fall into the hands of the man in the Spanish cape.

"You must forgive me for trembling, Michelangelo, but when this man came out of nowhere and seized your painting, and when

I heard your name uttered in the street, I knew more fear than I have known in my life. I never saw his face — could not describe him to you if I tried — but I am sure he meant evil. There are people who walk the earth only to commit evil, and sometimes, as you know, the devil himself walks through the streets of Naples to commit mischief.

"Of course it may have been one of the bravos hired by the Knights of Malta, and you must decide for yourself whether Naples is safe for you. You are welcome to my house, and may stay here as long as you please. Neither I nor Maddalena have any fear for what may happen to us, for we are too old to fear assassins. So go in peace, Michelangelo, and make your own decisions."

I kissed Fra Bartolomeo on the cheek and thanked him for his abundant care of my fortunes and his goodness. It was on the tip of my tongue to tell him that I would leave his house that same night, for a man has no right to put another in danger. I had used up his fund of generosity and placed him in mortal fear. As I went up the steep stairs to my small room under the eaves I had to fight back the desire to slip out of the house in broad daylight, and I think I knew the man in the Spanish cape would be waiting for me.

I spent the rest of the day quietly, and it was not until evening that I remembered Your Highness's commission to write the story of my life. My nerves were unstrung, and I was in no mood for pondering over the worthlessness of my existence. I painted feverishly, gazed out through the cracks of the window, and listened to Fra Bartolomeo as he moved restlessly downstairs. It occurred to me that I was painting better because I was in deadly fear. You will never know, and never guess, the excitement which comes to a painter when he knows that every brushstroke may be his last.

So I spent the day, and now with the small guttering candle on my midnight table, I shall try to summon up the images of my past.

First there was my father, a heavy portly man who moved slowly and heavily through life as though pursued by lingering nightmares. He was black-jowled like me, and had a spiky beard. His eyebrows were thick and straight, and gave him a brooding look, which was reinforced by the stern lines of his face. Yet there must have been some gentleness in him, for I remember together with his perpetual sternness the sweetness of his smile. He had a special fondness for apples and I remember him biting into an apple with great glee, and once I came upon him in the orchard gathering the windfalls and shouting like a boy at all that plenty, with tears of joy streaming from his eyes.

At some period of his life he must have learned mathematics, for he trained himself to be an architect and served the Conte di Caravaggio as the overseer of his estates. He built the granaries, put up fences, and was continually renovating the Conte's villa on the edge of the town, which was scarcely more than a large village set in the lowlands below Bergamo. My father taught us to respect the Conte and to bow deeply when he passed. He was a heavy man, lame and paunchy, with a firebrand for a nose, a huge dangling mustache, and a piping voice. He always carried a sword at his side, and in his youth he had been a famous swordsman. They said his lameness came from a wound suffered in the wars, and though we laughed at him behind his back, we felt a kind of reverence for him, as though he belonged to ancient history. There were white marble statues in the garden of his villa, and we would sometimes climb over the walls and wander among the statues, believing them to be the most beautiful objects in the world.

In those days few people ever came to Caravaggio, and the sight of a carriage coming along the dusty road always filled us with amazement. Bergamo, although only a few miles away, might have been as far away as Rome; and there were few people in the town who had ever been to Milan. We rarely saw soldiers, and indeed throughout its history Caravaggio, although lying in the plains, seems to have escaped the wars, perhaps because it was not worth capturing. There was only one street. There was the church of San Lorenzo with a painting above the altar showing the saint roasting on the gridiron, smiling and raising his hand in a kind of greeting. The saint seemed to be lying on a crimson bed, and if anyone was particularly fortunate the children of the town would say he was as happy as San Lorenzo.

There were not many happy people in the town, for the parish priest had put the fear of God into us. Father Fabiano was a little man, hunchbacked, red-haired and red-bearded, who held the Conte in contempt, accusing him of loose living and committing all the deadly sins including luxury and avarice, not forgetting the sins of the flesh. But in fact the Conte was more sinned against than sinning; there was no anger in him, no envy. He was a jaunty man with no love for the Church or the little humpbacked priest, and in his own way he would attempt to make us merry. He liked to give musical parties and was himself something of a musician, and so it sometimes happened that I would accompany my father to the villa on winter evenings to listen to the Conte's musical compositions played by his unmarried daughters, who were as ugly and charming as he was. At such musical evenings the Conte always made a little speech saying that of course Father Fabiano would disapprove of these sinful affairs calculated to incite us to ferocious lusts and devious acts of incontinence, and no doubt God would strike us all dead for our levity. But God did not strike us. We lived through the Conte's music, applauded his ugly daughters, and solaced our souls with melody. It was in that villa that I first came to love music above all the arts, so that even today

I regard composers and musicians as people set apart, of infinitely greater virtue than the rest. I do not believe the angels paint, but I know they sing.

I have spoken of my father, the Conte, and our misshapen red-bearded priest, but there was another person in the village who haunted our dreams. This was Paolina, the deaf-and-dumb girl with the withered leg, who lived with her father and some sheep dogs in a small shack on the cow pasture near the Great Pond. They were a strange pair, and we never knew whether they were happy like San Lorenzo or miserable like the damned, although I suspect that they knew more damnation than happiness. We saw little of the father. From time to time Paolina would come into the town on some errand or other, and we would watch her from a distance as she half ran, half walked, in her torn shift, her black hair flowing wildly. Sometimes her hair covered her face, and she was always making strange quick gestures with her hands. She had a reputation for stealing, and though she was lame she could move at a rapid pace, with a curious sideways motion, hopping with her one good leg while the withered one served to steady her. She had violet eyes and a face as white as paper.

There was a time when no one paid much attention to Paolina, but as she grew older and her body filled out she began to attract the attention of the boys, who would run after her and shout obscenities into her deaf ears, and they would even molest her, pulling at her clothes or her hair, terrifying her out of her wits, so that she would go running down the road with her mouth wide open, screaming silently. I remember the wide-open mouth, and the fear in her violet eyes, and the wild laughter of the boys as they galloped after her. The silent scream and the jerking of her poor body even now fills me with terror.

My father died when I was twelve. One day, while working at the villa, he fell from a scaffold. It was a short fall, no more than a few feet, but there was a bruise on his face which never healed. He went on working with his face swathed in bandages, but his character had changed. Normally stern, he became harsh and demanding, with an ugly temper, always roaring at the top of his voice. There was a devil in him. He bellowed after the women he saw in the streets, and they said he once followed poor Paolina in the streets and pulled up her shift. Once during Mass he suddenly shouted blasphemies, calling upon the devil to come out from under the priest's cassock and saying there were demons with fiery tongues licking the Sacred Host, and the dead were rising from their graves in millions. When he was quietened, my mother asked the priest to exorcise the devils in him, but the priest said sadly: "Have courage, for even God cannot help him now!" And these outbreaks, and many others that occurred later, terrified us, so that we began to believe that everyone in our family was tainted with the disease. People would look away from us or make the sign against the evil eye whenever we passed them in the street.

It was not only my father's character and behavior which changed. His appearance changed; he seemed to shrink visibly before our eyes. Suddenly he was old and wizened, a small gray man who walked with shuffling steps, his arms hanging limp at his side. Yet he retained his loud voice. On winter nights he would sit by the hearth, bellowing and cursing, and then falling into long and terrible silences. On the days when he shouted, we would put bread in our ears.

Once he tried to hang himself, but we cut him down just in time. A few days later he fell into the fire, but we rescued him so quickly that he suffered nothing worse than a burned hand. Strangely he was very docile when we bandaged the hand. On that day he talked kindly to us for the first time since he fell from the ladder, and we exchanged glances, telling ourselves that he was on the road to recovery, and there would be no more bellowing. A week later he vanished from the house; we searched everywhere, and then it occurred to us that he might have wandered to Bergamo, where he had a brother, a tavern keeper. Two days later we learned that he had drowned himself in Great Pond. His pockets were full of stones, but he was still clutching a crucifix. Father Fabiano was a merciful man, for he spread the story that my father had fallen accidentally into the lake while saying his prayers. Accordingly he was buried on consecrated ground, and the Conte di Caravaggio and all the other notables of the town attended the funeral.

For many weeks after my father's death I continued to live in the house with my mother, my brother and my two sisters, but when the spring came I took to absenting myself. Instead of going to school I wandered through the countryside and slept in the fields, stealing from the farmers. All through the summer I went wild. I would go into hiding when they came searching for me, and when I hid in the corn or in the shadows I could hear them shouting my name. Sometimes I wandered as far as Bergamo, climbing the steep path into the city, and there I felt safe. In summer it is not difficult to fend for oneself, but when the first frosts came I returned to Caravaggio.

My mother behaved with great nobility, for when I entered the house she said nothing at all, but seeing that I was half starved she set the table and all the time her lips were muttering prayers of gratitude.

She was a kindly woman with a long narrow face, deeply lined, and I have painted her often, though she died long ago. When I paint old women, I have sought out women like her. So in my paintings you will see her, but you will not see my father, for I cannot bring myself to paint him, or rather I see him in the portraits of myself, and even that glimpse of him terrifies me. In Hell,

I believe, my father rests in peace; and in a troubled Heaven my mother wanders like a ghost searching for the peace she will never attain.

She was a devout woman, and it was through her devotions that I became a painter. Though we were in no great poverty — my father had carefully husbanded his money, and the Conte gave my mother a small pension in memory of my father's services, and in addition the priest gave my mother a small stipend for attending to his vestments and the altar cloths — nevertheless my mother was hard put to it to keep us well fed and contented during the winter. When Christmas came, she said: "We must give a present to Father Fabiano, who has been so good to us," and she searched about for something that would please him, but found nothing. Now, my father being an architect, there were many paintbrushes, pots of paint and rolls of paper in our cupboards, and to amuse myself I painted a Madonna in watercolors. At the first stroke I felt a strange fever, and I remember my hand shook uncontrollably. Nevertheless I was able to paint a passable Madonna, not unlike the Madonnas on the church banners. She wore a blue gown, a high lace collar, earrings of the kind which we call "dragonflies," and a headdress such as our peasants wear on holy days, and if there was something coarse and powerful in her features, that was because I was thinking of Paolina when I painted her. It is a long time since I have seen this painting, but I remember it with affection. Even now, if it were placed before me, I would take pleasure in it, though it was painted by a child.

"You must take it at once to Father Fabiano," my mother said, and since my father also made frames for the Conte's collection of paintings, we had no trouble finding a suitable frame for it. We painted the frame with gold leaf, and that very day we went together to Father Fabiano's house. We had wrapped the painting in silk. As he drew the silk away, he whistled under his breath, smiled, made a reverence and sang out: "Oh dove of Christ, oh dove of Christ," over and over again, and I suppose he said these words because there were fat doves cooing under the eaves. Then he turned to my mother and said: "A gift from the grave — painted by your dear husband, may he rest in peace," and my mother shook her head sorrowfully and said: "By my son, Michelangelo."

I remember nothing more about our visit to Father Fabiano except that it was evening when we returned to our own house and far away across the silent snows a farmhouse was burning against an icy sky.

From that winter day I was like someone enthralled by paint, impatient to hold a brush in my hands, the day wasted unless I had paint around me. In a cobwebby cupboard I found some canvases that had once belonged to my father, and even some paints ground long ago, hardened with age, like lumps of rock, and we warmed them by the fire and melted them, wondering when my father had collected them, for they were so very old. When, for example, my father drew a design for a marble rotunda in the Conte's gardens, then he would paint small figures in the foreground, but neither my mother nor the Conte himself remembered him painting on canvas. It was all a mystery to us. Once the Conte said he thought he remembered a time long ago when my father had spoken of becoming a painter, but his work as architect and surveyor had taken so much of his time that he never succeeded in following his bent. And because the Conte was good to us and admired my paintings, I gave him some of my first paintings on canvas — a portrait of my sister, winter flowers in an earthenware pot, a man carrying a milk pail across a field. No doubt these paintings are still to be found in the Conte's villa.

In this way, Illustrissimo, I became a painter, and from that day to this I have never ceased painting. My painting began in winter, and that is why there is always something cold about them. In all my paintings you will see frost and ice. It may be no more than the white of a sleeve, or the white of an eyeball, but there is always the glint of winter in my paintings, for I am one of those who belong to the winter and the snow.

The Young Apprentices

ONE day, because this rage for painting came over me and there was no end to it, the Conte took pity on me and led me through the galleries of paintings in his villa. To see them we had to blow the dust away, for he had never paid much attention to his paintings. When I expressed a dislike for any of these paintings, he would make a reverence and say: "You are hard to please, your eminence. Does this one please you better?" I would say "yes" or "no" according to whether I truthfully thought it was painted by a man of value, a *valentuomo* who deserved the honor of holding a brush in his hands.

Altogether there were about fifty paintings in the Conte's galleries, and perhaps ten of them were of value. There were some ancient paintings set against a gold background made in Constantinople. They had come to him by way of Bergamo and Venice for the Venetians were lords of Bergamo, which bears to this day the Lion of St. Mark over its great gateway. There were other paintings by Milanese and Bergamesque artists of an earlier century, and these pleased me more. I remember especially a painting by Antonio Campi of a prison cell, the lanterns throwing their jumping flames against blood-stained walls, whole areas of the

painting covered with inky darkness, but in the foreground someone — perhaps John the Baptist — was lying with blood dripping
from his eyes and spewing from his mouth, and there was an executioner somewhere in the shadows. I remember I turned away,
and the Conte said: "Should you be afraid of paint, Michelangelo?" I answered: "It is not paint I am afraid of, but. blood."
Then he laughed and turned the painting to the wall, and we went
on through the galleries.

In those days I came to know the Conte as well as I knew anyone and better than I knew my brothers and sisters. He was related to the Sforzas of Milan, and like them he had the appearance
of a peasant. Only his eyes, pale blue, were mild and beautiful. He
had a flat head with strings of orange hair over his ears, a small
forehead, a large mouth, and heavy jowls. He was bowlegged, and
as I have said already he walked with a limp, and this gave him a
curious lurching motion, so that as we walked along the galleries
he was continually lurching from one side to the other. But it was
his huge red nose, shaped like the handle of a milk jug, and his
long dangling red mustaches which first attracted attention. Yet
when he smiled he gave an impression of benevolence such as I
have seen in no other man. From being physically repulsive, he
became suddenly beautiful; and indeed he was kind to everyone,
his purse open to every beggar.

One day, when the spring came, he called me to the villa and
said it was time I learned to take up painting seriously, and for that
reason he had made enquiries in Milan, whether among all the
painters there was one who could be entrusted to teach me without doing me any harm, for it is well known that there are painters
who drive their pupils to lunacy. God knows, he had not found
such a man! He had however found someone who could be of
some help to me in that he spoke the language of Bergamo, was

knowledgeable about the care and manufacture of paint, and was not altogether to be despised as a painter of trifles.

"Such a man may not please you, but at least he will be of service to you," the Conte said, screwing up his blue eyes and pretending to glare at me. "He will teach you how to paint in tempera and fresco, and you will learn something about chiaroscuro and the art of reproducing motion, for you must admit that your peasant walking across a field is very stiff and not so much walking as anchored into the earth —"

"Who is this man?" I asked. "Can he paint a man walking better than I?"

"He can paint an angel flying through the air, and with such skill that you really believe the winds are playing on the angel's garments. I have seen his angels, but I cannot speak so highly of his men and women. You must admit it is something to be able to paint an infuriated angel making his way across the spaces of the heavens —"

We were sitting in the Conte's library under a ceiling of crumbling cherubs and decomposing vine leaves. A fire was burning in the hearth and a servant was tending it, the same servant who, a few moments before, had poured the wine into our long-stemmed glasses. The Conte was wearing a fur-lined coat which reached to the ground, for it was a cold day and the wood was damp in the hearth. He was sighing as he absentmindedly turned the pages of a book. There was a long pause, and then he looked up from the page and said: "If you desire to go to Milan, you have only to say so. Everything has been arranged."

I remember every detail of that room, every flake of falling plaster, every book, and every movement of the servant as he bent over the fire, his blue buttocks tilted in the air like a blue peach, but most of all I remember the Conte sitting huddled in his chair, with the look of a man sitting in judgment over mysteries, pleased with himself because he had changed the whole course of my life.

"Then it is all settled," he said at last. "You have only to choose the day, and I'll send you to Milan with my factor. You will need clothes, of course. They dress well in Milan, but in the Spanish style —"

So he went on, telling me what to expect in Milan, where the Sforzas were no longer in power, and where, if one could believe him, the Spaniards had the Lombards by the throat, and not a day passed without riots and tumults. Meanwhile I reflected that all this had started with the gift of a painting to Father Fabiano, and God in His infinite mercy would direct my footsteps.

Two weeks later, in a new suit of clothes provided by the Conte, I was on my way to Milan with my brother Baptista and with Bartolomeo de Baschis, the Conte's factor, to sign the articles of apprenticeship with Simone Peterzano, the painter of angels and other confectionaries. The articles were drawn up with three lawyers in attendance and Bartolomeo's son Filippo added for full measure, and as though this were not enough they brought in a priest to correct the Latin and bless the enterprise with a holy candle. And so a whole afternoon and a part of an evening were spent in useless debate and much whispered consultation, and I learned (as I learned again later to my cost) that in the cities there is much whispering and no contract is ever drawn up without a priest, a candle, and three lawyers in attendance.

While they were debating the exact phrases to be used in the contract, I painted them in watercolors, for I had the habit of carrying colors with me at all times. I drew the thin lawyer with the goat beard leaning over the table while the two remaining lawyers gazed at him with the air of men pleading for their lives, and there was the priest in the center muttering prayers and holding the candle over his head. Simone Peterzano looked on like some ghostly stranger who has wandered into the room by accident and does not know what is happening: he knew little Latin, and from time to time in his brisk fashion he would ask for the meaning of a phrase, but the lawyers paid little enough attention to him. In a corner there was my brother, two years older than I, sunk in misery, and Bartolomeo and Filippo were in another corner raising their hands in despair. When I had completed the painting, I drew a noose hanging in midair, for it seemed to me that all these disputations had a deathly and menacing air. I gave the painting to my brother to give to the Conte on his return to Caravaggio. "You have a somber humor, my dear Michelangelo," the Conte wrote a few days later, "and I wish you would paint more playfully. Paint the gaieties of the flesh, not shadows. Paint the naked flesh, like the immortal Titian, or fruit, or flowers. If you should need anything, always remember I am at your service." I treasured the letter through all the years of my apprenticeship, and from much looking at it and unfolding it, it eventually disintegrated; and I was more sorry for the loss of this letter than for anything else that happened to me.

From time to time I would send presents of paintings to the Conte and he would reward me with small gifts: a silk cloak, or some cheeses, or some canvases when I was in need of them. Once every two or three months he would demand an accounting of my work, and I would write on the back of a painting how I had progressed. In this way I came to regard him as my real father, the author of my spiritual being. It seemed to me that he alone understood what I was attempting to do and had the power to influence my thoughts; and at night I would dream of him, the strange man with the mild eyes and the strings of reddish orange hair, the beaked nose and the paunch which sailed in front of him like a balloon. I tried to paint him from memory, but never succeeded in making him look anything but a buffoon. Yet to me he was the epitome of nobility and kindliness, and since any account of my life must also include my dreams, I speak of him here with an overwhelming gratitude. There was only one other man for whom I felt the same overwhelming affection.

Thus it came about that I, Michelangelo Merisi, son of the architect Firmo Merisi deceased, was apprenticed to the noble Simone Peterzano for the space of four years, and by these articles present I was to serve my new master, practicing the art of painting day and night according to his will, most faithfully carrying out all his orders, and never leaving his service except by the express will and intention of my lord and master, until I had learned the art of painting to his entire satisfaction, whereby I should become a member of the confraternity of excellent painters trained by him, handing down my knowledge to my successors in the high and noble manner appointed by the painters of the past, in full possession of many secret doctrines concerning the art of painting, and so on, and so on, to the very end of four parchment pages, each page being signed and sealed by the lawyers, and it was further agreed that Michelangelo Merisi, without a farthing to his name, should present twenty gold *scudi* for tuition and upkeep over four years to the aforesaid Simone Peterzano, and furthermore if the aforesaid Michelangelo should absent himself, then a further sum of forty *scudi* should be paid to the teacher of painting as balm for his soul, and all this *in nomine Domini* and *inviolabiter attendenda in hunc modum ut infra videlicet.*

So there was the beautiful white creamy parchment devoted to the four-year term of imprisonment of myself, the lamb, paid for by the Conte di Caravaggio, trussed, bound, quartered and roasted on the gridiron of Messer Simone Peterzano, a small wizened man with a bristling beard who could climb ladders like the youngest of his apprentices and paint well enough for a Milanese, which is to say that he could scarcely paint at all. He was a quick little man

with a pleasant smile and a way of rubbing his hands briskly together when he was excited. I learned nothing from him about
painting, but I learned a great deal about mixing colors. Others
knew him better than I, and while I had little enough respect for
him as a painter, I liked him as much as I liked anyone in Milan.
All through the years I have kept my copy of the agreement written by a lawyer's clerk in beautiful script. Among the signatures
you will find *Simone Peterzano pictor*, but you will not find my
signature, for no one asked me: the lamb does not sign to be admitted into the slaughterhouse. I am not one for signing things. I
never signed any of my paintings except once, and then the signature was written in my own blood.

In those days, at the beginning of my term of apprenticeship,
there were four apprentices, all of them older than I. Tomaso
Landolfino was a burly peasant from Brescia who had begun
painting late in his life, for he was sixteen or seventeen. He had
eyes of an uncommon brightness, and they said a priest, gazing
into his eyes, had discerned in them a gift for seeing bright colors,
and it is true that he painted in the colors of the rainbow and was
therefore especially skilled in painting clouds. I enjoyed Tomaso's
company because he was strong and smelled sweet and had a simple mind. Andrea Morosini came from Venice, and God knows
why a Venetian should learn painting at the hands of a Milanese!
He had a dark skin, dark eyes, dark mouth, dark temper, and his
arms were unusually long in proportion to his body, with the
result that he was always asked to paint the dark, unreachable corners of a church. Then there was Ambrosio Lotti, who was fourteen and looked like a cherub with his round pink face and innocent eyes: he taught us what little sin we came to know. Finally
there was Deodato di Dio, whose name meant clearly that he was a
foundling, though no one ever suffered less from being abandoned
on the steps of a cathedral since he was one of those who are born

with the gift of happiness. I never saw him frowning or giving way to ill temper; and I would watch him smiling in his sleep.

We were five apprentices, all living in the hayloft in the house of Simone Peterzano, over the stables. He fed us well, but not amply, so that our growing bodies went hungry at Lent and on Fridays, which he regarded as a day of fasting. But he was by nature kindly and protective, and we suffered little at his hands. We treated his two daughters with respect, but his fat wife Zustina liked to attend to the comforts of her "sons." Happily, Simone was a heavy sleeper.

All great cities smell of fear, and Milan was no exception. For me, when I first drove through the gates of the city, it was like being pounded on an anvil. The deafening noise of the streets, the clatter of carts on the cobblestones, the eternal sound of hammering, the air laden with stone dust, the cries of women and the curses of men, the windows crashing open and the soldiers marching — I thought I would never be able to bear these broken sounds. In Caravaggio the donkeys are provided with bells, and the music is sweet as they come along the village street. In Milan even at night the uproar is enough to make a man go mad.

Nevertheless the walls of the master's house helped to keep out the sound, and sometimes in the evening Deodato would play on his flute and Andrea would play on the viol, and I would sleep on the straw to the accompaniment of their music. We ate, slept, dreamed and worked together. On summer nights the confinement was too much for us and we would slip over the wall and join all the other roaring boys of Milan, but mostly we remained within the house or wherever our master ordered us to go, remembering that by the articles of our apprenticeship we were bound to obey his orders.

We had no real affection for him, for he was always brisk and assertive, rubbing his hands, telling us to get down to work, saying

things must be done in this way and no other way, and what liking
we had for him was mingled with a kind of distrust, for we were
all rebellious by nature and we knew he was one of those who are
doomed to be forgotten. He painted as briskly as he spoke. I have
seen him paint an angel in an hour and a *Descent of the Holy
Spirit* in a day. He would have his colors all ready, sketch out the
painting in charcoal, and then set to work with incredible speed.
But whether he was painting a Madonna or an angel or God the
Father, it was always the same painting.

Andrea would smile his dark smile and whisper in pretended
astonishment: "How beautifully you work, master, and how
quickly, too."

We would take up the chorus, while he smiled, rubbing his
hands and saying that if we applied ourselves and followed his
example we would do as well.

"Such energy, such grace, master," Andrea said, his eyes downcast, his face in shadow, his teeth gleaming. "God has surely
placed His hand upon your forehead, master."

"Perhaps He has," the poor painter Simone Peterzano replied in
confusion. "Yes, perhaps — sometimes I feel it on me!"

"There's no doubt about it," Andrea continued relentlessly.
"You can more than feel it, surely. Why, master, there's the shape
of God's hand written there, if you could see it. God has blessed
you!"

"Well, God's hand — yes, perhaps —"

"God's thumb mark, certainly. In the middle of your forehead,
master —"

"Yes, I do believe God has blessed me."

At such moments my poor master would smile in abject confusion, and with one hand he would touch his forehead and with the
other he would permit himself a little airy beckoning of the fingers, a salute, no doubt, to the divine hand still hovering above

him, and his face would crease into little smiles of self-approbation which, traveling outward from his eyes, settled finally on his lips; and when at last he walked away, Andrea, convulsed with laughter, would turn on tiptoes, imitating every gesture made by our master, and then twirling his hands over his own dark forehead in imitation of the hands of God, he would announce that he was the Lord's anointed, *magnificus pictor*, the divinely blessed Simone Peterzano.

But we did not often give way to horseplay. Indeed we were more like church mice, very quiet and reverent in his presence, though given to secret laughter when he was absent. And since Ambrosio was beautifully formed and sometimes served as a model for one of those angels the master was continually painting — he would be made to stand in an uncomfortable attitude, while yards of cloth were draped decorously around him — we would sometimes find ourselves watching him with bated breath, for strange things happened to the cloth around his loins.

Soon — and this happened especially at night when the day's work was done — I was painting the young apprentices in the hayloft. At first I painted their faces. Then I painted them as they lay in the straw. Later I painted them naked, for they were not averse to standing unclothed before me. Indeed, they would assume any posture I pleased for the sake of being painted by me, and the beautiful Ambrosio was especially fond of assuming the most ridiculous postures. I would make rapid watercolor sketches by the light of a candle stuck to the crossbeam, and the soft shimmering candlelight flowing over their young bodies was made golden by the glinting straw. It was a light which strongly appealed to me, for the colors of flesh glowed most vividly in candlelight. In tempera or watercolor one cannot paint the colors of human flesh with truth or depth; there are shadows which can only be rendered in oils. And so I took to painting oil paintings in the hayloft, for our master had encouraged us to paint in this way — paintings he would sell to the Spanish grandees — paintings of fruit and flowers, to give color to the darkness of their lives. From time to time, when there were no churches to be painted, he would make us paint flowers and baskets of fruit as industriously as we painted Madonnas and angels, or rather, he would stand over us while we worked, changing what we had done, getting into a rage, wiping out what we had painted with an oil-soaked rag, fuming and waving his arms, for he enjoyed our work well enough when we were painting the flowing gowns of angels, but he regarded the art of painting in oils as beyond our competence. Nevertheless, with patience, I was able to master the art.

In this way I painted them against the straw and the dark wooden walls of the hayloft, sometimes painting them when they were asleep, sprawling in their nakedness, lying on top of one another, assuming those strange and arbitrary attitudes which are assumed by drunkards and dreamers. In their sleep they always moved toward one another. What delighted me above all was their innocence, and the unexpectedness of their postures. Place four naked boys in a hayloft, and you will never guess the wonderfully absurd postures they will assume; and always their flesh was sprinkled with straw and golden in the light of the guttering candle.

Once, while I was painting them, the candle fell, there was a roaring flame, and the whole stable caught fire. It was summer, and there had been no rain for many weeks, the straw dry as tinder. I thought we would all be burned to cinders. The two piebald horses were neighing and whinnying in the stables below. Smoke and flame everywhere, and the smell of burning wood. I threw myself down into the courtyard, for I could no longer see what was happening in the hayloft. I thought they had been swallowed up in the sheets of flame, but somehow they had all scrambled out, and they were racing about in the yard rescuing the horses. Tomaso's hair was on fire. Andrea's face was bleeding. Deodato was limping badly, and Ambrosio was shouting insanely, his mouth wide open, his whole face contorted and unrecognizable. They pulled the horses away from the stable just in time, for a moment later the roof of the hayloft fell in. The flames were twice the height of the house, and to see the boys running wildly in the golden blaze was to see them more beautiful than ever. Rivers of sweat streamed over them and their faces glowed like hammered gold. There was a garden beyond the stable, and therefore no danger to other houses; and as the fire died down, we huddled together in the warm night, while the smoke rose and the embers glowed, and the windows of the nearby houses were white with candles. While we were bathing our wounds and Simone Peterzano, awakened by the uproar, was cursing us for letting his stable go up in flames, Ambrosio said: "Will you paint the conflagration, Michelangelo, and all of us in it?" I said I would. "And will you paint the manes of the horses on fire? Will you paint Andrea falling through the air? Will you paint us as we were?" It had all happened only a few moments before, but he spoke as though it had happened in another year.

I made some sketches the same night, and in a month I completed the painting. By that time we had rebuilt the stable. We had learned our lesson. Henceforth when anyone brought a candle to the hayloft he had to place a pail of water beneath it.

I thought I had never seen them looking more beautiful than during the fire in the hayloft, when they were naked and golden, but there were occasions when they dressed up in all their finery, wore brocades, damasks, and silks, put feathers in their hats, and paraded through the city in a painted cart drawn by the two piebald horses. This was our way of showing ourselves to the people. Standing in the cart, we would display our paintings and sell them, going from one marketplace to another; and in this way, selling eight or nine paintings, we might receive perhaps two *scudi* altogether: enough for a feast. At such times they resembled lords riding in triumph through a conquered city, and they were as beautiful in their finery as when they tumbled out of a burning hayloft.

From time to time Simone Peterzano would receive invitations to paint the small churches in the countryside. He grumbled about these commissions, for he rarely received more than a pittance, scarcely enough to pay for the paint and the food we consumed during the journey back and forth. At such times we all dressed up like lords. Andrea liked to wear a brass helmet and a flowing gown patterned with lilies. Ambrosio wore the black uniform of a Spanish grandee, and Deodato was robed in the vestments of a bishop, with a mitre as tall as a dunce's cap. For myself, I wore a hammered-gold cuirass and a robe of velvet, wonderfully spangled with gold and silver stars, and I carried a sword at my side. We were actors as well as painters; and our poor master would find himself wearing a scarlet cloak for fear of being drowned by our finery.

In this fashion we drove in the painted cart to whatever village desired our services. The church bells rang, feasts were set out before us, and every evening, when the work of painting was over, there would be dances with the village girls. Tomaso was a good fiddler, and Deodato had some skill on the trumpet. Sometimes, when we painted angels, we would wear the garments of angels, and there were village girls who truly believed we had come from heaven to entertain them.

In this way I spent the four years of my apprenticeship, learning, as I have said, nothing from Simone Peterzano except how to grind my paints. One day, exactly four years after I entered his service, I sought out my master, told him I was about to go to

Rome, and thanked him for teaching me so little, for in this way I was able to teach myself. He was sitting in his study, painting a small angel on olive wood, such an angel as he had painted a thousand times before and could easily have painted in his sleep.

"I was hoping you would stay with me," he said. "I thought of making you my assistant."

"To paint angels for a lifetime?"

"What's wrong with painting angels?" he said gravely, and he looked troubled. "They pay well for angels —"

"They pay better in Rome, and not for angels either," I replied. "I shall paint for the Pope and for great cardinals —"

"And starve to death, Michelangelo. Do you know how many painters there are in Rome? They tell me there are five thousand, and half of them are starving. If you stayed here, you could marry one of my daughters and inherit my shop when my time comes."

I laughed in his face, and on the next day I set out for Rome.

A Murder on the High Road

I CAME down the old Roman road from Milan with all my possessions bundled on the back of a black donkey. I had bought the donkey with the money received for a painting of red roses, and so I had twined roses on the donkey's mane. It was summer, and there was a heavy dust clogging the air, and I was haggard and unshaved after many days' wandering.

In those days I had no care in the world, for I could live on a few olives and some cheese from a friendly farmhouse. I had my palette and paints, and eight paintings rolled up in the saddlebags, and my best clothes, all carefully laundered, were rolled up with them, waiting for the day when I would present myself to some great official in Rome. At night I dreamed of the day when I would sit at table with the Pope, or at the very least with a cardinal. Heaven opened out before me. I saw myself riding on a white horse with a multitude of servants attending me. My life was a map with a single blue river threading through it, and I had only to follow the course of the river to reach any eminence I desired.

They said it was the hottest summer that ever was visited on Italy, and perhaps it was. I remember the heat of those days striking out of the earth and taking me by the throat, so that I was thankful for any shade. Sometimes I slept in the villages, but more often in the open fields. Before dawn I was ready to leave, and I would slip away with the first light. It pleased me to travel alone, without company.

One evening in a small village south of Genoa, when they brought me a tub of water, I found myself looking at my reflection and studying it earnestly. I thought I knew my appearance, but what I saw startled me. I had the shadow of a beard and a mustache, my hair lay matted over my forehead, and there was a strange wild look in my dark eyes. My eyebrows were shaggy, and my face was burned to the color of oak, and there were places where the skin was peeling and livid. I was so oppressed by the discovery of my own ugliness that I gazed at my reflection for a long time, absorbed by the strangeness printed indelibly on my features. It was not, I told myself, the face of anyone I cared to know.

For the first time I saw myself as a man, and was horrified. I ran my hand over my chin and felt an unexpected prickliness. The eyes were liquid black and very fine, and there was something to be said for the thick and heavy eyebrows, which arched nobly, but the nose was thick with heavy nostrils, the mouth would please no one but a prostitute, and the chin inspired no confidence. The hair was coarse and rough like tangled black wool left out in the sun. Some of these features, no doubt, would be concealed when the time came for me to grow a full beard, but what I saw in the water was the face of a common peasant with a trace of malignity and cruelty in his lips and a brooding violence in his eyes.

My father once told me we were descended from a certain Michele de Merisi who served in the army of the people against Frederick Barbarossa and was later ennobled, and he showed me a coat of arms with seven stars, a halberd and crossed swords on a golden shield. Thus I had always regarded myself as of noble descent, even if, as I sometimes suspected, it was the minor nobility, and the most minor of all. There was little enough nobility in the face that stared up at me from the water. I spat into the bucket and the face vanished.

That night I decided I would find a good room and give myself some reward for the discovery of my own ugliness. I rarely rode the black donkey, preferring to walk by its side; and I resolved that henceforth I would ride more often. I asked a farmer where I could find a room, and he pointed to the stables, laughing and saying that a man so verminous might find vermin to please him in the straw. He was a heavy built man with an orange beard and a face like a worm-eaten apple, and I said politely that I had marched all day and was in need of some comfort, but this only made him laugh all the louder. Then he made the sign against the evil eye and turned his back on me. I carried a dagger in my belt, and was in a mood to plunge it in the middle of his back, but thought better of it, being a stranger in the village.

It was growing dark when I found a villager who offered to provide me with a clean bed and an adequate supper. He was an old man with a kindly face who lived with his three sons and two daughters in a large house on the edge of the meadows. He had watery blue eyes and a tuft of beard, like a goat, but he smiled pleasantly. He told me his two oldest sons were priests and another daughter had entered a nunnery, and since so many of his children had entered the religious life, I felt he was to be trusted.

He led me to a small whitewashed room with a crucifix above the bed, explaining that it was the room used by his priestly sons on their rare visits to the village. A servant brought a bowl of milk. The bed smelled sweet, and the window looked out on a flower garden. I told myself this was exactly the kind of room I wanted, and no one could desire a more perfect lodging. With the black donkey tethered outside the window, and the saddlebags lying in a corner of the room, I was the master of all I surveyed; and indeed I was so pleased with the old man's kindness that I proposed to paint him and give him the painting as a keepsake.

When I had rested, I opened the saddlebags and examined what I had brought with me from Milan, for there had been no opportunity to perform this service before. There, in a small space, were all the possessions I owned on this earth. There were my paintings, carefully rolled up; pieces of brocade; a small ivory crucifix given to me by Messer Peterzano; mirrors; a bird's nest of rags used for cleaning my palette; my best clothes; a stiletto, an ax, a dagger and a rapier, and this was only a part of my armory, for I had carefully sewn five sharp-bladed knives inside my clothing in such a way that I could easily make use of them. I brought these weapons because it was common talk in Milan that a man traveling to Rome would have to defend his life at least three times. In addition, there were some jars of unguents to help my wounds to heal, if I should suffer them, and some strips of white cloth to be used as bandages. My money bags were silk ribbons provided with pouches which I wore round my waist next to my skin, and since I carried only twenty gold ecus, these being my total savings during the four years of my apprenticeship, there was little danger that they would be taken from me unawares.

I spread out my possessions on the bed, unrolled the paintings and studied them in candlelight, and while I was gazing at them there came to me the knowledge, the absolutely certain knowledge, that Rome would welcome me with open arms the moment I stepped through the Porta del Popolo, or at least a few hours or days after I had taken up my residence in Rome. I compared my paintings with those I had seen in churches and on the walls of private houses, and it seemed to me that I showed more skill and address in my paintings than any other living painter. I could paint flowers and fruit and boys with a skill that frightened me. One painting consisted only of a bunch of blue grapes on a plate, and yet each grape, living in its own nest of glowing shadow, possessed a perfection of roundness which astounded me. "If a man can paint a single grape perfectly," I told myself, "then there is no limit to his powers."

I was still ruminating over my paintings when the old man with the goatee and the watery blue eyes knocked on my door. I opened it, and he asked whether I would like to eat, for the whole family was sitting down to dinner. Then one by one he admired my paintings, praising them highly, saying that it was a great honor that I was staying in his poor farmhouse, and then he bowed and repeated his request that I dine with his family, saying it would be a great disappointment to his sons and daughters if they could not entertain me in a manner worthy of my honorable estate.

There was a long table in the dining room, which was white-washed from floor to ceiling, and there was a heavy wooden crucifix at the end of the room, testifying to the old farmer's devotion to his religion, and perhaps his devotion to his sons and his daughter who had entered the Church. The remaining sons were heavy-set, unusually handsome men, with dark eyes, fine straight noses and square chins; you could easily imagine them in breastplates and helmets, guarding the Castello in Milan. His daughters were plump and rosy cheeked, and they sat beside their husbands. There was the smell of warm bread and a rich soup, but what especially delighted me after seeing the faces of his sons was that the table was laden with flowers in profusion. Everything was done exactly after the fashion of the houses of the nobility. Grace was said; the servants attended us; there were clean plates. The old man told them I was a young painter from Milan making my way to Rome, where with God's blessing I would attract the attention of the papal court and great officers of state, and he had himself seen my paintings which he regarded with admiration, and therefore it was incumbent on all of them to make my stay pleasant. He plied me with wine and offered several toasts to me, and in turn I offered toasts to the old man and his family — that magnificent clear-eyed family, so well mannered, so kindly, and so decent that there could scarcely be another in Italy like it. So we spent the evening, and sometimes the old man spoke of the wars of his youth, recounting his battles and showing us his wounds, and with every wound we would drink another toast to him. Afterward there was some dancing in the courtyard, and I danced with all his daughters in turn.

At last when the old man took me to my room, all the time urging me to stay and paint his sons, I kissed his hand and told him that I regarded myself as his son, and he had given me more pleasure than I merited and I would obey his commands. He smiled and said: "We will talk about that in the morning, and meanwhile I wish you a good sleep in God's keeping."

I undressed and fell asleep the moment my body touched the sweet-smelling sheets.

When I awoke it was near dawn and the cocks were crowing. In my drowsy state of mind I meditated on my good fortune, and then I observed that someone was moving about in the dark corner of my room, near the saddlebags. I watched him carefully for a few moments, imagining at first that it was a servant who had forgotten something, or perhaps it was the farmer's son, one of the priests whose bedroom I occupied; and as the light grew brighter I saw it was one of those handsome sons who had entertained me that evening. He was searching through my saddlebags. I cursed myself for not locking the door, for not having a rapier under my pillow. It was a small room, and perhaps a quarter of the space was occupied by the bed. I slipped off the bed, naked as I was, and hurled myself at him. He shouted. I drove my fist into his throat, and he fell over, groaning. Then I heard footsteps, shouts, people running about the house. Soon the door burst open, and there was the old man with the candle and two of his sons, their faces lit by the candle, all peering into the room. There was another groan from the man on the floor. In a moment they were all on me, shouting and abusing me, for they seemed not to understand what had happened. Then one tore at the silk waistband which contained all the money I possessed, and another hurled me against the bed and began to pummel my face with fists like hammers. My forehead bled, and the blood ran into my eyes. My paintings, brocades and all the small odds and ends I had brought from Milan were scattered over the floor. What saved me was that they were all shouting and cursing, getting in each other's way, the old man alternately prompting them to punish me and to lift up the son I had attacked. At last they dragged him from the room and I was left in peace, while they debated loudly what they would do with me. I heard them shouting outside my room. One spoke of killing me, another said he would hold me upside down with my head in a bucket of water, while the old man screamed that I should be whipped with the bull-hide whip he kept in the stables.

By good fortune none of them knew I was well armed. Naked, my face beaten to a bloody pulp, I waited for them with a dagger in one hand and a rapier in another.

I did not wait for long. The strongest of them came lurching into the bedroom a few moments later, armed with a club. I believe he thought it would be a simple matter to beat my brains out. When I slashed his cheek with the rapier, he gave a howl of rage, dropped the club and fled cursing.

By this time the whole farmhouse was awake. People were running about everywhere. Sooner or later I would have to stand a state of siege with the whole village around me; and by force of numbers they were bound to prevail. I pushed the bed against the door, and then dressed hurriedly, gathered up as many of my possessions as I could easily gather into my saddlebag, slipped out through the window, mounted the donkey, and fled from the farmhouse. Happily, it was the last house in the village. It was early morning, and there was no one on the road.

An hour later I came to a small stream and washed the blood from my face; and when I looked at my reflection in the water it occurred to me that I was uglier and more repulsive than ever.

Two days later when I was traveling along a deserted road near the seacoast I came across a carriage lying by the roadside. It was one of those small, light, two-wheeled carriages which were becoming fashionable, with a single horse in the traces. But the horse had vanished; one of the wheels was broken; and two bodies lay inside, one huddled on top of the other. One was a man with a face of marble pallor, about twenty-five, with an expression which suggested an extreme refinement. I remember that he had a very thin nose and his white eyelids resembled heavy white petals. Indeed, the whole face had the transparency of wax, and at first I could not believe it was a real body lying there. He had been shot in the chest and his caked blood spilled over his white shirt.

The other was a woman about the same age, with fine silky yellow hair and there were still some traces of powder on her face. She must once have been beautiful, but since her throat was cut from ear to ear, and her lips were drawn back showing grimacing teeth, and her eyes were staring, I could not judge her beauty, and indeed I spent very little time looking at her. I made no effort to carry her out of the carriage, but left her lying there.

The sea lay below, the birds were singing, and a light mist lay over the broken fields. It was one of those summer mornings when the sky is a translucent green and white. The sun shone through the carriage window, which framed those two pale faces.

For a long time I stayed there, gazing at the carriage and its strange cargo. It was not difficult to imagine what had happened. In the late evening of the previous day they were attacked by robbers on horseback and forced off the road, and in this way one of the wheels was torn off and shattered against a stone boulder. What the robbers wanted was evidently the traveling bag attached to the roof of the carriage, for the leather straps were hanging free. Everything happened very quickly; there was no struggle; the man was shot and the woman's throat was cut before they had time to scramble from the carriage. It was all over in a few moments. The robbers had fled with the horse and the traveling bag and whatever other valuables they could find.

I say "they," but the more I contemplated the scene the more I was convinced that it was the work of a single robber, and one perhaps who had not intended to murder. It occurred to me that the murder was a thing of the moment, unexpected, unplanned, almost an afterthought. The smashing of the wheel, the screaming of the woman, the emptiness and loneliness of the deserted road conspired to fill him with a sensation of terror, and he had thereupon gone about his business quickly and methodically. He had not expected to kill, just as the man who rifled my saddlebag had not expected to start a murderous quarrel. He had cut the girl's throat because she had been screaming and he could not tolerate her screams, though on this deserted stretch of road no one would have heard them.

In this way, leaning on my donkey, I spent an hour gazing at the tumbled carriage, and from time to time I would look up at the hills covered with scrub oak or down at the sea which was like a sheet of glass.

I told myself that the murder was accidental, careless, almost an improvisation, a mere whim. I tried to imagine the murderer. Penniless, certainly. Unsure of himself, and therefore young. Someone who had cause to detest the habits of the rich. Perhaps a stableboy in the employment of the young aristocrat who had been driving along the seacoast. And from contemplating the habits of the murderer I began to imagine his features, the way he rode on horseback, his clothes, his habits, whether he was married, and what money he earned, until I could have drawn his portrait. Then it occurred to me that I was drawing a portrait of myself.

I am a painter, that is to say a man who studies carefully and watches the shapes of colors until, after long concentration, they reveal themselves. So on this headstrong summer day I contemplated a murderer and two dead people, seeing them only as colors. They did not terrify me, for they were made of paint.

So the long hour passed, and the strange sweet smell coming from the dead mingled with the salt smell of the sea. At last I went on my way down the road, and perhaps forty yards away I found a coat of brocade lying among thorns. The coat was bloodstained, and evidently it had been snatched off the dead man and then abandoned as being useless. I washed the coat in a stream and carried it with me to the next village.

When I came to the village I found that everyone was taking a siesta, the doors and shutters were closed, and no one paid any attention to the stranger who walked down the village street beside a black donkey, or at least no one was visible. It was a hot and sultry day. Sometimes I would look up at some shutters, and I knew they were watching me through the cracks, for this village was a little off the main road and few visitors came to it. I thought of beating on one of the doors and telling them about the broken carriage, and then it occurred to me that the villagers themselves were addicted to robbery, and I was afraid of being robbed of my few remaining possessions. I would have gone on to the next village if I had not seen a girl coming out of the tavern carrying a pail of milk. It was, as I have said, a lonely place, and I was startled by her presence. She walked with a slow and measured tread; she wore a green dress and her red hair fell down her back in waves; and there was an expression of grave refinement in her features. Greatly daring, I went up to her and said I was a painter, and it would please me if she would let me sketch her. As I was drawing her, leaning on the donkey, with the drawing board laid between the saddlebags, I told her about my journey from Milan, and how I was robbed in the farmhouse, and about many other things, to enlist her sympathy, but she seemed listless and remote, her mind wandering. She had not spoken a word. When I asked her to pose for me, she simply stood quite still in the middle of the road, while the sunlight poured round her.

Because she was listless and I wanted her to show more expression, I told her about the carriage. Suddenly she gave a scream, dropped the milk pail, and threw her hands toward me, and this gesture and her screams startled the donkey which began to gallop down the road. Recovering, she said: "Was it a black carriage?"

"Yes."

"With the arms of the di Lucca family painted on it?"

I did not remember whether there were any armorial bearings on the carriage.

"There was a man and a woman — they were about twenty-five," I said. "A wheel was broken. It must have happened yesterday, because the bodies were quite cold."

The villagers had heard her scream and now the shutters opened and people came running out into the street. The tavern opened its doors, and I half carried her inside. Then I told them what I had seen while they listened impassively, and I saw them exchanging glances and shaking their heads. The girl shivered uncontrollably, her face white as paper. The tavern keeper kept asking questions. At what hour had I seen the carriage? Had I seen anyone else during the journey? Surely I must have seen the armorial bearings painted on the carriage? He said the Marchese di

Lucca and his young wife had been expected in the village the previous day. They owned the castle which lay behind the village, and half the villagers were in his service. I went outside and recovered the brocaded coat, which still showed some bloodstains. At the sight of the coat the villagers fell silent, and then the tavern keeper said: "God rest their souls," and they all sighed, and their hands crept out to touch the coat.

The tavern keeper was a brutal man with a thick black beard. Suddenly the blood rushed to his face and he shouted: "How do we know that you did not murder them?" Immediately all the villagers began to stare at me accusingly. Some shook their fists at me, and they might have killed me on the spot if the girl had not taken my hand. They debated what to do. It was decided to send ten men on horseback to recover the bodies and scour the countryside, while three others were left to guard me. There was talk of whether they should inform the Marchese, the father of the dead man, but it was decided to wait until they had returned with the carriage.

In this way I waited in the tavern, while the three men continually threatened me, saying it was obvious that I was the murderer, for no one else had traveled along the road. I laughed and said I would be a poor murderer if I informed on myself, and besides they had only to examine my saddlebags to learn that I was penniless and had profited nothing by the murder. For some reason this remark enraged them, and they began to strike me, drawing blood. I gave myself up for lost, until the girl intervened and said they should at least wait until they had seen the bodies. Toward evening the carriage arrived, and the whole village gave itself up to wailing. In the small church there was chanting all night, and processions of mourners bearing candles made their way round the church walls. They bound me with ropes and threw me down on the floor of the tavern.

All that night I waited for them to cut my throat, and the guards whispered ominously that I would be lucky if they did not torture me. "You are a stranger here," they said, and I answered that in Caravaggio we opened our houses to strangers, because it was God's will that they should be well treated. They had never heard of Caravaggio, and knew only that Milan was somewhere far to the north. A constable came, and then once more I gave myself up for lost, for he asked questions and beat me when I failed to answer quickly enough for his satisfaction. They spoke of having a trial in which the villagers would be the judges, or of sending me in chains to the nearest town. They kept me in the tavern, and there were never less than three armed men guarding me.

A week passed, and then another, and then finally in the third week I felt that my life was no longer in danger. It was not that the guards treated me any better or that the food was more palatable, but the people who came to watch me as I lay bound on the floor no longer kicked me or spat at me, and there were some who murmured in sympathy. One night the old Marchese came down from the castle to see me. He was a frail man, his lips trembling with grief. He sat on a cane-bottomed chair and leaned on his staff, gazing at me sorrowfully. The guards kept away from him, standing in the shadows. He gazed deep in my eyes, as though he were searching into my heart, and at last he said: "Let the poor boy go. He did not murder my son."

I left the village the same night. I had a fever and could scarcely mount my donkey, and was too weak to travel more than a few miles a day.

In this way, Illustrissimo, after many more adventures, I came to Rome, and spent my first night sleeping on the steps of Santa Maria del Popolo, near the gate, for I was too weary and too ill to go further into the city. On the next day I was awakened by the pealing of the church bells, and the first thing I saw was the Pope riding a white horse as he entered the city. He raised his gloved hands in blessing, and I thought he gave me a special blessing, as one who has traveled dangerously to enter his service.

The Monsignor

ALL I had when I came to Rome were eight paintings and a black donkey, and now that I look around my small room I see that nothing has changed, because I still possess only eight paintings. I have traveled far, I have sat at dinner with the Pope and many cardinals and princes, and I have my paintings and nothing more. I have ridden on a white horse through the streets of Rome and scattered gold to the people, and been in prison, and died many times in the cellar of a hospital, and there is little enough to show for it. A few paintings: this is all I possess in the world.

A little while ago Maddalena came creeping up the stairs with a bowl of gruel and some artichokes which she found in the garden. She has grown more nervous recently, and I know that my days in the house of Fra Bartolomeo are numbered. She comes to me hesitantly and fearfully, and she always makes some excuse to avert her face when she enters my room. I have placed my paintings along the wall, and she prefers to look at the paintings rather than at me. Yet she always stays for a long time, crossing herself and muttering prayers for the good Lord to protect me.

This evening she came more stealthily than usual, and kept

looking over her shoulder, like someone afraid of being followed. Her skirts were damp with the night dews, for she had just come from the garden; and she carried with her, old and withered as she was, the scent of young rain. I could hear the rain falling and trickling through the straw, and the night was cool. Indeed, a wind had sprung up and the windows behind the black curtains were creaking.

At first she did not know where to set the bowl of gruel, for everything in the room was in disorder. I was working on an *Adoration of the Magi*, with the Virgin holding the Child, a donkey behind her, and of the Magi you could see only their offerings, their jeweled fingers, and a hint of their features. It was a small painting, and as usual when I painted anything small I would lay the canvas horizontally on the table.

For a few moments Maddalena wandered about the room, wondering where to put the gruel. Then I laughed softly, took it from her, and placed it squarely on the canvas. She threw up her hands in horror.

"What are you doing?" she exclaimed. "On the face of the Holy Virgin —"

"There's no harm in it," I answered. "Until the painting has been blessed, how can there be any harm in it? It is nothing but pigment."

Her lips were trembling.

"It's a sin against God," she whispered, "to do such a thing. Poor Michelangelo, you have no care for God or for your paintings. Sometimes I think you must be out of your mind when you do these terrible things."

To humor her I removed the bowl of gruel to some less offensive place on the painting, and she gave a little sigh of relief, but she continued to cross herself.

"And where shall I place the artichokes?" she asked.

"Why, place them anywhere you please on the painting. It will do it no harm. I've eaten many a meal off my canvases."

She stared at me in disbelief.

"I've rolled up canvases and used them for pillows," I went on. "I've wrapped them round me to keep warm. I've used them as weapons of offense, and I've held them over my head to protect me from the rain. What's canvas but cloth?"

Saying this, I took the artichokes from her hand and slapped them down on the painting, taking care however that they should not touch the Virgin's face.

While I supped Maddalena hovered over me, her lips indrawn in that familiar way suggesting that she had secrets to impart. I could hear the click of her beads and the flapping of her worn sandals on the floor.

"Something troubles you," I said at last, when I had finished the gruel.

"It's bad news," she answered. "Fra Bartolomeo has been to see the prior. It was about some church vestments — nothing important. But as Fra Bartolomeo was leaving, the prior called him back and said there were rumors that Michelangelo da Caravaggio was in the city. And the prior, Father Fabrizio, went on to say that it was likely enough that the poor painter would try to find lodging in the houses of priests or nuns, and perhaps Fra Bartolomeo knew something about it. That was all, but Fra Bartolomeo went on to say that the prior, who is a wonderfully kindly man, gave the impression that he knew you were hiding here — he did not say so directly, but that was the impression — and if he knows where you are, then perhaps there are others who know."

She said all this very haltingly and nervously, not in the way I have recounted it here, but in little quick gasps and sudden rushes of words, her hands flying to her hair and her damp skirts, from time to time uttering little prayers for my safety.

"It is God's will," I said, "and perhaps I may be able to hide in Father Fabrizio's house. At least for a few days we have heard nothing more about the man in the Spanish cape."

At these words she shivered and turned away, for the memory of the day when Fra Bartolomeo encountered the man in the cape was still fresh with her. I put my arms round her, to comfort her. Suddenly something on my canvas attracted her attention and her face lit up.

"God bless me, there's a donkey," she said, smiling through her tears.

"Why, so there is!" I answered in pretended surprise. "I hadn't noticed it before."

"A black donkey! A black donkey!" she repeated, and she was still muttering these words as she went slowly down the stairs.

I worked late into the night on the *Adoration of the Magi*, listening to the small rain falling and the wind rocking the trees in the garden below. There are donkeys in many of my paintings, but they are always the same donkey. I never needed a model, for I knew this donkey by heart, and when I painted it I could hear it braying and feel its wet muzzle against my face, and there came to me the raw smell of its breath and skin, and the sound of its plodding walk on the Roman cobblestones.

They say that black donkeys are sired by Satan, but I swear that this one was blessed by the living God. I never knew an animal more patient, more long suffering, more sweet-tempered. When we rode through the Porta del Popolo, it was covered with dust and you might have taken it for a white donkey, which I am told is the rarest of all beasts, even rarer than the unicorn; but a moment later, when I took it to the fountain, it was black again, with the scarlet sores glowing like rubies on its flanks. And having watered it, and found some fresh straw, I fastened it to a post and went into the church to pray for my safe arrival in Rome, being very hungry and having eaten nothing for two days.

On the following day, after the Pope had passed in procession, I unrolled my paintings and placed them on the steps of the church, holding them down with stones, in the hope that someone would buy them, or perhaps one of them, and thus provide me with food and lodgings, otherwise I would be forced to sell the donkey. But though many people passed up and down the steps, no one bought them. A young gallant put his foot squarely on the best of my paintings and laughed derisively, and some women examined them with peals of laughter. In this way I learned the habits of the Romans. Not until evening did anyone pause to admire them. I had seen him coming down the steps, and out of habit I shouted after him: "For the love of God, see my paintings!" and I expected him to turn away, as all the others had done, but instead he came at my bidding and examined each one in turn, pursing his lips and muttering under his breath.

He was a short round priest, and he had the pallor of men who have grown fat on too much food. Though he was about fifty, his cheeks were unwrinkled, and his blue eyes gleamed in the depths of his white skin. He wore a great ruff of white beard, and his hair, which fell over his ears, was silky and wonderfully combed. The long shadows were falling on the steps, and sometimes he bent low so that his head was almost touching the paintings.

"You have talent, boy," he said. "You have a wonderful way of painting fruit — and flowers, too. I can see you know the rudiments —"

"I know more than the rudiments!" I interrupted. "I can paint as well as any man living, if only the Romans will keep me from starving. Have grace, your lordship. Buy one of my paintings, and God will bless you!"

[61]

He turned, and I thought he was about to move away, but instead he swung round toward me, as though struck by an afterthought, by the desire to look more closely at the face of the young painter on the steps, who was dressed in rags and bleating like a sheep. It was a warm day, my chest was half bare, and patches of sunburned skin were shining through my rags. So he bent down to look at the wretched creature sitting on the steps with exactly the same expression he had employed when looking at my paintings. As he drew closer, I smelled the incense and perfume which clung to his cassock and saw his small white hands, which might have been the hands of a fifteen-year-old virgin, so white and spotless and sweet smelling they were.

Then, looking at me very closely, he said: "You are a very dirty and impudent scoundrel!"

He had a thin, reedy voice, and he could play on it like a musician, making exactly the right pauses, raising the pitch at exactly the right moment.

It was as though he had cut me across the face with a whip, and I rose, shuddering with anger. I did not care what happened to me so long as I could beat his face to pulp. I had not traveled all the way from Milan to be insulted by a fat silken priest. I had my donkey stick in my hands, and raised it, and then let it fall, because he was smiling at me so insolently, showing his little teeth, his little pink tongue, and he was wonderfully aware of his power over me.

He bent down and picked up my stick, and he was still smiling.

"So you were going to strike me, and then you thought better of it," he went on. "That shows, I suppose, that you have some decent impulses left. Where are you from?"

"Caravaggio."

"And where, may I ask, is Caravaggio?"

"Near Bergamo."

"Ah, so you come from the north. Penniless, too, by the look of you. No doubt you walked all the way, and you thought you would make your fortune in Rome with your miserable paintings."

"I rode on my donkey —" I said, and there were hot tears in my eyes.

"With paintings of flowers, as though Rome wasn't full of flower painters!"

"And I can paint everything there is — not only flowers. You can see for yourself that I can paint portraits, for you have studied two of them. Give me a place to paint, your lordship, and I'll astound the world! Otherwise there is nothing for me but to drown myself in the Tiber!"

"You will have difficulty in drowning yourself, because the Tiber at this moment is nothing more than a small muddy stream."

He laughed softly, and now for the first time there was a look of friendliness in his sharp blue eyes.

"Well, there's some spirit in you! You have talent, and though you are unwashed, I believe I can discern some virtue in your features! I'll see that you have some food and lodging for a few days! So roll up your paintings and follow me!"

He spoke like a great lord conferring a favor on one of his least favored servants, but I followed him willingly, nay, with alacrity, in the hope of food and a place to sleep. I rolled up the paintings, arranged my rags to better advantage, unroped the donkey, and it seems to me that I did all these things simultaneously. Then, walking beside the donkey, I followed him across the square, and once he turned with an expression of annoyance and disgust, but he paid no more attention to me until we came to the courtyard of a great house near the basilica of St. John Lateran, and there on the gateposts, emblazoned in gold, were the arms of Pope Sixtus, a lion rampant clutching three thistles.

[63]

I thought at first we had come to one of the houses occupied by the Pope, but I learned later that the house belonged to his sister, Camilla Peretti. She was an old woman, and I often caught a glimpse of her, very tall and proud and stiff, wearing the costume of an abbess. The monsignor who had accosted me on the steps of Santa Maria del Popolo was her majordomo, and he lived in one of the small courtyards behind the house, where I followed him. By this time it was growing dark and linkboys with torches led us through the courtyards. They were elegant youths, in blue silk, and they held their fingers to their noses as I walked beside them with my donkey.

"Get him washed and put into some good clothes," the monsignor said, addressing himself to a servant who looked like a butcher, and indeed he had just been preparing meats, for there was blood on his hands. "Give him some food, too. He hasn't eaten for two days."

The servant, whose name was Squallione, led me away into the servants' quarters, tore my clothes off me, pushed me into a tub of water, and amused himself by cutting off most of my hair, so that I looked like a German; then he put me in the red uniform worn by the stableboys. When I protested, saying I was a painter, Squallione replied: "Monsignor Randolfo Pucci has honored you by permitting you to enter his household, but let me warn you that he will not like you any better for your complaints." Then he put a dish of cold salad before me. From the other servants I learned that Monsignor Pucci was a beneficiary of St. Peter's, which is to say that he was the priest of a long-abandoned church, with no duties to perform except to supervise the household of Camilla Peretti, and that he had many revenues.

That same evening I was summoned into the presence of the monsignor, who gave me to understand that in exchange for my paintings and my services I would be permitted to enjoy the rank and food of a stableboy, but would not be asked to groom the horses; for which I thanked him pleasantly, only pausing to remark that I would prefer to wear no livery but my own, and as for the paintings I had brought with me, all rolled up together, they were my own property and if anyone desired them, then he must pay for them. He was so taken aback that some faint color appeared on his cheeks.

"You are an ungrateful scoundrel," he said. "I had expected at least a show of gratitude for all the trouble I have taken with you! But since you are a painter, I shall permit you to wear your own livery so long as it is decent and covers your body in a suitable manner!"

It was time for me to lay down my conditions for serving him.

"I shall also need fodder for my donkey," I said.

"It is granted."

"And a place to work in."

"Squallione will find you a place," the monsignor replied with an easy wave of his hand.

"And there must be a contract drawn up between us."

At this he stood up, his cheeks quivering and little puffs of smoke issuing from his nostrils.

"Enough, enough!" he shouted. "A child of charity does not lay down conditions! I have had pity on you! Must I be forced to turn against you? There will be no contract between us! I shall do my best for you, and you will do your best for me! That is our contract!"

"Then it should be sealed," I said. "We shall kiss hands on it."

"You are an extraordinary fellow. I do not even know your name, and you keep making demands of me."

"My name is Michelangelo Merisi da Caravaggio," I replied,

"and it is a name which you will not have occasion to forget. I want no more of this stableboy nonsense. Look at my paintings, and see whether I am not worthy of being well treated."

I stretched out the paintings one by one on his table, and arranged the candles so that the light should not shine directly on them. His little eyes were gleaming as he admired them.

"I shall give you a *scudi* for each of these paintings," he said at last.

"They are worth far more, and you know it. Give me ten *scudi* for each, and you will have made a profit!"

"I will give you two *scudi* for each —"

"Five!"

"Then I will give you four!"

I knew how to deal with such rascals and held to five, which he eventually paid me with ill grace, opening the little purple bag he carried inside his cassock and counting out the coins slowly, as though frightened that they might bite him. Then I kissed his hand fervently, and for the first time since leaving Milan I felt some gratitude to a man.

There was more hard bargaining in the weeks that followed. I demanded a large room, better food, money to buy a new cloak against the coming winter, and the services of one of the stableboys, Alessandro de Santis, to clean my brushes and act as my companion whenever I traveled through the city, for I was continually getting lost in my journeys. The last he refused to grant me, observing that the boy was unusually handsome and was the favorite of the Pope's sister; and this only increased my desire to have Alessandro beside me. In the end I obtained his services whenever I wanted them and he spent his nights with me. I also demanded permission to paint Camilla Peretti, saying that we would both acquire honor by presenting her portrait to the Pope. On this subject Monsignor Pucci remained unresolved, fearing perhaps that I would insist on having an audience with the Holy Father when the painting was finished. He also asked me to copy some religious paintings, which I did to humor him: a Crucifixion, a Deposition, and an Entombment were painted at intervals during the autumn and the winter. The monsignor was not pleased with them.

"They are not copies," he said. "They look more like your paintings, Michelangelo. It would be better if you copied them more faithfully."

"Then they would be worth less," I said, and went back to painting the beautiful Alessandro and my own portrait in a mirror.

In this way I spent my first year in Rome, living in the palace of the Pope's sister and acquiring some fame as a painter of portraits. But in the summer of the following year Sixtus died, and Monsignor Pucci lost his benefices, Camilla Peretti lost her palace, and I lost my protector, for I had come to know her well, although she refused to be painted. Monsignor Pucci went off to Recanati where he became a simple priest, and Camilla Peretti went to live on the family estate at Ancona. I was left alone with Alessandro, whose beauty I had celebrated in five paintings. One night I woke from my sleep to discover that Alessandro had vanished. He had taken all the money I had saved during a year of painting industriously.

They were not easy years for a painter. In the space of eighteen months three Popes ruled over Rome, and there was no peace in the city until the election of Ippolito Aldobrandini, who took the title of Clement VIII. I had reached that stage of fame, halfway up the ladder, which is exceedingly perilous, for while all admired me, no one would give me commissions; and from living in a palace I became a poor lodger in humble houses, making a living, if it can be called a living, in the workshops of others. At first I worked for Lorenzo Siciliano, then for Antiveduto Gramatica, and finally for the Cavaliere Guiseppe d'Arpino. They are names now, and if anything of theirs is still living, it is because I sometimes painted the flowers in the paintings they signed, or a boy's face, or some fruit in a wicker basket.

I earned little, for I suffered often from malaria. I would lie huddled in a rabbit-skin cloak in an evil-smelling bed, dreaming of the days when I sauntered through Rome with Alessandro at my side. Then the plague came, and men died by the thousands, and the black carts rumbled through the deserted streets. I decided, then, that Simone Peterzano had more sense than I ever imagined. I told myself I would return to Milan and begin my life afresh. I still had my donkey and some paintings. One day in October, with twelve *scudi* in my purse, still suffering from fever, all my possessions on the back of the donkey, I made my way to the Porta del Popolo. I was walking slowly under the archway with the black donkey beside me, when a carriage belonging to Prince Torlonia passed at great speed. I remember the foam flecking from the horse's mouth and the screaming of the coachman, but I remember nothing more. All that morning and for most of the afternoon I lay near the gate, and the few people who ventured abroad gave me a wide berth, thinking I had died of the plague.

The Tunnel

AT last toward evening, while I was still bleeding from the mouth, they took me to the Ospedale della Misericordia. Because the plague had swept through Rome, the hospital was overcrowded, and they found no place to put me except the tunnel which was once a secret alleyway to the nearby palace of Prince Colonna. By chance the prior of the hospital recognized me, for he was a friend of Monsignor Pucci, and I had just strength enough to greet him and implore his protection. I begged him not to put me among the victims of the plague.

"We are all victims of the plague, Michelangelo," he said, and then he ordered one of the nuns to bandage the ragged wound in my head. "We shall all die, and it is good to die in good company."

The prior, whose name was Camillo Contreras, was a Spaniard, with a long lean face and heavy eyebrows which met across the bridge of his nose, and he had the mournful expression of a man who encounters death daily. There was a wooden crucifix hanging over his white gown, and Christ's body was twisted in agony. He was about to leave me when I shouted after him: "I have some presents for you if you will save my life!" The donkey had followed me to the hospital, and my paintings were in my saddlebags. "For God's love take these paintings," I said. I gave him three of my paintings, and hoped he would remember me. The others I took with me to the tunnel.

I heard the rats running in the straw, and sometimes one of the watchmen would come down the tunnel and swing a lantern in our faces to see whether anyone had died during the interval between his rounds, and there would be pale splashes of silvery light moving along the damp walls. It was always dark in the tunnel except for an hour in midmorning when the opening of the tunnel caught the watery sun. Then all the straw would shine like liquid gold, the whole tunnel flaming with gold; and then for the rest of the day it would grow darker, yellowish gray in the late afternoon, then purple and maroon, until the light faded altogether.

They fed us irregularly on gruel, and sometimes I wished they would forget to feed us, for they would trundle the gruel cart down the narrow tunnel and force us to eat from the ladles which dripped with a yellow slime. Sometimes they brought us water with obscene things swimming in it. On very rare occasions we were given small slices of chicken and pork. Once we entered the tunnel we knew we would die there.

I suffered from raging headaches brought on by the kick of the horse, and fell into strange waking dreams: at such times the tunnel would vanish, and I would find myself wandering down a country lane with my black donkey, and usually there were emerald green apple trees nearby and white mountains in the distance, or else I would dream of the heads of St. Peter and St. Paul, which are shown in the Basilica of St. John Lateran at Easter, the head of St. Peter very rosy and well-fleshed, with a gray forked beard, and the head of St. Paul almost black with a thick black beard, and in my waking dreams blood spilled out of their eyes and ran along the paving stones of the church and drowned the worshipers, with only a small cat escaping into the square. I knew St. John Lateran well, for I had lived hard by, but I knew the heads of the saints better, for night after night they haunted my dreams. And sometimes it seemed to me that I could slip out of the tunnel at will to wander through the streets of Rome, returning at last into my body which lay on the evil-smelling straw.

An old woman was dying on one side of me, a boy on the other. The old woman must have been about seventy, dry and withered as an old corn stalk, with a face which must have been beautiful when she was young, a long narrow delicate face, parchment colored, with deep-set eyes; and because she was so quiet I would imagine she was the Virgin and peer at her closely, trying to remember every detail of her face so that I could paint it when I was well again. She was very close to death, sinking away, and I knew I would paint a Death of the Virgin in memory of her.

I never knew the name of the old woman, but I knew the name of the boy — Giovanni Battista degli Angeli. He was thirteen or fourteen, a special favorite of the nuns, for he never complained, even when being cupped, and he always gladly kissed the cross which the nuns held out to him, and when the nuns had gone he would smile at me and wink, and make a gesture with his thumb. He had been plump once, and there was still some beauty in his pale face, though it was covered with running sores, and because he scratched the sores the nuns sometimes tied his hands behind his back.

From day to day I watched the boy dying: the sweat gleaming in his yellow hair, the eyes growing more watery, the smile fainter, until he became almost a thing of bone. The flesh sunk along the cheekbones so that his nose seemed to become more prominent with every passing day, and gradually the carved nostrils took on the appearance of marble. I watched him in the candlelight: he knew I was watching him, and he would smile weakly in my direction and then turn away, a little shamefaced, for there was no boldness in him, and he possessed the modesty of the dying.

And, strangely, as the days passed his wounds healed, while the life went out of him, so that in the last days his face was the color of clean white parchment, and there were no more running sores. Towards the end he could scarcely speak, but he smiled often. It was as though he regarded me as an accomplice in the mysterious adventure he was pursuing. Once he said: "Shall we go out and steal the peaches off the trees?" I said: "Yes, we'll go out tomorrow." Then he looked at me searchingly for a long time and said: "Tomorrow may be too late. All the peaches will have fallen from the trees." "No," I said, "there will always be some left." This pleased him, and he lay back in the straw with a bony smile on his lips and there was a gleam of light in his watery eyes.

There was another occasion, late at night, when the candles were dripping, and everyone was asleep, when he turned to me and gripped my doublet with his small hands, and said: "Shall we go riding tomorrow?"

"Yes, we'll go riding," I said, to comfort him.

"I know where we can find the ponies," he went on. "They'll give us the ponies, eh? Fine bridles and saddlecloths, too, and good hay. There's a shop by Santa Trinità dei Monte where they will give us everything we want, eh?"

"I know the shop," I said. "We'll go there early one morning."

"No, we'll go tomorrow at the crack of dawn," he said, and there was some urgency in his voice and he was glaring at me as though he wanted my assent more than anything else in the world.

"Yes, we'll go at the crack of dawn," I said. "But now you should rest for a while."

"You'll promise to come with me?"

"Yes, I promise."

[72]

"And we'll ride together all day?"

"We'll ride as long as you like."

For a moment he seemed to be content, but I could not see him clearly. His hot breath was on my face, and there were little drops of pearly sweat on his hair and cheeks. Then he said: "When it gets too hot, we'll lie in the shade of the trees and I'll play my flute —"

"Yes, Giovanni, you'll play on your flute," I said, "but now you must go to sleep."

"You won't forget to come riding with me at the crack of dawn?"

"No, I won't forget, but sleep now and may the Lord give you pleasant dreams."

Then he slept, while the last candles were going out.

Now that I recall the face of this boy, I cannot remember whether he addressed me by name, and sometimes it seems to me that very few words passed between us: instead, we were continually exchanging smiles, since we had nothing else to exchange. Towards the end he became delirious, and once or twice he burst into song — a small, thin song which was almost drowned in the creaking of the straw and the coughing and choking sounds which erupt at intervals through the night; and the song was always about the pony which would take him over the hills.

Two days before he died a change came over him. I, who had watched him so closely over so many days, felt sure he would sink quietly into his death. I told myself I would awake one morning and see him lying lifeless in the straw, and then they would come and carry him to the lime pit and the earthly life of Giovanni Battista degli Angeli would be over. But it did not happen in this way. Quite suddenly his small and slender body acquired new strength, he began to breathe heavily, and this heavy breathing, far from disturbing me as perhaps it should have done, inspired me with new confidence in his recovery, a confidence which was not in the least shaken by my knowledge that he was dying. I knew he was dying, and I thought I knew he was recovering, and these two ideas went hand in hand; for it is possible to believe all things when one is ill. And the nuns too believed he was recovering, and exchanged quick glances in the shadow of their white hoods, because they were fond of the boy and because they were hopeful that one day he would serve at the altar or enter the priesthood.

On the last day of his life the breathing became even heavier, and there were long periods when he lost consciousness. The sound of his heavy breathing filled the whole tunnel; everyone was looking in his direction, and everyone was frightened. We had thought of death as a skeleton, not as the sound of a great drum booming. He had thrown off his ragged coat, and I could see the small beautiful chest slowly inflating like a bellows and just as slowly deflating, and there seemed to be no energy anywhere in his body except in his chest. It was not terrible to watch him. In the damp and flickering candlelight, with the sweat streaming over him, his chest was beautiful beyond anything in the dark tunnel. It was only when, quite suddenly and unaccountably, there ceased to be any movement in his chest that I became alarmed; and then after a long interval the heavy breathing would be resumed. It was as though he had simply forgotten to breathe, and suddenly remembered that it was his duty, his unavoidable task to do what was demanded of him. And this heavy breathing, when it was resumed, seemed to give him stature and purpose, making him great and terrible, so that it was impossible not to gaze at him open mouthed in awe.

I have seen men lying dead in the streets of Rome, and I have seen men being executed, but death had never pressed so close to me before. Now whenever I paint a human chest — God knows I

have painted men and boys often enough! — then I remember the
chest of Giovanni Battista degli Angeli, creamy white, the small
bones pushing through, the light of candles flickering silver on
every curved ridge, expanding as though a child were being born
within it, and it is so beautiful that it takes the breath away.

The last night was the most terrible. Then the breathing became louder than ever, and slower. He would lie very still, his
small fists clenched at his side, and suddenly there would come
echoing along the tunnel the vast voice of his breath, drowning all
other sounds. I watched him all night. One of the nuns brought
me a basin of cold water, and I would mop up the sweat streaming
over him. Toward morning I fell asleep. When I awoke he was in
convulsions, his arms and legs thrashing on the straw, and instead
of the heavy stentorian breath there was a kind of whistling.
There was only time for the nuns to recite a short prayer over
him; then he died.

I do not remember them taking the boy away, perhaps because
memory is merciful. I remember lying there in the straw, conscious that there was an empty place beside me which would soon
be filled, for there is always enough sickness in the world to fill the
empty places in hospitals. He had died and left nothing behind
him except the memory of his gentleness, and soon he would be
forgotten. And I, too, would be forgotten. A few people would
remember that I once painted fruit and flowers and portraits of
boys: they would remember, and then they would forget. I
thought I would die soon, and there was some comfort in it.

You might think that a tunnel creeping with rats and filled with
dying men is a sordid place, but the truth is that we were content.
When you are dying, you have very little care for your surroundings. We did not think of it as sordid. The nuns were kindly, and
sometimes a priest, an almoner or a visitor would make his way

along the tunnel to bring us news of the world outside. We were all rotting to death, but we did not think of ourselves as rotting to death. We belonged to that very special category of people who are ill and helpless, but otherwise in a satisfactory condition. We did not hate, or feel envy, or intrude ourselves on others, or desire. We felt no horror. Sudden screams did not perplex us. We understood perfectly why people screamed, and we were glad when the last echoes faded from the walls.

And for the most part we lay there very quietly, immersed in our own thoughts, but sometimes rousing ourselves to show solicitude for others. This was our only joy. You cannot imagine how we thirsted to protect others, to solace them, to give them food and water; and sometimes there were four or five of us crawling through the straw to be near someone who was dying or in pain. We knew — there was not one of us in the tunnel who did not know — that in a few days or weeks we would all have vanished into the lime pit. So we had reason to comfort one another.

Two or three days after the death of Giovanni Battista degli Angeli I felt my strength returning to me. It was only a little strength, and I shielded it as one shields a candle in a high wind. My hands were not nerveless any more. No longer listless, no longer having to force myself to action, I began to become aware of the whole tunnel, the great arch above all our heads, the length of it, and all the people lying there. Previously I had seen it through a dark glass, in fragmentary gleams. I saw a face, a hand, the hollow of a cheekbone. Now I saw that there were more than two hundred people lying there, all suffering, all preparing themselves for their final agonies, and most of them unmoving except for the fluttering of their hands. I tried to count them, but there were so many that the last of them disappeared into the distance.

I realized then, more than ever before, in what a terrible predicament men find themselves when they are ill. The horror of it brought new life to me. I would escape, if only into painting. I would treasure every moment of my life lived in the open air, and at the same time I would celebrate these poor devils who linger in the damp straw, helpless like beasts. I told myself I would devote myself to them, I would paint for them — the poor, the sick, the damned — and for no one else; and it seemed to me that by painting them I would be celebrating God.

For the first time in four weeks I found myself painting again. I painted on the back of those canvases I had brought with me, by candlelight. I painted the withered old woman who lay beside me. She was all bone and thin flesh, and very quiet, withdrawn from the world, seeming not to belong to it. She knew I was painting her, and sometimes she would smile at me approvingly. Sometimes the old have a very virginal look. I told myself, "Yes, truly she is the Virgin Mary and the Mother of Jesus, and Giovanni Battista was the Baptist, and we are all living in the time of Jesus." I do not know why I said this, but I know it was true, and it was all the more true at night when the white-robed nuns moved in procession between the rows of the dying and the uplifted crucifix gleamed like gold and there was no sound except their singing.

So the days passed, and every day I painted a little, and the fever and the festering sores left me.

Sister Clara saw that I had been painting.

"You may leave tomorrow," she said.

"No, I must paint here," I said.

She threw up her hands in horror.

"No, you must go," she said. "You are getting well, and so you must go."

"Who shall I paint, if I cannot paint here?" I said. "I have learned that I must paint these people. Shall I paint fruit and boys again?"

She shook her head sadly, said nothing more and went away. I knew she was going to talk to the almoner, or perhaps to the prior. That day they gave each of us a cupful of milk, and I felt my strength returning; nevertheless I was determined not to leave the tunnel. I have heard of prisoners who elect to remain in prison long after their sentence is over, and it was the same in the hospital. The damned are only happy among the damned.

The great flame of the sun shone for a few moments on the straw, and suddenly I saw the faces of those dying people as though they were suddenly transparent, shining in glory. How beautiful they were! One can gaze at an ear, a nose, a mouth, and go mad at the sight of so much beauty. A trickle of urine and excrement flowed at the bottom of the tunnel, and I would watch this river and think it more beautiful than all the great rivers of the world! And then the sun died away, and there was only the shadowy tunnel fading into darkness.

That evening something happened which was the beginning of my real life as a painter.

I was putting my brushes away and resting in a nest of fresh straw when I saw Sister Clara coming down the tunnel. She was not alone; she was followed by a man in a long cape. At first I thought it was the almoner, coming to tell me to leave the hospital. He was an old man, about seventy, and walked with hobbling strides, with difficulty keeping up with Sister Clara. I thought he was dressed in rags until he came closer, and then I saw that he was indeed splendidly dressed, his cape being of shot silk, all purple with swimming scarlet lights, and there was an intricately carved gold handle to his stick. He wore a wide-brimmed, black hat which concealed his features: I could distinguish only the gray beard, pointed and waxed. The cape reached his ankles, and swirled and bunched all round him, and there was a jeweled order hanging on a chain over his breast.

Few visitors came to the hospital, and I could make nothing of this old stranger who hobbled after the sister and sometimes paused to look over his shoulder at the poor devils in the straw as they settled down for the night. Sister Clara was smiling. When she was within a few feet of me, she pointed in my direction. The old man waved his stick and said: "Is this the one?"

For a moment he stood rooted there. I could make out something of his features under the wide-brimmed hat. It was a long face, more Spanish than Italian, a wide mouth, heavily lidded eyes, a nose as strong as a parrot's beak. His cheeks were the color of putty, and wisps of hair, lank and gray, fell to his shoulders. I was watching him through half-closed eyelids. I did not like him and liked him still less when he came closer.

"So you paint a little, boy?" he said, wheezing and bending over me.

He had foul breath and his teeth were rotted down like jagged stumps in his mouth.

"Yes," I said, "I am a painter by God's choice and my own necessity, having lived with the dead for five weeks."

"We have all lived with the dead," he answered. "It's a small matter. *Deo adjuva me!* The dead have nothing to do with painting. Come, boy, show me what you have done, and leave the dead to bury the dead. I have no time to waste on speeches of mortality."

As I have said, he was old and bent, dressed in the Spanish manner in clothes which rustled and smelled of freshness. Everything about him was singular, but most singular of all was his voice, which was not an old man's voice, but vigorous and resonant with the trace of a foreign accent, perhaps Spanish, perhaps French, the voice of a man about forty, with a pleasant sharpness to it, caring nothing for the opinions of others.

"Show me your paintings, boy!" he commanded. "Quickly, too! I am not one of those who prate on the marketplace!"

Then he prodded me with his stick as though I were some flea-bitten animal standing in his path.

I said I had no paintings, and even if I had, I would not show them to one who was so ill-mannered. I think he liked my defiance, for his voice grew gentler.

"God's truffles!" he said. "Don't trifle with me, boy! I haven't come out of my house on a windy night to banter arguments with a besotted son of Belial! The good sister told me you were a painter without a penny to your name, and dying of fever. That's why I have come. Not to play the merchant. I won't buy your paintings, if that's any comfort to you."

"It's no comfort to me," I said angrily. "If you won't buy my paintings, you are no use to me!"

"Now the boy is talking sense. You have a head on your shoulders — an ugly head, but still a head! Now show me what you have painted, and be thankful to the sister for bringing me here in God's good time."

"I'm thankful for nothing yet!" I said, and turned my head away to avoid his easy triumph.

I hated him for his calm manner, his hawklike head, his self-indulgence. He was enjoying himself in the role of patron. He smiled at me with the knowledge that he had only to bide his time, and I would be his willing bondman. If he liked the paintings he would buy them at a miserable fee; if not, he knew how to disengage himself from my poverty.

To humor me he said: "How old are you? I'd guess you're not

more than eighteen — you have a stripling's beard, with but a few decorative hairs hiding your chin. Well, how old are you?"

"I am nineteen."

"That's a good age for a painter. At nineteen he knows nothing, and if he is wise he will not presume beyond his knowledge."

"At nineteen," I shouted, "a painter knows as much as he will ever know!"

The old man was rubbing his hands together, making a strange cackling sound.

"You'll learn better, I dare say," he said with a mocking laugh. "Now show me your canvases."

"I have none with me —"

"Then you're a double-throated liar, boy, for I can smell paint a mile away, and I see canvases beside you. Now show them to me, and no more of this nonsense!"

It was strange how quickly he bent down like a dappled hawk, swift as lightning, to gather up my roll of paintings. When I tried to snatch them back again, he waved his trembling cane at me; and when I shouted in protest, the sister dropped to her knees and dabbed my forehead with a handkerchief, all the time whispering sweet nothings. I had the Church and Trade against me; I wanted neither of them; I wanted to rot in the tunnel alone, without them pretending to comfort me.

"God help the child!" the sister said, crossing herself.

"I don't need God's help!" I replied. "Leave me alone! I don't want this old man's patronage and pity! Leave me with the dead, or let me walk out of here into the sunlight!"

"God will have mercy on you!" the sister said.

"Let God have mercy on the dead!" I shouted. "God's mercy is in the lime pit — it's the only place where He shows Himself! Let the dead come to life, and then we'll see God's mercy!"

I cursed and raved, but the sister only smiled. It was, after all, her profession to smile upon men's ravings.

All the time the old man was examining my paintings, holding them up to the light, muttering to himself and pulling on his beard.

"Well, that's a good one. Ekh, ekh, there's no doubt he can paint a bit . . . He does fruit and boys well . . ."

I could not tolerate his mutterings at my expense. I tried to get to my feet and throw myself on the old man and retrieve the paintings, but the sister pressed me down. When I tried to push her away, I felt her breast in my hand, a firm breast, very full and ripe. It startled me that she had a shape beneath her habit. She was on her knees beside me, and suddenly I was aware that the entire habit was no more than a thin covering over her. God knows why it is, but the touch of her breast was like health to me. The old man had examined all the paintings and was rolling them up again.

"That will do for a beginning," he said. "You have some inkling of the art, boy. I'll find you a good master to work under, and give you a bed to sleep in, if it will bring you any comfort."

The sister was still kneeling beside me.

"Go with him," she said softly. "He'll bring you back to health — better than we can do."

"What if I don't want health?" I asked angrily, but there were no more outbursts.

One does not fight against Sister Clara. She helped me up, and soon three young fellows, the old man's servants, came at his summons, and two of them made a chair for me with their hands, and on this chair I left the tunnel. And as I passed all those poor dying people I made the sign of the cross in salutation.

Outside it was night and there was no moon, only the storm clouds scudding across the lightning-lit sky. We formed a small procession. The servant with the lantern went ahead, the old man followed, and I in my chair followed behind them. Then at last after much winding through narrow alleyways we came to a small and very tall house near the church of San Luigi dei Francesi in the shadow of the Giustiniani Palace. The old man carried my roll of paintings in his hand, and once when we came upon some ruffians on the road, he wielded the roll as though it were a sword; and I reflected that it was as good a use for my paintings as any.

The Footsteps of Giulia

I LOST count of the days, and even now I do not know how many weeks or months I stayed in the house of Maestro Valentino. I know my health came flooding back, and there were days when I could paint with a firm hand, and other days when all the strength seemed to have gone from me. They cupped and bled me, and stuck leeches on my back to draw the fever away, and through the mists of fever I saw the kindly face of a fork-bearded doctor with blue eyes like transparent circles of blue glass, and there was a servant girl Giulia who brought me baskets of fresh fruit, cream and cheese. They came and went, and the days followed one another in that strange, slow leisurely pace which is the pace of convalescence.

Sometimes Maestro Valentino would look into my room to ask how I was faring. He called himself Pietro Valentino, but his real name was Pierre Valentin, and he was a native of Dijon in France. They said he had come to Rome in the train of the French King, and was so enamored of the place that he decided to stay, but there were some who whispered that he was accused of embezzlement in France and had fled the country. For myself, I never learned his history and could as well believe one story as another.

[85]

There was always something in his gestures which suggested stealth, conspiracy, a mysterious passage of arms. He had a way of looking at you, of holding your hand and gazing into your eyes, which suggested that you were bound to him by a conspirator's oath. But I shall say nothing evil of him. He helped me when I needed help, and he was neither better nor worse in his financial dealings than all the other purveyors of paintings in Rome.

He had set aside for me a large room on the third floor, looking out on the Tiber and the Castel Sant' Angelo. The sunlight came flooding through the windows; the window boxes were scarlet with roses, which Giulia carefully watered; and the smell of paint hung heavy on the walls. There were stacked canvases along one side of the room, perhaps two hundred altogether, and there was something about this barren room which suggested that until recently it had been used for storing pictures and was rarely entered.

From downstairs there came a continual hubbub of voices. For the most part they were the bright, high-pitched voices of boys, who ground the paints and ran the Maestro's errands, carrying paintings from one prospective purchaser to another. There came the sound of hammering and the whine of the lathe and saw, for the Maestro also made ornamental frames; and so the heady smell of oil paint was enlivened with the sweeter smell of wood and wood shavings.

I saw Maestro Valentino rarely. Sometimes he would come in the evening as the sun was setting; he alone could climb that creaking staircase soundlessly. He would peer in, gaze round the room for a moment, and then he would be gone; or else he would sit down beside the bed like a doctor examining a patient and hold my hand. Though he was old and bent, there was a glow of health in him; soon I learned that he was bent from much studying, and

was not so old as he appeared, and the glow of health was compounded by the wine which inflamed his cheeks. I never saw a
beak so parrotlike, or a mouth so wide. When he smiled he
showed rows of jagged uneven teeth, which somehow reminded
me of a fish. But he carried himself with some elegance, and there
was always some jeweled order on his breast and his fingers, too,
glittered with jewels.

Once, when I had been about a month in his house, he came at
sunset with a gift of warm cakes in a basket. They were almond
cakes, very sweet, and like almonds they tasted faintly of poison.

He drew the bench from under the bed and sat down on it with
a purposeful air. I could see he intended to stay.

"I hope you are well, boy," he said. "They've cupped and bled
you enough, haven't they? You've put on weight, too, and so have
the leeches. God help us all, we'll all be gone soon enough! How's
the fever?"

"It's better today, Maestro Valentino."

"Thank God for that! You look as though there's some
strength left in you. They tell me you have been painting a bit.
Well, have you?"

"I tried to paint the flowers in the window box this morning."

"Flowers!" he said, his voice rising in alarm. "You'll never make
your fortune by painting flowers, boy. Who buys flowers?
There's no market for them. I have a hundred flower pieces in my
shop, and I sell perhaps one in three months. Paint the human figure — paint portraits — paint the saints! Let me tell you something. There's a market for Crucifixions. I have ten on order, and
for the life of me I can't find a painter who can do them worthily."

"I can't paint Crucifixions," I said, and his face fell.

It was growing dark. He heard one of the boys clambering up
the stairs and shouted to him to bring in a lamp. The boy ran

down the stairs three at a time, and for a little while longer I found myself gazing at the strange long Spanish-looking face of my protector, his beak glowing in the fading sunlight.

"You can't paint Crucifixions!" he said in a sharp voice. "There's nothing easier, if you would only set your mind to it. You have all the talent for it. I can smell a Crucifixion painter a mile away. Do you know Leonello Spada?"

"I've seen his paintings."

"What do you think of him?"

"A good draughtsman, but he knows nothing about painting."

"Exactly. There's no more talent in him than in my little finger. He can draw a pretty face, male or female, and there are some people who say he has a gift for drapery, and that's all there is to him. But now he's a Crucifixion painter commanding a hundred ecus for every painting. I taught him the trade, and I'll teach you if you'll only have the patience to listen."

I shook my head. The boy came running into the room with a lamp. It was a hot day, and the boy was naked to the waist, his young flesh glowing in the lamplight like fruit. There was no table in the room: only the bed, the stool, and the paintings stacked against the wall. The boy pretended to be looking for a place to set the lamp until Maestro Valentino growled: "Put the lamp on the floor, boy!"

For five weeks I had been in fever, lying on a straw bed among the dying in the Ospedale della Misericordia, and except for Giulia and Maestro Valentino I had seen no one since I came to live in the Maestro's house. There was something unnerving in the boy's health and vigor, and the grace of his movements, for I remember throwing out my hands towards him.

"So soon, Michelangelo?" said the old man. "So soon?"

I said nothing. The boy came up to me, held both my hands, gazed at me uncomprehendingly, as the young gaze on the sick, and then bent down and kissed me swiftly on the forehead; then he released his hands and one of them rested on my hair.

To Maestro Valentino he whispered: "His hair is damp." There was a note of horror in his voice.

"Of course his hair is damp," the old man said. "He is suffering from fever, and if you stay any longer the fever will get worse! Now get going!"

The boy fled, and we talked a little longer in the light of the small bubbling oil lamp.

Once Maestro Valentino said: "Can you think clearly and come to some conclusions about your future?"

I said: "I didn't know there was any future left. I won't paint Crucifixions."

"Why not?"

"It's not in me to paint Christ suffering. I cannot reach out so far. No more can I paint Christ ascending to heaven. I can only paint the Christ I know, the one who walked the earth. Let the other painters paint what no one has ever seen or felt on his own flesh."

Maestro Valentino held his head a little to one side, looking at me from the corner of his eyes.

"A hundred ecus for a Crucifixion — you must admit it's a fair price. A man could live a whole year on a hundred ecus. You'll change your mind, I hope. It's only reasonable that a painter should paint for the highest price, isn't that so?" Then he lowered his voice and said: "Would you copy a Crucifixion? I have two Flemish Crucifixions which are worth copying. I could get you fifty ecus for them?"

"I won't copy," I said. "I'll paint my own paintings. I haven't time enough, or desire enough, to follow in someone else's footsteps. I must go my own way."

"And what way is that?"

"God knows," I said, and turned my face to the wall, for I knew there was nothing to be gained by further argument.

Then for perhaps a whole minute I heard him muttering to himself, and at last, taking the lamp with him, he went silently down the stairs.

That night the fever came back again. I was once more in the Ospedale della Misericordia, seeing the dead and dying all round me. A great wind arose, and I saw them tossing in the wind like leaves, turning over and over, until at last none were left and there were only the bare damp walls of the tunnel, and myself alone with the memory of these people who were no more than dead leaves in the wind.

"Come back!" I shouted. "For God's sake come back! You are not leaves! You are human beings!"

I heard my own voice echoing interminably through the empty tunnel.

When I woke up, Giulia was mopping my brow with a sponge and there was a single candle burning in the room.

"Do you know," I said, "a candle is the source of all life?"

She said nothing, and I doubt whether she heard me, but sometimes I would remember those words later when I was painting. The beauty of a candle flame in a dark room is such that a man can go mad watching it. I watched Giulia sponging me, her lips pursed, her eyes lowered, her small face rounded with care, her small breasts moving in her shapeless gown. She was neither pretty nor ugly; she had one of those commonplace faces which you can see in any of the villages outside Rome, those faces which are stolid, almost expressionless, and curiously empty. And seeing her, I was aware only of wonder that there should be so much beauty in the commonplace. I said: "Giulia, I shall paint you. In a thousand years' time people will know how beautiful you are!"

She said nothing even when I reached up and stroked her face half hidden by her falling hair. My words were no more than dead leaves falling on the surface of a pool, scarcely touching her, and I no longer remember what I said — perhaps that she was beautiful and that she should not look so sorrowful. She had a strange commonplace beauty, but it haunted me, so that I found myself wondering how I would paint her. She had a habit of brushing her forehead lightly with the back of her hand, a gesture of the utmost weariness and yet it was performed with grace and composure, and I thought of painting her with her hand lifted in weariness, leaning against a wall when the day's work was done, all the strength drained from her. She was still sponging me. I said: "What do you do all day?"

"I work," she answered. "What else is there to do?"

"In the kitchen?"

"Yes, in the kitchen."

"And in the workshop?"

"Yes, in the workshop. I help the apprentices. I make the frames sometimes and run errands. They don't give me time to rest."

"All day and half the night?"

"Yes, all day and half the night."

She said nothing more for a little while. She finished sponging me, and now at last she sat down on a bench beside my bed with an expression of calm exhaustion, her head bent, leaning a little forward, with her hands folded on her lap; and then I knew this was how I would paint her, sitting down, slumped with weariness and yet with a kind of satisfaction, and all the folds of her gown would express her sadness, her weariness and her contentment.

"Do you want to paint me now?" she asked, and I knew from her tone that she was in no hurry to be painted.

"No, we'll start tomorrow, if Maestro Valentino will give his permission."

"He'll give it," she said, "but he will charge it against the money he gets for your paintings — he has already opened an account for you with your board and lodging subtracted from the price of a picture he sold."

"What picture?"

"I don't know. Only I know he sold the picture three days ago."

Her voice dropped again to a whisper. She was terrified, listening to every creaking of the stairs, afraid that Maestro Valentino would come up the stairs and see her alone with me long after the time when she should have gone back to her place in the kitchen.

I asked her how much Maestro Valentino would charge me for her services as a model.

She gave me a brief smile, threw up her head, and said: "Not much. I'm not worth anything."

She was gone a few moments later, carrying the basin of water and the sponge.

The next morning, when Maestro Valentino came to see me, I told him I wanted to paint a full-length portrait of Giulia. I believed I would be able to paint her in a week of sittings.

"I wanted you to paint Crucifixions," he muttered. "I hope you have been thinking of what I told you."

"Yes, I've thought about it, but I want to paint Giulia."

He pulled at his beard and said: "There's no money in painting a kitchen wench."

I was angry, but said nothing. He drew up the bench and leaned over the bed, his beard brushing against my face. His brow was furrowed, and his eyes were glittering.

"With your talent," he exclaimed, "you have no excuse for your follies. Paint kings, cardinals, and ambassadors — what have kitchen wenches to do with you? Paint Crucifixions and Last Suppers and Depositions — that's where the money is, my fine fellow! Put yourself in my hands and I'll make a fortune for you. How many times do I have to tell you that it is in my power to get you great commissions, my pretty cock sparrow? There is a prince of the Church — I cannot tell you his name — who has asked me to find a painter to be attached to his household. Your name came to my lips, and I very nearly uttered it. I was in grave danger of mentioning your name. Why, I told myself, there is no man in the world who can paint damasks and silks as you can, and then I looked at your paintings and remembered that you have never painted damasks or silks — always the bare flesh, a goblet or two, and a little piece of cheap cloth somewhere. You paint fruit well, and flowers too, and boys' faces, and somehow I was led to believe you could paint anything that walked the earth or the chambers of Heaven. You disappoint me. Why paint a kitchen wench when you can be painting cardinals?"

Maestro Valentino was not one of those men who can conceal their motives. I could see by the furrows in his brow that he was trying to hide something. He had already told me that a cardinal wanted to employ a painter in his household. He was one of those men who speak too quickly and are always surprised by their own words.

To soften the blow, I said: "I will paint Giulia, and you can call it the Magdalene."

"And how will you paint her?"

"As she is."

"Well, she's a little slut, and there's no grandeur or dignity in her — she's no more the Magdalene than I am. What's more, she is a virgin and thin, and as everyone knows the Magdalene was fat and far from being a virgin. Of course I cannot promise you she is a virgin. One of the apprentices tried to tumble her — to no good purpose, for she scratched his face with her dirty fingernails, and he will bear the scar for the rest of his life. Still, if you paint her kneeling before the feet of the blessed Savior with her back turned

towards you, you could make something of her. I can see the
painting now — a marble stairway, palm trees, and the dear Lord
sitting on his throne while the Magdalene wipes His feet with her
hair —"

"No, I want to paint Giulia alone," I said, "and I'll sell the painting to you for a hundred ecus. You would buy it, wouldn't you?"

"I don't buy paintings. I sell on commission. I charge four
tenths."

"Four tenths!" I exclaimed. "Why, that's nearly a half of the
worth of a painting!"

"So it is, but where would you be without that four tenths?
What's five tenths? What's six tenths? You are a painter, yet
you couldn't sell a painting to save your life. Who does the bargaining? Who has my knowledge of patrons? Who builds up the
clientele? And here you are, bargaining with me over the miserable pittance I charge, with a house and servants who have to be
paid. No, I won't buy your Magdalene, but I'll try to sell it for
you out of pity, if that's any comfort to you. You're a pig-headed
man, and you'll come to grief. I'll charge you for her sittings. Are
you sure you will have the painting ready in a week?"

"Yes, if you give me canvas and paint."

"I'll have to charge for them too," he said, and for the first time
I thought I detected a note of regret in his voice.

"You can set them against my account," I suggested. "They
cost little enough against a finished painting. It's a large account,
surely! Item, for rescuing Michelangelo from certain death, fifty
ecus. Item, for transporting Michelangelo from the Ospedale della
Misericordia, fifteen ecus. Item, for supplying the model, by name
Giulia, another three ecus. Item, for a roof above Michelangelo's
head, six ecus. For canvases, thirty ecus. For paint and varnish,
thirty ecus —"

He looked at me narrowly, the great beaklike nose mottled with anger and the lips curled derisively, but the eyes were laughing even though he pretended to be indignant. He interrupted my long catalogue of expenses, shouting: "Enough! Make an end to it! Will you haggle with me?"

"Yes, I'll haggle with you! It's more than my life is worth not to haggle with you sometimes! I want a fair price for my paintings!"

"You'll have a fair price, Michelangelo."

"For all of them?"

"Yes, for all of them."

"And you'll keep me informed whenever you sell one of my paintings?"

"On God's oath I'll keep you informed!"

"You'll tell me at once whenever you have sold a painting of mine?"

"Yes, by God's oath."

"Then why didn't you tell me you had already sold one of them?"

He looked startled. For the first and last time in my life I saw Maestro Valentino in the guise of a young Sebastian when the first arrows are winging their way toward him.

"How did you know?" he asked.

"A little frog jumped through the window an hour ago and told me."

He burst out laughing.

"Well, the truth is I had intended to tell you the moment I came into your room, but it slipped my mind. I sold your John the Baptist to Cardinal del Monte for fifty ecus."

"Then you owe me thirty ecus."

"You're quicker at subtraction than I thought you would be."

"And is Cardinal del Monte the man who wanted to employ a painter in his household?"

There was a long pause, and I knew he was debating with himself whether to tell me the truth.

"Yes," he said at last. "Yes, indeed. God's oath! I'm not a man who hides the truth. As for Giulia, paint her if you like! It will do no harm. As for the Cardinal, you will owe me a commission for every painting you do for him, but you'll have to be more presentable before I take you into his presence. You're nothing but fish bones! You'll have to eat and sleep more — that's for certain!"

Saying this, he left my bedside and made for the door, but not before shouting: "God's curse, what do you believe in?"

"I believe in God and His mercy," I said.

"That's a comfort. Sometimes when I am looking at you I wonder whether you are not on the side of the Devil!"

I heard him running down the stairs, sometimes slipping a stair or two, but always regaining his balance, cursing. I had penetrated his secrets, and that was reason enough for his grief. No doubt he is necessary; there must always be someone claiming his four tenths; but I was determined to make him earn his money.

The day began promisingly, with high clouds racing across an indigo blue sky, but during the afternoon the wind rose, bringing the smell of the Tiber to my small room. Soon there were thunderclaps, and by four o'clock the rain fell in torrents and the sky darkened. When Giulia came, it was already dark and the candles were flickering in the wind.

I was still feverish, but I was in a mood for painting. Already I had set up the easel, and the canvas was already in place.

Giulia was sitting on the bench, shivering, for the weather had turned unseasonably cold and the thunderclaps frightened her, so that she was continually crossing herself and muttering prayers. God knows what was going through her mind! She looked like a trapped animal, and no doubt in her confused, unhappy eyes I was only one more of those men who made unreasoning demands on her. Once or twice she would raise her head a little and gaze at me timidly, but a moment later she would drop her gaze. I think she trusted me, but I must have been a terrible sight in a blood-red dressing gown, barefoot, with a two week growth of beard and eyes which still glowed with fever. As I prepared the canvas, I usually had a paintbrush in each hand and another between my teeth, and soon in a most unaccountable fashion drops of paint would find a lodging place in my hair, my eyebrows, my cheeks and my beard, and my lips too would be covered with paint in all colors, so that I resembled a savage from the Indies. I am not the most handsome of men, but when I am painting I resemble a wild animal clothed in a Jacob's coat of colors.

So I went on painting, sometimes looking past the canvas at the silent, motionless figure of the girl sitting on the bench with her back to the window. She knew what was wanted of her, for she kept perfectly still except for the trembling of her lips; and by her silence I knew she had posed many times before. By this time all the sounds of the street had died down, and the thunder was moving away.

I had been painting for about half an hour, lost in that trance which descends upon all painters when they are truthfully submitting themselves to the model, when I saw that Giulia was no longer sitting on the bench. She had vanished, but her leave-taking had been very quiet and I heard no footsteps. I was not altogether surprised, for it sometimes happens to all painters to find themselves deserted by their models, either because nature has summoned them away or because they have become restless. I went on painting, because the image of her was burned in my brain. I would even look up from the canvas and see her sitting there, though she had vanished. She was wearing only a yellow shift and a bedraggled petticoat, but the shift was laced over the breast, having something of the effect of a bodice. All this I remembered. I remembered the curling shadows of her hair, the hollows of her neck, the thrust of the small shoulder blades, the way the candle-light fell on her forehead, and the way her hands lay open on her knees. Up to this time I had painted only her face and shoulders, for her body was not yet of any interest to me. I say I painted her face, but in fact it was only sketched in with heavy flesh colors and heavier shadows, though already her features were recogniz-able and the finished painting was already complete in my mind. She had vanished. I told myself I would work for another hour, for she had already given me so much of herself that I could con-tinue working without her.

And then I heard footsteps and looked up, expecting to see her sitting in her accustomed place on the bench, but she was not sit-ting. She was standing in front of me stark naked, solemn and un-moving, a strange smile playing on her lips, her hair falling over her thin shoulders. I said nothing, for I was dazzled by her beauty, her strangeness. For a whole minute I remained there like someone transfixed, looking her up and down, amazed by the small, thin, solemn beauty of her body.

She stood there trembling, her small face bent and shivering, and I felt no desire for her even though she offered herself. I felt only the overmastering desire to paint her as she was, the white body against the darkness of the night which streamed through the open window. I have no use for women, especially one so soft-fleshed and uncertain; I prefer to take my pleasure with boys. But there was in Giulia a strange fire of innocence so that one felt that whatever happened to her, she would be immune to the world's misfortunes, unreachable. There was holiness in her, and so I painted her as the Magdalene twice, once fully clothed, and then again in her nakedness. All the time she was fretting, for this was not what she wanted of me.

I worked through the night, and when morning came I was feverish again.

This was the worst of all the fevers I endured, worse even than the fever I suffered in the tunnel. It was as though all the liquid in my body was being dried into powder, as though I were watching my bones turning into water and steam. Day after day I was tormented by thirst. Maestro Valentino made plans for sending me back to the hospital, but Giulia, who nursed me through all those days, insisted that I was too weak to be moved. "He will die on your hands if you move him," she said, and she spent many days and nights by my bed, with cool water for my burning brows.

So the days passed, and every day, and many times a day, she came with gruel and little cakes, and sometimes there were eggs and fruit. Every day she would bring me a clean shirt to replace the one which had grown black and clammy with sweat. I heard carriages rumbling outside and people shouting in the street, and these sounds would assume the shapes of paintings. There would be the sudden high-pitched cry of a child, and immediately I would see an execution, or armed men scaling walls, or spears clashing. In those days the only sound I looked forward to was the sound of Giulia's footsteps on the stairs.

She would come into my room with the same grave solemnity which characterized all her movements, gliding rather than walking, assuming the attitudes of a nun performing a holy rite, very humble. She would tremble a little as she pushed the bowl toward me, whispering: "This is for you," or "Maestro Valentino has sent this for you," and I would take it eagerly and gaze at her in the light coming from the open window, or if she came late in the evening, by the light of a candle placed at the foot of the bed.

As my health returned, I was plagued with the most violent nightmares. The square window became a block, with a masked headman beside it. The headman was powerfully built, stark

[99]

naked, his body dark and covered with thick oily hairs, only his enormous genitals were scarlet and livid. Every night I saw the masked headman leaning on his ax, smiling and beckoning to me. "Come," he said. "Lay your head lightly on the block, and all your troubles will be over!" He smiled invitingly, showing his beautiful teeth. Sometimes, when I could bear his presence no longer, I would imagine myself hurling myself against him, wrestling with him and exerting all my strength, pounding him with my clenched fists, while the sound of his laughter roared through my ears. Then at last he would press my head down on the block with one powerful hand, carefully lifting the hair from the nape of my neck, then he would raise the ax high above his head. At this moment I would awake screaming, and sometimes Giulia would rush in with a towel soaked in cold water to cool my burning head. In this way I learned that she often slept outside my door.

The dreams of the old and dying are unendurable, but the nightmares of the young are also terrible. A strange light falls on dreams, and sometimes I have been able to recreate this light in my paintings.

There were not only the dreams of headmen and axes, of armed men marching in pursuit, seeing myself running down endless alleyways to escape from them, but there were also those other dreams, equally intimidating, although they promised happiness. Out of the darkness there would come a boy's face, and then gradually, inch by inch, a light from some unseen source would spread out over the whole of his body, uncovering his breast, his neck, his shoulders, a knee, a hand. He would come toward me with a smile playing on his lips, naked and beautiful, and when I put out my hand to touch him, he would vanish into thin air; and sometimes this dream, which was continually repeated, was more terrible to me than the dream of the headman. No women ever entered my dreams.

Thus between dreaming and waking, I entered the new life of a convalescent, whose hands trembled when he lifted a spoon and who had to be supported in order to stand upright. I slept most of the day and half the night, and all the while I was aware that strength was returning to me. It came slowly, drop by drop, but with every drop of newfound strength I knew I was returning to the world of the living. With all my strength I wanted to paint the light I had seen in my dreams.

One day, after Giulia had sponged me, I asked for a mirror. She shook her head slowly from side to side.

"No, not yet," she said. "Tomorrow perhaps."

"Why tomorrow?"

"Because tomorrow you will look better."

And when at last she gave me a mirror, I wondered at her courage in nursing me, for I could not recognize the gaunt, ravaged and hollow-cheeked stranger who stared out of the mirror in abject misery.

At first I thought someone was looking over my shoulder, someone with matted hair, great hollows instead of eyes and trembling lips, which were not red, but of some unearthly bluish color, like lead. Was this, I asked myself, the face of the great painter Michelangelo Merisi da Caravaggio? It was beyond belief that a man could look so much like a drowned and decomposing animal, and still be living. Horror-stricken, I returned the mirror, and she took it silently.

She cut my hair, trimmed and combed my beard, rubbed salves into the bruises which covered my body — for in my fever I had thrown myself against the wall — and saw that I was fed regularly. Maestro Valentino, who had kept away from me when I was ill, now resumed his visits. It appeared that there had been delicate negotiations concerning my future, but he took care to conceal the name of my future patron by mentioning so many names that I lost count of them. In this way I came to learn that Cardinal del Monte, Marchese Vicenzo Giustiniani and Prince Marzio Colonna had all seen my paintings and approved of them, and many others had expressed their interest. Maestro Valentino had not been idle while I was ill. He had shown them everywhere, and even the paintings I made of Giulia had been shown to his customers.

"How many have been sold?" I asked.

"No more than one or two," Maestro Valentino said airily. "Just enough to pay for your food and lodging."

I bounded off the bed and pushed him against the wall.

"Tell me truthfully how many you have sold?"

"Three," he answered, and when he saw that I was about to crack his skull against the wall, he said: "Four!"

"So you have sold four paintings and not paid me anything! If I had died, you wouldn't have paid for a single Mass for my soul! Tell me, how many Masses would you have paid for?"

He did not answer. He was blue with fear. Some of his boys came running up the stairs, for they heard us quarreling.

"Well, how many?" I shouted.

"I have sold five of your paintings, Michelangelo — that's the truth. I forgot one. I sold them all to Cardinal del Monte, and I have received a promise from Marchese Giustiniani for another."

"So it is the Cardinal del Monte who wants me to become his painter," I shouted, so that my voice could be heard in the street. "How much are you preparing to sell me for?" I stepped back to look at him better. "So you have sold altogether five paintings of mine to Cardinal del Monte, and what have I received?"

"I saved your life, young man," Maestro Valentino said.

"When you were hungry and ill, I took you into my own home. Isn't that worth something?"

I told him to make up my accounts within the hour. He could deduct whatever appeared reasonable for my food and lodging, and receive a gift of one of my paintings for all the services he had rendered me, but for the rest he would receive only his commission. I proposed to enter the service of Cardinal del Monte that very day.

Maestro Valentino threw up his hands in despair.

"You understand so little, Michelangelo," he said. "You are not well, and your mind is inflamed. Cardinal del Monte is not even in Rome — he can do nothing for you until he returns from Florence."

"How long will that be?"

"A month — two months — who knows? Stay with me here, Michelangelo. We shall arrange something to our mutual advantage."

If he had not said these words, I might have stayed with him. Instead, I left his house later in the day after sending a message to the chamberlain of the Cardinal's palace, indicating that I was ready to enter his service. The reply came back: "Come whenever you please. We are waiting for you." Then, with Giulia by my side, and with some of the boys helping to carry my paintings, wearing a borrowed cape and a feather in my cap, I went to the palace.

The Cardinal in Majesty

THE palace of Cardinal del Monte lay just behind the Piazza Navona and was called the Palazzo Madama. It was very large and beautifully appointed, and at the same time it gave the appearance of being much smaller than the other great palaces of Rome. This palace belonged to the Grand Duke of Tuscany, and accordingly the lilies of Florence appeared over the ornamental gateway. The Cardinal served as ambassador to the Holy See. They told me he was still young, and was at this very moment returning from Florence, being expected in Rome during the coming week.

When I reached the palace, the Cardinal's chamberlain, Monsignor Ettulio Scarpi, was waiting for me at the head of the stairs. He was a man from the Romagna, but by long acquaintance with the Cardinal, he had developed the habits and manners of a Florentine. He was small and precise, with an appearance of grave concern for the foibles of men, and a little uncomfortable in the presence of anyone who was not in holy orders. Yet he welcomed me warmly and said he had received instructions from the Cardinal about what should be done for me if the negotiations with Maestro Valentino proved successful. I was to receive a room in the palace, and such assistance as he could render. No final arrangements, of course, could be concluded until the Cardinal's return.

"We have already arranged a room for you," the monsignor said, "but whether it will serve your purpose is a matter which you alone can decide. At least there is a great deal of space, and as much privacy as you need. Other rooms may be available later, and you may discuss this with His Highness when he returns."

I thanked the monsignor and said I would like to see the room now, because I was anxious to resume painting.

"I shall take you there myself," he said, and there began the long and cavernous journey through the kitchens to the old guardroom which had been set aside for me. This room, which stood at the bottom of the stairs leading to the servants' quarters, did not at first impress me. It was perhaps forty feet wide and forty feet broad, and the only light came from a small high window looking onto the street. There clung to the bare walls the odor of young soldiers, of leather, of rusted swords, of rope and harness. The walls were bare, and there was no furniture except a bed and a chair. The barrenness of the place was strangely comforting, and I said I would remain there until something better was found. The monsignor promised to send tapestries to hang on the walls and whatever else I needed, and asked softly whether it was my intention to keep Giulia with me. I said she was a servant of Maestro Valentino and would bring me food when I needed it. I said I would find a new servant in due course. That night I began a new painting.

It must have been a week after I arrived when four men came hurrying down the stairs, carrying a wicker basket between them. There was an older man with spectacles on his nose, wearing a black doublet and a black collar trimmed with lace, and he was perhaps a cleric of some kind, very grave, and of fine Roman speech. The other men were younger, wearing smallclothes and doublets of patterned velvet in blue and white, and they must have been the servants of the house, for they had the look of servants.

They set the wicker basket down beside the bed, and then the older man addressed me, saying he had brought these clothes so that I should appear respectable for an audience with his most illustrious master, and he offered a thousand pardons because it had not been done earlier.

"I hear you are a young painter, and already famous," he said. "The Cardinal wishes me to say he hopes he will be of some service to you, but feeling that you needed to recover your health in quietness he thought it better to leave you in peace."

I thanked the cleric, and asked him when I would have the audience with the Cardinal.

"Now," he said, "as soon as you are fit to see him. The truth is the Cardinal is already waiting for you in the audience chamber."

I liked the cleric. He was a man of about fifty, already gray, with a long thin face and lips that puckered into a half-smile, yet with an expression of some sadness such as you find in those who must be obedient to their master's moods; obedience being a weight upon his shoulders which he bore gladly. His name was Fabrizio Crescenzi, as I learned later, and he had been in the service of the Cardinal and the Cardinal's family since his childhood.

As they busied themselves to prepare me for the audience with the Cardinal, they resembled cooks preparing a succulent meal out of a thin and bony calf. One came with a basin of hot water, another took an iron comb to my hair, a third cut my fingernails, a fourth scented me, a fifth laid out new clothes on the bed, with undershirt and drawers and a purple doublet with a white collar, with the trunk hose in the fashion of Seville, very full at the thigh and narrow at the knee, with boots of scarlet cotton double-soled

— a strange equipment for a painter attending upon a Cardinal. And all this, the washing and the hair clipping and the combing, the scenting and the trimming and the powdering, the pulling of my body into a starched and creaking undershirt, and then into the scented doublet and hose, all this could scarcely have lasted more than five minutes with all of them pushing and pulling, and the old cleric giving orders as though he had spent a lifetime dressing young men. Finally they gave me a blue velvet cap and a silver chain to wear around my neck.

I had no complaints against these clothes, for I understood well enough that I could scarcely appear in the clothes I had been wearing, which were the same clothes I had worn in the hospital, though they had been cleaned. I could not recognize myself when one of the servants held up a mirror: in the flickering candlelight I saw a face as smooth and ripe as waxed fruit.

"You have made me look as though I were being laid out for the grave," I said.

"Don't you recognize yourself?" the old cleric said kindly. "Well, there's no time to stare into mirrors. Remember to kiss the ring, and say 'Illustrissimo,' and keep your eyes lowered. Watch your tongue, too. His Highness likes to listen, but he is not over-burdened with patience. Above all, be brief and let your requests be simple."

It was a long walk from my cellar to the audience chamber on the second floor where the Cardinal was waiting for me. We walked through half-cellars and quarter-cellars and along stone corridors through kitchens white with steam, pigs, boars and whole oxen roasting on the spits, for every Cardinal has whole armies of retainers to feed, and as I approached in purple doublet and blood-red cotton boots the cooks bowed and greeted me in the manner of Naples, which was then becoming common in Rome — with a low sweeping of the arms and a generous inclination of the whole body dangerously calculated to bring about the complete collapse of all its members, yet it was done with such finesse that I confess to a feeling of admiration for such simulated benevolence, those looks full of deep tenderness which, directed upon the stranger in their midst, were intended to placate not the stranger but the Lord Cardinal Francesco del Monte, as though in some way it were possible for the stranger to carry their names and salutations into the august presence of one who fed them so bountifully; for they were as eager to please me in my new costume as previously they had been to spit at me.

Today I confess there was no lack of merit in their greetings, and for once they were behaving in conformity with the law which states that only those who are honorable shall be honored. Yet I did not answer their greetings, but simply pushed my way with my escort through the crowded throngs of servants, guards, cook boys and chamberlains as though it were my practice to act the prince in their company; and I reminded myself not to bow too indulgently to the Cardinal, and certainly not in the Neapolitan manner, for there are many Cardinals and few great painters.

In the large audience chamber there were two thrones, one more splendid than the other, no doubt because it was reserved for the Pope. It was a wide room with windows looking out on the street, brilliantly lit, the walls covered with tapestries, the floor deep in carpets. The Cardinal sat at the far end of the room on the smaller of the two thrones, alone except for a young priest at his side. His robes were a brave and glowing scarlet, and a jeweled crucifix blazed on his breast, flashing blue fire.

Until I set eyes on Cardinal del Monte, I thought there was no man who had the power to make me bend my knee. Sitting there at the end of the long room, he looked as though he had been there forever. He looked grave and old, with a white beard, and I thought he must be about seventy until I came closer and saw his unlined face, his pink cheeks, and his blue eyes which glittered with the same fires which came from the crucifix. He had a high forehead and a long, lean face, and an expression of great sweetness. His beard, they told me, turned prematurely white on the day he received the cardinalate, for at this time he was still in his forties, yet he always gave an impression of vigorous age. From the shape of his nose and the clean-cut line of his lips I knew he was a Florentine; and in his speech, too, there was more of Florence than of Rome.

I knelt and kissed his ring, and then he lifted me up and said something about my paintings. I was confused and said nothing, keeping my eyes lowered, not hearing him until he said: "Then you are accustomed to compliments? Strange that you should take them so lightly."

"Not lightly, Illustrissimo. It is simply that I did not know that anyone had seen them. I was in hospital so long, and I had lost hope for my paintings. Many were scattered to the winds, and God alone knows what has happened to them."

"God knows," the Cardinal said, and he rose and put a hand on my shoulder and then led me a little way from the throne, before pointing to the wall where, over the tapestries, hung the five paintings bought from Maestro Valentino, for which I had not yet been paid. Among them were paintings which I had taken with me to hospital, where they were rolled up and I had used them as a pillow. Now the canvases had been stretched, frame makers had placed them in elaborate gilded frames hanging by bronze chains, and there were little plates of bronze set into the frames with the name of the painter and the subject of the painting. "This was done because you signed none of your paintings," the Cardinal said, as he led me by the hand to a windowseat. From the seat it was possible to see all the five paintings hanging on the opposite wall.

"They look well against the tapestry," he went on, and because I was still standing and gazing at my paintings, he said: "Come and sit beside me. Tell me, are they well arranged?"

"Yes, Illustrissimo," I replied, and after a pause: "Better if you had hung only one on the wall."

"Why only one?"

"Because one painting is enough for a wall. There should be only one painting hanging in a room."

"Then I would need five rooms for your paintings?"

"That is so, Illustrissimo, and an extra room in which a man can think about them and meditate on their perfections."

He laughed softly and said: "At least you cannot claim that they are all perfect."

"They are as perfect as I can make them, which means that they are in their own way perfect."

"Perfection belongs to God," the Cardinal said softly, and looked at the ceiling.

Then for a long while there was a distance between us, an unbridgeable chasm. Though I was sitting beside him, it was as though he was walking away into the distance, door after door opening, the guards with their halberds saluting him as he passed through each doorway, through the hundred rooms of the Palazzo Madama. He had weighed up my virtues and vices, and found me wanting. Soon, no doubt, there would come a brief sermon on the dangers of pride, and I would be dismissed with an exquisite wave of a jeweled hand.

In this long interval, while he was moving away across the infinite distances of space, I studied him closely. I observed that his lips were full, yet gave an appearance of austerity, and that his eyes, which were the color of the sky at dawn, were clouded with thought and strangely withdrawn, until the moment came when they opened wide and glittered fiercely, and then he seemed to be another man altogether. He was the contemplative and the man of action, the dreamer and the warrior. I noticed too that his body moved easily beneath the heavy robes. He was one of those men who cannot be painted in a single portrait. It would be necessary to paint him many times, under many different conditions, against many backgrounds, in order to render the complexities of his nature. Kindly, even-tempered, fierce, unrelenting, suave, merciful and merciless — he was all these, and he would change abruptly from one extreme to the other. He frowned like Jove and smiled as sweetly as the Madonna, and I knew I would be in bondage to him for the rest of my life.

As I have said, I expected him to launch into a brief sermon against my immodesty and pride, but instead he said: "God loves the proud. St. Jerome speaks somewhere of a holy pride, and there is truly a pride which is very satisfying to God. These paintings are your offering to God, given proudly. I do not warn you against pride. I warn you against the world, which will demand that you abandon your humility before God and your holy pride."

I could make little of these words, although he spoke them very slowly and meaningfully. *A holy pride . . . I warn you against the world . . . Your offering to God, given proudly . . .* How many times I was to remember these words in the days to come! And yet always there was the knowledge that the words themselves were without meaning, and fruitless, unless I heard them spoken in the deep and resonant tones of the Cardinal's voice. In time I came to understand them, and sometimes it seems to me they were the greatest of all the gifts he gave me.

For a while I said nothing, for I was dazzled by the presence of the Cardinal in his majestic robes, by the tapestries, by the hundreds of candles burning in the audience chamber, and I must confess to being dazzled by my own paintings on the wall. From time to time the Cardinal rose from his throne and paced the floor, or gazed at my paintings, or else he would pause beside a window. He kept asking questions about my art: where I had worked, and who were my masters, and how it came about that he had never heard my name until it fell from the lips of Maestro Valentino. I told him about the year I had spent in the household of Monsignor Pucci, and he shook his head in bewilderment.

"How could it be?" he said. "They told me nothing about you, Michelangelo. I knew Monsignor Pucci — not well, but we were on good terms. He never spoke about your paintings, but kept you locked in his heart. For my part I promise I shall not keep you to myself."

He asked me about the old guardroom where I was living, and I said it served me well enough, but I would like sometimes to be closer to the sky. He laughed and said he would make arrangements with Fabrizio Crescenzi to find a better room for me, and perhaps they would be able to find a small room at the top of the palazzo, where I could rest from my labors in the bowels of the earth, but the truth was that I had come to like my cavern and was in no urgent need of change. The longer I lived there, the more I liked it.

And always he returned to my paintings, asking me in what order I had painted them, and whether I ground my own colors, and who were my assistants, and who were the painters I admired. He was surprised when I told him that I had no assistants, and even if they had been given to me I would not have been able to work with them. He seemed to like my painting of a basket of fruit less than the others, so I reminded him that it was as difficult to paint fruit as human beings.

"But at least the fruit keep still," he said, half smiling.

"No, they change according to the sun and the shadows," I answered. "They fade and lose their colors, and therefore they must be painted quickly. They are the worst models."

"And what are the best models?"

"The people in the streets — they have so much richness in their faces."

"Then you would prefer to paint the people you see in the streets rather than dignitaries."

"No, Illustrissimo, I will paint whatever is given me to paint, whether it is dignitaries or the poor people in the streets, for the painter does not choose his subjects — God chooses them for him."

So we talked in that blazing room with the yellow tapestries rippling on the wall while the wind poured through the open windows. There were perhaps twenty people in that room — servants and priests — but I was scarcely aware of them. Once or twice a priest would come floating toward him, whisper something and receive a whispered reply, or — and this happened more often — the Cardinal would make an intricate sign with his long and beautifully tapered fingers, and I counted altogether more than twenty-five of these mysterious gestures which took the place of speech among the high dignitaries of the Church. These gestures were so quick that only a trained eye could observe their exact meaning. The fourth finger would lightly touch the thumb, or the second finger would rise quickly and then bury itself in his palm, or he would join his hands to form a cat's cradle. This language of the fingers entranced me, and I decided that when the time came to paint his portrait I would pay especial attention to his hands and they would form a gesture which was known to me and him alone.

"I see you are watching my hands," the Cardinal said once.

"You should not watch them too closely, otherwise you will learn their secrets."

"And if I cannot help watching them?"

"Then you should turn away and look at your own paintings."

For me he was always someone strange and foreign, beyond knowing; and it pleased me that he found me equally mysterious. Sometimes he would pause and gaze into my face with an unbelieving air, as though he could not quite bring himself to believe in my existence or that I had painted the pictures; and when, after an argument on the merits of Raphael and Leonardo da Vinci, I said: "On matters of theology I shall bow to your wisdom, but on matters of painting you should bow to mine," he threw back his head and laughed softly, saying: "You are almost a Florentine!"

"What is it to be a Florentine?" I asked, for I had known very few in my life.

"It is to be impudent even to God," the Cardinal said, and he might have gone on to explain the meaning of these words, but at that moment a young priest came sidling up to him, whispered a question, and departed.

We had talked for an hour, and I thought he was about to dismiss me when he said: "Will you have supper with me, Michelangelo?" and then without waiting for a reply he moved toward a small door leading into a dining room lined with red damask. It was a small room, an antechamber to the audience hall, and no doubt it was used for many purposes. Two page boys with lighted candles stood by the table. The candles had been lit only a few moments before.

For the Cardinal it was, I suppose, a simple supper, but for a man who has spent a year starving in Rome such meals were undreamed of. Four enormous fish were set down on the table, and these were followed by veal, then pullets, then fruit covered with powdery snow, the fruit being eaten with small cakes in the Florentine manner. The Cardinal ate little, while I ate ravenously. The Cardinal was amused, and he would see that my plate was always full. In a gallery musicians played, and he asked me whether I had any love for music. I told him I adored it, and was never happier than when listening to it.

"Can you play any instruments?" he asked.

I said I had been tempted to learn, but so far had made no serious effort. Nor, to my sorrow, did I have a good singing voice, yet I enjoyed singing in company when my voice would be drowned by others.

"When I first saw your paintings," he said, "I was sure you were also a musician."

I said I would paint for him a group of musicians, and at that moment the entire composition of the painting came to me. I would paint three boys all singing and playing on their instruments, with the Cardinal listening in the background. So we conversed about music, and toward the end of the supper it occurred to me that I was sitting in his private apartments, and there was a handsome page boy with a lighted candle behind me and three servants busily attending me, and I thought: "I am still lying on the straw in the hospital," and soon I was shaking as though with a fever. The Cardinal was talking, but his voice came from a long way away.

"What is the matter with you?" he said. "Are you shivering? Are you ill? Have I said something to embarrass you?"

"No, Illustrissimo."

"Then what has come over you?"

"I am afraid —"

"You have nothing to be afraid of. You are among friends —"

He leaned over the table and pressed a glass of claret in my hands, but the shivering went on, and I could not lift the glass. I stared down at the table and watched the hands of the servants.

"Lift up your head," he said in a commanding tone, but I could not.

I told myself I was a slave, I belonged to the shadows, I had no right to be in this small and beautiful room lined with red damask, with servants waiting on me. I was strong and vigorous in my painting, but in my wisdom there was only weakness and in my way of life only sickness. I did not belong here. I belonged to the poor devils in the streets, who lie in the straw. I thought the Cardinal was about to throw me out of the room, but instead he said gently: "Give him some more claret!"

"It's not claret I want."

"Then what is it?"

"God knows," I said, and buried my face in my hands.

About a minute passed, while I tried to regain my composure. At last he said sternly: "I will not have you sitting at my table and not looking at me. Have you committed some crime, that you dare not look at me —" Then his voice grew gentle again, and he said: "Is it poverty? There's no crime in poverty. The Holy Father himself, the blessed Lord Clement VIII, was born in exile, a homeless fugitive, with no money. He, too, climbed the stairs of strangers. True, he belonged to the noble family of the Aldobrandini, but Rome is full of the dispossessed sons of the nobility living in poverty. What is there to be ashamed of in poverty?"

"It is not shame," I said. "It is nothing that has a name, Illustrissimo."

"All things have a name, but you must search for it," he said. "Are you ill? Is there anything I can do for you? Come here, Michelangelo."

I rose from the table and went to kneel at his feet, to kiss his ring and to hear whatever anguished words of rebuke he had for me, but there were none. He spoke about my paintings as gifts of God, for surely I had not the power to do them without God's help. He had known that I had been suffering from fever, and he therefore spoke with a gentle solicitude and yet with a certain troubled expression as though even now he could not bring himself to believe that this ugly, bearded, ungainly fellow at his feet was the painter who had painted those five pictures which hung on his walls. "That is why you must keep well," he said. "You have this gift, and it is given to you by God to be used for His purposes. Believe me, if there is anything you need, it will be given to you."

He said he would be my protector always, he would give me a salary and whatever provisions I needed if I chose to live in the Palazzo Madama, and if I chose to live elsewhere, then this too was according to God's will and he would remain my protector. But this was only the beginning, and to encourage me he spoke of his friends in high places who were already envious of his good fortune in finding such a painter.

"Keep well, for your art's sake," he went on. "Do not think of me or of yourself — only of your art. I suppose there will come a time when the Holy Father himself will want to steal you from me, and the Grand Duke of Tuscany also, but you must have no loyalty to me. Tell me, what are you thinking about?"

"I am thinking about Your Highness's benevolence."

"And what else?"

"The straw in the hospital."

"Yes," he murmured, "I have heard about the hospital."

The musicians were no longer playing. They were watching the strange spectacle below, the Cardinal drawing back his chair while my huddled body lay at his feet. My tears fell on his scarlet robe, and his jeweled fingers lay on my damp hair.

At last, when I had composed myself, he said: "I shall leave you now. I shall not hold it against you that you are still feverish. You have an honorable place in my establishment, and you will always be welcome in my chambers." He said too that I could approach him at any time except during audiences and during his devotions and he would always greet me with open arms; and the more he heaped these honors on me, the more I trembled.

At last he rose and lifted me up and said: "I thank you for the painting of the musicians." Then he blessed me, his hand forming the sign of the Cross very slowly and with great energy. Then in a swirl of scarlet he left the small dining room. From another door, as though at a secret sign, Fabrizio Crescenzi entered, to lead the way to my dark cellar.

"How did you find the Cardinal?" he asked me, as we walked through vast corridors and passageways.

"More generous than I hoped, and kinder than I dared to imagine —"

Fabrizio Crescenzi put his finger to his lips.

"There's no doubt of his kindness," he said, "but of his generosity there are different opinions. He pays us when he can. He owes us many months of salary, and no doubt you will find yourself as poor as the rest of us. Still, if you are in his good graces, your fortune is made. I've heard that he pays his painters before he pays his other servants."

"Has he had painters before?"

"Many — and he kept them a week before dismissing them. He will keep you longer, because he is deeply attached to you. They tell me he has spent hours gazing at your paintings, and when a visitor comes he leads him directly to the paintings and asks his opinion, and if he agrees with his visitor, then it is well with him. Once he asked one of his priests whether it was likely you would ever have a desire to enter holy orders."

[119]

"And what did the priest say?"

"He said, Michelangelo, that it would be a sad day for the Church if you became a priest."

We had reached the kitchens, and now it was only a few steps to my room.

"Well, you're close to the cooks, so you won't ever starve again," he said. "Are they feeding you well?"

"As well as anyone could desire —"

"Then take this advice. Don't grow fat, Michelangelo. The Cardinal hates fat men. Did you notice that all his clerics are thin? If you have hollow cheekbones, His Highness will love you. Well, good night, Michelangelo. No doubt you will have better quarters tomorrow."

"Good night," I said, and soon I threw myself on the bed and fell asleep, dreaming of a vast yellow audience chamber filled from floor to ceiling with my paintings and the Pope, or rather the Cardinal dressed in papal robes, was standing in the middle of the room, admiring them. In my dreams I heard the Cardinal saying again: "You must have no loyalty to me," and I knew I would be loyal to him until I died.

The Villa Medici

DURING the following weeks, while I was working on my painting of the musicians, I learned many things about the Cardinal which I had never suspected. I learned, for example, that he was very close to the Pope and only the Cardinal San Severino was closer; that he read Greek as easily as I read Italian; that he sometimes walked incognito in Rome, wearing the clothes of a merchant, with a fur-lined cape, and these secret journeys were performed more often in winter than in summer; and when he wearied of the Palazzo Madama, he would take up his residence in the Villa Medici, which also belonged to the Grand Duke of Tuscany.

There were other things I learned, which were even more to my liking. He not only possessed his own musicians and his own singers, but he would often permit his servants to attend their concerts, and nothing gave him greater pleasure than to be among musicians. They said, too, that he was skilled in the sciences, and that there was a secret room in the Villa Medici where he practiced the art of alchemy, transforming lead into gold, but they added he was not overly successful, otherwise his servants would be better paid. They also said that he was at work on a history of the Florentine Republic and had already written some thousands of pages. When Fabrizio Crescenzi spoke about him, it was always with expressions of awe and incredulity. He seemed larger than anyone else in Rome and carried his magnificence lightly.

I mention these things only because they were a part of my life and of my dreams. I lived in his shadow, and was perfectly content to remain his servitor. I had seen him but once, and if I never saw him again I would still be happy in the knowledge that I was attached to his court. He was one of those men who leave a shining on the air, and sometimes I would think of him as a meteor who flashed high in the heavens and never really settled upon the earth.

I expected that many weeks would pass before he remembered my existence, but nearly every day Fabrizio Crescenzi would come to me with some small present, saying it was His Highness's wish that I should possess it. In this way I received some damask curtains, a rosary, a pair of hose, a cape from Florence, a box filled with sweetmeats, an old Roman helmet which had turned green with age, and a small ivory crucifix. There were many other small presents, but most often he would send me gifts of flowers from the gardens of the Villa Medici, saying that he hoped they would bring the sunlight to my dark cave. Sometimes there would come brief notes in his own handwriting, addressed to "the most honorable painter Michelangelo Merisi living in the darkness beneath the earth."

Meanwhile I worked on the painting, using as models two boys plucked off the streets. They were both handsome, but in different ways, for one was full-fleshed, with chestnut-colored hair and blue liquid eyes, and the other was delicate and dark, with something about him which reminded me of Giulia. Neither could play a musical instrument, but in time they learned to play a little. What I liked about them was a certain gentleness of expression, a kind of brooding innocence, though they were far from being innocent. They had that tenderness which is appropriate to music, and while I painted them I saw to it that musicians played behind a curtain. The younger and more meditative boy was painted twice, in a sweet and melancholy mood on the left of the painting, and then you see him again with his back turned in the corner of the painting. The boy in the center was draped with the red damask curtains sent by the Cardinal. I painted the notes of music carefully so that men should know what they are singing.

One day, while I was still painting these youthful musicians, the Cardinal sent me a pannier full of grapes. Accordingly I arranged that the boy at the left should be plucking aimlessly at a bunch of grapes, and when I think of this painting, I remember the sweet smell of the grapes which came from the first vintage, and the youthful flesh of the boy Giorgio, who was depicted unclothed except for a loose toga around his waist; and in painting his flesh I sought to render the same delicate pearly light which fell on the grapes.

In those days I knew few painters, and indeed I kept apart from them, having encountered none in Rome who were worthy of my admiration. One day the painter Leonello Spada sought me out. He was about my own age, tall and well built, with thick curly hair and the merest suggestion of a golden beard, but what especially attracted me to him was his manner, which was gentle and confident and always on the edge of laughter. He had large violet-colored eyes and a nose which was wonderfully distinguished, being sharp as the nose of an aristocratic prelate. He said he had heard good things about me from Maestro Valentino, and having observed my paintings, he had felt an overwhelming desire to meet me, but for some reason he had felt afraid. Now at last he had taken his courage in his hands, and he hoped I would honor him with my friendship.

I said I was busy, but if it pleased him he could look at the few paintings I still owned. I had not yet finished painting Giorgio, and every moment of the day was spent in contemplating this painting I had promised for the Cardinal, or painting it, or busying myself with the affairs of my two models. He had come at an inopportune time, and I would gladly have sent him on his way.

He examined four or five paintings, saying nothing, and I thought he was about to leave when he caught sight of the painting of the musicians standing on the easel. It was not a very large painting, but it gave an impression of magnitude and seemed to dominate the room, and this came about, I believe, because the red damask curtain was a blaze of color and because the flesh tones were intensely luminous. If you set this painting on a wall, it would dominate and devour any other painting in the same room.

"My God, what have you done?" Leonello Spada exclaimed when he saw the painting, and he stood in front of it with his mouth open as though thunderstruck.

"It is not finished," I said. "There is much more to be done, especially with the head of the boy on the right. I had hoped to put Cardinal del Monte in it, but there is no room for him."

"You're dissatisfied with the painting?"

"Yes — it's too heavy for the frame. The boys are too much in the foreground, and they are almost spilling out of the picture."

"You find a good many things wrong with it?"

"Yes."

"Then you are a fool," Leonello Spada said quietly. "You are a bigger fool than I thought! Don't you realize that if you died now, and all your other paintings were lost, and there was only this one, then you would still be immortal? Don't you realize that?"

I said I realized all this well enough, but it was not a question of immortality — it was a question of my own dissatisfaction with my painting, because the canvas was too crowded, because there was scarcely a square inch of the painting which was not filled with the three boys, and because there was not enough air for them to breathe. It was all my fault, because I had chosen too small a canvas. I had intended to paint the Cardinal attending a concert given by these three boys, but I had been carried away by their youthful beauty and the colors of their flesh.

"And this surprises you?" Leonello Spada said, as though he were a great teacher commiserating with the failure of a novice. "You are astonished because the colors of the flesh appear on the canvas and there is no place for the Cardinal?"

"I am astonished because I had hoped to convey the sound of music, but instead I have conveyed silence."

"What has music to do with painting?" Leonello Spada exclaimed, and I was so angry that I threw a paintbrush at his face.

"My God, if you don't know what music has to do with painting, then you might as well hang yourself!" I shouted. "You might as well ask what sculpture has to do with painting. You're a fool, and there is nothing inside your head except the contents of half a dozen addled eggs! Now get out!"

I expected him to scurry up the steps and vanish, for I screamed at him more abuse than most men can stand. He looked ridiculous with the thick smear of white paint on his face. The room was dark. Only a few lamps were lit. Giorgio was sleeping on the bed with his face turned to the wall, in the shadows. Hearing me shouting, he jumped up, terrified. He had thrown the light coverlet away and was staring at Leonello Spada as though he were an intruder, and then suddenly, like a rocket, he hurled himself at the intruder, bringing him to the floor. Giorgio was stark naked, and because it was a warm day, and especially warm in my cavern, his young body was silver with sweat. He slithered like a fish. He was all over Leonello Spada, who was too surprised to defend himself. When I think of it now, I see Leonello Spada lying on the floor with something like an immense silver spider, all arms and legs, pummeling him and pounding his head against the floor. All the time Giorgio was shouting at the top of his voice.

The truth was that the boy looked beautiful, and he was assuming attitudes and gestures that I had never seen before, and so I watched him in admiration, letting him fight for a little while longer. And then fearing that my visitor might be seriously hurt, I lifted Giorgio up bodily and threw him on the bed. He crouched there with his hair falling over his eyes, and I made a mental note that I would one day paint him in that posture.

Leonello Spada got up, and ruefully examined his clothes. His doublet was torn, and there was dust all over him, but there was no damage except for a bruise on his chin.

"What a spitfire!" he said, laughing. "Well, thank God, he isn't very strong. How old is he?"

"Twelve."

"He is the model for your musicians?"

"For two of them."

"And is he living with you?"

"Yes, if that is any concern of yours."

"I like to know who my friends are living with," he said, and once again there was that clear laughter. "Who is the boy in the middle of the painting?"

"He is the son of the baker in the Piazza Navona. He is not here because he is working in his father's bakery."

"You take your boys off the streets?"

"Yes, because I like them with muscle. I wouldn't paint a nobleman's son."

I wondered why I was bothering to talk with this insolent stranger who could say, as though it was the most natural thing in the world: "I like to know who my friends are living with." And yet the more I saw of him, the more I was struck by his good breeding and his intelligence. He talked directly, from the shoulder, and when he laughed he gave an impression of wonderful good humor. And when he went up to my painting, his eyes blazing with admiration, and said: "You must leave it as it is — not another stroke of the brush," I knew that he spoke from the heart.

I told Giorgio to dress himself decently and bring some wine for the guest, and then I sent him to the Cardinal's kitchens to get some food, and we all ate off an old canvas which was supported on two wooden horses.

"I drink to your painting," Leonello Spada said, "and to the master of us all, Michelangelo Merisi."

I thanked him, and said I knew well enough what I had composed and was in no need of compliments. They might have been of some help to me in the Ospedale della Misericordia, but now they came too late. All I asked was that I should be left alone to serve Cardinal del Monte and to paint as I pleased.

"And no friends?" Leonello Spada asked.

"What are friends to me?"

"What they are to all of us — people we can rely on to the very death. When you are in despair, when you are in danger —"

"I live every moment of my life in despair and danger," I answered. "There is despair and danger in the tip of my brush."

"Yes, but when you are not painting?"

"I am always painting."

So we argued, while the food grew cold on the canvas table and Giorgio brought more lamps and candles. Soon the baker's son,

Antonio, arrived to share our meal, and Leonello Spada drank a toast to him, and another to Giorgio, saying that he was offering a toast to the far-distant future when people would look upon these Roman boys and admire them, though they were long dead.

He asked me why I painted in a cellar with no light coming from the street except through a high window, and I said I owed the cellar to the generosity of Cardinal del Monte, whose servant I was, and that it was as good a place as any. I painted by oil-light and candlelight, and in this way I could direct the light where I wished. I was not dependent on the vagaries of the sun. True, the place was nearly unbearable in summer: full of smoke and fumes and the odors of the kitchen. The Cardinal had promised me another room in the palace, and no doubt in time I would live in greater state.

"And so you are content?" Leonello Spada said at last.

"Supremely content," I replied, "and if I stay here in the bowels of the earth for the rest of my life, I shall be content."

In the following days I saw Leonello Spada often, for he was a pleasant companion and he came with gifts. He was a good painter in his own way, and he knew all the painters and architects in Rome. Through him I came to know Antonio Tempesta, Onorio Longhi, Adam Elsheimer, and many others, but these are the three I like to remember. I was closest to Leonello Spada, and we swore blood brotherhood. If one of us should ever be in danger, the other would immediately rush to his rescue: and more than that, for we would cherish and honor one another all the days of our lives.

One day shortly after Leonello Spada came into my life, I received a summons from Cardinal del Monte, who was anxious to see the painting of the musicians. It was almost finished, and therefore I had no hesitation in showing it to him. I insisted that it should be seen on an easel in the middle of his great audience chamber, facing the window, for I did not want it hanging on the wall, and I especially asked that there should be no other paintings in the room except my own.

I wrapped the painting in the red damask curtain and carried it by myself out of the palace, for it was beneath my dignity to enter the Cardinal's chamber through the kitchens with so precious a burden. The guards had been warned of my coming, and they saluted me agreeably. So I walked up the great carpeted stairway slowly, and at last placed the painting on the easel which the Cardinal had already provided in exactly the position I demanded. Then I slowly unwrapped the red damask curtain and watched him through the corner of my eye.

He stood there near the window with an expression of grave Florentine passivity, his face untroubled by any cares, one hand softly stroking his silver beard, lost in his own dreams. Then when the last corner of the damask curtain was lifted away, he stepped back as though struck by some object flung across the room, gasped, smiled, raised his hand in a kind of benediction, ran up to the painting, stepped back, and peered at it for a long time. On the previous night, dissatisfied with the composition, I had added another portrait to the painting, for there, peering above the shoulder of Antonio, was my own dark face. I had originally intended to show the Cardinal among musicians; instead I depicted myself.

"You have outdone yourself," the Cardinal said, and there were tears of excitement in his eyes. "Is there anything you cannot paint?"

There was a long silence. Servants brought wine on golden salvers. The priests who were always to be found in the Cardinal's entourage crowded around the painting. One small dark priest with a pinched face pointed to the purple love knot around Antonio's waist and murmured something about the indelicacy of the knot painted with so much care and abandon.

"If you could paint as well, then I would permit you to tie love knots around your choristers," the Cardinal said, and the priest covered his mouth with his hand. "And remember," the Cardinal went on, "that Michelangelo Merisi can and does paint for the Church, and he will paint altarpieces and you will kneel before them."

Then he dismissed the priests, so that, besides ourselves, there was only one handsome serving boy in attendance. This pleased me, and I felt more at home.

The Cardinal said very little about the painting of the musicians, although he sometimes walked away from it for the pleasure of returning to it, and once he asked my permission to close the windows in order to see it by candlelight. When all the candles were lit, he gazed at it for a long time and then he said: "It is even better now. The red burns more hotly. The colors of the flesh are richer, too. It seems that there is one kind of painting which looks better in candlelight, and another which looks better in sunlight. I don't know why, but I know it is so."

He did not pursue the argument with himself, but instead he turned to me and said: "I am going to the Villa Medici. If you come with me, I will show you the paintings belonging to the Duke of Tuscany."

We drove to the Villa Medici in the Cardinal's carriage, for though he enjoyed walking it was not permissible for a Cardinal in his vestments to be seen walking through the streets of Rome. In the carriage he seemed lost in thought. Something of great moment was evidently occupying his mind, and I imagined he was pondering weighty affairs of state, for there were important political matters which were then being discussed with the Pope. I watched him closely, observing him at close quarters, his marble skin, the straight nose, the brow unfurrowed, and the eyes clear. His beard had the silvery white of birch bark and his eyes were the brilliant blue of juniper berries, but in the shadowy carriage I could see little of his eyes and his head was bent forward almost in such a way as to conceal the beard. I had never seen him so absorbed in thought, or so silent.

When we reached the Villa Medici he was still lost in thought. The footmen came with their lighted candles, as they always do when a Cardinal appears, even if it is broad daylight. Usually they attend him wherever he goes, but on this occasion he waved them away. We walked along the gallery of paintings, and from time to time he paused and asked my opinion of a painting, and usually I would answer that it had no particular value, and in fact there were very few paintings which merited attention; nor was this surprising, since the greater part of the Duke of Tuscany's collection had long since been removed to Florence.

"Then you find no merit in them?" the Cardinal said, watching me closely. "Not even in the *Sleeping Woman* by Giorgione, for which, I believe, the Grand Duke paid five thousand *scudi*."

"No," I said, "I do not value it, for if it were a true Giorgione then I would have removed my boots and knelt humbly before it, but I felt no such need. You must understand, Illustrissimo, that Giorgione is to be accounted a god among painters, perhaps the greatest who ever lived, and therefore worthy of the greatest reverence, but the painting you showed me is merely the copy of a copy."

"So there is not one of these paintings which are worthy of adorning the palace of the Grand Duke in Florence?"

"None."

"And if I offered you any one of these paintings, there is not one you would accept."

"That is true, Illustrissimo. Here there are only bad paintings or copies of good paintings badly executed. So let us leave this butcher's shop!"

He thought for a moment and then he said: "If I did not know you so well, I would have thought you spoke out of pride, believing yourself a greater painter than any of these. Does nothing please you?"

I said hotly: "All paintings by a painter who has truly learned his trade please me. I could name you twenty painters I revere, and twenty more I look upon with pleasure. Great art is the greatest gift which God has given to the world, and for this life is worth living and death is worth dying. But there are only a few great works of art, and no generation can produce more than a few great artists."

We came to the gallery of sculpture. There were a few languid works carved in our time together with some antique sculptures, a Venus, a Niobe, the heads of Roman emperors. The Cardinal stood in admiration before the Venus, not that he possessed an affection for naked flesh, but because the name Praxiteles cast a spell on him.

"I suppose you detest this Venus as much as you detest the paintings in the picture gallery?"

"I do, Illustrissimo. We have better Venuses in the streets of Rome. You will see a hundred women more beautiful than this in the Piazza Navona. This Venus has the softness of pig's fat, but the women in the Piazza Navona have sturdy muscles and sweet flesh. Take any woman from the Piazza Navona, strip off her clothes and set her beside this Venus, and you will see a work of art. This is not a work by Praxiteles, or by Phidias either, for there are no bones beneath the flesh, and no life flows through her."

At this the Cardinal threw up his red-gloved hands in horror, exclaiming: "You must not ask me to strip off a woman's clothes."

"Nevertheless you must know the human body and the colors of the flesh. This is what painting is about. It is always a celebration of the flesh. Man is made in the image of God, and God is made flesh."

He said very gravely, as though pondering some problem which had long absorbed him: "They tell me that Raphael was lecherous, and Leonardo slept with boys, and there is scarcely a painter of eminence who possessed a shred of modesty. All have committed great sins, and you yourself, Michelangelo, on the evidence of your paintings, have committed sins with boys, and there is no end to it. And yet the Church needs you and protects you. It is all a mystery to me!"

At this very moment I caught sight of a statue half hidden behind some ornamental carvings designed for a fountain. I saw at first only the head and shoulder of a young athlete, but it was enough to take my breath away. Then, when I drew closer, I felt the chill which comes with viewing a great work of art. It was a marble statue of two wrestlers in fierce and vigorous combat. One had been brought to his knees, the other crouched over him, pressing down with all his strength. The wrestlers were naked, and the marble had the glow of flesh. But what was most remarkable was the energy pouring out of the unmoving marble, the thrust of muscles, the crisped tendons, the ripple of flesh. Hot breath came from them. The sweat and agony of combat were in them, though their faces showed no emotion, and perhaps it was precisely because their faces were impassive that they resembled young gods.

"I see that you like the statue," the Cardinal said with a faint gesture of distaste.

"I would give all the other statues for this one," I answered, and indeed I have never seen a statue which moved me so profoundly.

"To me," said the Cardinal, "it is no more than boys coupling, and there is enough of that to be seen in the streets of Rome." And then he added softly: "No doubt it is a question of taste."

"On the contrary," I said, "it is a question of the greatest art. The boys are not coupling. There is not the least suggestion of erotic feeling. They are in combat, and at the same time they are composed, very quiet within themselves. Look for example at the feet. They are rendered with anatomical precision and at the same time with tremendous power — they are not plaster casts of feet. Look at the toes of the boy digging into the earth. Every toe is fighting, and every muscle is drawn tight. Each toe has a character, almost a face, of its own."

Standing beside the marble statue, I delivered myself of a lecture on the human foot, which has always delighted me because it is so complex and resilient, so strong, so delicate, so gentle, and so determined. The foot spreads out like a leaf, is compact like a clenched fist, is supple as a sponge. It is all bone and muscle with only the thinnest covering of flesh. Look at the feet of a peasant and then at the feet of some pampered woman in a boudoir; study the similarities, the differences, the revelations of character. There was a good deal more of it, and the Cardinal showed an exquisite forbearance as I went on to explain the careful anatomy of the feet and the mechanics of walking. Then he smiled and said: "I had always thought that our feet were an afterthought of the Creator."

He said these words gently, almost sorrowfully. I had an impulse to continue lecturing him on the subject of the human body, but instead I remained silent, content to admire the statue of the Wrestlers, the warmth and vigor of those youths, so young and innocent, and so displeasing to the Cardinal and the Grand Duke of Tuscany that they were kept hidden in a corner of the Villa Medici.

And then very slowly, in the manner which he employed when he was in deep and ceremonious thought, he pressed his gloved hands together and lifted them until his fingers rested against his lips, and said: "Tell me, Michelangelo, what are the chains which bind a painter to the Church? You deal in the colors of the flesh, and the Church deals in the Holy Spirit — how can there be any commerce between us?"

"The flesh exalts the spirit," I said, "and there is no escape from it until death. So let us live with it. And did not Christ assume human flesh? Shall we throw the flesh away and live only in the spirit — to what purpose?"

"To praise God," he replied, and the long red gloves were still lifted to his lips.

"And cannot we praise God through paintings? Cannot the flesh praise God? We live in the flesh, and we must abide by it. When I paint the head of John the Baptist, is it any the less flesh because the blood is spilling out of the wounds? And is it any the less spirit? When I paint a Crucifixion or a Deposition, I must paint the body of the flesh. If I could paint the spirit I would do so, but it is invisible."

"No, Michelangelo, you paint the flesh because you are in love with the flesh, and you painted the musicians because you loved those boys."

"I painted them to please you —"

"So you did, but the love for the boys was greater than the pleasure. There is something strange and devilish in you, and sometimes I think I should exorcise the devils in you! It should be done now — before it is too late! And then I think of all the other painters, all eaten up by devils, and how the Church has always clasped them to her breast, and I wonder why. I have often asked myself whether we need paintings at all, and I do not know the answer."

"I know the answer very well," I said hotly. "How else can we glorify the flesh except in painting and sculpture? What else is art but the glorification of God and man? I tell you, my lord Cardinal, that everything I have painted was done for the glory of God, and it would be folly otherwise!"

"And for the glory of man?" he said smiling, but it was a sad smile.

"Yes, and for the glory of man."

Then we went into the gardens and we watched the gardeners at their work, and we were about to reenter the carriage when he turned and said: "I have been hesitating for some time before telling you what I have in store for you. You have said much that offended me, and much that delighted me, and I did not know where to turn. The truth is that you are still a mystery to me. But this I can tell you — a great and important commission is at my disposal. In God's time you shall learn what I have in store for you."

The Contarelli Chapel

"IN God's time" — and it occurred to me that God's time might be very long, and if I waited for this commission I might be old and gray before I put the first brushstroke to the wall. I was sure it would be a painting covering the whole length of a wall, or the four walls of a room. I thought of the papal apartments painted by Raphael, and the Sistine Chapel painted by Michelangelo Buonarroti, and I was sure that the Cardinal had something equally vast and impressive for me. Perhaps the tapestries in his audience chamber would be torn down, and the whole of that magnificent room would become mine. So I dreamed, and as the days passed I gradually found myself thinking of painting vast battle scenes and triumphant processions, another Judgment or the entire life of Christ from floor to ceiling.

But these were dreams, and the real work of painting went on. Since I had given of my best to Cardinal del Monte, I felt it was time to earn a large sum of money by painting something which would please the Marchese Vicenzo Giustiniani, who had shown me many signs of favor. His palace stood nearby in the Via Dogana Vecchia. It was a somber place, very dark and with few servants, for the Marchese Giustiniani preferred to save his money for works of art. He had a vast collection of paintings, and many Roman statues, which he kept in cupboards. He was equally secretive about his paintings, which he kept stored away. Only a few of his best paintings hung on his walls.

About the palace of the Marchese Giustiniani there hung an air of sorrowful brooding, so that whenever I entered it I felt I would soon come upon decaying corpses and women lamenting. He was even more solemn than his brother, the Cardinal, and I never saw him laughing or giving way to emotion. The palace always seemed damp and lifeless, and the smell of ancient incense hung about the place. In the Piazza Navona they spoke of him as "the old woman," using a contemptuous word which signified a woman with evil-smelling skirts, but I found him simple and sweet-tempered, though overweighed with sorrows almost too great to be borne. In the middle of a sentence he would sigh and make a little gesture of helplessness. I suspected that he must have committed some terrible crime when he was young, but when I came to know him better I realized that he was oppressed by the thought that his collection of works of art would be dispersed at his death. He loved painting more than anyone in Rome, and he spent nearly all his waking hours gazing at the works of the masters.

I sent Antonio with a message saying that I was now ready to paint according to his command, having in mind a painting of a lute player with Antonio serving as the model. I expected a reply in a few days, but to my surprise the reply came immediately, written in his own hand, saying that he had long expected to receive a message from me and had been grieved by my silence. From Maestro Valentino he had bought two paintings of fruit, and he wrote of the pleasure they had given him, for his mouth watered whenever he saw them. He would be pleased to accept the portrait of Antonio as a lute player, but would have preferred a painting of a young woman of great beauty "although I understand you have a preference for painting boys, finding them no doubt more amenable to your instructions and more patient in assuming a pose." He added that he would send his chamberlain to discuss the price for the painting.

The chamberlain was a gentle soul, the price was satisfactory, and I immediately set to work on the painting. Since Antonio possessed that perfection of beauty which is neither masculine nor feminine, and could be painted equally as a girl or a boy, I simply gave him a wig of chestnut-colored hair and tied in it a love knot of white silk. During this period Leonello Spada came frequently, saying that he desired nothing more than to watch me at work; and whatever faults the painting has are due to his friendship, for we often talked when I should have been working.

He asked me why I never painted out of doors in the sun, but always in an enclosed space, against a dark wall, with lights of my own choosing directed on the model, usually from above, sometimes from the sides and more rarely from below; and I answered that I lived in the Cardinal's cellar, where I had all the privacy I needed, and saw no reason to rent another room filled with sunlight. It was not that I objected to the methods of the Academy; the academicians could do as they pleased; they did not live in cellars. But I had learned much from my stay in the cellar, and I had learned even more in the tunnel at the Ospedale della Misericordia, with the river of blood and dung and piss running down it, and the dying lying in the damp straw. If I loved the colors of healthy flesh, it was because I had seen too much diseased and broken flesh, and too many dead people.

It was the custom in the tunnel to remove the dead at once, and so whenever we heard the beginning of a death rattle, then all of us from the youngest to the oldest would set up a fierce cry and the watchmen would come running in to remove the body. They would come down the tunnel swinging their lanterns, throwing their vast, racing shadows on the wall, and in a moment they had lifted the body from the straw; and as they carried it away, walking with their legs straddled wide apart to avoid stepping into the muck, I would have a glimpse of a dangling arm, silvery white or rosy yellow in the lantern light, or perhaps a nose and a forehead, nothing more, or simply the dark shape of a body outlined as though with silver wire. I had seen, then, how darkness and a single lantern gave depth to a human figure. The most startling and memorable thing in the world was a dead face seen suddenly in the swinging light of a lantern.

I went on to speak of the beauty of the clothes worn by the poor wretches in the tunnel: clothes which were torn and caked with excrement, sweat and mucus. I spoke of the peculiar beauty of clothes which have been well worn, and of how I had gazed for hours at a rusted iron pot, which assumed unbelievably rich colors. I told him, too, that I had long since abandoned the practice of outlining a figure on the canvas, but instead worked straight from the model, and this was because I wanted nothing to come between me and nature. It was the first time I had ever attempted to put my ideas into words. Finally I said: "I realize very well what I am doing. I have come to destroy painting."

There was a long silence, and I remember Antonio leaning forward with a strange smile on his parted lips and Leonello Spada leaning back, lost in thought, his face impassive, as though carved out of stone.

"So you regard sculpture as a greater art than painting?" he said at last, and I nodded.

"Will you become a sculptor?" he asked.

"No, because I shall never have the time. But I truly believe it is a greater and more enduring art than painting, and the more closely painting approaches sculpture so the more closely it approaches greatness."

Then he smiled and said: "If you are not careful, Michelangelo, there will come a time when all the young painters in Rome will find themselves cellars and paint by candlelight."

While I was painting Antonio as a lute player, there came no word from Cardinal del Monte. From time to time there would come those small gifts which demonstrated his continuing affection for me, but where previously they had been gifts intended to please me, now they appeared to be accompanied by invisible messages. Item, a skull, the size of a pebble, carved out of ivory in a small velvet-lined box. Item, a book of prayers in vellum. Item, a purse empty except for a single gold coin depicting Alexander the Great. Item, a hand, excellently modeled, from an antique statue. Item, a skullcap lined with fur.

I could make nothing of these gifts, and I asked Fabrizio Crescenzi whether it was intended that I should attach any meaning to them. He answered that a special meaning was attached to everything the Cardinal did, and sometimes there were two, or even three meanings. If he sent a skull the size of a pebble, he was not only conveying the idea that it was proper for me to meditate on death, but also that I should meditate on the insignificance of human life in comparison with the vast splendor of God.

"And no doubt," I said, "the significance of the skullcap is that it warms the head and tickles the ears, and in addition it may be used to snuff out candles."

"You should not laugh at His Highness's gifts," Fabrizio Crescenzi said, "for truly he has a high regard for you and he daily prays for your salvation."

"Daily?"

"Why, yes, I have heard him at his prayers."

"I suppose he prays for that poor devil of a Michelangelo Merisi, now beginning to be known simply as Caravaggio, who belongs among the fallen angels."

"On the contrary he prays for your spiritual health and he earnestly beseeches God to strengthen your faith, to put love into your heart, and to lead you to the divine mercy."

Fabrizio Crescenzi said all this in low tones, as though he was not sure whether he had permission to recite the private prayers of a Cardinal.

"And what is still more important," he went on, dropping to a whisper, "His Highness has great things in store for you — such great things as you cannot imagine."

"I am to be asked to paint the Cardinal's audience chamber?" I suggested, for the truth was that I was growing weary of these promises and wished for certainties.

"It is nothing like that," he replied. "No doubt if you painted his audience chamber, you would perform a work which would redound infinitely to your credit, but only His Highness and his visitors would observe it. What he has in mind is something which will proclaim your genius to all the people of Rome. It is a project he has been working on for many months, but there are legal difficulties which I cannot tell you about. I have been sworn to secrecy."

"But you know what it is?"

"Yes, of course, I know. How could I help knowing!"

Saying this, he gave a little sigh and his face reddened, as though he had said too much, and a moment later he hurried up my stairs.

In this way I came to know that some vast project was being prepared for me, that Fabrizio Crescenzi knew all about it and had been sworn to secrecy, and that many months had passed since the matter was first broached. Beyond this, unless the strange gifts the Cardinal was sending me provided some clue, there was no way of telling me what lay in store. And so when Leonello Spada came, we arranged the gifts on a table — the fur cap, the ivory skull, the coin showing the face of Alexander, and all the others, as though in some way they might spell out the mystery, but to no avail. When I saw the Marchese Vincenzo Giustiniani I asked him whether he knew anything about the project. He looked at me with that blank expression which men commonly simulate when they possess secret knowledge.

"I know nothing," he said. "Well, let us say I know very little. Tell me, how did you come here?"

I thought he was out of his mind. The Palazzo Giustiniani is not far from the Palazzo Madama, and there is only one way to walk there.

"I walked," I said.

"Yes, of course you walked. I did not expect you to make such a short journey in a carriage. But tell me, how did you come?"

"The usual way."

"Of course, my dear fellow, but just tell me how you came. What buildings did you pass? What did you see on the road? Did you perhaps see the Cardinal del Monte during your journey?"

"I did not see him, and as for the buildings I passed you know them as well as I. All this has nothing to do with the great project he has been speaking about."

"On the contrary, it has a great deal to do with the project, but I have already spoken too much. You will learn in God's time. Have patience, Michelangelo."

Then he took my arm, led me to his dining room, and showed me an empty space on the wall reserved for the painting of Antonio.

"So you see," he said, "I have absolute faith in your work, and if you serve me well, I too shall see that great projects are given to you. But you must remember that all these things take time, for the Church dispenses its money with great care, and for every project a hundred lawyers must be consulted. There are contracts to be drawn up, and there are even contracts to permit the drawing up of contracts."

"Contracts with whom?"

"Contracts with everyone. When it is an affair of importance, then you can be assured that there are enough contracts to go round."

"And they concern some building between here and the Palazzo Madama?"

"I have already talked too much, Michelangelo. We have all sworn oaths of secrecy. Permit me to observe that you have come into my presence in doublet and hose streaked with paint, and if you were not Michelangelo Merisi, the servants would have thrown you out. I shall have great pleasure in presenting you with a new doublet and a new pair of hose."

Suddenly the light dawned on me. I kissed the hand of the Marchese Giustiniani and hurried three steps at a time down his stairs. It had occurred to me that there was only one building between the Palazzo Giustiniani and the Palazzo Madama where I might be invited to paint a series of important canvases, and this was the Church of San Luigi dei Francesi, which had been built only a few years before. At long last all the pieces in the puzzle began to fit together. There had been lawsuits connected with the foundation of the church, and more than once Fabrizio Crescenzi had spoken to me about those interminable lawsuits in which his family — his cousins and uncles — were all implicated, for they were the trustees and beneficiaries of the foundation. Now at last I saw clearly what was expected of me! I would be asked to paint the life of St. Louis of France, who died miserably of the plague somewhere in North Africa; and as I raced down the stairs I was already composing the painting which showed him lying on the straw, in some vast tunnel, with the ghostly faces of his courtiers around him. A shaft of the dying sun would illuminate the face of the dying king, and here and there the spectator would see the gleam of armor. In the foreground there would be a Turkish slave leaning on a curving sword, and behind St. Louis there would be a priest offering the last sacrament.

I ran to the church which stood hard by the Palazzo Giustiniani, and found the gates closed. Through a side door some workmen were removing the dismantled scaffolding from one of the chapels. No one was guarding the door, and it was easy to slip inside that large and gloomy church, which had never yet heard a simple Mass. Pleased with my composition, I looked for the place where the painting would stand, and decided that it must be above the high altar, while the incidents of the saint's life would be painted in the chapels, on the walls, and perhaps even on the columns.

There were only a few workmen in the church, and they went about their work lethargically, as though they had all eternity before them. Although quite new, the church gave the impression of being old and abandoned; the birds had made their nests in it, and their droppings turned the floor into a white glistening sea. I filled the walls with paintings of battles and ships of war, and as I gazed around the church bare of all ornament, I seemed to see the walls springing to life and color. The truth was that I knew very little about St. Louis of France and could give my imagination free rein.

I was still meditating on the beauty of the church transformed by my paintings when I saw the Cardinal bearing down on me. He seemed to have sprung out of the earth. Probably he had been in the sacristy, or perhaps he had been talking to the foreman of laborers behind the altar. There was some dust on his crimson robes. He walked with rapid strides, his brow furrowed, his blue eyes glaring.

[145]

"What are you doing here, Michelangelo?" he said, his voice cracking like a whip.

"Illustrissimo, I merely came out of the sun to rest my eyes."

"To pray for your sins in an empty church?"

"To pray for my sins and to rest —"

There was a half-smile on his lips.

"Then let us pray together, Michelangelo, but not here among these bird droppings. Come to the sacristy."

I followed him to the sacristy, which was empty. On the table lay the plans for some restorations. There was no one about, and this was strange, for the Cardinal never went anywhere without a retinue of priests and footmen, unless it was to visit the Villa Medici, where more priests and footmen were in residence.

"Come, tell me why you came here," the Cardinal said sternly.

"Illustrissimo, it suddenly occurred to me that these empty walls would benefit from my paintings. I have already composed in my head a painting of the death of St. Louis."

"And what else?"

"Many incidents in the life of St. Louis."

"And what else?"

"A battle scene showing the army of St. Louis fighting the Saracens."

He looked at me with the air of someone listening to the babbling of a lunatic.

"Then you should know," he said after a long pause, "that the Society of the Congregation of St. Peter, which is now in charge of this church, has never once considered any paintings or frescoes or altarpieces connected with the life of St. Louis of France. All we are concerned about is the chapel named after the late lamented Cardinal Matthew Contarelli, who was a Frenchman and who, out of his devotion to St. Matthew, left a sum of money for the painting of an altarpiece and two side paintings to the honor of his saint. And all this is a secret, and you must tell no one. Will you promise?"

"I promise."

"Even if I tell you that I shall commission you to paint the three paintings?"

"Yes, I promise."

"Well, let us hope for your sake that you keep your promise. Meanwhile meditate upon the Gospel According to St. Matthew. Read it carefully. Spend an hour every day in holy meditation, and ask for the saint's blessing."

Then he blessed me and sent me on my way, accompanying me to the door of the sacristy. He looked very lonely and sad, but there was no anger in him.

No one ever kept a secret better. Obedient to the Cardinal's commands I read the Gospel According to St. Matthew until I knew it by heart. I visited the Cardinal's library and read the commentaries written by learned authors and the legends of the saint written by men who had never known him. In this way I learned that St. Matthew was murdered at the orders of King Hirtacus of Ethiopia, a pagan, for having denounced the marriage between the king and the virtuous Christian princess Iphigenia. No doubt the altarpiece would show St. Matthew communing with his angel, and the two side paintings would show incidents in the life of the saint. Since there are not many incidents connected with St. Matthew, I soon came to the conclusion that his Calling and his Martyrdom would provide me with proper subjects for my painting.

A month passed, and then another, and there was still no news from the Cardinal. I finished the painting of the lute player and presented it to the Marchese Giustiniani, who immediately commissioned another painting after inquiring whether I was under any compulsion to present the Cardinal with any new picture.

"I understand they are commissioning you to do the paintings in the Contarelli chapel. The legal documents were signed yesterday, but you will have time to do one more painting. Indeed, you may have time to do many, because the subjects have not yet been decided."

I said I knew nothing of all this, or rather I had sworn secrecy to Cardinal del Monte, my protector, and could not speak about the Contarelli chapel.

"You have done well, Michelangelo," he said, "for I assure you, if you had whispered a single word, the Cardinal would have learned·about it. Cardinals love secrecy. It is their food and drink. Nothing delights them more than to carry great secrets in their hearts, and since there are very few things which can be called great secrets, they must invent them."

He asked for a painting to be called Earthly Love as a companion piece to a painting called Spiritual Love which he already owned. It would take the form of a winged Cupid, with all the emblems of earthly love scattered around him. Musical instruments, armor, architecture, books, poetry, a globe, and many other things, would be represented in this painting celebrating the triumph of earthly things.

"Paint the flesh tones well — that is all I ask of you," the Marchese said.

So I painted Giorgio naked, with one leg cocked up on a bed, laughing in derision of the world, with pages of music and many musical instruments crowding at his feet. When it was completed, the Marchese received it gratefully, remarking that the brilliance of the flesh tones put all the other paintings to shame, and therefore he felt constrained to hang a green curtain over it. But I suspect there was another purpose for the green curtain. His unmarried sister sometimes came to visit him, and he wanted to protect her from the sight of a lewd boy cocking a leg at the world.

Meanwhile the arrangements for the Contarelli chapel proceeded slowly, and three more months passed before the contract was finally signed. Then I went to work as I had never worked before. For the altarpiece I painted Giorgio as the angel guiding the hand of St. Matthew, and for the *Calling of St. Matthew* I painted a scene in my own cellar with the Cardinal himself as St. Matthew, with myself, Leonello Spada, Fabrizio Crescenzi, and Antonio as his assistants in the counting house, while on the right, in darkness, Christ and St. Peter appear to summon the saint into God's service. Of all my works this was the one which gave me the most intense pleasure.

For there, in this somber cellar, lit by a light from the top of the stairs, with Christ raising His hand in command, urgently bestowing His blessing, with St. Peter no more than a shadow leading the way, and St. Matthew and his servants displaying their earthly riches by the brilliance of their clothing, I accomplished exactly what I set out to do — I showed the world in all its youthful glory and Christ in His divinity, and the world and Christ were joined together.

One evening I prevailed upon the Cardinal to pose for me in my cellar. I explained that I needed him for St. Matthew, and I cannot paint unless I have the model before me.

"You can paint me here," he said, "and there is no need for me to go down to your infernal cellar."

"Nevertheless," I explained patiently, "the scene is the cellar, and the light in the cellar is unlike the light in your audience chamber. It is not only that I must paint you, but also the air around you."

He made some more excuses, offered to send one of his priests, a distant relative, who bore a remote resemblance to him, and he hinted that I must be at my wits' ends if I could not find a better model for St. Matthew.

"And I suppose," he went on, "you will ask me to discard my

robe and put on those extraordinary clothes which decorate the boys in your paintings."

"Not for a moment," I replied, "for I cannot see Your Highness except in your robes. I shall paint you as you are, only your face, and then, too —" I went on, my voice dropping to a whisper, "I need you for the Christ."

At first he was shocked, then pleased, then a look of bewilderment crossed his face.

"I am wholly unworthy," he said.

"Let me at least be the judge of your unworthiness, Illustrissimo," I said.

He came at about seven o'clock in the evening, and I was still painting him at midnight. For the portrait of Christ he stood perfectly still for three hours, then rested for about twenty minutes before sitting at the table, so that I could paint him as St. Matthew between Fabrizio Crescenzi and the handsome Antonio. They were no more than sketches for portraits which would be filled in later. I call them sketches, but others might call them finished paintings, for all the essentials were recorded by my brush.

The Cardinal was cordial, and he was especially solicitous of Leonello Spada, asking him many questions about his paintings, and this pleased me. He drank wine — diluted with water — but maintained his pose. Giorgio, who had acquired some skill as a lutanist, played for him. So the night passed, and by three o'clock in the morning he was beginning to nod. His head — that splendid head with the silvery beard — fell forward, and then jerked up.

"How much longer, Michelangelo?" he complained, but there was not the least sign of annoyance in his complaint.

"Only a few more minutes, Illustrissimo."

"Then let them be very short minutes, my son," he said, and for a few more minutes he maintained the pose.

Soon his head began to sink forward slowly until it touched the table. He was in a profound sleep. We carried him to the bed, but even though Giorgio played strident music we could not awake him.

We doused the lights, and I kept watch by his bed. When dawn broke I fell asleep beside him.

This was how I painted the *Calling of St. Matthew.* In later years the Cardinal would reproach me for having kept him awake through the long night. Sometimes, when we were alone, he would say: "Michelangelo, my bedfellow." Sometimes, too, he would go alone to the Church of San Luigi dei Francesi and contemplate the painting in which he is both St. Matthew and Christ.

The Flood

I KNEW it was raining because I could hear the thunder and the sound of waters swirling through the street and the cries of people running for shelter, but in my cellar all these sounds were muted. I was painting the great scarlet curtain behind a portrait of Cardinal del Monte in his scarlet vestments, standing beside a table on which a gold crucifix studded with emeralds was mounted; and there was a lapdog at his feet, and somewhere in the background his servants were hovering. I remember the painting was only half finished, and the skirts of the Cardinal were sketched in roughly. Only the face, the jeweled hand, and the crucifix were completed to my satisfaction. It was already late in the evening, and the room was turning white with the fume of candles.

It was the dead of winter, and very cold, so cold that I wore gloves while I painted and wrapped myself in a dressing gown lined with rabbit fur. There was a bronze bowl of charcoal glowing at my feet, and another lay near the bed, where the boy Giovanni was sleeping. He was a peasant boy from some lost village in the Sabine hills, and he had entered my service in the autumn. He was thirteen or fourteen, with the face of an impudent angel, but it was not his impudence or beauty which pleased me so much as the expression of his eyes, which were trusting and gentle, like a woman's. I knew from the moment I picked him off the streets that he would serve me faithfully and honestly. He was not one of those *putti* who need to be caressed and kissed and put to bed. I had had trouble with the other boys who served me: they stole, told lies, offered their bodies to anyone who stepped down my stairs, and continually complaining of the darkness of my cellar, they were always running off to sit in the sunlight or sprawl in the taverns. Some were poxed, others had running sores which they concealed as best they could. So I had rid myself of them, and for a while Giulia had come every day from the house of Maestro Valentino to bring me food and to attend to my chores. But she, too, detested the darkness and candlelit solemnity of my lodgings, and she would make excuses for not coming or move silently and fearfully about the place as though it were tenanted with ghosts.

I had lived alone, and with a pack of roaring boys, and then with Giulia visiting me, and none of these were satisfactory for my work. For a while I had thought of abandoning Rome altogether and living in some remote cottage in the Campagna. Then I would remember the great honor done to me by Cardinal del Monte, and how at least once a week he would descend to my cavern and examine my paintings, and sometimes I would be invited to dine with him in the great hall upstairs. I knew no greater pleasure than his company.

So I remained in my dark cave, where the walls were high and there was more space than I needed, and where I had only to run up three flights of stairs to find myself in the presence of the Cardinal. And I must admit that it pleased me to live below the surface of the earth, as in a grave. It pleased me, too, that when I was asked my address, I would answer simply that I lived in the Palazzo Madama. In my eyes this was the most desirable residence in

Rome, better by far than if I had been living within the walls of the Vatican or the Belvedere.

But on that winter evening with a damp chill in the air, I was not so certain that I wanted to continue living there. A few days before there had been a cloudburst, and the rain came cascading down the stairs. Happily, all the paintings were out of reach of the rain, but it had taken a whole day to drain off the water with buckets. Damp is bad for paintings, and accordingly they were all removed to the Cardinal's private apartments, and while the cellar was being cleaned, I was permitted to live in one of the rooms reserved for the servants of the Duke of Tuscany.

"I may have to find you a place to live in the Villa Medici," the Cardinal said. "At least it is on higher ground."

I thanked him and said I was content with my cellar, except when it rained, for I wanted nothing better than to serve him.

"Could you not serve me as well in the Villa Medici?" he asked smiling. "No, the truth is that you like the people on the Piazza Navona, and you would be unhappy anywhere else. So I serve two functions. I provide you with my palace and I also provide you with the Piazza Navona, and what more can a poor cardinal do?"

Then he smiled, made a sweeping gesture with his hands at the eight or nine paintings which were now hanging on the walls of his apartment, and said: "When visitors come, they always ask about your paintings, Michelangelo. At first they frown. They look uncomfortably at one another. Then they look away, but they are soon looking at them again. Then they ask me about you, and every day I have to spend a few minutes explaining who you are and how you came to live in my palace. And I must tell you truthfully that I find myself in great honor through your paintings, and I believe they come more to see the work of your hands than to hear the words of my lips."

That night I dined with him alone, and he bought another head of John the Baptist as a present for the Grand Duke, and inquired delicately about the progress of his own portrait, for which over a period of three months he had given me perhaps ten sittings.

"Why is it," he asked, "that for others you will paint a John the Baptist in twenty-four hours, and I must wait many months for my portrait?"

"It is because I reverence Your Highness so much," I answered, "and I therefore paint you with great care and thought. What I have done before — a John the Baptist or a Magdalene — I can repeat swiftly. It is no trouble to me, for all the problems have been worked out. But what is new is always troublesome to me —"

"Am I so new to you after all these years?" he laughed. "How many years is it since you came to live with me?"

"Four years."

"So you have had time in four years to study me to your heart's content, and you are no closer to an understanding of me?"

"I know Your Highness's features as I know the shape of my hand, but it is altogether another matter to describe Your Highness's soul. I would want my painting of you to be seen in a thousand years, and so I must work to put eternity into it."

Thereafter he would sometimes gaze at my paintings and say of one which seemed to him not quite successful: "Have you put eternity in this one, Michelangelo?" And that evening he gave me a small jeweled box, of silver set with small emeralds, very slender, with a chain permitting it to be worn round the neck, and inside there was a miniature portrait of him and beneath glass there was a thin sliver of a bone of St. Apollonia and small stones which came, he said, from a holy rock in Jerusalem.

"If you should need my help urgently at any time," he said,

"then you have only to send me this silver box, and I shall know that you are in need."

Then he blessed me and my work, as he always did in parting, and I kissed his ring. As I knelt before him, I was so moved by the gift of the silver box that my hot tears scalded his hand.

I heard the rain falling, and Giovanni was moving restlessly on his bed. My cellar looked empty, for most of the paintings were still in the Cardinal's apartment. Once or twice I left the painting of the Cardinal to gaze at Giovanni as he slept, the face so innocent, the young body so beautiful as he lay there in the splendor of unconsciousness. I decided I would paint him as soon as I had finished the Cardinal's portrait.

When the scarlet curtain was finished, I decided it was time to take a stroll outside. The candles were dying out, because there was so much smoke in the room. Then I observed that there were no sounds coming from the kitchens, and it was unusually quiet in the palace. Usually the Cardinal's kitchens are kept busy during the night, either at bread-making or preparing the food for the following day. It occurred to me that perhaps the Cardinal was not in residence, and this puzzled me, for I was usually informed of his absences. Or perhaps the Cardinal was spending the evening at the Villa Medici, or he was attending some ceremony at the Vatican. It was three days before Christmas, a time when there are many festivities.

For a little while longer I worked, painting in the reflected lights on the Cardinal's silver beard. I made plans for completing the table and the lapdog. There was a whimper from the bed. Giovanni was no longer facing the wall, but lying on his back with his legs sprawled out and one forearm covering his eyes. He whimpered again, and then the black bitch starting from under the bed knocked over one of the candles, barking furiously, and immediately afterward Giovanni woke up and began to shout, and the cellar was in a bedlam. I cuffed the bitch, set up the long silver candlestick which was the height of a man, and went to the bed. Giovanni was sitting up. His face was flushed, and his hair damp on his forehead. He was still whimpering.

"What is it, Giovanni?"

"Signor, I had a dream. All Rome was underwater."

He caught his breath. He looked frightened. The white shift was sticking to his flesh.

"It's raining," I said, "and that's why you dreamed that Rome was underwater. Now go to sleep."

He was still sitting up with that strange, startled expression on his face. I made a mental note of the expression, for it was exactly such an expression as I intended to paint on the face of an angel in an altarpiece for the Grand Duke. I went up to the bed, and he threw his arms round me and clung to me like a child. His body was hot and he felt feverish. We could hear the rain falling outside, slowly, steadily.

"I saw the water come up higher than the palace, higher than St. Peter's," he said. "I tell you the whole city, even the highest parts, were all underwater. We were all drowned — everyone was drowned."

He whimpered again, and the bitch whimpered under the bed.

"There hasn't been a flood for seventy years," I said, "and it's not likely that the good God will send a flood now that the Holy Father has returned in triumph from Ferrara — it would be a punishment on the Holy Father, wouldn't it, and what's more it will soon be Christmas and the people will be celebrating, and how can they celebrate if Rome is underwater? Get dressed, and we'll go out, and then you'll know whether there is a flood or not."

While he was getting dressed, the rain stopped. I snuffed out all except one of the candles and kicked under the bed to warn the black bitch we were going out. Dressed in a short doublet which he had forgotten to button and in drawers that came down to his knees, barefoot, the boy came up the stairs with me, the bitch at our heels. We went through the kitchens; there was no one there and only a single lamp was burning. In the light of the lamp Giovanni's face was flushed, his lips moist and trembling.

"The rain has stopped," I said. "It's silly to think anything is going to happen to the city."

"Why is everyone away?" he asked, staring round the empty kitchen.

"They have all gone to sleep early, so that they can celebrate Christmas. Anyway, they have all gone."

We went out by the side door. One of the Cardinal's guards was standing there, but as usual he had fallen asleep, leaning against the wall. By this side door anyone could enter the palace, and because it annoyed me that the palace should be unguarded, I kicked the fellow awake. His halberd clattered to the floor. He awoke out of a drunken stupor, lunged at me, his great fist brushing against my face, and it was necessary that he should be punished. I threw him back against the wall, so that his head made a sound as though it were cracking wide open. Giovanni was clutching at my hand, and I shook him off.

"If you sleep," I shouted at the guard, "who will defend the Cardinal? It is more than your life is worth to sleep when you are on duty!"

He muttered something under his breath and made the sign against the evil eye, so that I was tempted to push his head into the wall, but Giovanni was still clutching at my hand.

"It's late, master," he said. "He has had his lesson. Don't punish him any more."

When a man works late in the night, he has little enough feeling for the passing of time. I thought it was near midnight, but in fact it was near four in the morning and the streets were deserted except for the occasional shadow of one of the *sbirri*. Here and there the clouds were giving place to the clear winter sky, and a few stars were shining.

"So you see the rain has stopped, and there is a full moon struggling to free itself of the clouds," I said.

Giovanni shivered in the cold wind sweeping across the Piazza Navona, and I thought of sending him back for a cloak, and then thought better of it.

We walked through the deserted streets. Usually when we walked together at night, keeping to the shadows, Giovanni would be a few paces behind me with his hand on his dagger, ready to spring forward the moment I was attacked, but now, because it was bitterly cold and there was a raw wind, we walked arm in arm. Sometimes I would gaze at him with a feeling of great tenderness. His father was dead, his mother had long since abandoned him. He was well built, strong and sturdy, and he could maintain a pose longer than anyone else, and in addition he had a clear golden skin. I had painted him twice as a young John the Baptist, and the Marchese Giustiniani had liked the paintings so much that he wanted both of them. I had already planned many more paintings of Giovanni. I would paint him as an angel, or as a young courtier, or as a silk-coated bravo smiling at a martyr's agony. There was no end to the paintings I intended to make of him.

We made our way down the narrow lanes to the Tiber, where the air was fresher, seeing only a few stray dogs and cats. It was very quiet that night. We had reached the river when we heard a low booming sound, like a cannonade, in the distance. It was very faint, and seemed to come from beyond the Sabine hills. Even while we were standing by the river bank, the sound grew louder, and all the time the dark river was boiling.

The moon emerged from behind the clouds, and then vanished again as more clouds drifted hurriedly across the face of the sky.

"The river is rising," Giovanni said, and since he was a farm boy, who knew the ways of the moon, the stars, the rain, and the clouds, I listened to him with pleasure and attention.

"I can see it is rising," I said, "but it rises every year, and sometimes many times."

"But now it will rise higher than ever and drown us all."

I thought he was joking.

"All of us?" I said. "Shall we all die?"

"Yes, we shall all die," he went on, and he was still listening to the distant cannonade.

He was smiling, and I had the feeling that he was still searching for an explanation for the distant booming sound. At dawn we returned to the Palazzo Madama. All that morning the skies remained clear, but the river rose. I decided to paint a portrait of Giovanni. This time there was no ram, no fleece, no wilderness in the background: only Giovanni himself, in his insolence and youthful pride. I remember I was on edge. The painting went badly. In despair I returned to contemplate the portrait of the Cardinal and made some half-hearted attempts to finish it. Then I returned to Giovanni, and for a while the work went easily. In the afternoon we went down to the river.

The river was beginning to overflow its banks, but no one was particularly disturbed. There were crowds lining the banks, and it amused them to watch the swollen river with the dead tree trunks floating past, and sometimes a drowned ox. Everyone was saying that at nightfall the river would quietly subside.

Toward evening thick black clouds filled the sky, and the rain began to fall. At the Palazzo Madama the Cardinal ordered everyone to work at filling up canvas bags with sand kept in a storehouse for exactly this purpose. The work went on through the night. Inside the palace the windows shook and the candles shuddered with every clap of thunder. We heard that the inns along the Tiber were falling into the river, and the great stone bridges might be swept away, so strong was the force of the current.

We worked all night, and in the morning it was still raining. All the streets and squares near the river were underwater, and people were being given bread and wine at their windows by boatmen who had difficulty in maneuvering their small wherries. All this was done by. order of the Pope. And all the time the rain was coming down and the river was rising. Every hour another street vanished underwater. But at the Palazzo Madama, the great timbers shoring up the walls, the mountains of sandbags piled all round, we felt safe. My cellar was safe, for we had set up sandbags across the window, and it was inconceivable that the flood could enter the palace, which was protected like a fortress. Yet for safety's sake most of my possessions were removed to the second floor of the palace.

The rain did not fall violently. On the contrary it fell gently, persistently, as in spring. We did not fear the rain so much as the flooded river. Rain and warm winds had melted the snow in the high Umbrian mountains, and now every stream, rivulet and torrent was being discharged into the Tiber. The river seemed determined to swallow the city.

What was strange was the dreadful silence which fell on Rome, especially at night. Everything became damp and sodden. The lamps set before the sacred images in the streets went out. The smell of the sewers filled the air, and the only sounds came from the boatmen and the sudden explosion as a wall crumbled into the water. In the Palazzo Madama there were candles in all the windows, and guards stood there to watch the rising river. We were a blaze of light in a desert of darkness.

Bread came from the bakers in the hills, and they said the fish we consumed had been caught in the Piazza Navona, which was eight feet underwater. The black boats of the Companions of Death patrolled the streets; it was the first time we ever heard of them possessing boats. The Pope gave orders that the churches should be opened to the poor, and that bread and wine should be distributed in all the churches which were not underwater. They said the entire Square of St. Peter's was underwater, and the Tiber was climbing the stairway of the Vatican.

The Cardinal went about the business of defending his palace and the surrounding area like a general commanding an army. Boats — wherries, skiffs, rowboats of all kinds — were assembled in the courtyard; food from the Cardinal's kitchens was piled into them; and we fed the people who lived on the Piazza Navona. On Christmas evening, and again when the water was dropping the next day, the Cardinal went out in a boat and blessed the people, calling on them to be of good heart, for the waters would surely subside. And indeed on St. Stephen's Day there was only five feet of water in the Piazza Navona. A pale green sun came out, and for the first time in three days we saw a watery sky. The Pope, who had taken refuge in the Quirinal, was said to be returning to St. Peter's.

So the days passed, and between working in a room off the Cardinal's reception room — but the air was too humid for any work of value — and helping to defend the palace I passed my time with Giovanni at my side. The Cardinal warned us that the dangerous time would come when the waters were subsiding. He said: "Be on guard to the end!" and so we were. On the fourth day we learned that some sandbags had burst and water was entering the kitchens. Then we heard that water was filling up the cellars in the north of the palace, and once more we hurried to make chains of buckets, with the Cardinal himself giving the orders. Toward evening we heard that water was flooding into my own cellar. I looked around for Giovanni, but he was nowhere to be seen. I imagined he was upstairs, or in the courtyard with the boatmen. We hurried away to my cellar, with the Cardinal leading the way. We had candles and lanterns, and someone was holding an immense pitch-pine torch above his head. The water was pouring down the steps, making a golden cascade in the light of the torches.

"Did you leave anything behind?" the Cardinal said, at the head of the stairs.

"Nothing of value, Illustrissimo," I replied. We peered into the darkness to see what could be done, because the water was now coming with great force down the steps. There was little we could do except to seal off the door at the head of the steps. I saw a bed, a table, some old frames and paintbrushes floating on the surface.

"There is something white over there!" the Cardinal said.

I gave a yell and threw myself down the steps, and the Cardinal followed me. We swam across my cellar and we both reached Giovanni at the same time. Together we brought him back to the steps. All my life I shall remember the Cardinal carrying Giovanni up the steps in the light of the golden candles. In silence we carried him through the kitchens and up the long flight of steps to the audience chamber, where we laid him under a painting of the youthful John the Baptist. The Cardinal knelt at his feet and offered the prayers for the dead.

The Coming of Benedetto

W HEN the spring came, you would have thought that Rome had never suffered from the flood. The streets were cleaned, the dead were decently buried, the cellars were purged and fumigated, and wherever the flood water left its mark, the mark was erased. Rome rose from the flood more beautiful, or at least more habitable, than ever. Roofs were retiled, and there was new paint everywhere. That spring the flowers in the gardens of the Villa Medici were brighter than ever before.

I grieved for Giovanni, but not for long. One day, when visiting a cardinal at St. Peter's, I encountered near the Castel Sant' Angelo, a stableboy leading a piebald mare. He had a lean dark face, blue eyes, and a shock of golden hair. He had large hands and good shoulders, and there was something about his walk and his smile which suggested that he was not born to be a stableboy, and indeed I learned later that he came from a noble Venetian family which had fallen into misfortune.

"I'll buy your mare," I told him, "and I'll pay twice its value on the market."

He said it was not his mare, and being merely a stableboy he was in no position to sell it. I asked him the name of his master, and he said it was Cardinal San Severino.

"Then come with me," I said, "for I am paying a visit to the Cardinal this very hour. I shall ask him if I can buy the mare and your services, too."

The boy smiled pleasantly and accompanied me to the Cardinal's small palace in St. Peter's. Cardinal San Severino was a very old man, but he still enjoyed a daily ride in the gardens of the Belvedere. When I presented the boy to the Cardinal, saying that I would like to buy the mare and the services of the stableboy, he threw up his hands in a gesture of horror and said: "What next? Shall we see Michelangelo Merisi the possessor of a fleet of horses? I never believed you liked riding."

"Nor do I," I replied, "but I need both of them for my paintings."

"A horse for your paintings?" he said incredulously. "I can understand that you might have some need for my stableboy. But a horse —"

Then I told him that Marchese Giustiniani had arranged that I should paint for the Church of Santa Maria del Popolo two scenes from the life of St. Paul, and since everyone knew that St. Paul rode on horseback to Damascus I had been searching in Rome for the most magnificent horse in existence. If I could not buy the mare, could I at least be given the opportunity of painting it?

The Cardinal enquired about the progress of the paintings at San Luigi dei Francesi, and asked how it was possible to paint so many paintings of so high a quality in so short a time, and I therefore lectured him on his ignorance, for although I had received many commissions I had not completed them easily or quickly, and had indeed completed many of them long after the day mentioned on the contract. Just as a man may say many prayers in a day, so a good painter should be able to compose many good paintings in a year. As for the painting of *The Martyrdom of St. Matthew*, I had twice changed the entire composition and was now at work on a third composition, and might be engaged on a fourth or a fifth in years to come.

The Cardinal promised me the use of the piebald mare whenever I needed it, while as for the boy I must make my own arrangements. Then he asked what paintings I could sell him, and I said I would sell him a portrait of David holding up the head of Goliath, with the stableboy serving as the model for David.

"In that case I willingly give you Benedetto," he said, and from that day Benedetto lived in my cellar.

For the painting of *The Conversion of St. Paul* I needed a saint, a piebald mare, and a man of great age and wisdom to portray the groom. The next day I found the old man in the Piazza del Popolo. He was a one-legged beggar with shaggy hair and purple veins which stood out on his face. He had served in the galleys and had been many times imprisoned for stealing. He was half blind, and when he was in his cups he talked about the strange lands he had seen while a captive of the Turks. And what especially pleased me was that he had been to Damascus, and that he bore the scars of many wounds and many floggings. His name was Antonio Tocchi, and he would sometimes stay in my cellar on a bed of straw.

For this painting I used Leonello Spada as the model for St. Paul.

One day, after I had been painting for thirty hours nearly continuously, I discovered that all my models were asleep. The mare was asleep, Antonio Tocchi was lying in his bed of straw, and Leonello Spada was snoring in a bed of crimson damask curtains. Only Benedetto was awake.

This was how I painted — in long spells, not caring about food or drink or the rising and falling of the sun. In my cellar the world was blotted out: there was only the immense canvas, the mare and the two men caught up in the silence of painting, the shapes gradually taking form before my eyes. Benedetto would bring me a bowl of milk or a loaf of bread, and then vanish into the shadows. They say I work fast, but God knows I work slowly. Hours would pass while I studied a few square inches of canvas before touching it with my brush; they thought I was dreaming, but I was working relentlessly. I was never able to say: "I shall work for two hours, and then I shall rest." The painting mastered me. I would paint for ten hours, or twenty, or thirty, and thank God that my hand could still hold the brush and that my eyes could still see the shining flanks of the mare.

There are paintings in which one puts almost all of oneself, and other paintings where only fragments of oneself are permitted to appear, but into *The Conversion of St. Paul* I put all of myself. There were times when I was so absorbed in the mare that I became her, and it would not have surprised me in the least if I had grown hooves and a silky mane. I knew what they would say of my painting; they would say it was the portrait of a mare, and not fit to be hung in a chapel in Santa Maria del Popolo: some poor devil held the mare by the bridle, and another lay at the mare's feet, and who would dare to proclaim that this was St. Paul, especially since he wore the cuirass of a soldier? But there was that bright light falling on the mare's flanks and on the man lying pitifully at the mare's feet in the attitude of one struck dumb and blinded by God's fire, and it was enough for me if I could represent the sudden blaze of divine light: not daylight nor moonlight nor any light known to man, but the perfect and instantaneous light of Heaven striking down on mortal flesh and revealing the glory of God's creation.

In that crowded canvas there was only a mare and two men, and yet there were whole worlds. The mare was not a mare only, nor was she an uncomprehending beast unredeemed by divinity.

She, too, was a glory, and the old man who held her by the bridle was not merely Antonio Tocchi: he was one of the patriarchs and prophets, an angel sent down to earth to witness the sudden conversion of Paul, and therefore he must be painted in a way to suggest that he was more than a man, and perhaps even more than an angel. So he stands there quietly in the shadows, very old and bent, looking down at Paul dispassionately and yet with a kind of quiet sympathy. He has known this will happen, and therefore he shows no surprise. And then again there is no horror or amazement on the face of Paul, no beseeching. He lies there in a calm stupor, as I have seen men struck by lightning who wear a strange smile on their lips long after they are dead. But Paul is not dead. He has fallen from his horse, and in the act of falling he has climbed to the gates of Heaven.

All this, of course, I explained to Cardinal del Monte, and I remember how he pleaded with me to make the mare smaller, saying: "You could paint her running away into the distance — very far away. Why do you have to fill the whole canvas with the horse?" "Because there is no other way," I said, "to render the majesty of God." "Is the horse therefore God?" he said. "No," I replied, "but the light falling on the mare's flanks is God." And then for a long time he was silent, stroking his silver beard.

I never worked so feverishly on a painting, never gave such prolonged thought to any other work of mine. There were many technical problems which were almost beyond solution. Above all there was the difficulty of rendering the light in such a way that God's presence would be known, and this is why I worked unceasingly, hour after hour, in an effort to give a fierce opacity to the light. There were times when I had to lean against the easel for support, but the strength always returned. It was strange how it came unfailingly, bubbling out of some unknown wellspring.

There came a time when it was necessary to sleep and I threw myself down on the pallet bed, whispering to Benedetto to douse the lamps. I must have slept for twelve hours. When I woke up the sun was streaming through the window — that window which I painted so accurately and so painstakingly in *The Calling of St. Matthew* — and I then discovered that everyone except Benedetto was gone. I shouted to Benedetto: "Get breakfast, and then to work!" There was a stone pitcher in the corner of the room, and I dipped my head in the cold water, and so did Benedetto. I kissed him, for he looked beautiful in the sunlight with his shirt wide open and his face shining with water.

"Where's Leonello?"

"He went, and took the mare with him."

"And where's old Antonio?"

"God knows, master. He fell asleep on his feet and pitched right over during the night, splitting his nose. Can you paint him without a nose, master?"

Benedetto was in no mood for working that day.

"Shall we go on holiday?" he said, peering up at me with an easy smile.

"What kind of holiday?"

"Why, the best kind," he answered. "Riding and feasting and whoring — there's no better kind. We've worked for two days without stop. It is time we went abroad, master."

"No, we work," I said, "and if the work goes well, then we'll go feasting in the evening."

I thought that was the end of the matter, and turned my back on him. I wanted to look closely at the painting in the sunlight. There were a hundred details which I wanted to explore. I wanted to be sure that the three figures were anchored to the canvas, and then too I wanted to discover exactly how the reflections of St. Paul's armor should be glimpsed on the underbelly of the mare; and indeed it was precisely for the sake of these reflections that I made St. Paul wear armor. The truth was that the painting absorbed me more than any other I had ever painted, not only because I was more certain than ever that I was now a master, worthy to be compared with the masters of the past, with Titian and Raphael and perhaps three others whom I accounted as their fellows, but also because I believed I had opened out a path for myself which I could follow in many hazardous directions. I had no patience with Benedetto, and I was in no mood to permit him to interrupt my work.

So for perhaps five minutes I studied the canvas, and I was preparing to study it for another hour, quietly and contemplatively, according to my habit, when Benedetto suddenly pulled at my arm and said: "For God's sake, master, when do we go riding? You can't work with the mare gone, and Antonio Tocchi has gone, and Leonello, too!"

"For God's sake go away!" I shouted, turning on him in anger, for I had had enough of his whining.

"You said we would go riding," he answered. "You promised it! I swear you promised it!"

"I didn't!"

"Oh, but you did, master!"

Saying this, he smiled his most captivating smile — the smile that told me he was lying, and knew he was lying.

I wanted to work. God knows, a painter should have the right to work without the interference of his servant. I was more angry than ever now and struck him across the cheek. I had meant to give him nothing more than a light tap, but the blow must have been harder than I thought, for he stood there with a puzzled look, holding his hand to his burning cheek. A moment later his lips were trembling, and tears spurted from his eyes.

I knew then what married men suffer: the weepings and the remonstrances of their women. The sight of him standing in the sunlight with that reproachful look disturbed me, and I struck him again, so that he went reeling across the room to tumble at last on his pallet bed after tripping over a coil of rope. He wept like a maniac. I could see his small shoulders moving and his feet beating the straw, and I had no sympathy for him. Once I saw him looking back at me, his damp hair falling over his eyes, his cheeks flushed, his mouth wide open in surprise and anger, and I should have paid attention to him, but I didn't. I was thinking only of my painting. It annoyed me that Antonio Tocchi and Leonello Spada had vanished — with no by-your-leave and no message to say when they would return, and I was still more annoyed because the beautiful mare had vanished, leaving her droppings. I took up my paintbrush. I was accustomed to paint by the light of candles and hanging lamps, but the sunlight sometimes shows me my errors, and there were some details of the face which I hoped to improve. I was working on Antonio Tocchi's face when I heard a rustling in the straw and a sound like a quick muffled intake of breath. I swung around just in time.

Benedetto was coming toward me with the rapier which he had taken from the wall, crouching low, one shoulder higher than the other, his posture so ungainly and twisted that I scarcely recognized him. The heavy rapier trembling in his hand seemed to possess a life of its own. His eyes were staring, curiously blank, and what was even more surprising was that he was baring his teeth like an animal. He was coming for me, and I just had time to turn aside. He was holding the rapier with both hands. I kicked out, and luckily my boot caught his hands, and the rapier went spinning into the air, and I remember very little of the next moments except that he fell to the ground, face down, arse up, with his legs sprawled in different directions. He was screaming at the top of his voice, and there was blood coming from his hands.

I would have murdered him if he had not fallen in the straw. I threw myself on him, but I do not think we wrestled for long: no more than the space of a few breaths. He was white and trembling, ragged, bloodstained and dirty, and I remember especially the smear of blood across his mouth.

"Would you have killed me?" I asked.

"Yes, I would have killed you," he said, and his breath came hard and choking.

I kissed him full on the mouth. He was silent then, and unresisting. I tore off his clothes, while he lay very quiet in the straw, the yellow sunlight falling on his nakedness which I knew so well from having painted it so often; and he made no protest when I turned him over. It was like pushing one's thumb into a soft apple. He opened easily: only sometimes there came a little whimper from him. And afterward he turned and clung to me like a woman, his eyes closed, while the tears clung to his long black eyelashes. On his face there was the expression which I have seen on paintings of St. Sebastian. I left him there and went on painting.

But that evening, since neither the mare nor Leonello Spada nor Antonio Tocchi had returned, I decided, because the painting was already far advanced, to go on holiday. I sauntered out, dressed in my best clothes, with Benedetto performing the service of my page. It was about dusk when we set out. I wore my rapier, and Benedetto was armed with a short dagger; he walked ten paces behind me. I must admit to a curious feeling of pleasure at the thought that he might attack me again, for there was no telling whether there might not spring up in him, humbled and contrite as he was, a remembered motive for revenge, while I, accustomed to a life of uncertainty, took pleasure in danger.

They will never understand my paintings until they know that I lived in danger every moment of my life as a painter. Each brushstroke was a brush against death, and every figure had within it the potentialities of shipwreck. My paintings are the shapes I have summoned out of storms.

It was one of those sultry evenings when the air is heavy with the smells of the Tiber. I saw the cutthroats hovering in the shadows, and they would look at me balefully till they saw the armed page who walked behind me. Then they would scamper away down the alleyways, for they feared a battle. Three or four times we were accosted in this way. Then at the corner of the Via Tiburina a drunken man came lurching out of a house of prostitution. He was tall and heavily built, his purple doublet stained with wine, and he was shouting at a woman inside the house.

Such men are not usually dangerous, though sometimes our Roman cutthroats pretend to be drunk the better to display their mischief. At first I did not recognize him, and then I saw that he was Giovanni Baglione, a wretched painter, who would be better employed painting coffin lids than the walls of churches. I had known him briefly when I was working in the house of Monsignor Pucci. Seeing me, he hurled himself on me like a long-lost brother. I avoided him by ducking out of his reach. For some reason this made him even more affectionate, so that he came hurrying after me, his long arms pawing the air, his body bent forward, so that he resembled an enormous hunting dog about to leap on its prey. He had forgotten about the woman in the house; his only thought was to hinder me. He was jumping from one side of the narrow lane to the other. Somehow he succeeded in getting in front of me. "I know you well, Michelangelo!" he screamed. "Have you lost your courtesy? Don't you meet your friends civilly when you encounter them on the road?"

I shook him off, but he came running after me, gripped my arm with a steel-like grip, and said: "Don't you remember me? For God's love, say you remember me!"

He was a bad painter, and therefore I said: "Yes, I remember you! You must be the pimp, Sigismundo, who plies his trade in the Forum. May God had mercy on your poverty!"

The words must have enraged him, for he screamed like a stuck pig.

"What did you say? Sigismundo? Why, you know me well enough! Where's your courtesy?"

"I have no courtesy for bad painters!"

"What's that you said? A bad painter, eh? Did you say I was Sigismundo? Dare you say such things in public?"

I reminded him that we were not in public, and he reminded me that I had not greeted him when we met. I explained that I do not bow when I meet strangers, or even when I meet friends; they bow to me first, calling me by name and then reminding me of the names they were christened with. I gave him a push which sent him sprawling against a wall, and suddenly a window opened and a woman in an upper room emptied a chamber pot on his head. He must have thought I had done it, for he came roaring at me. Benedetto came running up. I shouted: "Don't touch him! A woman emptied a chamber pot over him!" But Benedetto will never heed a warning. He was in a light-hearted mood and it pleased him to dance around the wretched man with his dagger held at arm's length, pricking him, driving him to fury, and all the time smiling his angelic smile, until at last, from clutching the air and cursing interminably, poor Baglione dropped to the ground and buried his head in his hands for fear of another pinprick from the rapier. Squatting there, one leg under him, the other stretched out, he howled like a dog which has been run over by a cart wheel. He was like something left on the road, and since there was no more fight in him, we were content to leave him there.

"Shall I prick him a little more?" Benedetto asked me.

"No," I said, "you have pricked him enough — more than is good for him or for us."

"Why, there's no danger in him now. He's no more than a whipped dog."

"So he is, but even whipped dogs can bite, Benedetto. Let us hope he does not bear us too much malice."

Because Benedetto was so determined to bring more misery to Baglione, I took his dagger from him. Surprisingly he made no protest. Arm in arm we walked down the deserted lane, which brought us to the Tiber. The dark tower of the prison of Tor di Nona rose against the sky, all the windows dark except one, high up in the tower, from which there came the reddish glow of a fire. We were passing under the prison walls when we heard a blood-curdling scream which seemed to linger on the night air, and Benedetto pressed himself against me and said: "They are torturing a man," and I answered: "It is not a man, and it is not torture. It is a woman alone in her cell, and not knowing whether she will ever go free."

"How do you know these things?" Benedetto asked me.

"How can one not know when one has lived some years in Rome?" I answered. "I tell you, the real language of Rome is in the screams you hear every day. Men cry in the night, and sometimes they pray, and what are prayers but screams for help?"

About a hundred yards from Tor di Nona stands the Osteria del Orso with the crimson bear on the signboard swinging in the wind. There is no courtyard; the place is more like a large shop with a fire blazing in the hearth. The servants wear scarlet livery with the shape of a bear embroidered on their doublets. There are seven or eight long tables huddled close together, and though the food is good, one is likely to suffer from a cramped stomach because the tables press so hard against the belly. It is not a place where anyone can dine in comfort: the noise is deafening, and the servants are forever butting you and spilling food over you, and the wenches are always trying to sit in your lap. But behind this large room there is a smaller room with only three tables. This room faces the river, and because it was in my mind to reward Benedetto for his good offices during the day, I told him we would take our seats "by the river," according to the custom of the rich. But as it happened Prince Mario Buontempi, a buffoon, was entertaining some friends recently arrived from Florence in this room, and we were refused admittance. I cursed, but there was nothing to be gained by cursing. We found a place in the corner near the hearth fire, where the pigs were roasting. We ate well, and drank better. The sweat poured out of our faces, and we could scarcely breathe in the sweltering heat of the place. There was only one advantage. In the light of the flames I studied Benedetto's face, and sometimes I would look toward the door. I had a strange feeling that Baglione would appear armed to the teeth, determined to wipe out the indignities he had suffered earlier in the evening.

There were a few people I knew in the inn. The Cavaliere Giambattista Marino was among those who came to pay their respects to me. He has the face of a well-bred white horse, all nose and teeth, with a bitter smile. His hands, which are long and tapering, are more eloquent than his face. They are feminine hands, and his voice when he recites his poems is also feminine, high-pitched and shrill. Yet this man with the delicate hands and the face of a horse has the courage of a lion. We embraced. He asked about my health and about my paintings, and when I told him about our encounter with Baglione, he smiled and then grew serious, saying he was not a man to be trifled with and possessed a long memory.

"Then what would you have me do?" I asked.

"If you are wise," he said, "you will send him a small present in order to make amends."

"And if I don't —"

"Then you will suffer for it. But since, as you say, he was very

[177]

drunk, it is unlikely that he will remember. Only you must be sure that he doesn't remember." Saying this, with a wave of his hands he dismissed the subject of Baglione and asked whether he could come and visit me. "There is no better painter in Rome, and it is always an honor to be permitted into your cellar."

I said: "You know you can come whenever you please."

"Then it is decided. I shall come tomorrow. I shall sit in a corner and compose poems in your honor while you paint." And then just before leaving, he said: "Be careful, Michelangelo. Do not provoke too many enemies. One or two enemies is enough for one lifetime."

"Then God help me," I said, "for I have at least fifty."

For a moment he gazed at me steadily, and then he said: "All your enemies are my enemies." Then he was gone, and for perhaps an hour, warmed by wine and with Benedetto beside me, I knew a glow of happiness such as I had not experienced for many months.

Ever since we entered the Osteria del Orso, I had the feeling that some strange accident would occur. I could not guess the nature of the accident. Baglione would suddenly enter the inn, cold sober, with a sword in his hand, or perhaps all my fifty enemies would appear simultaneously. Or some prince or other would offer me a commission to paint his entire palace, or a cardinal would invite me to paint an entire chapel within the Vatican. Whether good or evil would befall me I did not know. I knew only that something untoward was about to happen.

The crowds were thinning out, and there were no more than thirty or forty people left in the inn when the strange accident occurred. At the time I did not recognize that anything unusual was happening. A small boy, about eleven or twelve, came up to me, begging for alms. He looked a little like Giovanni Battista degli Angeli, who died by my side in the Ospedale della Misericordia, only this boy was red-haired — it was long, silky red hair which fell to his shoulders. He was ragged and dirty, his backside showing through his rags. Every night the beggar boys come to the Osteria del Orso to feed on scraps from the table, and this boy was no different from the others.

He had a whining singsong voice, but there was about him a delicate grace of movement. He was well built, though he needed more flesh. I tossed him a farthing. He said very seriously: "What canst thou do with a farthing, master?"

"You can buy a bowl of milk," I said, "and put flesh on your bones."

He looked at me wearily. He was shaking with a fever, and his small freckled face was pinched with hunger. His voice was hoarse — it was like an old man's voice. He smiled, clutched my hand, kissed the hollow of my palm, and stood there as though waiting for me to speak. I had thrown out my legs to warm them by the dying fire, and he stood between them.

"God keep you," I said carelessly, for I had seen enough of these ragamuffins in the streets. "What do you want with me?"

"To serve you, master."

He kissed my hand again.

"In what way will you serve me?"

"In any way —"

I told him I already had a servant. I needed no other. All the time I was thinking that out of some dark corner of the room someone would emerge with a face of menace or promise. I did not know that the boy was menace and promise. I decided to humor him.

"If I take you into my service, what will you do for me?" I said in a bantering voice, not intending to be taken seriously.

"I'll do more than anyone has ever done for you," he answered. "I'll rob for you, master. I'll find women for you. I'll sleep beside your bed and guard you, master."

I turned to Benedetto, who was smiling indulgently. Though he had attempted to murder me, he knew he was secure in my affections. He tossed another farthing to the boy, who caught it easily, and then tossed another, which fell into the fire. Like lightning the boy's hand went under the blazing log and out again. Clutching his farthings and paying no attention to Benedetto, he came and stood between my knees again with that odd, expectant look on his face.

"You have had your farthings," I said. "Now you can go!"

Sheepishly he began to stroke my doublet.

"It will do you no good," I went on. "You can stroke the cloth till your skin is worn to the bone, but I'll give you no more money."

"I don't want money," he said. "I want to serve you —"

"Then you are out of your mind!" I said, pushing him away, so that he almost fell into the fire. "You're too thin to sleep with, and too ugly to have around me. For God's sake be gone!"

I stood up then, for I knew I would have no peace while the boy was importuning me. He took my hand and pointed to a woman sitting in a far corner. The smoke from the candles half obscured her face. I saw a wild tangle of red-gold hair reaching to her shoulders, a green bodice, a face that was downcast so that I could not see whether she was plain or beautiful. She was in repose, lost in dreams, unmoving. She might have been a servant girl snatching a few quiet minutes after her labors in the kitchen; except for her hair, there was nothing to distinguish her from all the other women who passed through the Osteria del Orso that evening. Yet there must have been something about her to attract my attention, for I found myself being led willingly by the boy across the room. Once I looked back. Benedetto was sitting by the fire with his legs stretched out in front of him, basking in the warmth of the fire, his eyes closed, a smile playing on his lips.

"Maddalena!" the boy said, and the sound of his voice must have startled her from her sleep, for she gave a little shudder.

The moment she looked up I knew I was her prisoner. She had a face made to be painted, a broad forehead, a long straight nose, well-modeled lips. Her skin was that milky gold which is sometimes found in people with red hair. An oval face, but strong, for there was something of the peasant in her. But the most extraordinary thing about her, except for her beauty, was her quietness, the sense of exquisite calm and composure. It was the face of a Madonna, and she seemed to have stepped out of a painting. And there was that great crown of fiery gold hair flowing like waves over her shoulders.

The boy crept along the bench to sit beside her. I bowed, taking my place on the bench opposite her. At first, while I drank in her beauty, no words were exchanged. The boy was whispering to her, leaning up and cupping his thin hands to her ear, and as she bent to listen to him, some strands of gold hair fell over her face. She brushed them away carelessly. Every gesture was perfect. Yet there was a strange indifference about her. She asked for nothing. The boy kept whispering and pointing to me, and she nodded gently, as though she had listened to him so many times that his words had lost their meaning. At last the boy said: "She will go with you —"

I was in no mood to have her: that milky skin, that golden hair, that ripeness in the green bodice, were not made for my pleasure. The boy, I told myself, was a pimp, and soon enough he would be announcing a price. She lowered her eyes again and gazed down at her hands lying loosely on her lap, while the boy said: "Will you take her?"

"No, I won't take her," I said, but I could not take my eyes from her face.

Already I was composing a painting of the Madonna with Maddalena as my model, and then from one painting I composed another, and then another. There was that terrible stillness about her, such as I have seen in no other woman. It was a kind of holy quietness.

I said casually: "If I need her as a model, where shall I find her?" I thought of Leonello Spada and Antonio Tocchi and the unfinished painting of *The Conversion of St. Paul* waiting for me in my cellar, and all the days lying ahead when I would need to devote myself to them. I had never painted a Madonna, never desired to.

"You won't find us," the boy said, "unless you take us both."

"Why should you think I would want either of you?"

"Because you need us," he said insistently.

I looked at the woman, wondering whether she was aware what the boy was saying. She nodded, and it was clear that she understood.

The boy was very like her, and was perhaps her son. She was twenty-seven or twenty-eight, full breasted, big boned, and a sculptor in ancient Greece would have used her for a model of Minerva. I thought of Giulia, so thin and frail, tentatively warming her hands over life, and then of this woman who seemed so secure, so content, so perfectly designed to be a Madonna. One was the Magdalene, the other was the Virgin. Through the corner of my eye I watched Benedetto closely. At first he detested the boy; then he had looked suspiciously at Maddalena; then he, too, was caught up in the strange beauty of this woman.

At last I said: "You can have everything you want. You can live in my cellar, if you like. I'll paint her, but God knows when."

Then in a small silent procession we made our way to the Palazzo Madama.

The Palace of Prince Colonna

IN this way Maddalena became a part of our life in the cellar, cooking for us, mending our clothes, sweeping the floor, but always unobtrusively. The boy, Sandro, was her son, and she had long ago forgotten the name of the father. She was not faithful to us, and she would leave us whenever she pleased, working as a flower seller in the Piazza Navona, or wandering off into the country to visit some relatives in Palestrina, returning with huge baskets of flowers and fruit. She talked only when it was necessary, and then always in a soft, low, musical voice.

What attracted us to her was her beauty and something we could scarcely name — a holiness. It was not that when she entered the room we immediately set about behaving ourselves; it was simply that we became aware of her radiance, her quietness, her gentleness. She had a strange power of entering a room without being seen. I would be painting, and suddenly I would say: "Maddalena has just come in," and then I would turn to see her in a corner of the cellar sitting over a knitting basket. She had been sitting there quietly for an hour. She knew she could do this just as she knew, after seeing my paintings in the Church of San Luigi dei Francesi, that I would one day paint her as the Madonna.

But at this time I was still too busy with *The Conversion of St. Paul* to contemplate a large altarpiece with Maddalena as the Madonna. There were small commissions which had to be completed; there were large canvases for the Church of Santa Maria del Popolo; and in addition there were new commissions from people who could not easily be refused. I was working harder than ever. Cardinal del Monte had asked me to paint a *Deposition of Christ* for the Chiesa Nuova and a head of a Medusa to be sent as a gift to the Grand Duke of Tuscany. These, too, had to be completed. I thought I had more work than I could ever accomplish when I received a letter from the chamberlain of Prince Marzio Colonna, saying that he wished some paintings by my hand. So it happened that in five weeks I painted five pictures for him — a Judith, a David, a small Crucifixion, a portrait of the prince and another of his mistress Lucrezio Mirandola, formerly a woman of the streets. Some of these paintings I had begun before entering his service, but all were completed while I was staying in his palace.

I had never met the prince. I heard that he was old and ill, given to terrible bouts of ill temper, and likely to offer a starving painter ten *scudi* for an altarpiece. They said he lived in greater luxury than the Pope, and this was true, and that he had a collection of paintings rivaling that of Cardinal Scipione, and this also was true. To me he was always generous, loyal and forgiving. When I painted his portrait, I painted him as I saw him, and he forgave me willingly.

At first I set the letter aside, not believing that the prince would have any need of my services and scarcely trusting the words of a chamberlain. But two days later it happened that Cardinal del Monte came to my cellar. As usual he had asked permission to see the paintings, sending word by his chamberlain, and as usual I replied by sending Benedetto with the message that I looked forward to his visits as the Children of Israel looked forward to the descent of manna. I hung the huge crimson curtains round the cellar, lit the candles, and welcomed him as he came down the stairs, accompanied as always by footmen with lighted candles, but in the blaze of light I had prepared for him these candles were like the faint stars one can sometimes see on a summer's day.

At the foot of the stairs I knelt and kissed his ring, and led him to the throne where my models sat. He paid no attention to me, but was immediately absorbed in the paintings which, except for the Deposition, were stacked carefully one behind another, some twelve paintings altogether, most of them unfinished, but all of them in a condition to be seen, for the features and the essential shapes were painted in and there remained in each case only the working out of limbs or clothes or some scenery in the back-ground. He watched in silence as I showed one canvas after an-other, giving him perhaps a minute to see each one before passing on to the next. And in his silence there was great sympathy. With each painting he leaned forward a little more.

I left the Medusa to the last, for I knew he was anxious to see its progress. When he saw the painting, his mouth fell open and he made a gesture, as of irritation, with both hands, and then when the hands had grown calm again they settled on his knees and I could see the fingers clutching the skirts of his gown — these were the only movements he made during the showing of the paintings. He said nothing, but all the blood ran from his face.

On a circular shield, against a sulphurous green background, I painted the Medusa at the moment when Perseus has cut off her head, giving her features an expression of liveliness, the mouth wide open, eyes starting from their sockets, and the serpents around her head leaping out toward the beholder in such a way that he must feel menaced by their fangs. So Leonardo da Vinci had painted her, but that painting was lost and it was left to me to invent another. The footmen had shown little interest in my paintings, but they were alarmed when they saw my Medusa and quickly crossed themselves.

"I am not surprised that they crossed themselves," the Cardinal said, when I had given the shield to Benedetto, who turned it to the wall. "There is evil in that face — more evil than I wish to contemplate."

"Would you have me paint a kinder Medusa, Illustrissimo?" I said, and there was some mockery in my voice, but no more than the occasion warranted. "You asked for the *terribiltà*, and I have painted her according to the specifications you gave me."

"So you did, but I did not think at my age I would be frightened by anything you painted, Michelangelo. No doubt the Grand Duke of Tuscany will be equally frightened, and —" Here the Cardinal paused, and added in a softer voice: "And equally pleased." There was a ghostly smile playing on his lips, and the blood was coming back to his face.

He asked when the painting would be completed and I said I hoped to give it to him in a week. He expressed his satisfaction and esteem for my art, and asked to see a John the Baptist sitting naked and contemplative beside a lamb, and he said he observed some similarity between John the Baptist and Benedetto, which caused Benedetto to fling out his legs in a little dance, but when I enquired whether there were any other paintings he would like to see again, he answered that he had some affairs to attend to and would see them later. He was about to leave when I remembered the letter from the chamberlain of Prince Marzio Colonna and I said I intended, if it so pleased the Prince, to paint for him, if he rewarded me well enough, but there were altogether so many rumors of his ferocious temper and ill manners that I was likely to find myself in bad company. I phrased the sentences elegantly in the Florentine manner, saying the opposite of what I intended to convey, and the Cardinal was amused.

"I see you have no high opinion of the poor Prince," he said, "but you should have some sympathy for him. He is very ill and not likely to live long."

"Then I should see him?"

"Of course you should see him. He is rich, and he has twenty palaces, and those are excellent reasons why you should see him. But if you see him and he commissions a painting from you, what will happen to the twelve unfinished paintings? If you die now, Michelangelo, there will be twelve paintings which can neither be sold nor can they decorate a chapel or an altar nor can they be hung on a wall. You should finish what you do."

"Let me paint in my own way, Illustrissimo," I said sharply.

He was taken aback and said nothing for a few moments, then he beckoned to me and when I knelt and kissed his ring, he bent down and kissed my forehead, and he did the same for Benedetto, and afterwards he blessed the cellar, raising his right hand very stiffly and solemnly, making the sign of the cross. He performed this service with an exquisite grace and tact. Then in silence he turned and mounted the stairs. I thought he was angry with me, and perhaps he was, but when he was halfway up the stairs he turned and said: "Be in good heart and avoid mischief, Michelangelo, for my sake, and when you have seen Prince Colonna come and see me."

And I knelt, and Benedetto knelt beside me, until we could no longer hear his footsteps along the stone corridor.

On the following day, accompanied by Benedetto, I went to the palace of Prince Colonna with no expectation of seeing the prince, but in order to pay my respects to the chamberlain. He was an old man, about fifty, with a beard half white, half gray, grizzled and with bent shoulders, wearing the scarlet livery of the princely family. Benedetto carried three paintings to show the chamberlain who would no doubt show them to the prince, for such is the normal fashion among painters in Rome. In a day or two, if he was satisfied with the paintings, the prince would summon me to an audience and he would announce the subject of the painting he desired and how much he would pay for it, and this audience was usually very brief.

The chamberlain, whose name was Taddeo Falliano, had no sooner set eyes on us than he declared that the prince was anxious to see me, having received a letter from Cardinal del Monte recommending me to his service.

"The prince will see you now — at this very moment," the chamberlain said. "But I must warn you not to be surprised by his appearance. He is suffering from the *lupa*."

Benedetto drew back and began to make the sign against all the maledictions of the flesh.

"You don't have to worry," the chamberlain went on. "The *lupa* is not like the plague, it will not harm you, the humors are contained within the flesh and have no way of reaching the air. In spite of his appearance the prince is exceptionally understanding and intelligent."

So indeed he was, but at first sight of him I held back, not only because he was monstrously swollen and his skin was a strange bluish color, for I am accustomed to monsters, but also because there came from him the smell of the many rancid ointments used to mitigate the disease. There was something else which was very strange about him, for he was wearing spectacles with thick lenses, so that his eyes, which were pale green, seemed to be hovering an inch away from his face. In that small darkened room with a thin watery light coming through the curtains he resembled an immense fish sitting on an ornate golden chair.

We bowed low before him, and he smiled benignly, saying in a thin voice that he was pleased to see us, and all the time he was addressing himself to Benedetto. I stepped forward and explained that Benedetto was my servant. He peered up at me through his enormous spectacles and said: "Then you are certainly uglier than your servant." And thinking I would be enraged, the chamberlain said quickly: "The light is very bad. If we could have candles, then you would see that Michelangelo is by no means as ugly as you think."

"Then by all means bring candles," the prince said. "The light is bad for me, but I shall not be able to see his paintings unless we have more light. It will hurt my eyes, but these are sacrifices I must pay to art."

Soon a page boy brought in a seven-branched candlestick, entering the room slowly, so that the prince could grow slowly accustomed to the light. Then the chamberlain showed him the three paintings I had brought, and he expressed his admiration for them by clicking his tongue while examining them so closely that I was afraid his head would break through the canvas. And after he had examined each one, he made me a little salutation, to indicate his pleasure.

"I shall not tell you which I regard as the best," he said, after he had examined all the paintings, "for there can be no question of one being better or worse than another. You are an enviable man, Michelangelo, for you have accomplished perfection."

He spoke with courtesy and friendliness, his head inclined a little to one side, his bloated blue face shining in the light of the candles. And giving a little laugh, he said: "In the state in which I now find myself, I cannot commission you to paint me, nor do I think you would have the courage to do so. If God made man in His likeness, then God forbid that I should be included among men. But you would honor me if you painted the members of my family —"

He went on to talk about my paintings. What surprised me was that he knew so much about them, had examined so many, and could recite all the churches and private collections where they could be found. He talked about them learnedly, and he remembered paintings I had forgotten. He had acquired three of my paintings of flowers, and wanted others.

"I shall not be satisfied until I have acquired as many as Cardinal del Monte," he said, "but I realize that the Cardinal has a great advantage over me. You live in his palace, and therefore he is in a stronger position to acquire them. As for me, I can merely hope to obtain the crumbs from the Cardinal's table."

"I shall serve Your Highness to the best of my ability," I said.

"Nonsense! You will always serve yourself! As for me, I shall, if I am lucky, get a few remnants left over, even though I am far richer than the Cardinal. Also — for I know you much better than you know yourself — you will not pay the slightest attention to my desires. You despise princes, and we are all beggars at your feet. Nevertheless I should like you to paint for me, and I am prepared to pay for the honor you will do me."

There was a long pause, and I thought the audience with the prince had come to an end. I was about to make my departure when he beckoned to me to come closer and said in a whisper: "I would like you to paint me — just as I am. Do not be alarmed! If you refuse my request, I shall not be put out. As for the three paintings you have brought today, I will gladly buy them."

At this moment another page boy entered the room, bearing on a silver tray some syrups in gold goblets. It was a hot day; the syrups were powdered with snow; and the pleasure of drinking from a gold goblet was equal to the pleasure of drinking the syrup. With his usual good manners the prince had arranged that there should be this pause to enable me to collect my thoughts.

"While you are painting me, you may have everything you please," the prince said softly, when the tray with the goblets was removed.

I should have known these words were dangerous.

"Everything?" I murmured.

"Yes, everything that a rich prince can bestow on a great painter."

"I can live in your palace?"

"Of course."

"I can have a white horse, the most beautiful courtesan in Rome, banquets every day, musicians to play for me?"

"I grant you all these."

"I may examine all Your Highness's paintings at my leisure?"

"You would be honoring me —"

"I may paint you at any hour of the day I please?"

"Of course."

"I may awake in the middle of the night and decide that this is the proper time to paint you?"

"This is the least of your requests, Michelangelo, for I scarcely sleep. It would please me if you painted me in the middle of the night, for it would give me something to do apart from praying for my immortal soul. How long would it take you to paint me?"

"About five weeks."

"Then it is arranged that you stay in my palace for five weeks—"

"And furthermore it is understood that I am beholden to no one except the Cardinal?"

"Yes."

"And thereafter the permission of the Cardinal must first be obtained."

"We shall have no trouble on that score, Michelangelo. He owes me some favors, and he will grant it readily."

"And at the end of five weeks I am a free man with permission to return to the Cardinal's house?"

"All this is granted to you, and will be put down in writing."

Indeed, the chamberlain was already writing it down. Already the contract was being drawn up, such a contract as no other painter in all Christendom had ever received. I mentioned that the paintings I had brought with me, the David, the Judith and the small crucifixion, were still unfinished, and he said: "Whether they are finished or not, I will accept them. If you complete them, so much the better. I am at your service. If there is anything else you wish to be added to the contract, you have only to say so."

I blushed when I mentioned the price I proposed to ask for the prince's portrait, but he simply nodded briskly and said: "Write down the figure he asks. As for all the other matters, the chamberlain will answer for me."

Saying this, he made a sign to the pages who helped him out of the chair and accompanied him from the room, all the time supporting him by the elbows.

"The contract will be sent to you tomorrow," the chamberlain said, "unless of course you would like to receive it earlier."

I replied that it would not be necessary to send it, for I intended that very evening, after performing some errands, to take up my residence in the palace.

"And when will you start painting the prince?"

"Tonight."

So it was arranged, and the terms of the contract, which was drawn up with the help of many lawyers and the priest attached to the prince's household, were followed to the letter. I began painting the prince at three o'clock in the morning, and at six o'clock the white horse, already saddled and caparisoned, was led into the courtyard, and with Benedetto riding a bay, we gave ourselves the pleasure of parading through Rome in the most exquisite finery to the astonishment of everyone who watched our progress. On this occasion it amused me to wear the prince's livery, but on other occasions I would ride out in whatever I was wearing.

We wore immense ostrich plumes in our caps and tossed coins to the crowd as we rode through the Piazza Navona. Sometimes we saw people we recognized, and they would gaze after us with expressions of disbelief, their mouths falling open, and we passed them by, pretending not to have seen them.

We spent the following days in the calm enjoyment of luxury. Everything that I or Benedetto desired was given to us either by the prince himself, or by the chamberlain, or by the prince's servants. To the banquets I invited all the roaring boys and maids who caught my fancy; the prince made no protest. On the contrary he sometimes appeared in the gallery to applaud our feasts. The prince's musicians played for me at the banquets, and while I painted, and while I slept. The room where I painted the prince was hung at my orders with paintings from his collection, which were changed every day, except for a Madonna by Leonardo da Vinci, a youthful knight by Giorgione, and an Annunciation by Piero della Francesca, which were left hanging on the walls. There were never less than ten paintings in the room.

The more I contemplated the prince the less I was intimidated by his appearance, for his evident goodness and courtesy shone through his swollen features. In his youth he was handsome, though in middle age he had acquired the pox as well as the *lupa*. His entire face, even his eyelids and his swollen ears, was pitted with pockmarks, and so were his hands. Yet he carried himself with great dignity and everyone who came into his presence was aware of his desire to please, not out of simplemindedness but out of a genuine desire to show affection; and he treated his grooms with the same deference as he treated his guests.

I painted him without those spectacles which made him resemble a fish, wearing his purple robes of state, his princely crown on a table beside him, a scarlet curtain falling in such a way that part of his face remained in shadow. Behind him in the darkness, very faint, were depicted the arms of the Colonna family. Since the light troubled him, he preferred to pose with his eyes closed, with the inevitable result that the painting conveys a brooding, melancholy expression, the lips sagging at the corners, the eyelids heavy, the chin drooping. I painted him with lowered lids, with only a flicker of his green eyes.

Ten days after we began living in the prince's palace I had so far advanced with the painting that there was time to resume work on the Judith and the David. There were no more banquets, and I no longer rode out on a white horse. The musicians still played for me, exquisite meals were still set before me, and the prince's collection of paintings was still at my beck and call. It was about this time, when luxury was beginning to pall, when I had grown weary of sleeping in a bed stuffed with swan's down, and when I had exhausted all the pleasures provided by the prince's servants, that the old chamberlain came to me and asked whether there was anything further I needed for my comfort. I answered quickly: "The only comfort is to hold a paintbrush in my hands."

The chamberlain answered: "At your age I used to think of other things besides the comfort of my hands."

I was examining the Madonna by Leonardo da Vinci and saw no need to pursue the conversation further, but later in the day, while walking across one of the prince's courtyards, I caught a glimpse of a woman of about twenty-five with dark reddish-gold hair and a clear golden skin, wearing a gown of striped red and green. She glanced over her shoulder, saw me, and hurried away. I asked who she was, and they told me it was Lucrezia Mirandola, the prince's mistress. Even in that brief glimpse I was aware of the grace of her carriage and her aristocratic bearing, so that, although she was a woman of the people, someone the prince had seen in the marketplace while riding to St. Peter's, she appeared to have descended from generations of princes. They said, too, that

at the time when the prince found her she was employed by a
fishmonger and spent her days gutting fish.

At the next sitting with the prince I said I would like to paint
her.

"I was afraid you would ask for her," he said irritably, and he
put his hand up to his eyes as though to conceal his grief, for he
knew exactly what I would ask of him. "I suppose you will want
to sleep with her?" he went on in a very low voice.

"I will paint her as Venus," I said. "I shall expect her to pose for
me at midnight."

"You shall have your wish, Michelangelo."

"And furthermore no one else shall be present while I paint
her."

"That, too."

"And she will pose for me until dawn."

"Yes," he said, "dawn is a good time for her to sleep. You shall
have your wish."

"And furthermore, with Your Highness's permission, she will
never be asked any questions about what happened between us."

"I have told you already, Michelangelo, that you shall have all
your wishes. It is not even necessary for you to state them, for
they have been promised to you."

I painted Lucrezia Mirandola lying on a red damask curtain,
with invisible cushions supporting her. She lay there in an attitude
of perfect abandonment, her red hair disheveled and streaming
across the curtain, her legs apart, her arms spread out, her eyes
half closed. Like many Roman women of the people she refused
to remove the hair of her armpits, and accordingly I painted her as
she was. For seven nights I painted her without benefit of musicians, and sometimes I would find myself falling into a kind of
stupor from long gazing at her. She breathed very lightly, and in
the glow of the flickering candles she seemed in perpetual move-

ment, though she was quieter than any model I ever painted. It seemed to me that her perfect beauty aroused those same sentiments of terror and glory which a man feels when he contemplates a crucified Christ: that her very perfection was a testimony of God's magnificence. And I must confess that I painted her, even in her attitude of abandonment, with a deeply religious emotion, and my greatest care was to work in fearful silence so as not to disturb her.

The prince was pleased with my painting of her, showering me with the most flattering compliments and expressions of esteem. He hung the painting in his gallery, but a red curtain was hung over it.

"Now that you have enjoyed nearly every luxury possible to man, I suppose you will now return to your dreary cellar," the prince said.

"Yes," I replied, "and I am most grateful to Your Highness for permitting me to enjoy the dreary luxuries of princely life. I envy you nothing. I know that the supreme luxury is to be a painter."

"I had expected you to say that, Michelangelo, and therefore I do not hold it against you. You know that whenever there is anything you need, you have only to come to me and it will be given you."

I thanked him, and then he asked what I liked most in the world after painting. He implied that if it was within his power he would give it to me.

"What I enjoy most is living in my cellar," I replied, "and then, whenever it pleases me, I climb the stairs to the Cardinal's apartments and live for a while in perfect luxury. Then I return to my cellar, where all the ragamuffins of Rome congregate around me. I like to leap from the lowest dregs to the heights and then back again."

"Beware that you do not fall too low or rise too high," the prince said.

I should have taken his advice, for three days later I wandered out into the street alone just after nightfall. A roof tile had fallen on a constable patrolling the streets, and by ill chance I was standing close by and the constable thought I had thrown the tile at him. I laughed at him, but there was blood on his face and he was beyond laughter.

"Did you throw the tile at me?" he shouted.

"What if I did?" I said, and at that moment three more constables appeared out of nowhere.

I drew my rapier and defended myself as well as I could, a dagger in one hand and a rapier in the other, but I was no match for four men armed with heavy swords. One struck me with the flat of his sword, and I fell to the ground. Then they were all on top of me, debating whether they would kill me on the spot and throw my body into the Tiber or whether they would carry me to prison at great inconvenience to themselves. One had a long stout stave, and after beating me with it, he decided that it might be more profitable to take me to prison. So I was trussed to the stave like a pig on its way to market, and carried along the same streets through which only a few days before I had ridden on Prince Colonna's white horse.

In this way I was taken to the Tor di Nona prison.

The Prison of Tor di Nona

WHEN the door clanged, I became aware for the first time in my life of the foul odor of corruption in the stench of the prison. Men had died around me in the Ospedale della Misericordia, but their smells were of a different kind, and more bearable: a prison has a special smell. A small candle was burning on a bench; the walls were smoke-blackened; the low pallet bed beneath the barred window was still warm from the previous occupant. The cell was perhaps ten feet square and the barred window was out of reach, high up; cobwebs dripped languidly from the ceiling, waving a little, though there was scarcely any wind.

To the end of my days I shall remember my first night in the Tor di Nona. At first I walked around the cell with my hands behind my back as though they were still tied, carefully avoiding the bench with the spluttering candle as though this small light had to be protected at all costs. I wondered what it was doing there and who had lit the flame — certainly not the jailer. I amused myself by gazing at my leaping shadows, which vanished, then rose abruptly, and then at the curious scratchings on the wall, the crucifix, the bleeding heart of Christ, the profile of a girl or some sentence carved with a sharpened nail. Soon I discovered that the whole wall was covered with the writings of prisoners who had been there before me — hundreds upon hundreds of sentences, prayers, names, dates, and some of these dates went back more than a hundred years. Some were written in a cursive script difficult to read, and others were very faint. In a period of a hundred years three or four hundred prisoners had written on the wall, and no doubt there were many who had not bothered to write. I was still reading when the candle flickered out and died.

I cursed the evil-smelling darkness, and for a few moments I felt like a drowning man with all the breath knocked out of him. I could feel the walls pressing in on me; to the foul prison smell there was added the greasy smell of the burnt-out candle. There was no air to breathe. I was choking, and hurled myself at the wooden door, hammering on it with my fists, shouting myself hoarse. I expected nothing, except that the earth would open out and swallow me. I cursed the corporal, the sergeant, the jailer, the governor of Tor di Nona, and all the poor wretches who had lived in my cell. I was like a child weeping with rage. No one heard me. Ten, twenty minutes passed, and then I heard the clanking of chains and the muttered curses of the jailer as he mounted the stone stairs, taking his time and breathing heavily. The judas opened and I saw the yellow flare of a lantern, a shaggy gray eyebrow, a blue eye.

"It won't do you any good," he muttered. "You don't have to shout!"

He spoke sadly, as though he had said the words many times before.

"I want air," I said. "I can't breathe! For God's sake let me out! Send a message to Cardinal del Monte! Do you know who I am?"

"They all say that," he replied. "You're all very important when you want the doors unlocked! You're all princes and lords spiritual! I knew a cutthroat once who claimed he was the unnatural son of the Holy Father, and perhaps he was, but we cut off his head all the same!"

The iron judas closed with a bang, and I heard him shuffling down the steps again, muttering to himself, cursing me for invading his sleep, and all the time I could think only of the yellow flare of the lantern lighting up a few inches of my cell and the blue eye which was angry and bloodshot, but somehow comforting. I told myself that if he returned, I would speak more pleasantly, for I enjoyed his company and wished he had stayed longer.

I tried to sleep, but no sleep came. I tried to think of my paintings stacked against the wall in the Cardinal's cellar, and of Maddalena, and of Leonello Spada, and of a hundred other people, but I could only think of the overwhelming horror of my cell; and soon enough I was on my feet again, hammering with my fists on the door, calling upon Christ's mercy, repeating over and over again that I was innocent and that a cursed corporal had no right to arrest me because a tile had fallen from a roof. I shouted to the jailer to bring me a candle, some food, clean water, a broom to clean out my cell. God knows what I shouted! I heard him coming up the stairs. I kept shouting. I hammered at the walls, and tried to pull the bars away, and all the time I was in a kind of delirium. At last to my relief I heard the jailer just outside my cell, and there were other men with him — two or three or perhaps even four men, for I heard them talking. And then the judas moved and I saw the yellow light of his lantern and the bloodshot eye, and after a moment there was the rattling of keys.

When the door opened, I was blinded by the light, for they held three or four lanterns among them. The yellow light seemed to be racing around the cell like colored ribbons. Someone was holding a tray, and another was holding a folding table, and there was a silver dish on the tray and a carafe of wine and goblets. And while the prison servants set up the table, the jailer gazed at me

calmly, pulling on his beard, his small bloodshot eyes lighting up
with amusement.

"We treat our prisoners well," he said, "and we expect to be
treated well in return. We do our best for them, you must admit
that! You have to be grateful — that's the important thing, to be
grateful!"

"I'm grateful enough," I said.

"Of course you are. You have a sensible head on your shoulders. We know how difficult it is in prison — the first night is the
worst. That's why we try to make people comfortable the first
night —"

He waved toward the table which was being set up under the
barred window, and smiled with his yellow teeth. He put a hand
on my shoulders and came closer.

"You shouldn't shout so much, signor," he went on. "You're
waking all the other prisoners, and what good does it do? So you
must be reasonable and try to understand my position. I do the
best I can, with my limited means. I have brought you some food
and wine, signor — they may help you to sleep — and if there is
anything else I can do for you —"

"I want a broom to clean up the filth in the cell, and a candle,
and some paper and ink to write a letter to the Cardinal, and a
decent bed."

"Is that all you want?"

"Yes, that's all."

"Well, it does no harm to ask for these things, and the truth is
that some prisoners ask for far more. We'll do what we can for
you within the limits of the law. You mustn't think we can do
everything at once, though. There may be delays — it may be a
month or two before we can get all of them, though in your case,
since the crime was merely an assault on a corporal, and far worse
crimes are being committed every day, you may have the broom

much sooner. The law works slowly, but it always catches up with you. There's one thing you don't have to fear — they won't cut off your head! It was such a small crime, signor!"

"If it was a small crime," I said, "why do they bother to keep me in prison at all?"

"We have to follow the processes of the law," he replied. "Where would we be if we didn't follow the law, eh? Why, the whole state would be in anarchy without the law, that's the truth of it. A small crime is like a big crime — have you ever thought what would happen if you had committed some very terrible crime like assaulting the Holy Father? Have you thought what would happen? Why, you would be treated exactly as you are being treated now. They would bring you here, and they would examine you, and then they would lock you up and do no harm to you. They wouldn't punish you for a long while, because the processes of the law have to be followed. Is that clear?"

"Yes, that's clear."

"And they would look after you, and feed you regularly, as we are feeding you, and they would take no end of trouble to keep you in good health, and all this not because they have any love for you, but because they love the law. Sometimes my wife asks me why I have not followed a less arduous profession, and I always tell her I am performing a service to the state by looking after the prisoners entrusted to my care. Do you follow me? I am only the servant of the law, and that is why you should have more sympathy for me instead of keeping me awake at night and shouting yourself hoarse. But I have long ago learned that the best treatment is kindness even in the face of ingratitude, and that is why I have brought food and wine for you."

And then saying: "It is a privilege to serve you," the jailer advanced toward the table which had been set up under the dark window. Three prison guards dressed in their yellow uniforms

[205]

were standing against the wall, all of them smiling pleasantly. They were young farm boys, and one of them, who could not have been more than sixteen, possessed an extraordinary clear-cut beauty, so that it was on my lips to ask him to pose for me as a young David. I was about to turn and say something to the jailer about my gratitude for his kindness when the church bells began ringing. It was two o'clock in the morning. At first there were the great bells of St. Peter's, and these were followed at intervals by the bells of St. John Lateran, and soon a hundred churches were tolling the night hours. The jailer was hovering over the table. I thought I could smell the hot meats under the silver dish. The jailer said: "The servants will look after you," and then, he lifted the silver dish. There was no food on the table.

My first thought was that I was dreaming, and then it occurred to me that someone in the kitchen had made a mistake which would soon be rectified. It was absurd and beyond reason that they should go to so much pains for my sake. Involuntarily I stepped back. The jailer's mouth opened wide, and I saw only the blue eyes and the blood-red tongue and the stumps of teeth. Then they were all over me, hitting me with the whips they had concealed behind their backs, tearing at my clothes, while they roared with laughter. I fought them, but a single man is no match for four men armed with whips in a small cell. I thought I could fight better in the dark and tried to throw the lanterns down — two were on the table, and these fell to the floor, and a third, set down in a corner, I overturned, but before it went out, it set fire to the straw mattress.

They fought like madmen. They pulled me down across the table and beat me over the back and shoulders, and then because the fabric of my doublet was padded, they tore at the doublet until I was half naked. The jailer was dancing round me. He kept shouting: "More! More!" but whether he was shouting for more light or for more clothes to be stripped off me I never learned. At last the jailer took the one remaining lantern and retired to the far corner of the cell, where he stamped out the flames from the burning pallet, shouting hoarsely: "Go at him, boys!" and then I knew he was a coward, in mortal fear of his life, and I decided I must somehow hurl myself at him if I was to save myself. I had visions of finding his keys and escaping down the long winding stairway. While I kicked and struggled, the boys used their elbows and whips, and sometimes in their excitement they would whip one another. I rolled off the table, and then they fell over me, and for a brief moment I had the advantage. I sprang like a cat from the floor and threw myself at the jailer. The lantern dropped out of his hand, and he cursed by all the devils of Hell, but the lantern did not go out. The farm boys saved him. One was incapacitated, for I had dug my heel in his stomach, but the two others were unspoiled. I kept kicking at the lantern, to bring darkness down on all of us, but they caught me before I succeeded and lifted me bodily back to the table, which was strong enough to support my weight and theirs for a little while longer. All the time the room was filling with so much smoke that even the one remaining lantern seemed dull and diffuse in the half-light.

This time I thought they were going to kill me. They had thrown their whips away, and were happy to use their fists, their teeth, their elbows and their fingers. They stripped me naked and split my legs apart, and while one hammered my face, the other, standing between my knees, began twisting my privates until I caught him in the chest and sent him staggering against the wall. Then he was back at me, kicking me from the side, screaming that I was not worthy to live and it was best to finish me, while the older one shouted over his shoulder at the jailer, asking whether he had permission to snuff out the little life that was left, and at that moment the boy who had been lying unconscious on the floor sprang up and hurled himself at me. The jailer was jumping up and down, shouting: "Don't kill him — it's more than our lives are worth to kill him!" and then I was grateful, and the fight went out of me.

I covered my head with my arms, and let them do what they pleased with the rest of me. As long as my eyes and my hands survived, I did not care what they did to me. One straddled me, making grunting noises, and another pulled my mouth open while the third pissed down my throat; and while they fingered me and dabbled their hands in my blood and I choked up the piss, I knew that if I could endure for a little while longer, I would live through the night. It was the hot, tingling freshness of the urine on my face that cleared my brain of its smoking humors. For the first time since they entered the room I was able to think clearly. For a little while longer they fingered me, but at last, as though in disgust, they threw me off the table onto the still-smoking straw, and laughed at the poor, naked, twitching thing I was. Then the jailer bent over me and said: "You won't hammer again on the door, will you? Go to sleep!"

I heard the key turning in the lock and their laughter as they walked unsteadily down the stairs. The room was full of smoke, and dark. I crawled across the floor and wrapped my arms round one of the lanterns they had left behind, for it was cold in the cell and the lantern was still warm. Then I saw that some straw was still burning, and by blowing on it I was able to light the lantern again. The table was still standing, but the empty goblets and the silver dish lay where they had fallen. By the light of the lantern I looked to see what damage they had done and felt my bones. There were great bruises on my legs, but only a few whip cuts. There was some clotted white stuff on my thighs, and whip cuts all over my chest and back. I was trembling as though with fever, but my mind was clear; and I could remember some of their gestures — the heave of a shoulder, the lacing of the neck muscles, the way a hand rises when it holds an instrument of torture, and for a long while I sat there with my arms folded round the lantern, remembering the passion in their dark peasant faces as they pawed and mauled my whipped flesh. I made note of their expressions, and how they balanced themselves on their heels when they were coming at me and when they were flung away, for it seemed to me that these were subjects worthy of a painter's attention. Gradually in my dazed mind they were becoming paintings.

At first there was little pain from the whip cuts, but later I had to clench my teeth to prevent myself from crying out against the pain. I tried to stand, but could not, and went crawling across the floor in search of my tattered doublet and what was left of my hose, which I wrapped around my lower parts for warmth. I thought of Maddalena, and wondered what she would say if she could see me there, and of Benedetto and Tomaso and Leonello Spada, all safe in their beds, for it would not occur to them to search for me until the morning. And I thought: "Can it happen to a man that he can be beaten nearly to death because a tile has fallen from a roof?"

The church bells rang again, and once or twice I thought I heard a boatman singing far below. The lantern was going out, for half the oil had spilled out of it during the fighting, and so I went in search of the other lantern they had left near the door, but there was even less oil in it. I dreaded the dark. I was afraid that when the darkness came down again I would find myself hammering on the door. All night I was wide awake. I watched for the coming of morning as other men watch for the coming of immense caravans which, after many dangers, many encounters with bandits and wild beasts, emerge through the sunveils of the desert. And while I watched, I listened for any creaking on the stairs, any footfalls. I knew they would come again.

I must have slept toward morning, for I remember being awakened by the turning of the key in the lock. A new jailer came in, accompanied by a young guard, who may have been the brother of one of the guards who whipped me during the night, for they had the same peasant faces, only this boy was younger, more delicate, with a hint of refinement on his coarse features. With his feet the boy pushed a bowl of stale porridge toward me, and they were about to go away when they observed the disorder in the cell, the lanterns, the burned mattress, the bloodstains on the floor and the shreds of torn clothing. What particularly surprised them was the table standing below the window, and the bits of clothing I had wrapped around me, for they kept looking from the table to me and back again.

"What happened?" the jailer asked. "Were you up to some mischief?"

He was a man of about thirty with a three-day growth of beard, cadaverous and sickly looking. He resembled a bearded skull, and his voice had the rattle of a man with consumption. I have learned since that sick jailers are the best: they know suffering and they have a little compassion.

I tore open what was left of my doublet and said: "Do you think I whipped myself? They came in — four of them — promising me food and God knows what else, and then they fell upon me! Is that how they treat people in the Tor di Nona? Get me hot water and ointment for my wounds, and some clothes, and some good food, and send a messenger to the chamberlain of Cardinal del Monte, whose servant I am. And go quickly, for God's sake, for every hour I am here will have to be paid for!"

The mind of a jailer works slowly, and I could hear his thoughts clucking before he said: "I suppose you tried to set fire to the cell, so they punished you."

"It's a lie! They came with lanterns, so that they could see what they were doing when they were tearing me to ribbons."

The boy came up to me, pulled my torn doublet aside, and ran his fingers over the caked blood. The jailer sighed, and shook his head from side to side. I had a feeling that he spent a good part of the day sighing and shaking his head.

"Then you didn't set fire to the mattress?" he said, and his voice was plaintive.

"Of course I didn't! How could I? I kicked over the lanterns! For God's sake get me hot water and ointments, and clothes. I am Michelangelo da Caravaggio, a painter in the household of Cardinal del Monte. Some stupid constable thought I had thrown a tile which fell from the roof. Is that a reason for putting a man in prison?"

The jailer thought about this in the same way that he thought about everything else — slowly, with grave difficulty, groping for something that nearly always escaped him. At last his gaze settled on the chipped earthenware bowl of porridge, and he said: "There are no spoons today. You'll have to eat it with your fingers. The spoons have gone. Everything gets stolen in prison."

"By the prisoners?"

"God knows who steals — perhaps the guards."

He was about to leave when I shouted after him: "Hot water, ointment, clothes, the chamberlain of Cardinal del Monte."

"Yes, yes, all in good time!"

I spent a week in the prison. I was not beaten again, and I never saw the fat, blue-eyed jailer again. The cadaverous jailer came in the afternoon with some oddments of clothes, a bloodstained cape and a doublet which was two sizes too big for me. I gripped his arm and said: "For God's sake bring water!" It did not come until the second day, when the sores were suppurating. Sometime to-

ward the end of the week the jailer said a message had been sent to
the chamberlain of Cardinal del Monte, and he whispered that my
friends were coming to the office of the prison governor and clamoring for my release, but the governor was away and his assistant
had no authority to order my release.

"And the chamberlain?"

"The chamberlain is away, too," the jailer said.

"You are sure you wrote to him?" I shouted, for I no longer
believed his words.

"You may say what you like," he said, "but if you could see the
people running in and out of the governor's office and inquiring
about the great painter Michelangelo da Caravaggio, you would
have no doubts on that score. But there's nothing they can do
down there — they can only keep you until the governor returns.
They've tried everything. Bribes and favors and all manner of in-
ducements, but you must understand we are not people who can
be bribed — everyone must take his turn."

"And what if the governor never comes back?" I shouted. "Do
I have to rot to death?"

"No," he said, shrugging his shoulders. "There's no question of
your rotting to death. As it is, you ought to be thankful you are
alive."

Saying this, he went quickly to the door, only to return a moment later with a long silver spoon like a ladle which he had been
carrying in an inner pocket.

"This is for you," he said timidly, a forced smile gradually ap-
pearing on his cadaverous features.

I hated him then, hated him for all his cunning, his lying smiles,
his malignant desire to please. He was no better than the fat blue-
eyed jailer, and the little kindness in him derived from the knowledge that he might one day find himself cooped up in a cell. I

took the spoon and hurled it to the floor, where it broke into three pieces, and then I turned my back on him.

"Get me clothes fit for a great painter," I shouted at the empty walls. "God's curse on you! Get me clothes and better food and wine, and do it for your soul's sake!"

I had asked for these things before without effect, but now for the first time I knew I had them in my power. The silver spoon told me what I wanted to know: that they were afraid, and could be bribed. Jailers are the most miserable of all God's creatures, for they see their own damnation in the eyes of their prisoners. So I was merciless, and for the remaining hours I was in prison I spoke to none of them except to give commands.

The clothes came an hour later: they were not bloodstained, but good new clothes such as a simple workman might wear. The food came before evening. In the afternoon a prison servant, an old woman breathless from climbing the long stairs, came with a broom and a dipping bowl and fresh rushes: she swept the room clean, then sprinkled the rushes evenly over the floor, all the while muttering prayers. The old burned pallet bed was removed, and two young guards brought in a new one made of fresh straw. The jailer bowed when he entered the cell and bowed again when he departed, and he bowed at intervals while addressing me. I flattered myself that all this was brought about solely as a result of my threatening gesture with the spoon, but it was not so. There were many reasons for their change of attitude toward me. Item, the prison governor was about to return. Item, Leonello Spada had spread the rumor that Cardinal del Monte was on his way from Florence. Item, Prince Colonna, asked by Benedetto to come to my aid, had written a letter to the Holy Office inquiring about "a travesty of justice concerning the good and faithful Michelangelo da Caravaggio, arrested for no ascertainable cause." Item,

Marchese Vicenzo Giustiniani and Orazio Costa, both bankers and collectors of paintings, were moved to declare that my prolonged imprisonment without trial could result only in discredit for the governor and "such sickness and distress as would leave our friend permanently incapable of painting." Item, every morning and evening there were crowds outside Tor di Nona clamoring for my release. But all this was unknown to me at the time. I did not know, and could hardly have guessed, that half of Rome was talking about me.

I was released at seven o'clock in the evening on Sunday, when all the church bells were ringing. The prison governor returned late in the afternoon, and immediately ordered that I should be given my freedom at a time when the people were in church, thus avoiding a demonstration. And so I was led out through a small side door into the darkness of the evening, alone, carrying my sword and dagger which only a few moments before were returned to me. Looking up at the lowering clouds and the few stars, I said aloud: "Pray God that no more tiles drop from the rooftops."

The Holy Father

WHEN you asked me, Illustrissimo, whether I had suffered grievously in prison, I lied and said cheerfully that they did me no more harm than I had done myself, and in future I would run whenever a roof tile fell to the earth. Then you smiled and threw back your head in laughter, and afterward you said: "God has preserved you, and this is perhaps one of His greatest miracles!"

"Surely," I said, "if He has preserved me so far, then He will preserve me to the end."

"So He will, but only if you have faith in Him. It is not enough simply to pray and to attend the Mass. You must have the most absolute faith in Him."

"I have more faith in God's mercy than I ever dared to hope for, and why should I not have faith, since I am His painter?"

Then you were silent and a long while later you looked up and said: "When you have too much faith, then it is perhaps most dangerous."

Those were the days when I was completing my painting of the Deposition, the naked Christ being lowered into the tomb, the great stone of anointing jutting out in such a way that it broke out of the picture altogether so that the eye was led into the depths of the painting by following the line of the stone, and was then arrested by the figure of Christ bathed in a naked light. In the shadows St. John held the head of Christ, while Nicodemus supported Him round the thighs, and the three Marys sorrowed in the background. You objected, I remember, to the nakedness of Christ: not that He was unclothed, but that He was so starkly naked, with nothing to redeem His nakedness, so human, so mortal He seemed to be in your eyes. I replied that I wished only that I could have made Him more naked.

"What you are saying," you said, "is so terrible that it is beyond my comprehension. Would you paint the private parts of Christ?"

"I would, and shall, and have," I said, "for I see no harm in rendering Him as He was. We are told that He took upon Himself all the sufferings of mankind, and shall we exclude that suffering? God knows, men suffer enough from it."

"So they do," you answered, "but I cannot believe that He suffered in this way."

"Nevertheless He suffered as men suffered, otherwise He was not God."

You showed surprise, and I remember how you trembled, gazing at the painting of the Deposition in my cellar, while Benedetto stood beside you as solemn as an altar boy. Maddalena was sitting in a corner of the cellar, but I doubt whether she heard us, for she was sewing something and all her attention was occupied by her sewing. It was dark except for the candles which flickered in front of the Deposition.

I had painted Christ with the agony still marked upon His body, the dew of death on Him, the eyes closed, the head falling backward, protected by the hovering hand of His mother who blessed the air above Him. I had rendered Him in His ultimate nakedness, stripped of everything except His death. As you

looked at the painting, tears streamed down your cheeks, and you
said that of all the hundreds of paintings of the dead Christ you
had seen, none had affected you so deeply as this, and this truly
was a work of faith. And then later you asked me again whether I
could not make Him less naked, and I said it was not possible.

"And have you really painted a dead Christ with His private
parts?"

"No, Illustrissimo, but I have painted the living Christ with
His private parts."

"Will you show it to me?"

"No, because I fear you will be offended, and I have no reason
to cause you any offense."

"But if I insist —"

"Illustrissimo, you have never insisted on anything before. You
have given me freedom to do as I please, and God knows a painter
cannot paint except in freedom. Later I may show it to you, but
not now."

Then I took you by the hand and led you once again to my
painting of the dead Christ, and you said: "To one who paints like
this everything may be forgiven," and then your voice dropped a
tone, and you added: "even murder."

In those days you were still lamenting the death of Pope
Clement VIII, and you suffered from sleeplessness and spent long
hours in prayer. The new Pope, Paul V, had shown many signs of
benevolence toward you, but he had not succeeded in allaying
your grief. And so, to forget your grief, you spent many hours in
my cellar, and it was your habit to speak very gently to Benedetto
and Maddalena, and when other painters came to visit me, you
would sit there and listen to their talk, saying: "I am nothing more
than a poor priest, and I learn from painters."

One day, when you were absent, a messenger came from Cardinal Scipione Borghese. He was a small, thin, hollow-cheeked priest, and from the moment he entered my cellar he looked disapproving. I was painting an angel, and accordingly Benedetto had been hoisted up on pulleys and seemed to be descending stark naked through the air. The priest could not take his eyes from the angelic youth.

"Must you really paint angels in this way?" the priest said angrily. "Surely you know that angels are never naked. Their appearance is the most decorous imaginable, whereas this creature —" he was almost spitting the words "this creature" — "is scarcely in a state of grace." And saying this he sighed and tried to turn away from the spectacle of Benedetto, who was smiling his most enchanted smile and waving his feet in the air.

I said I was not aware that clothing was manufactured in heaven, that the body was holy and beautiful, and that I needed no advice on how or what to paint. As for those ropes and pulleys, I begged him to regard them as necessary evils employed by all painters when they were attempting to depict an angel flying down from heaven.

"But at least," said the priest, whose name was Father Girolamo, "you should have the courtesy to hide what is most offensive to the eyes."

"And what, pray, is that?"

"You know perfectly well which part of him is offensive to me."

I pretended not to understand what he was saying, and demanded the most precise details: whether it was the glint of the boy's teeth or the light in his eyes or the exquisite roundness of his thighs, until Father Girolamo cried out in despair: "It is terrible! I have never in my life seen anything so offensive as this boy's sex."

"You would like me to hide his sex?"

"Of course I would, or better still you would have the goodness to let him down and to clothe him properly."

I had a small scarf of blue patterned silk which Maddalena had given me, and so I wrapped this scarf lightly round Benedetto's legs.

"Is that better?" I asked.

"It is a little better," Father Girolamo admitted, and then he went on nervously to discuss his master's business, saying that Cardinal Scipione Borghese had always possessed a high opinion of my art, that he rejoiced in the possession of the paintings I had made for him, especially the *David with the Head of Goliath*, and that he was willing to pay liberally for a portrait of someone who was very close to him, a man so illustrious that he would not even mention the name; and while the priest was speaking, reciting these propositions as though by rote, his eyes would sometimes stray toward Benedetto and the remarkable blue scarf, which rose and fell and waved from side to side as though life had been breathed into it. The blue scarf was like a small flag waving urgently in the wind. The priest would turn away with a startled expression, but he always looked back again, and he was continually losing his train of thought.

"Will your illustrious Cardinal pay for the painting?" I asked, for the Cardinal had the reputation of being one of those who pay with promises. "Will he pay on account?"

"Of course he will, and most liberally, too," Father Girolamo replied, and he went on to hint that if the painting was satisfactory to him, then it would please him to give me more commissions, so many commissions that my entire life might be spent in his service; whereupon I reminded him that Cardinal del Monte was my patron and benefactor, and I would first have to seek his permission.

"So you should," the priest said, rubbing his hands together and throwing a fleeting smile in the direction of Benedetto. "Why, yes, of course you should. All this is very understandable. When you learn the nature of the task my master requires of you, I am sure all difficulties will be smoothed over." Then he turned directly to Benedetto and said: "Boy, boy, for God's sake keep still! Do you know what you are doing?"

"I know," said Benedetto, smiling, and he gave such a monstrous kick to the little scarf that it flew in the air and fell slowly, and very gracefully, at Father Girolamo's feet; and the poor father, not knowing what he was doing, his blue cheeks reddening, stooped down and picked up the little fluttering scarf with an expression of pity, as though it had been sorely used, and then absentmindedly stuffed it in his pocket.

"My illustrious Cardinal will expect you to wait upon him in the midmorning to learn the nature of the paintings he requires of you," Father Girolamo said, and without another word he went running up the steps while Benedetto shouted after him: "Bring me the flag, monsignor! Bring me the flag!" And then a little later he said: "I kicked well, didn't I, master?"

I pulled his ear.

"You kicked so well," I said, "that Cardinal Borghese will not thank me for a picture because within an hour all of Rome will know what you did to the scarf."

I let down the ropes so that he could rest his legs.

"All of Rome, eh?"

"Why, yes, for the good father will tell everyone, raising his arms to heaven, imploring maledictions on you and me and painters everywhere. You'll go down in history as the best kicker of them all."

"Then give me another scarf, master, and let me practice for the sweet father's sake, so that I shall be worthy of him," Benedetto said, and then, perhaps because he was exhausted by the exercise, he promptly fell asleep.

On the next day I presented myself with Benedetto in the apartments of Cardinal Borghese, at the Vatican.

Up to this time I had thought the apartments of my lord benefactor, Cardinal del Monte, were the most luxurious in Rome, and indeed the Palazzo Madama was altogether larger and more handsomely conceived than any of these apartments attached to the Vatican. Nevertheless Cardinal Scipione Borghese had far the greater collection of paintings. They crowded the walls, stood against chairs, or hung on easels in every corner; and the greater number of them were boxed in ornate gilded frames so that to enter these apartments was to enter a world of shimmering gold.

The Cardinal was very plump, and like many plump people he laughed easily and boisterously. His face however was deadly white, and seemed all the whiter in contrast with his scarlet vestments. We knelt and kissed his ring, an enormous emerald, and then when we stepped back he drew the sign of the cross vigorously in the air above all heads, all the time smiling a secret smile, his lips pursed and wrinkled; and this was strange, for in making the sign of the cross he seemed suddenly to become someone else altogether, and at such moments we were not aware of his perfumed hands or the shimmering gold frames. A little Negro girl came, bringing us wines, and when I drank to the Cardinal's health he said quickly: "No, no, for the love of God do not speak about my health —" as though the subject displeased him, or perhaps he was genuinely modest and felt that it was a waste of time to discuss anything so mundane as his health.

I watched the Cardinal closely, for he was a man of discernment and taste, uncomfortable in his heavy brocaded vestments, inclined to gout, ceremonious in his movements, ill at ease when meeting people; and so he would often turn away from me to contemplate the paintings hanging on the wall. He had a lisp and spoke rapidly in a thin, high-pitched voice, but what was most remarkable about him was the expression of his eyes, which were very small and very dark, full of remarkable intelligence and fire. They said he was fat from too much eating, but though he kept a good table he showed very little interest in food. His passion, his hunger, was to acquire paintings, sculptures, rich brocades, and jewels. He was fond of young women and boys, but his interest in them was experimental, and he had no attachments.

So much I knew or learned on the rare occasions in which I was permitted into the Cardinal's presence, which were no more than four or five times altogether. Toward me he showed only kindness, and he would sometimes look at me with an expression which said: "How is it possible that you have made these extraordinary paintings?" For my part I treated him with respect and forbearance, as a collector who possessed an exquisite talent for collecting the best paintings as well as the worst.

Yet for some reason he did not talk about the commission he intended to give me. He spoke expansively about his collection, about the painters whose work he admired, and about the difficulty of acquiring paintings when everyone else was busily attempting to acquire them. He asked me what new painters were emerging in Rome. Once, folding his hands over his ample stomach, he sighed and said: "The Holy Father has not the least interest in building up a collection. The truth is that he dislikes the arts, and this is perfectly understandable since he is a deeply religious man who would be happier worshiping Our Savior in a small whitewashed cell than amid the adornments of the Vatican." And then he went on to speak of the acts of piety and benevolence performed by the Pope, and of how he was continually irritated by the demands made upon him during his official duties. "I really believe he would be happier as a monk," the Cardinal continued, and then he turned to me and said: "Have you ever seen him at close quarters? You would be surprised by his humility. Truly he is the servant of the servants of God."

All this time the hot sun was flashing through the windows, and we were half blinded by the dazzling display of colors in the room. The Cardinal had a particular penchant for scarlet — he would buy a painting for no better reason than that there was a good deal of scarlet in it — and since all, or nearly all, his paintings were in heavy gold frames, we seemed to be swimming in a lake of scarlet and gold. For about an hour we had been in attendance on the Cardinal; nothing of importance had been discussed, and I was about to take my leave when I heard the clip-clop of horses in the courtyard below. The Cardinal put a finger to his lips and hurried to the window, and soon a whole army of horsemen could be heard clattering on the cobblestones, so that for a moment I thought the Vatican was being attacked. Benedetto began to run to the window, but suddenly stopped, overwhelmed by some sense of impropriety, caught there, spinning on his heels, his arms outstretched and the hands dangling, so that he resembled a dancer or an angel alighting on earth, and so I cried out: "Stay where you are! Don't move!" I must have shouted, for the Cardinal turned sharply, thinking I was addressing him. He frowned, raised his finger to his lips, and continued to gaze out of the window though his cheeks had reddened with impatience or anger. And Benedetto remained silent, hovering there like some creature belonging to another world, the sunlight forming a nimbus around his yellow hair and catching the gold buttons of his scarlet doublet. In those moments I seemed to myself to be painting him: the canvas was cut to shape, the palette prepared, the shimmering background sketched in, and from the Vatican I was mysteriously translated back into my cellar, while the roar of hooves echoed across the courtyard and the silver trumpets blew.

Above the clamor of the trumpets I heard the Cardinal saying: "Come to the window, Michelangelo!"

I hurried to do the Cardinal's bidding, for no one ever refuses such a command. I looked down at the courtyard swimming in blue and scarlet. There were at least a hundred men at arms there, all on horseback, lances on their thighs, young faces shining in the sun, and in the midst of them rode the Pope wearing a wide-brimmed red tasseled hat, a white gown and red velvet hood. With his bristling beard he looked less like a Pope than the commander of an army. He rode his horse well. Just as I reached the window, he looked up, caught sight of the Cardinal, smiled, raised his hand in benediction, throwing a blessing at the Cardinal, and then another at me, and a third at Benedetto, who shouted at the top of his voice: "Long live the Pope!" and soon they were all shouting it, and because there were so many horses in an enclosed space and because the shouting disturbed them, there was a sudden panic, a spasm running through the courtyard, horses swinging up on their hind legs and biting one another, while some riders fell between the horses' legs and were in danger of being trampled to death all because Benedetto had shouted at an inopportune moment.

There were so many horses milling in the courtyard, so much tumult, so many men at arms beating their horses' necks with their bare fists, so much wild neighing and cursing and stamping of hooves on the cobblestones, that the place began to resemble a battlefield. Someone, perhaps the papal chamberlain, shouted that the Pope was in danger, and this was the worst thing that could have happened, for some of the men at arms attempted to ride up close to the Pope to protect him, while others, realizing that the courtyard might soon become a place of carnage, began to wheel their horses round and attempt to make their way out of the courtyard, and once more there was confusion and terror, shouts, alarums. Happily one of the trumpeters had the sense to slip off his horse and make his way outside the courtyard, where he blew the tally-ho. At once half the horses turned about and drove out of the courtyard like lightning, their manes flying, while the rest, held fast by spurs and reins, stood their ground. And once more the Pope smiled and looked up at our window, waving to the Cardinal to assure him of his safety before dismounting. He did not need the services of a groom. He simply vaulted off the horse, alighting on his toes. Then he vanished out of sight, leading the horse into the shadows of the arcade beneath us.

I feared for Benedetto, who was the cause of all the disturbance, but the Cardinal paid no attention to him and evidently, in his relief over the Pope's safety, he was not disposed to blame anyone. He returned to the middle of the room with a pleased expression.

"That is how I would have you paint him, Michelangelo," he said. "On horseback, ready for war."

It was the first hint that I was to paint the Pope. The Cardinal was rubbing his hands together.

"On a charger," he went on. "Perhaps on the dappled gray he was riding this afternoon. You have painted horses before. I saw your *St. Paul on the Road to Damascus*, though I must confess that there is more of the dray horse than of St. Paul. It's a strange painting, not to my taste, but it put me in mind of a painting of my uncle which would do credit to him as well as to you."

I had forgotten that Cardinal Scipione Borghese was the nephew of Pope Paul V. I bowed low and said: "If your lordship desires —"

"What is more," the Cardinal continued, "if the painting is as magnificent as a man of your talent can be expected to make it, that will only be the beginning. I have other paintings in mind, notably a whole series of paintings on the life and martyrdom of St. Paul, for as you know my uncle has a particular veneration for the saint, and there are other paintings which we can discuss later. Does it please you to paint the Pope, Michelangelo?"

"Nothing could please me more," I answered, but the Cardinal must have noted some hesitation in my voice, for he said abruptly: "You can discuss the fee with my chamberlain. No doubt it will be a suitable one, in addition to the honor and glory."

It was on the tip of my tongue to say that I had sufficient honor and glory, and hoped I would be paid according to my merits, but the Cardinal was in no mood to dispute about payment. He was in fact rapt in contemplation of the painting. As he envisaged it, it would be some twelve or fifteen feet high and eight or twelve feet broad. There would be thunderclouds in the sky, and the setting would be the forests of the Campagna where the Pope was accustomed to hunt, while in the background there would be a Crucifixion, thus disposing the beholder to see the Pope riding to the rescue of Our Lord, and perhaps — though the Cardinal was not quite certain whether it was desirable — there should be a dove flying above the Holy Father to symbolize the descent of the Holy Spirit. The Cardinal enjoyed these little flights of fancy, and was tireless in inventing new ones, as for example when he suggested that there might be an angel beside the dove pointing in the direction of the Crucifixion. He might have gone on to invent more and more symbols when suddenly there came an ear-splitting burst of silver trumpets from two trumpeters standing by the door, and the Pope entered the room.

Benedetto was the first to see him. He fell to his knees with such abandon that his face struck the bare wooden floor and his nose bled. I fell more decorously. The Cardinal fell slowly and gracefully, not as though he were kneeling, but as though he were sinking through the floorboards, while the Pope, coming swiftly across the room, made windmill gestures with his hands, bidding us to rise.

It was the first time I had seen the Pope at close quarters. He was a tall, heavily built man, exuding health, with no fat on him, entirely unlike his nephew in appearance and manner. He was brisk and cordial, urgent in all his movements, very quick on his toes. Some of the men who had been hunting came with him, but they remained by the doorway, restless and ill at ease, still dust-stained from the journey. The Pope sat on one of the two thrones which stood against the wall, facing the windows. Servants appeared, bearing vessels of scented water. The Pope removed his broad-brimmed red hat and red velvet hood, washed his hands, splashed water on his face and then wrung out the water from his beard. Cardinal Scipione Borghese was in a strange position, half kneeling beside the Pope while at the same time sitting in the smaller of the two thrones.

The Cardinal was whispering to the Pope, no doubt about the painting, for he sometimes motioned in my direction. The Pope nodded briskly. He gave an impression of impatience, but I was to learn later that there was scarcely a moment of the day when he was not impatient over something, and I imagine that even when he sleeps there is that look of impatience mingled with surprise at the thought that the world moves so slowly.

I was studying him closely, for I knew the sittings would be brief. His hair was dark brown, his beard was brown with a shade of auburn, his forehead both high and broad, his features strongly marked, his nose long, clear and straight, his lower lip thick, his complexion fair and ruddy. The most remarkable feature of his face was that it was in perpetual movement, with not a muscle at rest. His hands were beautiful, the fingers tapering, of the color of wax, and he was perfectly aware of their beauty, admiring and contemplating them. As for his eyes, which were very large and of the clearest blue, so full that they were like the eyes of men who are very shortsighted, they too were in perpetual movement. I had the feeling that even when he was washing his face and hands he was aware of everything that happened in the room, even those things which were outside the range of his vision.

When the Pope had finished washing, the Cardinal beckoned to me. I knelt at the Pope's feet and kissed each of the scarlet leather crosses sewn on the toes of his riding boots, and then with a brisk slicing of the air he made the sign of the cross above my head.

"We have admired your work, which We have had the pleasure of seeing in Our nephew's apartments," the Pope said, waving in the direction of the paintings on the wall. "We are not informed on the subject of painting and rely on Our nephew's knowledge, and since he speaks highly of you, then We too will find it in Our hearts to speak highly of you and give you a special blessing since you have devoted your talents to the glory of the true revelations of Our Savior —"

He went on to say many more things, demonstrating his ignorance of the painter's art, his knowledge of revealed religion, and his dependence on his nephew's taste. Then he said: "We have given thought to the painting which Our nephew proposes, bearing in mind that he is extremely desirous that We should be painted on horseback, but on reflection We do not believe that an equestrian portrait is in conformity with established usage or even with the example of Our Savior, Who often went riding, but never so far as We know took part in hunting. Therefore We propose —" and here the Pope nodded in the direction of the Cardinal, his lips curling into a smile and his teeth glinting, "that you should paint Our portrait in any fashion which seems proper to you and in accordance with the practice of Our predecessors, who have always looked kindly on painters and held them in honor. And may God have you in His keeping and cherish you!"

And saying this, the Pope blessed me for the third or fourth time, his right hand making a little chopping movement in the air.

I was about to express my gratitude and to explain the kind of portrait I had in mind, but the audience was already over. Once more the Pope was engaged in a whispered conversation with the Cardinal. With Benedetto beside me, I made my way backwards toward the door. I did not bow or kneel, but stood upright, for it seemed to me that no purpose is served by bowing or kneeling to those who pay no attention to your presence; nor had anyone told me that it was the established custom to kneel at intervals when retiring from any room where the Pope is enthroned. The huntsmen, who were gathered at the door, were impatient over my impudence and murmured against me. One of them punched me in the stomach, saying: "Show more reverence to His Holiness next time!" It was a heavy punch. I gasped. It must have been a very loud gasp, for both the Pope and the Cardinal turned in our direction, and I heard the Cardinal saying: "What has happened?" Someone put a hand over my mouth, and another of the huntsmen said: "It is nothing, my lord. He tripped over his sword." The Cardinal smiled and resumed his conversation with his uncle, while we fled down the stairway and into the courtyard, lucky to suffer no further blows from the hired bravos.

Of course nothing had been decided upon, and as we rode back to the Palazzo Madama I reflected upon the indignities suffered by painters, who must attend upon princes for their rewards. I told myself that nothing would come of the venture: soon the Pope would be engrossed in another hunting foray, while Cardinal Scipione Borghese would soon forget that he had once amused himself by inviting a painter to his apartments. Yet I had much to be thankful for. I was still in the service of Cardinal del Monte, and I had more commissions than I could accomplish. I would never paint the Pope on a white charger, and I felt sure I would never see him again except at a distance. Benedetto was far from sharing my melancholy.

"We'll go to Heaven for sure!" he exclaimed happily.

"What makes you think so?"

"Why, didn't he bless us, master? Didn't he bless us so close that we could feel the warmth of it on our faces? 'Twas like a trickle of fire!"

Saying this, he clapped his hand to his face in remembered pleasure and agony.

"And you felt it?"

"Yes, I felt it, master, and didn't you feel it, too?"

"I felt nothing, Benedetto, except a punch in the belly," I answered, still mortified by the knowledge that I did not know which of the eight or nine huntsmen had struck me, though I have now come to the conclusion that it must have been the tall, sallow, German-looking fellow who shouted that I had tripped over my sword.

Not surprisingly Benedetto showed no interest in the incident at the doorway; perhaps he had not even observed it. He could talk only about the blessings he had received from the Pope.

"And what a man, eh? There's lean muscle on him. He's not one of your skinny Jeromes either. A fine one for hunting, too. We'll go riding with him, master, if we please him, and drink wine with him, eh? Women, too. Didn't you know that his lips were as scarlet as his vestments? There's a Pope for you!"

So Benedetto went singing on his way, his cheeks flushed, his golden hair flying in the wind, while I was filled with premonitions and forebodings, knowing that those huntsmen would stop at nothing if they felt called upon to punish someone who had shown insufficient reverence to the Pope, however unwittingly. And then I would find myself forgetting my fears, remembering my joy in the Pope's presence and reflecting on how best to paint his portrait. I told myself I would paint him in the open air with the thunderclouds boiling above his head, alone in all the wilderness of nature, and far, far away, on some rocky hill almost lost in the background there would be the scene of the Crucifixion. It pleased me to paint him in this way following Cardinal Scipione Borghese's suggestion, for I had never painted such a painting before; and the thought came to me that I would paint him from memory, full of fire and energy, his robes swirling, and there would be a dappled gray horse in the middle distance under those lowering skies. In my imagination I was already at work, and by the time we reached my cellar I had almost finished the painting.

But once in my cellar, I was in no mood for work. The Deposition hung on the wall, and I remember studying it minutely, wondering why I should trouble to paint a mortal man when Christ and the saints provided a greater challenge to my brush. Portraiture was not my study. I had other things to attend to besides pleasing my sitters with subtle and exhausting flattery. The Pope, a man of action, who scarcely ever gave himself to meditations, would want to be represented in a meditative mood, wearing a halo of holiness, with a book of prayers in one hand while with the other he blessed his flock. I wondered whether His Holiness had ever read a book in his life. I saw him only as a man of action, resolute to conquer. I could easily imagine him leading a Crusade against the Turks. Yet there were no depths to him, no shadows, nothing for the painter to grope for; and so it happened that I found myself building up his face and subtly changing it, giving it an authority lacking in the man I saw. He was of the earth, but my imagination chose to depict him as though he had descended from heaven.

For weeks I heard nothing more from Cardinal Scipione Borghese. The truth is that I was in no way alarmed by the Cardinal's silence, for it is the custom of collectors to keep their painters in ignorance of their attentions until the last possible moment. Once Father Girolamo came to my cellar to return the blue scarf, saying he had unaccountably taken possession of it during his former visit and had intended to return it earlier, and though he remembered perfectly how he had come to possess it, he pretended that he had merely picked it up in a fit of absentmindedness. He was still making his explanations when Benedetto sauntered into the room. It was a hot day. Benedetto threw off his shirt and lay down on the bed with his face turned to the wall; from time to time Father Girolamo would find himself gazing at the boy's naked back with a look of inexpressible anguish, as though the quiet flesh were a torment to him, and then with an effort he would explain that Cardinal Scipione Borghese had often expressed himself in my favor and never ceased admiring my paintings which were given a place of honor in his apartments, and he hoped shortly to be the messenger of tidings which would please me. And there was a great deal more of this meaningless conversation, customary among our Roman prelates. At last, with a final fearful glance at Benedetto, Father Girolamo made his way to the carriage waiting for him outside the Palazzo Madama.

I never learned why he came: for surely it was not to return the blue scarf, which could only fill him with apprehension. For him the blue scarf must have been a badge of evil, the mark of an extinguishable shame. There were dark rings under his eyes, and he looked thinner and paler than before. Perhaps he came because he was tempted by Benedetto's beauty.

Once Father Girolamo was gone, Benedetto jumped up from the bed, laughing deliriously. He pounced on the blue scarf and went round the room waving it like a banner, singing and shouting at the top of his voice. He put it to his nose: it smelled of church incense, and he bellowed uproariously. I shouted after him: "My God, what has come over you?" Drunk with pagan joy, he could only jump around the room in happy delirium, the tears of laughter turning his cheeks silver. And between gusts of laughter he would say: "What a gift, eh? Smells of incense, too! Poor priest, poor priest! God save him for a blue scarf! What a world we live in, eh? Well, what to do?"

Saying this, the boy slipped off the rest of his clothes, tied the blue scarf with a single knot to his member, and pranced around the room in the must ludicrous manner imaginable, his belly sticking out, the scarf waving and jerking, now falling softly, now rising high like a battle flag, as though it possessed a life of its own; and so, leaping from the bed to the floor and back again like a dancer, he celebrated the return of the scarf with wild rejoicing. There was a battered helmet hanging on the wall; he stuck it on his head at a rakish angle. In one hand he waved a broadsword, and with the other he balanced the old brown skull I had used in painting a Saint Jerome for the Conventual Sisters. Thus accoutered, he was like a ship with all sails flying, dancing round the room and sometimes pausing in front of the mirror to examine himself with an experienced eye, and I think he would have gone wandering out into the street if he had not fallen against a chair leg and crashed to the floor.

"I did well, didn't I?" Benedetto exclaimed, sprawled out on the floor, the banner still waving.

"No one could have done better," I said, and I helped him to the bed.

Maddalena

WHEN Maddalena entered our lives, everything changed. It was as though some very special token had been granted to us. There are some women who are born with a kind of radiance, and we recognize them by the brilliance of their eyes, the light glowing in their faces, and their natural grace of movement; they seem not to walk but to hover over the earth. So it was with Maddalena. We all recognized that she was one of those rare beings who belong to the world but also in some mysterious way to the company of the angels.

There was about her an astonishing gentleness, and a maddening firmness. If she wanted anything, nothing could stop her. She loved the poor beggars in the streets and was always tending to their wounds, and if any of her friends needed money she found it for them. It always startled her that there was poverty in the world. Yet she did not give the impression of being deeply religious. She attended Mass and Vespers, and then hurried away with a smile on her lips as though she was relieved that it was over. She rarely crossed herself. She always spoke in a low, musical voice, which had more of the accent of Lombardy than of Rome; and whenever we asked her where she came from, she would smile and change the subject. She said she had a mother living in Trasta-vere, and perhaps she had, but we never saw her mother and she never spoke of her father. She did not even possess a surname. She was "Maddalena" or "the red-haired one," and in our quarter no one ever called her by any other names.

What was especially strange about her was that in repose she was not particularly beautiful, but the moment she walked or talked her face seemed to fill with an unearthly radiance — she was so alive, so filled with quivering life. Sometimes she was quiet as a cat. She could enter a room unobserved, and leave just as si-lently, just as invisibly. She had her bed in the cellar, but we never knew when she would come to occupy it. She would model for me, and while I was painting her she would sometimes vanish as though she had melted into the walls, returning some hours later with a smile. There was nothing in the least mysterious in her smile, for she was nearly always smiling; and if I asked her where she had been, she would simply shake her head and talk about something else altogether.

On Benedetto the effect of her coming to live in the cellar was shattering. He seemed to change character overnight. No longer boisterous and impudent, he became quiet and attentive. He was careful to dress properly, to button up all his buttons, and to speak respectfully. In the past he was always bringing in boys from the street, and they would vanish into dark corners or behind stacked canvases, where I would hear them squealing with excitement. But all this was changed now. Benedetto went about on tiptoe. He became the slave of Maddalena. He was also the slave of the black bitch, Ruffo, who attached herself to my household about this time, taking her place under my easel, guarding me better than any of the young bravos who accompanied me through the streets of Rome.

Ruffo was one of those shaggy, half-wild dogs which you see in the farms: long-haired, damp-nosed, with beautiful violet eyes. She would sit below the easel, wide awake, keeping watch, and if anyone came down my stairs she would go up the stairs and examine them to see whether he was a friend or a stranger; and if I slept with Benedetto or Maddalena, she would leap into bed beside us.

At last, when the commissions for the two churches were completed, and the Deposition hung in the Chiesa Nuova, I was ready to paint Maddalena. Altogether I made seven paintings of her. I painted her as the Madonna of the Rosary, as the Madonna of the Pilgrims, and in *The Madonna and Child with St. Anne.* These were large paintings, and in addition there were three smaller ones in which she was usually represented with a child in her arms. She was the most patient and regal of models, and she would maintain a pose uncomplaining for ten or even twelve hours. Sometimes when I painted her the cellar would fill with my friends, who came to visit me for the pleasure of seeing her, or rather, since her quiet beauty filled them with awe, they came for the purpose of venerating in her the image of the Madonna.

Inevitably there were many who importuned her, and she was often followed in the streets. About this time a beak-nosed lawyer of some wealth offered me a hundred *scudi* for a night with her and two hundred *scudi* if I could arrange for him to marry her. I derived some satisfaction by breaking my sword over his skull.

One day, when she had been absent for some days, I was painting a small shield representing the Lamb of God for the Cardinal, who wished to present it to the Grand Duke of Tuscany. I had therefore procured a lamb, which was tethered to my easel. It bleated miserably, but I continued to paint patiently. Benedetto, for some reason, was as miserable and nervous as the lamb. Suddenly he could contain himself no longer, and said: "Where's Maddalena? Where is she? Where does she go?"

"It is her business where she goes," I said.

"No, it is our business," he said. "Who else's. At night, too. Sometime she is away all night. When I follow her, master, she always goes through the Campo dei Fiori, and I lose her there. I've watched her through the corner of my eyes, but I never know what is on her mind."

"Do you know what is in mine?"

"Yes, master, there is no hiding your thoughts. I see them plain. But Maddalena's thoughts are beyond understanding! God knows what she is thinking when she is sitting here!"

I said I thought Maddalena probably went to Trastavere to see her mother.

He shook his head.

"She wouldn't run so fast to see her mother," he announced categorically. "Do you think I don't follow her? She walks to the Campo dei Fiori. Then when she sees a press of people she runs up to them, makes her way through them, and vanishes from sight. She runs like the wind, too."

"And rightly so," I said. "Anyone who is followed by you is duty bound to run for his life. I, too, if I was followed by you would run like the wind."

He took these words with ill grace, his cheeks flushing purple. He pressed his clenched fists against his cheeks and went off into the shadows with his head bent low, to commune with his sorrows, while I worked on the Lamb of God. It was one of those small commissions which Cardinal del Monte was always giving me. These commissions were sometimes irksome, for I was happier with a large canvas.

Benedetto was not in love with Maddalena — it was more terrible than love. She was like a sister, a mother, a friend on whom he implicitly relied. There was moreover a strange understanding between them. She would be gone for two or three days, leaving Benedetto in despair, and suddenly, as though he had heard her footsteps, he would say: "She is coming." But he had not heard her footsteps. Ten or twenty minutes would pass, and sure enough Maddalena would appear at the head of the stairs. It is a phenomenon common among lovers, rare among friends.

That afternoon it happened again that Benedetto knew she was returning when she must have been a mile away. He suddenly jumped out, shouted something, stalked up to my canvas, said: "She is on her way!" and immediately his whole body began to tremble. I pretended to pay no attention to him, but continued painting. I knew he was there, very close to me, for I could feel his breath on me. The lamb was bleating. The oil lamps were making a curious spluttering sound. I could hear the carriages moving outside. Benedetto flung his hands over his eyes, and said: "The blood of the Lamb" over and over again. I thought he had gone out of his mind. There were tears rolling down his cheeks, for by this time I had turned to look at him. I said: "You must rest, Benedetto." He said: "You don't understand — she is hurt!" "How do you know these things?" I asked, and I only made an effort to take him by the arm to steady him, but he jumped away as though I was about to attack him. Then he vanished in the shadows.

I went on painting. I was obscurely aware that something had gone wrong, that Benedetto was in pain, and that very probably Maddalena had suffered an accident, but I am neither a magician nor an alchemist and I have no power to see anything which is not in front of my eyes; and it happened that I was growing accustomed to the agonies of Benedetto in Maddalena's absence. Once before he had suddenly grown pale and said: "My God, something terrible is happening to her!" when in fact nothing whatever had happened to her and she slipped into the cellar an hour later without attracting any attention to herself.

So I told myself that these strange premonitions were no more than delusions, not to be trusted. The painting absorbed me to the

exclusion of anything else, and I soon forgot Benedetto's hysteri-
cal behavior, for although the boy was keen-spirited and handsome above the average he possessed no logical faculty whatso-
ever. He was like a woman; he knew everything through his skin.
From time to time I would become aware of him prowling in the
shadows, but it was only a dim awareness. Like the beds and the
easels he had become a part of the furniture.

God knows how long I painted — an hour, two hours. The
lamp burned. There was no morning nor afternoon nor evening; it
was always night. There was the lamp above my painting and another, a much smaller one, hanging at the head of the stairs, so that
if a visitor came he would not plunge headlong down the steps.

There comes to those who work with paintbrush and oil paint a
curious withdrawal from the world. Paint, canvas, models, colors
— all vanish, giving place to *something other*, another world, the
kingdom of whatever is seen with abiding affection. Once you
have stepped into this kingdom, the ordinary world falls away,
and it is all one to you whether you are hungry or thirsty, ill
clothed or dressed in finery. Absorbed by the painting, living
within the small enclosed world of your own creation, you would
scarcely turn a hair if someone drove a bolt through your head.
You are so intent on what you are doing that if someone were to
enter the room and shout that the house was on fire, you would
pay no attention to him; and if you heard and understood the
words they would have no meaning. So it is when a man is praying
with all his heart and soul, since painting, too, is a form of prayer.

It must have been about the eighth hour when I stood back
from the canvas, obscurely aware that something had changed in
the room. I glanced over my shoulder. Nothing had changed:
only the unmoving shadows beyond the reach of the lamplight.
The black bitch as usual lay curled up at the foot of the bed. The
draperies hanging on the walls, the helmets and swords, the second

easel, the stacks of paintings — all were in their accustomed places. Then I looked to the stairs, and gasped, for an apparition seemed to be standing there. It was Maddalena.

She wore a wreath of flowers in her hair, but it was neither the wreath nor the ragged dress which sent my heart pounding against my breast. Blood was pouring down her face; there was blood, too, on her bare and outstretched arms, on her bare feet, on her knees and all that part of her that could be seen through the torn dress. She stood there in silence, lit by the oil lamp at the head of the stairs, and at first I thought it was a painting or one of those statues which can sometimes be seen on the prows of ships. She was larger than life, fierce and terrible in the magnificence of her bloodstained garments, her face scarlet. I wondered what kept her there without falling, and only later I realized that she was leaning against the wall and her arms were outstretched only because she was holding on to one of the ringbolts embedded in the wall. A moment passed; then from the shadows there came a cry of despair. It was Benedetto, who now set eyes on her for the first time. Then it was the turn of the black bitch, who began to yelp pitiably. Afterwards came shouts from the upper galleries — the Cardinal's men had followed the trail of blood, and suddenly they burst into my cellar.

"Maddalena!" Benedetto shouted at the top of his voice.

He hurled himself up the stairs, caught her in his arms as she was about to fall, and began screaming at the top of his lungs.

Soon the cellar was full of people running in all directions. Everyone was shouting. The bitch was barking. One of the lamps went out. Maddalena was carried down the stairs by the white-faced Benedetto and laid on the bed. She did not make any sound; she never moaned and seemed to be in a trance. There was so much blood, so many people were hurrying round the bed, and there were so many prayers delivered beside her, that I imagined she was dying. It was inconceivable that anyone so drenched in blood could possibly survive. "Send for the priest," someone shouted, and about the same time one of the kitchen servants came hurrying down the steps with a basin of hot water. A moment before I had felt alone in my room; now twenty or thirty people were running about in all directions. Only Maddalena was quiet. She lay like a queen robed in scarlet on the high bed.

They washed the blood from her face, cut open her dress, sponged her, slapped her to bring her back to consciousness, and otherwise busied themselves about her. I was sure she was dead or dying, beyond praying for. I could not bring myself to go up to her. In the midst of the uproar I turned to the painting, added a few brushstrokes, and then stepped back to see the effect of these strokes.

Benedetto came running up.

"She is asking for you," he said gravely, plucking at my sleeve.

I went to her, the brush still in my hand. I thought I would hear her last words, and imagined her dying in my arms. The blood had been washed away, there was color in her cheeks, she was smiling a little; and in her face and her whole body there was the appearance of exhaustion which comes to a woman after childbirth. There were purple bruises on her arms and legs, a great cut across her forehead, more bruises on her left hand. Those who had been washing her forgot to remove the caked blood from her ears, and this startled me. She said: "It was nothing — only a carriage coming through the marketplace. I was dancing with some children — there were twenty or thirty children. The driver of the carriage was drunken or demented. I shouted to him to stop, but he wouldn't. One of the children was nearly under the wheels, but God be praised I rescued her in time. I think I fell under the wheel, but I have strong bones, Michelangelo, and they will mend. The driver did not know what he was doing. He leaned over and cut me with his whip. The children ran away and left me for dead."

She spoke in whispers, but even as she spoke I could see the strength coming back to her.

For modesty's sake they had covered her with one of the hangings torn down from the wall.

Soon afterward a doctor came, examined her wounds, prescribed ointments and ordered a purge so that the evil humors would be removed from her body, and as he was leaving one of the priests of Cardinal del Monte descended to the cellar, having been informed of the accident by the house servants. He gave her the benediction, and seemed to be annoyed to find her still living. Then one by one the people who had crowded into the cellar left us; most of them knelt and kissed her hand before they departed.

That night while she slept I painted her by the light of a single candle. It seemed to me that her face had assumed the aspect of sanctity, so calm, so beautiful, so withdrawn from the world of men. She was not restless, but moved her head only a little. There was still blood in her hair, but there were no more bloodstains on her face or body. I painted her with an exquisite care, thinking of how I would surprise her when she awakened from her deep sleep, while Benedetto watched me silently.

For a long time I had been contemplating a painting of the death of the Virgin, and it seemed to me that Maddalena living had all the beauty of the dying Virgin. When I painted the dead Christ, I used Leonello Spada as my model, while making many studies of the dead in the Ospedale della Misericordia. Now when I painted Maddalena, I was aware of the quiet richness of her life, her insatiable gentleness, her abundant goodness. She was more alive than anyone else I had ever known.

Toward morning, when Benedetto had at last fallen asleep, Maddalena died.

All that day Benedetto slept heavily, and all that day I continued to paint Maddalena. I painted her as though she were alive, knowing she was dead. During the day Leonello Spada came to my cellar. I put my finger to my lips, and from that moment he knew she was dead, and he remained with me, and kept watch. And in the evening, when Benedetto awoke and saw that she was dead, he did not weep.

There were many aspects of the death of Maddalena which remained mysterious and inexplicable.

Item: her body remained uncorrupted three days after her death.

Item: the blood formed a cross on the floor, though no wounds were visible.

Item: one day after her death, while I was still painting her, she cried out in a voice neither high nor low the word "sancta." At this time Leonello Spada, Onorio Longhi, Giambattista Marino, Antonio Tocchi, and many others were with me in the cellar.

Item: she gave herself to anyone who wanted her in her life, and in her death she offered herself as an example of holiness and unblemished beauty.

Item: no one ever heard from her a word of complaint, nor did she take the name of God or the saints in vain, nor did she suffer anyone else to do so in her presence.

Item: when she was carried through the streets of Rome, lying in a cart, banners and flags flew from the houses, the crowds gathered and threw flowers at her, and rejoiced with her, though she was dead.

Item: the people of Rome knelt in the streets and humbly crossed themselves.

Item: she was dead.

Yet the incontestable fact of her death was, of all things, the least observable, since she gave every appearance of sleeping. Neither then nor at any other time were we constrained to behave as though she were dead: we did not lower our voices, nor did we entertain reminiscences of her, nor did we light candles. During the three days while I painted her we went about our affairs exactly as before. Benedetto did not weep, Leonello Spada did not stop making jokes, the bitch did not bark. As she lay dead, it was as though she had taken up her abode in my cellar, even more quietly than before, and she belonged to us all the more because some mysterious change had come over her which possessed no name and was beyond all understanding.

In the end, when we buried her, it was almost an afterthought. We went about it quite naturally, in the same way that we would go about taking a walk in the country. We had hoped that Cardinal del Monte would perform the funeral ceremony, but he had left for Florence a week before and the ceremony was performed by Cardinal Abbiati, who was a close friend of Prince Marzio Colonna. By the graveside there were five princes, four cardinals, two bishops, and all the priests of all the churches for which I had painted. They wore their most splendid robes, but they did not appear with solemn faces. They rejoiced with Maddalena. It was a lovely spring day with unclouded skies and a fresh wind blowing through the dusty streets. For myself I had the curious feeling that we were playing a charade, and that Maddalena would be waiting for us when we returned to the cellar.

There was no funeral feast. Gradually as the days passed we grew accustomed to the thought that she would never return. We did not so much console one another as console her for her absence. We would say: "Maddalena would have liked that," or "Maddalena would have done this or that," and we would say these things calmly, not sorrowfully, in exactly the same tones we would employ when talking about the weather.

In the following weeks, after acquiring an immense canvas, the largest I have ever used, I painted *The Death of the Virgin*, employing the studies I had made of the dead Maddalena. At the top of that canvas, which measured twelve feet by eight feet, I placed the flaming red curtain which the Cardinal had given me long ago. Around her, as she lay dying, I set her friends including Antonio Tocchi, the Cardinal, Leonello Spada, myself, and many others from the Piazza Navona, and I arranged the light to fall fiercely upon her and on the sorrowing Magdalene, who weeps in the foreground. At the foot of the Virgin's bed was a brass bowl into which some drops of her blood have fallen.

In this way, without subtlety, describing only what I have seen with my eyes, I depicted the grief which passes beyond all imaginable grief. I painted Maddalena, but I painted the Virgin. It was my intention that the painting should hang in the Church of Santa Maria della Scala in Trastavere, where she had sometimes lived, but when the painting was offered to the priests they said I had committed a blasphemy for painting as the Virgin "a common prostitute who had died in a sordid accident."

I confess the news did not please me, and though I painted well enough in the following days I was a prey to melancholy thoughts. Leonello Spada came to live with me, saying that Benedetto was not strong enough, or wise enough, to prevent me from committing some folly.

"We shall find you a new Maddalena," he said, and he spoke as though at any moment she would appear at the head of my stairs.

"There will never be a new Maddalena," I said, and I returned to painting skulls and St. Jeromes.

One day three weeks after the death of Maddalena I left the Palazzo Madama and made my way in the direction of the Piazza del Popolo, intending to see my paintings in the Church of Santa Maria del Popolo, for a long time had passed since I had seen them. I was in no mood for company, but wandered alone, sunk in grief, scarcely caring what happened to me. There had been a storm during the afternoon, and the clouds were still scudding low, no more than a few yards above the rooftops. For some reason the church was closed, and for a while I wandered along the banks of the Tiber until I came to a tavern. God knows what I wanted that afternoon, but I told myself there was no harm in entering a tavern and seeing new faces. I would sit in a dark corner, drink wine, study faces, and forget my sorrows.

As always after storms there was a freshness in the air, and the smell of violets. There were few people in the streets, for the rain had left great puddles. I wore a Spanish cape slashed with gold embroidery, a broad-brimmed hat, a scarlet doublet, a thin Florentine dagger at my belt, and I remember I wondered why I had come out in all this finery. In this fashion I entered the Osteria del Orso, found a corner seat and delivered myself to the study of the handful of people who had entered the inn before me.

I had been there five minutes when my friend Onorio Longhi, the architect, came over to my table, saying that he had observed me sunk in misery and he felt duty bound to entertain me. He wagged his red beard, spoke of his eleven children, and invited me to his table where his friends were waiting for him.

"They are all good fellows," he said, "and they will entertain you merrily. What is more, they have insisted on paying their respects to you and they hold you in great honor."

I went over to their table and found them to be agreeable companions — being young and kindly disposed toward me. There was a certain captain of the Castel Sant' Angelo, a Bolognese, with a well-cut beard. There were two young students for the priesthood, and in addition there was a remarkable elegant youth called Ranuccio Tomassoni, with a high forehead, deep blue eyes, a well-formed mouth, and a dazzling smile. He was sweet-tempered and modest, and it occurred to me that if I ever painted Christ again, I would ask him to grow a beard and serve as my model, for I could not expect to see a more divine face. He had a low and pleasing voice, and he spoke with some knowledge about my paintings.

"Since Michelangelo is succumbing to his grief, I suggest that we all go and play tennis, for everyone knows that tennis dissolves grief," Onorio Longhi said.

Immediately everyone began to clamor for the game of tennis, and we went off to the Campo Marzio. On the way Ranuccio Tomassoni invited me to stay with him in his villa at Terni, and I accepted his offer, saying only that I still had a few paintings to finish for Cardinal del Monte.

It was decided that Ranuccio Tomassoni should be the leader of one side, while I led the other. It was growing late, with long shadows sweeping across the court, and we therefore played more violently than usual, knowing that the time was short. As usual, bets had been laid, with the winner receiving ten *scudi* from the loser, but it was understood that the winner would entertain the loser to dinner that evening.

So we played, as carefree as children on holiday, shouting at the top of our lungs, with the score going first one way and then the other. Onorio Longhi, having the loudest voice, kept the score and the Bolognese captain kept shouting: "Strike! Strike!" as though he were an onlooker, not a participant. We had thrown our cloaks away at the beginning of the game, and later we threw off our doublets, playing in our shirts. The game was going badly for Onorio Longhi and me when we made five strikes in succession, and in this way we caught up with our opponents, to the discomfiture of the Bolognese captain, who took off his shirt and displayed his fine torso.

I shouted: "If you take off anything more, you will be playing bare arse!"

He was angry and turned on me, uttering a curse, and a moment later we were playing in deadly earnest, as though our lives depended on it. It was getting so dark that we could hardly see the balls. We lost two strikes, gained three, and were about to bring the game to an end when Ranuccio Tomassoni ran up to me and shouted: "You cheated!" His beautiful face was so distorted that I could scarcely recognize him.

"If I cheated, then we have all cheated and we shall all go down to Hell!" I said.

He flung down his bat and his hand went to his dagger. I did not see the blade until it flashed through the air and caught me in the neck and tore my ear. I felt the sharp pain before I was able to reach my own dagger. Then he aimed again for my face, and I knew I was fighting for my life. I heard Onorio Longhi bellowing as he tried to pull me away from my enemy, and all the time I was thinking: "I must not touch his face!"

So we fought like madmen, stabbing and jabbing at one another, while the Bolognese captain attempted to come between us, and Onorio Longhi bellowed, and the two students for the priesthood came running up, waving their arms frantically, doing nothing. I lunged forward, and felt the thin Florentine dagger sinking into flesh, and for a brief moment Ranuccio Tomassoni stood quite still with his dagger clenched in his fist within an inch of my face. Then the dagger fell to the ground, he screamed, clapped both hands to his groin, and reeled backward. A moment later he was dead and there was a puddle of blood between his legs.

Flight

YOU have never killed a man, Illustrissimo, and therefore you will never know the degradation of guilt in the loneliness of murder. A man who has killed is unalterably changed from the man he was before; he wears his guilt like a dagger at his side. He guards this dagger well, and ten times an hour he runs his finger over the blade to see if it is still sharp. All through his waking hours he remembers the look on the face of the man he has murdered, the accusing look which says: "You have taken from me all I possess. Could you not have taken less?" The face of a dead man has a hundred mouths.

It is strange the heaviness which settles in the bones of a murderer. My soul is heavier than ever, because it must also embrace the soul of Ranuccio Tomassoni. I know now that there are alterations in the blood of dying men, and I believe there are also alterations in the blood of murderers. So I thought as I made my way through the darkening streets to my cellar, blood dripping from my neck and ear, leaving a bloody trail. I never knew whether I would meet someone I knew at the turning of the road.

Happily, it was a Sunday evening, with all the church bells ringing, the people at their prayers, and therefore there were only a few wandering through the streets. Few saw the man who kept in the shadows, holding up a bloodstained hand to hide the gash in his neck and ear. He had become a shadow — more than a shadow. He was a dark stain which entered into the fabric of the walls.

I thought I would sleep in my cellar, but I knew the *sbirri* would find me too easily. I had hidden some gold *scudi* in a pot, perhaps a hundred, and I dug them out of the pot, surprised to see my hands so white and nerveless, without feeling. The sound of the church bells was deafening. No lamps were burning. It was dark in my cellar. I could see the shapes of the canvases stacked against the wall, and the thrones where the models sat, and the bars across the high windows, and seeing those bars I threw myself in despair upon the bed and wept uncontrollably, not for myself, but for Ranuccio Tomassoni, a man I liked and scarcely knew, and would like to have known better, now lifeless, because I had killed him. What were they doing to him? Where had they taken him? They say a body is still warm for three days after death. Therefore for three days there is still some semblance of life in him. On the third day he dies forever.

For about an hour I shivered in my bed, listening to the church bells. Sometimes there would come to my confused mind the thought that I should make my way to you and throw myself upon your mercy and seek absolution for my sins. I saw you standing at the head of the stairs, robed in scarlet and gold, with the flames of mercy streaming from your fingertips. And then I looked closer at your familiar face and saw you slowly shaking your head from side to side.

I heard footsteps coming down the steps, and thinking the *sbirri* had come to arrest me I groped my way to the edge of the bed, ready to drop to the floor and hide in the shadows. At night, without a candle, there are places in my room which are in pitch darkness. I watched a shadow moving across the room, and it was only much later that I realized the shadow was speaking, saying over and over again: "Michelangelo, where are you?" He spoke very softly, and yet with assurance. It was a young voice, and from the intonation it was clear he belonged to the Piazza Navona. For a while I kept quiet, watching the shadow blundering across my room, breathing heavily, so dark and shapeless that I could not make out whether he was short or tall. At last I heard him climbing up the stairs, and I must have given a little sigh of relief, for he paused and said loudly and clearly: "You are there! I know you are there!"

Even then I said nothing, for I had become a creature of shadow, lost among shadows, hoping never to emerge from them.

For a little while longer he paused, and then he said clearly but still in a whisper: "I am Andrea Rufetti, the friend of Onorio Longhi —"

I jumped up from the bed, and he must have heard me crashing among the furniture, for soon he was running down the stairs. I could not see him. We were still shadows confronting one another, moving warily.

"Yes, I believe you," I said, and held out my hand, clutching at the empty air. "I'll light a candle. Wait! It will be better when I can see you!"

"No," he said, "it is better to be in darkness. Have you strength enough to walk? If you can walk, you must come quickly. Onorio Longhi sent me."

In the past I had seen much of Andrea Rufetti, and he had posed for me. He was round-faced with dark curly hair; he played the viol, and for this reason I had included him among the musicians in one of the paintings I made for the Cardinal del Monte. In those days he was happy only sleeping with boys. Then the customary miracle took place and he married the daughter of a dressmaker on the Piazza Colonna. Meanwhile I had lost all track of him and he was no longer among the circle of my acquaintances.

It occurred to me that I could find no better place to hide than the house of Andrea Rufetti.

"Walk ten paces behind me, and come quickly," he said. "Follow me, and have trust in me."

I followed him into the street. I had thrown a dark cloak around my shoulders, and no one paid any attention to us. Within ten minutes I was climbing the stairs of a house I had never entered before. A door opened, and I saw a candle gleaming at a table, with a fair-haired girl sitting beside it. She looked pale and terrified, and she must have known who I was, and why I was taking refuge in her house. She nodded in the direction of a small inner room, and I followed Andrea into it. By this time we were accustomed to habits of silence, and he merely pointed to the bed, which lay in the shadows. Then he went out, returning a little later with his wife and a bowl of water and a towel, and while they were bathing my wound, Andrea whispered: "Onorio Longhi has sent a message to Prince Marzio Colonna. It is the best way. You can have no faith in the Church —"

"The Church is best," I said, "for the Church has the power to grant mercy."

"Perhaps," he said, putting a finger to his lips, "but not now, not for many months. The Church can be merciless, and princes are more merciful."

I closed my eyes in weariness. I had murdered a man, and he was talking about princes. I watched the bowl of water turning scarlet, and thought: "Strange that I should be wounded in the throat. I have always known the knife would descend on my throat."

I had the feeling that the skin had been torn from my throat, that it was all raw and bleeding, and many muscles had been cut through; but when I put my finger to the wound I discovered the blood had already congealed, and there was only the dull ache of an old wound — a wound two hours' old.

Andrea's wife sat there beside the bed, not looking at me, her fair hair falling over her face. She had the look of a penitent Magdalene, very quiet and withdrawn, mechanically squeezing out the bloody towel which Andrea handed to her, then handing it back to him. Somewhere I could hear a child whimpering.

I made mental notes of how I would paint her with the bloody bowl lying on her lap — a bloody bowl, and the head of Holofernes resting at her feet — and I was especially engrossed in the study of the light falling in the bowl until I remembered it was my own blood, and it was not Holofernes but Ranuccio Tomassoni who seemed to be lying there, and in the darkness outside the house the *sbirri* were searching for me.

"It would be best if you left Rome tonight," Andrea Rufetti said. "But where would you go? Onorio Longhi has no word from the prince —"

He seemed to be talking to himself, lost in his own thoughts. Sometimes he would throw a quick glance at his wife, so that they seemed to be conspirators.

I was still thinking how I would paint his wife — the yellow hair in candlelight, one eye completely invisible, only the tip of her nose and the curve of her cheek being outlined clearly through the great fountain of falling hair; and then it occurred to me that I had no paints, no brushes, no canvas, and very soon I would have no possessions at all. In a few hours or days the papal police would sequester all my paintings and every article of value I possessed. Someone else would occupy my cellar. God knows where I would be! A fugitive from justice wandering at night from one dark village to another, alone and unknown! I thought of the days when I left Milan and wandered with a black donkey to Rome, and how I had worked over the years to make a name for myself, and now it was all over!

I struggled to get off the bed, but they pushed me back, and I was too weak to resist.

"It's no use, Michelangelo," Andrea said. "It is better to rest and sleep."

"What is sleep good for?" I asked, and turned my face to the wall.

It was a kind of delirium, the candlelight on the woman's hair, the knocking of the blood at my throat, the death's head on the floor. A stupid quarrel on a tennis court, and once more I must be thrown into the pot of boiling lead. I said to the wall: "No, no, it mustn't be! There are too many faces to be painted. I must have my paintings back. How can I live without them?"

"You must not speak," Andrea said relentlessly. "Onorio will do everything he can to remove the paintings and send them to you, wherever you are. If he cannot find the Prince, he will find the chamberlain, and if not the chamberlain, he will find the factor. The important thing is to go into hiding at once. We are already spreading the rumor that you are on your way to Florence. You understand, you have already left Rome."

"At night?" I asked. "With all the gates closed?"

He laughed softly.

"You scaled the walls, like everyone else who escapes from Rome," he said. "Whether you escaped or not, they are scouring the countryside."

A maidservant came with some broth, and I drank it straight from the bowl. He was talking about Prince Colonna's villas in the Sabine hills. There were three or four villas, with servants always in attendance, because the prince never knew until the last moment which villa he would go to. They were called villas, but in fact they were large palaces, with many rooms and many workmen's dwellings. A man could drown in these villas and never rise to the surface again.

"There is no safer place in Italy," Andrea said. "You have nothing to fear."

With those words echoing in my ears I fell into a fitful sleep, awaking at intervals to see Andrea and his wife sitting there in the shadows, keeping watch over me, their heads nodding. There was a candle in another room throwing a faint light on them. And seeing them, I would whisper to myself: "There is nothing to fear," and go to sleep again.

A man does not sleep soundly when he has killed a man. When I was young I would drop into a pit of sleep so deep that it must have reached the center of the earth, but from that day I have never slept more than a few inches deep. It was as though I were in a grave, the earth covering me, but only lightly. One eye slept, while the other kept watch.

I awoke at midday to see the light streaming through the windows. I heard some carts lumbering across the Piazza Colonna, and then for some reason a strange quiet descended on the house. Suddenly there was shouting on the stairs, and then once again there was silence. "There is nothing to fear," I told myself, and walked to the window, taking care to keep to the shadows. I was still looking out of the window at the sunlit square when there was a commotion in the next room, more shouts, the sound of a stick thumping on the floor. I wheeled round to see the door bursting open, and there was Andrea and his wife and a small priest with a heavy staff. Andrea was standing behind the priest, making signs to me to keep quiet, his fingers at his lips. His wife's face had turned white, as though drained of blood, and there were bruises under her eyes, as though she had been weeping.

The priest said: "I knew he was here. It seems I have come just in time."

He was not an ordinary priest, for he wore on his left breast the crossed swords which indicated that he came from the criminal court.

He was a young man, about twenty-five, clean-shaven, with the blue cheeks of a man with a strong beard, if he would only permit it to grow. The face was narrow, cavernous, very dark and swarthy, so that he looked more like a Spaniard than a Roman, and although he was undersized he carried himself with an air of great authority and decision. I thought it was all over. He would arrest me and take me to prison, very simply, without any need for guards, for these clerks from the criminal court are accustomed to being obeyed and they are held in high regard by the people, who always cooperate with them. And as he stood there in the doorway, smiling with satisfaction, nodding his head from side to side, I thought it would be simpler altogether if I hurled myself out of the window and broke my neck on the street below; and I must have made a movement toward the window, for he was instantly upon me, pushing me away from the wall, saying: "Take care, Michelangelo. A man can fall straight to Hell through a window."

Andrea still had a finger to his lips, so I said nothing, sitting on the edge of the bed and staring at him.

"You have been wounded," the priest said. "You must tell me how it happened."

"I wounded myself with my sword when falling in the street," I replied. "I don't know where it happened, and no one else was present."

He wrote down the words I had spoken in his minute handwriting.

"Is that the only explanation you can give?"

"I can say no more."

"Evidently you can say no more because you have committed a

crime. Very well, you will remain in this house for further examination later, and if you leave this house at any time you will be forced to pay a fine of five hundred *scudi*. You should be aware that the courts can never condone murder."

Saying this, he left the house, leaving a constable at the door below.

"There are many ways to escape from here," Andrea said. "Rest today, for you may need all your strength tonight. In any event they won't come back till tomorrow."

During the afternoon I learned that Onorio Longhi and the Bolognese captain had both been arrested, and because Andrea thought it would soon be my turn he arranged that I should hide in an apartment below.

I sent a message to Benedetto, saying that I intended to escape from Rome. He at once went to Cardinal San Severino, hoping to obtain a pardon for me. The Cardinal had already learned about the duel from the courts, and ordered Benedetto under pain of imprisonment to have no further contact with me and to remain in the Cardinal's palace at St. Peter's. Cardinal del Monte was still in Florence, and although an urgent letter was sent to him through Fabrizio Crescenzi there was clearly nothing he could do. Nor under any conditions would he have acted impetuously. Only Prince Marzio Colonna, who was ill and dying, sent a message saying that I was welcome to stay in any of his villas in the Sabine hills.

That night I slipped out of Rome with the help of Leonello Spada and Andrea Rufetti, with Antonio Tocchi leading the way. The old man knew the sewers as well as he knew the side streets of Rome; he had spent half his life as a thief, and the thieves know the roads under the earth. Donkeys were waiting for us in a small village just outside of Rome. I expected to make the journey alone, but both Leonello Spada and Andrea Rufetti insisted upon accompanying me. A week later Andrea Rufetti returned to his house, but Leonello Spada remained with me.

We stayed in the Prince's villa at Palestrina. I painted in one of the high towers overlooking the valley, but the painting went badly. There was no Maddalena to inspire me, no Benedetto to bring joy to me. I, who had spent the greater part of my life in a cellar, now found myself dreaming of walking through the streets of Rome. I missed the people and the churches. I missed the bells and fountains and the sounds of the ox wagons through the streets. Above all I missed my familiar surroundings, for I had become the slave of my cellar. In Rome I knew where everything could be found, and in Palestrina it was a day's work to find a good paintbrush or a canvas, and the work had to be done deviously for fear of arousing suspicion.

I heard that Cardinal del Monte had returned to Rome, and because I was in the utmost despair and hoped to receive a pardon from the Holy Father, who alone can dispense pardons, I sent him the small silver box he had given me, saying that it should be sent to him whenever I was in dire need. Ten days later the message came: "I can do nothing now. Have patience, and pray."

I spent my days in prayer and painting, and sometimes — so great was the dryness of my soul — I would find myself incapable of painting or of prayer. In this mood, at night in my high tower, I painted an *Incredulity of St. Thomas*, pointing my own hand at the wound. I painted sorrowfully, and the hand is a sorrowing hand.

God knows why Leonello Spada stayed with me! He had some talent as a painter, but no more than you will find in a hundred others. He had grace and dignity, and he jested easily, and perhaps the jests interfered with his paintings. I would say: "You must paint as though it was the last time, as though you were at the stake and your feet were already in the fire," and he would shake his head and say: "I paint with whatever talent I have. It is for you to paint with the flames."

Then some days later we heard that Prince Marzio Colonna had died, and a few days afterward there came another message from the Cardinal, this time in someone else's handwriting and without the signature, saying that *The Death of the Virgin*, had been refused by the priests of the Church of Santa Maria della Scala, and accordingly it had been sold to the Duke of Mantua for his collection. The painting was seen by the Dutch painter, Peter Paul Rubens, who earnestly begged the duke to buy it so that it should be in safe hands. He had asked the Cardinal to permit a public showing of the painting since the painters of Rome desired to see it. All Rome flocked to see the painting. "It is the painting of the hour and of the age," the Cardinal wrote, adding that never in history had so many people gathered together at one time to see a single painting. It hung in the courtyard of the Palazzo Madama with an awning to protect it from the sun and the rain, and thirty thousand people came in three days to admire it. Before it was taken to Mantua, the Cardinal arranged that it should be seen by the Pope in the hope that he would grant a pardon while he gazed at it. "But unfortunately, my dear Michelangelo, he belongs among those who believe you should have chosen a woman of greater virtue, and accordingly he refuses to grant a pardon at this time. Meanwhile your name is on the lips of everyone in Rome, and I am asked daily for news of you." In the last words of the letter he said that some people seemed to know where I was hiding, and it would be better if I settled for a few months in the Spanish dominion in the south, out of reach of the Roman courts.

The warning was clear, and within an hour we were already making our way to Naples, walking by night and sleeping in the woods by day.

Naples oppressed me. In those narrow, restless streets I wandered like a man who has lost his soul, silent as in a grave; and though I was no longer in hiding, and therefore free to walk openly, I felt that I was in continual danger and that at any moment the police would find me. We had lodgings in the Osteria del Ceriglio, near the waterfront. All the dregs of Naples congregated in this inn owned by a German, who had his own army of ruffians. In the evenings I would amuse myself by finding a dark corner of the tavern and from this vantage point observe the strumpets, the sailors, the merchants and the roaring boys, and I would attempt to read the scribblings in a hundred languages on the walls. The German treated us well enough; we were given a large room over the courtyard, and there I painted. There was no lack of commissions, and in a period of three months I painted three altarpieces. My fame had preceded me. The German bowed low whenever I passed him, and I painted his fat, piglike face in *The Seven Acts of Mercy*, which hangs now above the high altar in the Chiesa della Misericordia. In the center I placed Leonello Spada, and at the right I painted one of the strumpets of the tavern; and above all those people performing or rejoicing in acts of mercy I painted the Virgin and Child supported on the wings of two angels; and once more the Virgin wears the face of Maddalena. I painted the Virgin with great tenderness and energy, from memory.

Sometimes when I was sunk in melancholy Leonello Spada would say: "Let me send for some boys or girls, or both at once, and drive all this madness away. God knows, they are cheap enough. The German will send us all the wines we want, and not even trouble to ask us for money because you painted him. You could live like the Pope here, if you only set your mind to it."

I would go on painting, with the look of a man about to be hanged.

One day, when we were walking through the port and Vesuvius was smoking, a blue cloud in the distance, Leonello Spada gripped my arm and said: "What are you grieving for? For Mad-dalena or Ranuccio Tomassoni?"

"For all the dead," I said.

"Then for God's grace, let us leave the dead behind us. Let us leave Italy altogether, and go somewhere where no one dies."

"Where is that?"

"We'll find it. I've heard there are islands where no one dies. At least let us leave Naples and go somewhere far out of reach of the Roman courts and your memories. Go now. Go tomorrow. But no more of this brooding."

On the following day we took all our luggage and went down to the port, determined to take the first ship leaving for the islands. In this way we came to Malta.

The Palace of the Grand Master

THE air of Rome, my lord, is white with the dust of ages, but the air of Malta is silver and gold and blue, and the fresh winds come in from the sea. In Rome you can believe that men are made to die; in Malta you can only believe that God intended them to live forever. So, in those early days, we lived in a fever of intoxication. We visited the churches to see what paintings hung there, but we spent the greater part of our days wandering along the shore and admiring the colors of the sky.

We had intended once we arrived to seek out the Grand Master of the Order of the Knights of Malta and to present ourselves as his court painters, but we soon learned that no one is ever permitted to enter his presence without his invitation, and many have suffered from having presumed on his friendship. The Grand Master is more unapproachable than the Doge of Venice or the Turkish Sultan; every corridor, every chamber of his palace is guarded; armed men guard his sleep and his waking, and stand invisible behind his throne; and when he walks abroad he is accompanied by never less than ten men all carrying an armory of swords beneath their innocent black robes.

Through Monsignor Strozzi we obtained a small commission to

paint a Catherine in the cathedral, and prepared to learn how to approach the Grand Master to best effect. We must know whether to bow or kneel, and what titles to employ when addressing him, whether *Illustrissimo, Reverendissimo, Devoto, Sincero, Nobile, Delecto*, or all of them, for the princes of the empire are accustomed to live in great state and they attach extraordinary importance to titles of honor. During those weeks while we painted the chapel of St. Catherine, we learned only two more useful things about the Grand Master — that he held audiences on the third Thursday of each month, and that he sometimes drove out of his palace to inspect the waterworks he was building on the island, and this usually happened in the late afternoon, and he avoided all the main roads and reached the waterworks by a circuitous route; and they said he spoke to no one during these journeys except the engineers.

Leonello Spada was of the opinion that we would never break through the wall surrounding the Grand Master, and that indeed it was beyond anyone's ability to do so unless he was provided with letters of commission from the highest sources. The prelates and princes of Rome, and even the Pope himself, were more approachable. The Knights rode through the streets of Valletta with trains of Turkish slaves, in a panoply that beggared all description, like conquerors riding though a captured city, throwing disdainful glances at the people crowding the narrow streets or gazing impassively into the distance. Long ago they had defeated the Turks, and they regarded themselves as lords temporal and spiritual owing allegiance to no one except the Grand Master. They were masters of the Mediterranean Sea, and they feared no one in the world.

After four weeks in Malta, we were still as far as ever from meeting the Grand Master or even a single knight. We saw only the church officials, the shopkeepers, the servants at the inn. In all of Malta, according to Monsignor Strozzi, there were no other painters of talent. "It is a desert," the monsignor said, "and it is beyond me why you should want to stay in this desert. Go to Lombardy or Venice or Rome, if you wish to find employment. But not here, not in Malta. I tell you, these men are interested only in cutting throats!"

He said such things many times. Indeed, whenever we mentioned our desire to seek further employment, he would throw up his hands in a gesture of annoyance. He was an old man with lined cheeks and gray hair and the narrow, stooped shoulders of a scholar. But his eyes were alert and candid, and I detected in him more intelligence than he displayed openly; he possessed a deep and corrosive knowledge of the islanders; he preferred not to speak of them. Sometimes he watched us painting, pretending to be studying his Missal as he sat in the nave, his head bent over the book while watching us from under his thick, shaggy eyebrows with an expression of quiet cunning. He thought I did not see him, but I saw him well.

"We shall get nowhere with him," Leonello Spada said. "In his heart of hearts he thinks all painters belong to the devil."

"On the contrary," I said, "he adores us, and will do everything possible for us except to bring us into the presence of the Grand Master."

This was true, for although the monsignor delighted in serving us and sometimes watched us painting with a bemused and happy expression, he was strangely silent whenever the discussion turned on the Grand Master. At the inn we were told that the Grand Master, Alof de Wignacourt, was a man of about fifty, silent, taciturn, with a commanding presence befitting a man who was the undisputed master of an island and a fleet. They, too, spoke of him in hushed voices. They saw him rarely. What they remembered most about him was that he had once, while engaged in combat with the Turks, crushed the skull of an enemy captain with a single blow of his fist.

We asked for more information and heard that he was seven feet tall, had six fingers on one hand, and a harem of Turkish women. This information so pleased Leonello Spada that he swore on oath that he would not leave Malta until he had seen him. Monsignor Strozzi had pity on us, and said he would arrange for us to attend a Mass in the cathedral, placing us close enough to the altar to permit a good view of him.

"But you understand," he said, putting a finger to his lips, "that this is the most I can do. I cannot bring you into his presence, and I have heard nothing to suggest that he has an abiding love for painters."

On that Sunday therefore we were permitted to stand in one of the chapels near the high altar and to observe him at his devotions. He was not seven feet tall, but he was taller than anyone else in the cathedral. Heavily bearded, with eyes like blue ice, he carried himself with more dignity than an emperor. His beard jutted out, and there was about all his movements, even when he was kneeling before the high altar, the suggestion of a powerful animal about to attack. He would have taken the Sacred Host by force, if it had been necessary.

No wonder people were frightened of him and spoke about him in whispers. Light flashed from his eyes, his hands assumed commanding gestures, and he knew he was the unchallenged object of everyone's gaze.

We watched him as he walked down the nave, wearing his ducal crown glittering with rubies and emeralds, the Maltese cross embroidered on his black gown in gold thread, with red and blue jewels smoking from his fingers, and he wore a heavy gold chain over his breast. But it was not the blaze of jewels which caught our attention so much as the fire in his eyes. One does not argue with such men; one obeys.

"What do you think of our Grand Master?" Monsignor Strozzi asked when the procession had vanished through the cathedral doors.

"Better that he should be on our side than on the side of the Turks," I answered softly.

This answer pleased Monsignor Strozzi, and in time it reached the ears of Monsignor da Rimini, who in turn communicated it to the great chamberlain of the court, and so with some additional decoration it reached the ears of the Grand Master himself.

By this time, of course, seven or eight weeks had passed, and we were reduced to painting the mistresses and daughters of the church dignitaries. Leonello Spada had acquired so much facility that he could paint a passable portrait in two or three sittings; he had the gift of rendering a likeness, while I, more ponderous, achieved likenesses with extreme difficulty, plagued by the desire to change a face more to my liking. I would wrestle with a face, tear it apart and put it together again, constantly erasing and re-shaping it, until, exhausted, I would turn away and concentrate upon a foot, a shoulder or a thigh, for these always gave me pleasure. Yet, when I was compelled to face the issue, I gave strength and solidity to my portraits, anchoring them to the canvas so that no tempests could ever blow them away. It could be said of my portraits that they went beyond the skin and were all different, while Leonello's portraits were merely pictures of the skin and were always the same.

Though we were painters with different temperaments, we were brothers in arms in a strange country, and we therefore depended upon one another. We rejoiced in each other's successes and commiserated with each other's failures. When we were particularly unlucky — as when Monsignor Strozzi informed us that the Grand Master had been shown the painting of St. Catherine in the cathedral and had expressed disapproval, saying that we had failed to express the strength and boldness of the saint — then we retired to a tavern and got royally drunk.

"God help us both," said Leonello Spada, "for all it needs is that the Grand Master should lift his little finger and we would both become Knights of Malta overnight. There's a knighthood for you. We could forget Rome and stay on this island forever. It's warm in winter and not too hot in summer, and the women are pretty enough!"

It seemed to us both that nothing was so desirable as to become a servant of the Grand Master. I told myself I would become a Knight of St. John and ride in a black cape with a plumed hat through the streets of Valletta, with Turkish slaves attending me, like all the other knights I had seen parading in their finery. I was a painter, and by God's grace the best in Italy. But I was prepared to sacrifice Italy for the sake of Malta, where the air is clear and all the buildings are new and there are no white relics of the past.

Saying nothing to Leonello Spada, I determined on a ruse. I noticed that many clerks entered the Palace of the Grand Master. Wearing a black robe and carrying *The Beatitudes* of St. Thomas Aquinas, I expected no one to pay any attention to me. I had seen the clerks enter. They were not knights of the Order of St. John, but like the knights they wore black capes, though without the large Maltese crosses embroidered on them. Instead they wore small silver badges on their capes, these badges being about two inches high and placed on the left breast. Generally the clerks were older men, bent and bearded, but there were a few younger ones among them. I, too, wore a black cape over a black doublet. It was a hot day. The guards at the entrance paid no attention to me. I walked slowly up the steps, and paused once to consult my small leather-bound book, and I believe it was that pause, while I searched for a page, which convinced the guards that I was one of the clerks attached to the Grand Master's court, for they scarcely looked at me.

Once inside the palace I walked boldly, purposefully. There were long corridors, chapels and offices opened out from them, and the Great Hall was, as I knew, in the rear of the building. There were so many guards standing in those wide corridors that they merely compounded their inability to detect an intruder, for those who saw that I had passed twenty guards assumed that I must have some reason to be there, and those who were dubious and watched me closely thought better of it. A young rosy-cheeked clerk with a sheaf of documents under his arm came hurrying down a corridor. I bowed; he slowed his pace and bowed in return; then he was tripping away as fast as his feet would carry him. And sometimes if I saw in the distance a guard who might prove to be unruly, I slackened my pace, consulted my book, turned down a page, muttered something, and went on with an air of clerk-like absentmindedness. Much later I came to know that I had played my part almost too well; the palace was full of these clerks; they were like ants; and the guards were almost unconscious of their existence.

I had penetrated deep within the palace when I realized that I was lost. There came a moment when, having walked down those immense and innumerable corridors until my feet were aching, it occurred to me that I was as far as ever from penetrating the holy of holies. I simply did not know where the Grand Master held his audiences. It was shortly after noon. There were fewer and fewer people walking about; a sense of lethargy was beginning to descend upon the palace at the hour of the siesta; and for some reason this quietness filled with the faint rustling of silks and the soft echoing of footfalls disturbed me, so that I was compelled to rest on one of those marble benches which stand at long intervals in the corridors. I never saw anyone else sit on them; and I doubt whether they are often used. In that bustling palace everyone was in a hurry, except the guards.

Like Theseus I had entered the maze, but there was no Princess Ariadne to show me the way out. I knew, or thought I knew, a great deal about the palace; the servants at the inn talked about it at length; Monsignor Strozzi had described the Great Hall, without however informing me that it was on the second floor. There was no grand ducal staircase. In all my wanderings in the palace I never caught a glimpse of a staircase. I had seen a hundred doors, a hundred bronze lanterns, a hundred tapestries on a hundred walls. Sitting on the marble bench I became intoxicated by a sense of failure, by the knowledge that I could only break out of the impasse by a sudden unhoped-for stroke of good fortune. A clerk came hurrying past me. He was a fat and portly man, accustomed to his own dignity, full of admiration for his dewlaps, his bushy eyebrows, the hard set of his eyes and mouth; he had a fine sweeping forehead, and he walked like a farmer. He had seen me through the corner of his eyes, for he was one of those men who observe everything; and he may have detected my mute plea for help, or perhaps he was weary of walking down marble corridors. He sat down beside me. I pretended to be immersed in my leather-bound book.

"God be with you," he said, in the tone of a man desiring to open a conversation.

I looked up and repeated the salutation.

"What are you reading?" he asked.

"A work by St. Thomas Aquinas on the Beatitudes," I said quickly, and looked down at the book.

"Well, my friend, do you usually read St. Thomas upside down?"

He leaned over gently, took the book, turned it the right way, and went on: "I see you are nervous. It is nothing to be ashamed of. All the clerks are nervous during their first days. By your voice I know you came from Rome, and by your manner that you were born somewhere in the north — was it Milan?"

"No, not Milan — in Caravaggio."

He nodded and smiled, for it pleased him that he had described me with some accuracy. And more inquisitively than ever, he went on: "I believe you are attached to His Highness's library?"

"No," I said.

"Then you must be attached to the hospital?"

"No, not to the hospital?"

"Then to the refectory?"

"No, not to the refectory."

"Then no doubt you must be attached to His Highness's private office?"

"I am attached to none of these," I said. "I am a painter, and I have just completed a painting in the Chapel of St. Catherine. With God's blessing I hope to paint the Grand Master, and that is why I have come here."

Hearing this, the fat clerk whistled under his breath and gave me a look compounded of admiration and fear in equal proportions. Unspoken questions rose to his lips; he gazed at me searchingly, turned away, gazed again, looked down at his hands, and whispered: "I have seen the painting, and I hear that the Grand Master was particularly pleased by your rendering of the armor, though there was much about the painting he disliked."

"I have heard the same," I said. "But it is almost as much as a man's life is worth to make his acquaintance."

"Then you have never met him?"

"That is true, nor do I have any hope of meeting him unless God aids me. They say he is always at his prayers, and hides from men, and never shows himself."

I said this in order to learn more about the Grand Master, and my clerk fell neatly into the trap I had laid for him.

"Why," he declared, "there is no man in the world who lives less in seclusion. No doubt he spends some time at his prayers, and he never shows himself among people unless he has something to say to them, but to say that he hides from men only shows your ignorance. There's no man more up and doing. One moment he is with his architect, the next with his armorer, the next with his shipwrights. He is a water engineer, a builder, a cannoneer, a doctor. Every day he spends an hour in the hospital of St. John, either on a tour of inspection or tending the wounds and sicknesses of the patients, for all the high officers of state humble themselves in this way. Only yesterday he complained that life was too short for all the things he intended to do. 'If God gave me enough time, I would make this island so strong and secure that it would rule the Mediterranean,' he said, and we believed him, and we are only afraid he will wear himself out by attempting too much."

"Then you are well acquainted with him?" I asked cautiously.

"I know him no better and no worse than others know him," the clerk replied. "Sometimes in the evening he calls me to read to him, but that is not knowing a man; and sometimes he will discuss questions of theology with me, and that, too, is not knowing a man. He is a man who lives deep in himself, and only his confessor knows his soul, and perhaps even the confessor —"

Suddenly the clerk's voice dropped to a whisper, his face grew red, and he held my hand. It was strange how excited he had become, his eyes staring, his mouth agape. At first I thought he was suffering from a stroke, for he was rigid and his eyes were glassy.

I turned quickly and saw the Grand Master coming out from a

small door, his head bent down, his shoulders hunched; he did not so much come through the door as hurtle out of it, followed by some clerks and guards all in the black uniform of the Order, and they too held their heads low, and the clerks walked with their hands folded on their breasts. But I paid no more than a passing glance at the clerks, those shadowy creatures who hugged the walls and carried themselves like serious schoolchildren. My eyes were fixed on the Grand Master. He wore the long black gown of the Order, and there was a gold chain hanging around his neck and the eight-pointed star was on his breast, but I did not become aware of these things until long afterward. All I saw was the face, ruddy, blue-eyed, with a reddish bristling beard, and a look of power. He was more like a force of nature than a man. He strode down the corridor as though at any moment he would turn aside into the walls, which would fall before him. He was a head taller than any of the clerks and guards who accompanied him. He gave the impression of a man who was completely alone, unconscious of the presence of the retainers, superbly unaware of the existence of any power except his own; and there was a faint smile hovering on the corners of his lips.

My friend the fat little clerk was trembling as he rose to his feet. It occurred to me that one does not remain sitting in the presence of the Grand Master, and I too rose unsteadily to my feet. We bowed while he strode past us, and I thought I might never see him again, but the little clerk said something in a high-pitched voice and he suddenly turned toward us. The clerk had spoken truthfully. He knew the Grand Master; they had spent many hours together.

"What are you doing here, Claudio?" the Grand Master exclaimed.

It was a heavy, rich, molten voice. He spoke in Italian, but there was more than a trace of a French accent.

"I was resting here with my friend," the clerk said, making a gesture in my direction.

"This is no time for resting," the Grand Master replied. "Come with me to the shipyard and bring your friend with you, if this is your pleasure."

For the first time the Grand Master observed my presence. He looked me up and down, and held me with his eyes.

"Your Highness," I said, "it is my greatest desire to paint you."

There was a long pause. He looked straight into my eyes, as though searching into the impenetrable depths of my soul, and he seemed to find something which satisfied him, for he said: "Very well, you shall!"

The arrangements were made through Monsignor da Rimini, who conducted the affair as though I was the ambassador of an unfriendly state. Nevertheless, it was agreed that I should paint the Grand Master in five sittings, he would wear armor during the first and last of the sittings, and when I learned that he had a favorite grandson Leonardo, the son of his daughter Blanche and her husband Jérôme Varèse, the Procurator of the Treasury of the Order of St. John, and that the boy might be willing to serve as the Grand Master's page, I begged Monsignor da Rimini to secure the boy's services. For myself I was given the use of a Turkish slave, Achmed, for I always needed a servant about me.

"You are asking far more than anyone has ever dared to ask before," Monsignor da Rimini said.

"You must remember," I answered, "that I shall so paint the Grand Master that people living five hundred years from now shall see him as he is. I am painting him for the centuries to come."

Monsignor da Rimini sighed, and looking vexed, he muttered into his beard and quickly changed the subject, after first observing that nothing was more dangerous than to make demands on the Grand Master and warning me never to talk to him unless first spoken to.

The sittings would take place in the Grand Master's robing room, a small room behind the Great Hall. I complained that I needed space to move about in, for a painter must step back to see the effect of his painting, and there was scarcely room to swing a cat. A larger room would be necessary. Monsignor da Rimini said all the large rooms were occupied, that the Grand Master had already decided on the robing room, and it was too late to make any changes. I said I would paint the Grand Master if we were both locked up in a closet, but it was not fair to present him entirely in shadow. Monsignor da Rimini sighed again and said: "You always ask too much. Nothing good will come out of this."

Nevertheless a larger room was found without difficulty in this palace which consisted of large rooms. It was one of those bright high-ceilinged rooms, all white and gold, overlooking the harbor, and it was therefore necessary to cover the windows with sackcloth, so that I could work by the light of my own lamps. At the appointed time, ten o'clock in the morning, the Grand Master entered the room accompanied by his grandson, and because he was in full armor he immediately ordered the windows to be opened. Seven or eight people, including Monsignor da Rimini, accompanied him. It was a very hot day. They were all fanning themselves and complaining about the heat. I said: "I cannot paint you, Illustrissimo, except in my own way." By chance I had with me a half-finished painting of the slave Achmed, wearing only a white shirt and sitting cross-legged, against a dark and shadowy wall. Showing him this painting, I explained that I must have darkness to paint in. He nodded, and made a sign to all the rest to leave. Then I arranged the lamps and stood the boy Leonardo beside him, and immediately he fell into the pose I wanted, holding a golden baton in his mailed fists, in armor up to his throat, only his head bare. The boy Leonardo served as his page, holding in his hands the great helmet decorated with white and scarlet plumes.

The sitting was to be for two hours, and I feared for him. I could see the sweat trickling down his beard and sometimes he would sway a little in the heat, while Achmed silently fanned him. Meanwhile he said little, for he was a man accustomed to giving orders and there were no orders he could give me. He knew that he looked magnificent and enviable in armor, the blue steel shining like shot silk, chiseled, gilded, and damascened, with inlaid etchings of gold arabesques. It was such a suit of armor as a king might wear after a great triumph. Golden fruit and flowers, and even galleys, were etched into the steel, which shimmered in the light of my oil lamps. He maintained the pose well, and when his grandson fidgeted, there would be a warning half-smile, as though he were saying: "Be strong, like me!"

As for the boy, he resembled his grandfather to perfection, except that he was weak where his grandfather was strong. They had the same long faces, the same broad foreheads, the same heavily lidded eyes, the same mouth, and the same color. But where the grandfather was all power and dignity, the boy showed an almost feminine diffidence and malice, always watching me cunningly through the corner of his eye. I suspected evil of the boy, but there was none in the grandfather.

At last when the sitting was over, the Grand Master gave a shout, the servants came rushing in, the armor was unbuckled, and the windows were thrown wide open. Then dressed simply in a long black robe with the Maltese cross in gold upon his breast, he advanced toward the canvas with that same powerful and menacing air which characterized him at all times, and after staring at it for a moment or two he said abruptly: "You have done well in so short a time." I had painted his face high up on the canvas and sketched out the armor, and the boy's face, too, was sketched out carefully. Later in the day Monsignor da Rimini came hurrying in to say that the Grand Master had expressed his satisfaction with the progress of the painting, and ordered that every assistance should be given to me.

"He smiled when he spoke about you," Monsignor da Rimini said with a dazed expression. "He even threw back his head and laughed as he described how you painted, splashing paint all over you and making grimaces all the time. Oh, he watched you very carefully! He was suffocating in his armor, and he promises never to wear it again! But he thinks you suffered even more than he did, because you were working so prodigiously hard, and the truth is that he has the greatest admiration for you!"

I was pleased with these testimonies of the Grand Master's admiration, but felt no overwhelming impulse to rest on my laurels. He was a hard taskmaster, and I knew I would have to perform miracles of valor in order to remain in his good graces. So I worked on the painting for the rest of the day, having acquired the services of one of his sailors, who was of the same build, and somewhat the same appearance, buckling him into the armor and placing him in exactly the same pose. I studied the armor with a kind of desperate passion, for I have very rarely painted armor. I was fascinated by its intricacy and strength, its bellying curves and overlapping scales. I studied it at all hours of the day — in sunlight, in candlelight, by the light of oil lamps, and in the moonlight, when it was most beautiful. The blue of steel and the blue of moonlight married, caught fire, and produced colors which were neither those of moonlight nor of steel. Intoxicated with the discovery of the beauty of armor, I was determined to render it with the curious light which flows from the moon.

Achmed did not share my admiration for armor. It amused him to parade around the room wearing the Grand Master's plumed

helmet — a dangerous occupation, for if anyone had seen him he
would have been in trouble. He had a dark golden skin, an impudent face, rather round and childish, and when his features were
composed, he would assume an expression of great sweetness and
nobility. I painted two portraits of him. He had a quality of stillness, and was the most perfect model who ever sat for me. First
I painted him sitting cross-legged, wearing only a white shirt, his
head a little to one side; and in the painting he seemed to be so
brimming with life that I could have sworn the painting could
speak. Later I painted him naked, as a young John the Baptist.
They were very hot days, and the sweat ran in rivers down his
golden body.

But in those days I was busy with the portrait of the Grand
Master, who continued to spend two hours every morning in the
makeshift studio with the closed windows. One day — I think it
was the third day — he asked me whether I might need more sittings, and then without waiting for an answer he said: "You paint
like a man storming the Turkish galleons." I said I would like two
more sittings beside the five he had already promised. "Then you
shall have them," he said, and for the first time he smiled. It was a
smile of great sweetness, and then I understood why he smiled so
rarely.

When at last the painting was completed, he pronounced himself well satisfied with it and ordered that it should be hung permanently in a new gallery to be called the Hall of the Grand Masters. He asked me to paint another portrait of him, and when
this was finished to his satisfaction he commissioned me to paint a
Beheading of John the Baptist for the Chapel of the Baptist in the
Cathedral of St. John, saying that if this painting pleased him he
intended to give me some special mark of his favor.

Already he had given me an apartment in the palace, a precious
chain of gold, a chestnut-colored bay, and the title of court

painter. The boy Achmed, who had been my servant for six weeks, was made my slave, and at my request Leonello Spada, whose paintings were without merit in the eyes of the Grand Master, was also granted the honor of being a court painter. Once more I was painting for eighteen hours a day. I was scarcely aware of all the splendor around me, for I thought only of my art. At night I would throw myself down on my bed, worn out by a mortal weariness. Achmed slept at the foot of my bed. He watched over me and over my paintings as though nothing else in the world gave him any pleasure.

Never since the day when I first mounted the stairs of the Palazzo Madama had I known this exaltation, this certainty of my own powers. I told myself that now at last I knew how to paint. I no longer hesitated, no longer brooded. *The Beheading of John the Baptist* was a work to which I had given much thought in the past, and I had long ago arrived at the general shape of the painting — a prison courtyard lit by the flames of braziers, a barred window to the right with prisoners looking out, and in the foreground the beardless John the Baptist lying supine, while the executioner bends over him, naked and gleaming. Beside him the prison governor stands in icy contemplation of the scene, while the red-haired Salome moves forward with a golden bowl to receive the head of the Baptist. So it had always been as long as I could remember — the red-haired Salome, John with a sheepskin round his loins, the huge muscular body of the executioner gleaming in the light of braziers. Behind them all there would be a prison gateway, the huge stones pressing down heavily to give a sense of doom and terror to the drama enacted below.

I wanted this painting to be my masterpiece, the one work which would survive if all the others were lost, and I therefore poured into it all my accumulated knowledge and feeling. I measured the chapel carefully, and learned to my delight that I would need the largest canvas I had ever painted on. It was twelve feet by seventeen feet, and the figures were therefore life-size. Leonello Spada posed for the executioner and for the prison governor; Achmed posed for John the Baptist, while a kitchen girl from the Grand Master's palace posed as Salome. At the last moment I introduced a fifth figure, an old woman with a pale ravaged face, lifting her hands to her face in horror. I had seen her while riding down an alleyway in Valletta, and her look of helpless misery haunted me, so that later in the evening I sent Achmed to find her. Then she was brought to me, more miserable than ever because she feared for her life. I told her what I wanted of her, gave her a few coins, and painted her in a single sitting.

Indeed, I was never conscious of painting *The Beheading of John the Baptist*. It was as though the painting, so long contemplated, came to life on the canvas of its own accord, and I seemed to observe it from a distance. I remember that as he lay there, Achmed groaned, and we were all charged with the terror of the Baptist's death. Once the Grand Master entered the room where I was painting, and having taken one look at the scene — the naked boy lying on the ground, his throat already cut and the blood spilling from the wound, while the executioner bent down to cut the head from the body — he gave a gasp and tiptoed quietly away. I had arranged the lamps so that the murder should take place in a brilliant light.

Many others who saw the painting gasped and turned pale; many made the sign of the cross, and some screamed. Therefore I thought it best to keep the painting veiled until the Grand Master himself unveiled it in the cathedral on the feast of the Beheading of John the Baptist, at the end of August. Meanwhile the Grand Master came more and more often to visit me while I was at work, and he would ask to see the painting and gaze at it quietly, and sometimes he would question me, saying for example: "Why is there a rope hanging down the prison wall?" or "Why are the bars of the gate of different sizes?" or "Why is the prison governor wearing a blue cloak around his shoulders?" I answered his questions as best I could, and he would talk about the colors which give pleasure and those which strike terror in the heart, until I reminded him that every color had it in its power to be pleasant or terrible according to the genius of the painter. What was terrible about my painting was not the colors, but the fact that I had created living people quietly determined upon a savage murder; and if there was artifice, it was in showing John the Baptist so young and so helpless, with his arms roped behind his back, lying peacefully on the ground. Then he would go away and come back the next day with more questions.

He ordered a huge ornamental frame for the painting, and because he was especially pleased with it he commanded that the painting should be placed high up in the chapel and special honors should be paid to it. He remembered his promise to grant me a special mark of his favor, and accordingly in July, while they were still working on the gilded frame, he told me that he had already given orders to grant me the badge of nobility. I would become a Knight of Grace of the Order of St. John Hospitaler, with all the rights and privileges of knighthood.

A few weeks later, on the eve of the unveiling, on a night of storm and violence, with the thunder echoing out to sea, I knelt before the altar in the cathedral, wearing a white shift. Out of the shadows the Grand Master emerged and granted me what I desired most in the world — a light tap on the right shoulder with the flat blade of his ceremonial sword. I remember the glinting of the rubies and emeralds on the sword, and his smiling face in the light of the altar lamps, and a moment later, while I was still kneeling, someone placed the black mantle of the Knights of St. John around my shoulders. Above the heart, in white silk, there was the eight-pointed Maltese cross.

I had become a knight not by virtue of the accolade or the black mantle, but by my own endeavors. So I told myself as I sat in the refectory and my brother knights served me with bread, water and salt in token of the poverty of St. John, and the Grand Master whispered in my ear: "Be not proud, Michelangelo. Serve God humbly." Then he added in a whisper, while the church bells rang and the storm gathered over Valletta: "As you have always done."

On the night before the unveiling, as *The Beheading of John the Baptist* was being lifted up to its place above the chapel, a white dove which had wandered into the cathedral suddenly dashed against the painting, leaving the mark of its wings across the face of the executioner. The Grand Master, who was standing beside me, asked me whether I would like the painting to be let down. I said: "It is a good omen. I shall not touch the painting again." He smiled, turned to the Archbishop, and said: "The dove has blessed the painting."

As a Knight of Grace I was henceforth under the protection of the Grand Master, and outside the papal states I could travel where I pleased and be received everywhere with honor. I had wealth and honor in abundance. Another slave was given to me — a boy called Mahmud, dark-skinned and beautiful, who soon showed some talent for painting. He was younger than Achmed and spoke Italian spasmodically, often breaking into Turkish and looking at me with a puzzled expression because I could not understand him. He spent his time sitting cross-legged on the floor, rising swiftly whenever I wanted some service from him.

And always there was this fever of painting. I painted a *St. Jerome Gazing at a Skull*, giving to the saint the features of Alof de Wignacourt. I painted Achmed and Mahmud separately and to-gether. When Blanche Varèse gave birth to another son, I painted him in his cradle. But all these were minor works: I dreamed of vast canvases like *The Beheading of John the Baptist.* I told myself that I was now strong enough to paint a Crucifixion, larger than life and fit to stand above the high altar of the cathedral.

The Grand Master begged me to paint another portrait of his grandson Leonardo, to be sent as a present to relatives in Picardy. At first I refused, saying that I had too many other works to at-tend to. The truth was that I had no great liking for the boy, whose smile when he greeted me was faintly amused, as though he wanted to suggest that he knew all my secrets and would not re-veal them. He had the disdainful air of the true aristocrat, remote and inaccessible. I discussed the matter with Leonello Spada.

"You should paint him," he said. "People are envious of you, and they ask one another how you have reached so high so quickly. You have more enemies than you think."

"How can I have enemies when I see no one except the people who sit for me?"

"That is why you have enemies," Leonello Spada replied. "Do whatever the Grand Master requires, for he alone can protect you from your enemies."

It never occurred to me that I had enemies among the knights. I had been on the island for only a few months, and I had scarcely spoken to anyone except a few old monsignors, the Grand Master, and my slaves. I had made many enemies in Rome, but it never occurred to me that I had made any enemies in Malta. Neverthe-less I agreed with Leonello Spada when he said I should work al-ways under the protection of the Grand Master.

Accordingly I agreed to paint the boy Leonardo. One evening toward the end of September I began to paint him in the darkened room by the light of a single lamp which caught his face and left the rest of him in shadow. He wore the uniform of a Knight of Justice, the highest order of the Knights of St. John Hospitaler, with a gold chain round his neck. The eight-pointed Maltese cross was outlined on his left breast. Such was the painting, which was already formed in my mind. A face, the insignia of rank, the shadowy outline of his young body, nothing more.

At the first sitting Leonardo kept the pose well, a faint smile playing on the corners of his lips. It was hot in the enclosed room, and from time to time Mahmud or Achmed would dab the sweat gathering on his face. I let him talk as long as he held the pose, and he talked charmingly in a mixture of Italian and French, repeating some of the things his grandfather had said about my work. He asked whether he might learn painting from me, and I promised at the very least to give him paint and canvases.

At the second sitting, which took place two days later, he seemed nervous and I thought I detected a nervous smile on the corners of his lips. He was unusually pale, and I suggested it might be better if we postponed the sitting.

"Then you are afraid to go on?" he said sharply.

"No, I am not afraid, Leonardo," I said. "You are pale, and I think you are feverish."

I put my hand on his forehead, but there was no fever. He snatched my hand away.

"How dare you touch me?" he exclaimed. "I am the son of the Grand Master!"

I explained patiently that he was not the son but the grandson of the Grand Master, and as a Knight of Justice he had taken the oath to deal kindly and gently to all those of lesser rank. He seemed to acquiesce to my arguments, regained his composure, and continued to pose with a brooding expression.

Half an hour later he complained of being ill, began to cry, and suddenly began screaming at the top of his voice. Mahmud rushed forward and clapped a hand over his mouth, and a moment later Achmed carried him to the bed which lay in the shadows of the room. The boy was struggling ferociously, and from time to time there would be more screams. Soon the guards rushed in. Leonardo was still screaming and writhing on the pallet bed, and he soon succeeded in ripping off the black mantle. He wore nothing under the mantle.

Within less than five minutes the boy's father, Jérôme Varèse, the Procurator of the Treasury of the Order of St. John Hospitaler, a fiery man with an orange beard, swept into the room. The boy lay white and naked on the bed, still screaming.

"What has happened to you, my son?" Jérôme Varèse said.

In a calm voice, pointing his finger at me, the boy said: "He tried to rape me." Then he screamed again.

Jérôme Varèse turned to one of the guards and said: "Take him to the prison of Sant' Angelo."

I remember nothing of the journey to the prison of Sant' Angelo, for the guard had clubbed me over the head.

The Prison of Sant' Angelo

IT was a large cell, as I discovered the next morning when I awoke with my head throbbing and the smell of caked blood in my nostrils — a cell which could hold perhaps fifty people standing upright, wide enough for a man to pace up and down in, and very high, with low barred windows twelve feet above the level of the floor, and the ceiling darkened by smoke, so that I guessed that this was once the seneschal's apartment. The walls were roughhewn, and here and there were inscriptions in Turkish or Arabic scratched out with nails by the poor wretches captured by the Knights of Malta. There was a thin carpet of old straw on the floor, and in one corner a pallet bed where some rats had made their nest.

By this time I had been in enough prisons to know what they are made of. I knew myself well enough to know what poor resources I had against those towering walls of stone, and how little hope there was of being able to break through them. It was early in the morning when I awoke with a silvery mist blowing in from the sea, and when I touched the walls they were damp and left a rust-red stain on my hands, and through the barred window the mist flowed like the breath of a man on a cold morning; and I looked up at the flowing mist, and thought that if the mist could flow into the cell, then I could flow out of it, and it had better be soon, for the Grand Master, I knew, would punish me with more than a taste of his prisons.

As the light thickened in the cell, I began to make my preparations for leaving it. First, I felt myself all over to see whether any bones were broken, but found nothing worse than a few bruises. Then I counted my possessions: some paintbrushes in the inner lining of my doublet, twenty *scudi* and four gold coins given to me by the Grand Master, besides a rag cloth smeared with paint, and useless for anything except wiping paintbrushes. I wore the gold collar under my shirt, and reflected that it might serve as a bribe, being worth at least a thousand *scudi*. I found a small mirror — it was the one given me by Maddalena — and when I looked in it, I scarcely recognized myself. My beard was matted, my eyes were bloodshot, there was filth over my forehead, and most of my face was caked with dried blood. They had thrown me down face forward into the cell, and I must have spent the night with my face in the bloody straw.

As for my clothes, they too were bespattered with filth and blood, my doublet torn, my hose in shreds, one of my shoes broken across the heel and the other so clean and new that it might have been polished by my servant only a moment ago. The doublet had split open across the silver blazon of the Cross of St. John embroidered in heavy thread; and so I reminded myself that I was a Knight of the Order of St. John Hospitaler with the right to succor all pilgrims wherever they may be found and to be aided by my fellow knights in whatever extremity I found myself; but these were small comforts. It was growing lighter and the rats were beginning to awake and creep around their nests.

I had been in prisons before, but always there were powerful protectors like the Cardinal del Monte and Prince Marzio Colonna to open the bars or to pay a bribe against the offer of a painting. This time I recognized I had no protectors, for there was no one in the court of the Grand Master who would dare to oppose his wishes or who would not rejoice over my downfall. I could expect no help from Leonello Spada, and my slaves Achmed and Mahmud were powerless to assist me. The Grand Master had given them to me, and no doubt he had already taken them back. I thought: "I have only one weapon, and that is my gold collar. There are men who would risk their lives for so much gold."

About an hour after I awoke, the key grated in the lock, the door opened, and the jailer came in accompanied by two guards. The jailer was a small dark man, a Maltese, with a thick bristling beard and black eyebrows; he spoke neither French nor Italian; no doubt he spoke in the language of the islanders and perhaps this was the reason why he had been chosen, so that he would understand nothing that was said to him. As for the guards, they were as surly as the jailer, being small bearded men with the typical faces of Sicilians. One of them carried a bowl of steaming gruel, which he offered to me. I was supposed to take it from his hands and be grateful. Instead I shouted at them at the top of my lungs, hurled the bowl to the floor where it broke into a hundred pieces, and told them I expected at least a truckle bed and a change of linen and a meal decently served, for was I not a Knight of St. John? And I mingled curses with my demands, which they understood perfectly, though they pretended not to. With my face caked with blood, my doublet torn, and my whole body shaking, I must have seemed to them a madman. I told them I needed water to wash myself in, and clean towels, and one of my slaves to assist me, and my easel and paintbrushes and a new canvas; and when I

had finished telling them what I wanted, I repeated the long catalogue all over again, ordering them to leave me in peace until they
had brought all I demanded.

They stood there open-mouthed, and I knew I had some mastery over them, though I had no way of knowing how deeply I
had affected them. They exchanged glances. Once, when I was
more than usually threatening, shaking my fist in their faces, one
of the guards drew a thick-bladed knife from his belt, and for a
moment I thought I would suffer the fate of John the Baptist. I
saw myself being thrown to the ground, my head cut off with a
single stroke of a rusty blade, and no doubt the Grand Master
would be pleased to receive it on a silver salver. But the knife went
back to the belt, and from that moment I knew they had received
no instructions to kill me, whatever the provocation. On the contrary, they were eager to please me, they were afraid of me, and at
the same time, like all those who gain their bread by guarding prisoners, they wore their guilt on their faces. So I shouted all the
louder and threatened them more boldly, almost pushing them out
of my cell, and one of the guards said he would see what could be
done. Then I heard the key turn again in the lock and they were
whispering together as they walked away.

I was not hungry, and did not miss the gruel which had spilled
over the stone floor. This prison was still new to me. I told myself
I would explore it at my leisure until they brought me what I
demanded, and my future conduct would depend on what they
brought. And indeed, in less than half an hour, they returned with
clean towels, a bowl of water, another bowl of gruel, a clean shirt
and doublet, a chair and a small table. From what they had
brought me I knew they had consulted no one except themselves;
they had not dared to approach any higher authority. So, when
they had arranged the chair and the small table, placing the bowl
of water beside the bowl of gruel, and doing all this in silence, I

asked them why they had not brought me my easel and paint-brushes. I must have my slaves and all my possessions around me.

"You can count on it that you will lose your heads," I shouted at them, "unless you bring me my possessions. You know well enough that I am not an ordinary prisoner. And then, too," I added, for a brilliant idea had suddenly struck me, "I must have fresh straw, not this niggardly straw which has grown moldy with age. And where is the truckle bed I asked for?"

"There are no truckle beds here," one of the surly guards answered.

"Then get me my own bed," I commanded, "and be quick about it! Get someone to sweep out the old straw! Get me paper to write on, and ink! Get me my paints! Hurry!"

When they had gone, I wondered how long it had been since a Knight of St. John had been imprisoned in the fortress of Sant' Angelo. Probably not a single knight had ever been imprisoned; and this was to my advantage. The guards did not fear me; what they feared was the silver cross embroidered on my doublet, even though it was torn; and they were afraid, too, that I might be restored to my former eminence. They would do my bidding, as long as it did not conflict with the orders they had received from the governor of the prison. But what orders? It was my business to discover what those orders were.

In fact I was already engaged upon this occupation. By commanding them to serve me, I was attempting to discover what they knew and what they had been told. So far everything they brought me came from the prison stores. They had no need to tell anyone what they had done: they had merely performed these small services to placate me. But if my easel and paintbrushes appeared, or if my slaves came to me, or my own bed, or indeed anything from my own quarters, then it meant that they had gone beyond their instructions and had appealed to a higher authority.

I stripped off my bloodstained clothes, washed myself all over, and then put on the clean shirt and doublet. Then I ate the gruel, and then taking care to make no sound I took the chair and carried it just beneath the barred window, to see whether there might not be some way of escaping through it. But even with the help of the chair I needed three or four feet to reach the bars, which had all the appearance of being firmly anchored in the walls. Even then I was convinced that this small window was my only means of escape.

The truth was that I was well content with my examination of the cell. With the table, the chair and the two bowls, it was beginning to have the look of a room which has been lived in, familiar to me, and by its very familiarity I was in a better position to know how to break out of it. I would make use of what there was, and my own resources. In the end, however, everything depended upon help from outside: not so much the help of friends as the help from enemies unwittingly given.

About an hour passed when I suddenly realized they had already given me more help than I could reasonably expect. I was thunderstruck. I remember clapping my hands to my forehead and groaning over my own simplicity and stupidity. I had been sitting at the table, and it had never occurred to me until this moment that a table and chair constituted a ladder. A moment later I had placed the table below the window and mounted the chair on it. The table legs were strong. There was no danger of falling. I climbed on the chair and found I could almost reach the lowest of the bars. With another six inches I would be able to grasp it firmly. The discovery amused me, and I remember leaning against the wall and laughing quietly until the tears ran out of my eyes. Then I heard footsteps in the corridor outside my cell, and I hurriedly dismantled my improvised ladder.

Once more the key turned in the lock with a grating sound.

When the door opened, I was the picture of innocence, sitting in the middle of the cell, leaning my elbows on the table, my cheeks cupped in my hands. The jailer and the two guards came in, followed by two old men carrying bales of fresh straw which gave off such a rich and intoxicating smell that I could scarcely believe I was in prison. Everything about the straw pleased me. It was a bright creamy yellow, it rustled, and was strong and supple, being this year's crop. One bale of straw was thrown down in a corner, to form a bed, while the other bale was broken and scattered over the floor. While all this was going on, I deliberately concealed my pleasure. I pretended that this was the least service they could render me, and far more was demanded of them than the mere gift of straw.

"Now hurry," I said. "Get my easel and paints, and send my slaves to me, and bring me paper and ink at once! Remove these soiled clothes and have them cleaned! Be quick about it!"

They took the clothes, and one of the guards muttered that he was busying himself with my commands: from his tone I realized that they had not yet approached the prison governor. By luck or good fortune I remembered the name of the prison governor. It was Giovanni Duvilliers. He was a Frenchman from Provence, who had been chosen for the task because he was small, powerfully built, and hard-faced, with no more imagination than a sparrow, and therefore he was perfectly suited to be a prison governor.

"And tell Giovanni Duvilliers that I have to see him on a matter of the greatest urgency."

I said these words as they were leaving. They looked stunned and frightened. Either they had not expected me to mention the dreaded name or they were disturbed by the way I spoke, as though he was someone familiar to me. Tongue-tied, they stood there watching me.

"How can we tell him to come here?" the surly guard said. "We are only the guards."

I had no patience with these fawning ruffians. There was only one way to impose upon these creatures.

"You tell him," I said, "as you would tell anyone else. You go up to him, you bow low, you salute him, you utter his name, and then you take a deep breath and say that Michelangelo Merisi da Caravaggio needs to see him on a matter of the greatest urgency — and by God, if you don't tell him, I'll see that you are made into sausage meat!"

The words must have had some effect, for the guard turned pale, muttered something under his breath and crossed himself, as a man does when he is charged with an important mission. Then they were gone and I heard them whispering as they went down the corridor.

I spent the next hour in a state of elation. They had already presented me with my means of escape — the straw. Already, too, by their manner of answering my questions, they had shown they were afraid of me and would obey my wishes. Clearly the Grand Master had made no decision about my fate. He had forgotten about my existence, or more likely he was engaged upon more pressing affairs and would deal with me at his leisure when for some reason he was reminded that I was still in prison, or when for some reason he needed me or remembered my paintings, for one does not forget my paintings easily.

All these thoughts raced through my brain while I waited jubilantly in my cell for the moment when I would escape or be admitted once more into the Grand Master's good graces; and already my hands were busy weaving the straw into a rope. With the rope, once I had broken through the bars, I would let myself down onto the jagged rocks which, I knew, surrounded the Fortress of Sant' Angelo. Then it would be no difficult matter to swim out to sea and find a friendly fishing boat which would take me to Sicily. The prospect of escape pleased me more than the thought of returning to the service of the Grand Master, and I began to plan my escape for that night, finding some satisfaction in the thought of being a prisoner for scarcely more than twenty-four hours.

I calculated that the rope would have to be at least twenty-four feet long to reach the rocks below, and I spent the rest of the afternoon weaving the straw into rope, taking care that if anyone should enter I would seem to be resting on the straw, as though sleeping. And as the rope grew longer, I concealed it under the remaining straw. What troubled me was that all the straw in the room was in danger of becoming a rope, and there would be no way to hide it.

Sometimes it would occur to me that if I did nothing, if I simply remained quiet, there would come a time when my honor would be vindicated. Leonardo's hysteria would end, the Grand Master and the Procurator of the Treasury would come to my cell and ask my forgiveness, and once more I would be the court painter of the Most Illustrious, Most Reverend, Devout, Sincere, Noble and Pleasant Alof de Wignacourt, Prince of the Empire.

In this mood, while weaving the straw, I would paint in my imagination the great Crucifixion over the altar of the Cathedral, a canvas larger than any I had yet attempted. Since Malta is an island, and the cathedral belongs to the Order of St. John Hospitaler, I would paint the crucifix rising from the waves, and clearly visible at the bottom there would be the galleons of the Grand Master attacking the infidels at Mahometa in Barbary. The Crucifixion would be lit by the light of a storm at sea, and I promised myself that I would spend the winter studying the storm light on naked flesh. Achmed would be my model, and the sea coast of Malta would be my study.

So I dreamed, and I might have gone on dreaming indefinitely about the painting if I had not heard footsteps in the corridor outside. I had time to conceal the rope before the door opened and two guards entered with drawn swords. Because it was growing dark, both guards also carried lanterns.

As soon as I saw them, it occurred to me that they had come to lead me away for trial, for I could not imagine that I, a Knight of Grace, would be punished without trial. But in fact they had come to guard Jérôme Varèse, the Procurator of the Treasury, who appeared a few moments later, sweeping into the cell like a whirlwind. He stood on the other side of the table, a ghostly figure in the light of the swaying, jerking lamps.

"I have come to hear your confession," he shouted, and all the time I was thinking how to paint him in his anger, the gold wires of his beard, the blue caverns of his eyes.

"You know as well as I that there will be no confession," I answered. "The boy lied. You know that as well as I do."

"The boy told the truth," he roared at me. "My son had no reason to lie. Admit that you have slept with boys, with Achmed and Mahmud, who were given to you by the Grand Master in their innocence and purity."

I laughed aloud.

"Then you do not know Turkish boys! One does with a Turkish slave what one pleases, and God knows they do not come in purity and innocence!"

He said grimly: "You shall not see them again," and I wondered, and still wonder, whether they had been put to death as accomplices of my crime.

Then, sitting in the chair, he asked me how many times I had been arrested in Rome for sodomy or buggery or unnatural vices, and I answered that I had been arrested by a constable when a tile fell from the roof, and once I was arrested for carrying a sword, and at another time I was arrested for throwing a dish of artichokes at a waiter, but these were all small matters, and I had resided at the Palazzo Madama under the protection of Cardinal del Monte, who would surely have withdrawn his protection if I had ever committed a serious crime.

But as I professed my innocence, Jérôme Varèse leaned forward across the table, his eye gleaming with the excitement which comes from possessing a card up his sleeve.

"You have been arrested for murder?" he said at last, and there was a note of triumph in his voice.

"I have killed a man, but I have not been arrested. I told the Grand Master all about the affair, and I held nothing back. He knows all about me, and he must know I committed no sin upon your son."

There was a long silence. The Procurator of the Treasury was a heavily built man who consciously adopted the habits of the Grand Master, sitting very straight in his chair, permitting scarcely any expression to appear on his hard features. He wanted at all costs to give an impression of iron self-control, but emotions of hate, despair, pity and revulsion would break through his composure. His lower lip trembled, his wide flaring nostrils expanded as he found difficulty in breathing in this humid cell, and sometimes his hands made jerking movements on the table. He was gazing at me, looking deep in my eyes, and what he saw there gave him no comfort.

At last I said bitterly: "Why do you make an enemy of a friend? I can accomplish for Malta more than any knight has accomplished. Do you suppose it is reasonable that I should rape the grandson of my protector, the man I honor most in the world?"

"Then you are saying that it never happened?"

"I am saying that it is beyond belief — that no one in his senses would believe such an accusation — that you know very well that it never happened."

"Then you say my son is a liar?"

"No, that he was ill, and did not know what he was saying."

I thought he would be reasonable, but I had misjudged him. In his heart of hearts he no longer believed that I had committed the crime.

Suddenly he rose and said: "Then there is no hope for you!"

Once more the red-hot flush of anger cut across his cheeks, and for a moment I thought he would strike me.

"Why don't you kill me now," I said, "since you will never bring yourself to believe that I am innocent."

Some words touched his lips, but he never spoke them. He gave me a piercing glance full of ungovernable hate, then made a sign to the guards to unbolt the door. In a few moments I heard his footsteps dying away along the corridor.

It was dark in the cell, the choking darkness of a hell pit. I could feel danger welling round me as though it were palpable. What I feared most was that I would be strangled in my cell, for I had no weapons except a chair, a table, and a coil of rope. So I resolved to escape before dawn.

When I grew calmer, I realized that there was still much to be done. I did not know yet whether I could break the bars. Once out of my cell, there was still the problem of finding a fishing boat. Perhaps I would be able to make my way along the rocks and reach the center of the town, and go into hiding. For a brief moment it amused me to think of escaping and then marching up the steps of the palace and presenting myself to the Grand Master. Meanwhile I was still weaving the straw into rope.

An hour after the Procurator of the Treasury left me, the

guards came again. This time they brought food on a tray: there were slices of beef, lentils, a bowl of milk, bread, and an apple. They also left me a small earthenware lamp, the flame burning low. I drank the milk as soon as the guards were gone, for I was overcome by thirst, and I was about to push the bowl away when I saw that somone had written in blue ink in the hollow of the bowl: "A boat is waiting for you. Hurry." The words in blue ink were in the handwriting of Leonello Spada.

In the apple I found a razor-sharp blade, and in the bread there was a file which would enable me to cut through the bars. I examined the meat and the lentils carefully, but they concealed no weapons.

In the knowledge that a boat was already waiting for me outside the prison of Sant' Angelo, I decided to leave that very night. For the next two hours I wove the straw so rapidly that my fingers bled. I needed to preserve the lamp, and because there was little oil in it, I held the wick very low so that there was only a small blue bud of flame. Long before midnight I had twenty-four feet of hard rope.

With the help of the chair and the table, and by using the coiled rope to give me the extra three or four feet needed to reach the bars, the rope resting on the chair and serving as a cushion, I was soon able to examine the bars. There were four of them. One was loose, and gave way readily, but the two bars in the center had to be cut through with the file and this took by my reckoning more than two hours of exhausting and silent labor. At last, tying the rope firmly to the fourth bar, I squeezed my way out of the window and let myself down the wall. No more than thirty-three hours had passed since I was thrown bloody and unconscious into the cell.

As Leonello Spada had promised, a boat was waiting for me

offshore. I swam to it, a friendly Maltese fisherman hauled me on board, and soon we had cleared the channel and were sailing into the open sea.

Long before dawn Malta had disappeared from sight.

Wandering

THE fisherman was a man of about fifty, with a face the color of an ancient oak tree. He spoke only in Maltese, and therefore we communicated by signs. For most of the day he sat crooning beside the tiller, from time to time pulling on the ropes of the sail. He gave the impression of a man who spoke rarely and saw no reason to move his body unless compelled by overwhelming force, and as I remember him he remained all that day and all the following night in the same position. When he crooned, he reminded me of Achmed, and indeed there is much similarity between the crooning of the Maltese and of the Turks.

Malta is only eighty miles from the southern coast of Sicily, and we could expect to reach the mainland in about twenty hours with a following wind. In fact, we reached Cape Pessaro at dawn the next day and by the late afternoon we were lying at anchor off Syracuse. When it grew dark I thanked the fisherman, gave him as a reward the four or five gold coins I found in my pockets — for he refused the gold collar, making signs which indicated that he had already been well paid for his endeavors — and went ashore. In my possession there was a razor-sharp blade, a file, a gold collar worth a fortune, and some twenty *scudi.*

I regarded Sicily as a third world to conquer, for had I not conquered Rome and then Malta? I had come to Rome and Malta penniless, and in despair. I came to Syracuse with wealth and in high spirits. So I spent the night wandering through the streets of the port, and in the morning I slept in a lemon grove.

By the afternoon, when I woke up, I was hungry and made my way to the nearest church, which happened to be the Church of St. Lucy, outside the walls. I found the priest, Father Piero Gentile, in the sacristy, and he resembled his name, being old and gray and very gentle. I asked him to hear my confession, and at the end he said: "God be praised, my son, that you escaped from Malta unharmed. Truly God has preserved you, and that He should have sent you here is a mark of His special knowledge of all that happens in the world below. For only God knows that I have spent half my life seeking a painter." Then he went on to say that he had hoped before he died to see a painting of the martyred St. Lucy hanging above the high altar of his church. The senate of Messina had long ago promised him the money for the painting, but no suitable artist had appeared. As it happened, he had been on a visit to Rome when my painting *The Death of the Virgin* was being shown before it entered the collection of the Duke of Mantua. "I wept when I saw the painting," Father Gentile said, "and when I heard that you had killed a man and were living in hiding, then I wept again."

"And now that I am here, will you weep for me?" I asked, for many people have suffered at my hands.

"No, my son, I shall rejoice because God has given you to me."

These were not fit words to be spoken in a confessional by a priest to a murderer, and so we soon moved to his house adjoining the church. There in a courtyard, among the walnut trees, he spoke very gravely about St. Lucy, who had been martyred only a few yards away. He spoke of the inscription which had been found on the stone covering her bones, and of the miraculous gifts showered on her worshipers. She had suffered martyrdom in the reign of Diocletian. Summoned to appear before the prefect of Syracuse, she refused to obey. They found her kneeling in adoration before a crucifix, and when they went to lift her up and drag her to the judgment seat, they found she was immovable like a heavy stone anchored to the earth. They poured boiling oil and flaming pitch on her, but the oil rolled off her and the pitch could not ignite her. "But God could not protect her forever," Father Gentile said, "and so it happened that one day when she was sleeping the Roman soldiers broke into her room, tore out her eyes, and stabbed her in the heart. That same night the Christians buried her secretly, and from that day to this there has been a succession of miracles in Syracuse."

He spoke as though he had seen it happen with his own eyes, as an old man will remember something that happened in his youth. His voice fell to a whisper when he spoke of the burial of St. Lucy in the silence of the night, and for some reason it was evidently this scene which he remembered most vividly. I saw her lying there, blinded, dead, while a blinding light came from her. Almost at once I had formed the composition of the painting: the frail and shining Lucy, the two huge gravediggers arching over her, and in the background the mourners watching and waiting, while a bishop with the curling beard of Father Gentile blesses her. It was a composition not unlike *The Beheading of John the Baptist*, but more crowded, more jagged, more impatient of mortality. I would have the common people of Syracuse bending over her, dazzled by the brightness of her face.

I related all this to Father Gentile, saying that I would paint her in such a blinding light that everyone would recognize her sanctity, and I would see to it that the whole church would be flooded by this light. I would paint the burial of St. Lucy around the text: "God could not preserve her forever."

"This is not a text of Holy Writ, my son," he said. "It is only my awkward way of explaining what cannot be explained. God protected her from the boiling oil and the flaming pitch, but He could not protect her from the swords of the soldiers. I can no more explain this than explain how a man is born into the world —"

"Nevertheless I shall paint it around those words," I said, and already I had the strange feeling, which visited me very often when I was planning a painting, that it was already finished, already hanging in its chosen place.

We sat in the courtyard until nightfall, and the wind came in from the sea. Now at last I was at peace with myself, the long years of turmoil over. I told myself I would settle in Syracuse and make my peace with the world, far from the Roman and the Maltese courts. In Malta they told me that every year the Grand Master had to send the Emperor a gift of a golden falcon as tribute, and this falcon was the badge of his servitude. Well, I would be the servant of no one. I would paint only what I wanted to paint, here among the lemon groves on the edge of the sea.

"So you will do me the honor of staying with me," Father Gentile said, "at least until you have finished the painting?"

"With pleasure, and as long as you wish," I replied, and then we went into the house.

He talked agreeably during supper, and I was about to go to bed when he took my arm and said: "Are you in danger from the Knights of St. John?"

"They are well rid of me," I laughed.

"You should take care," he said. "I have heard that they are

[306]

unforgiving. They have their agents everywhere in Sicily. It would be better, Michelangelo, if you did not advertise your presence in Syracuse."

I paid little attention to Father Gentile's words. My task was painting, and it was my habit to waste as little energy as possible on other affairs. I would paint *The Burial of St. Lucy*, because God had pointed the way, and as for my private affairs they were of no more consequence than the buzzing of flies.

The next day was a Sunday, and I was up early. The light in Malta is blue and gold, but that of Syracuse is blue and silver and white. I walked down by the sea and watched the fishing boats and bathed my face in Arethusa's pool of sweet water, which lies only a few yards away from the salt sea, and visited the cathedral, where the white columns of an ancient temple to Jupiter support the Christian roof, and in the marketplace the doves fluttered, and the gaily painted carts were bringing the worshipers to Mass. Then, from the darkness of the cathedral, I hurried across the town to the church of St. Lucy.

During the Mass I watched Father Gentile's parishioners and selected my models. They were farmers, lemon growers, fishermen, dark-eyed like the Maltese sailor who brought me to Sicily, burned brown by the sun. I chose a dozen, and could have chosen a dozen more. For St. Lucy I chose the daughter of a washerwoman, and for my servant I chose an altar boy called Anselmo di Guardi, who was pleasant and well mannered and spoke good Italian, for he had spent his childhood in Rome.

Although *The Burial of St. Lucy* was a somber and tragic painting, I painted it joyfully. What pleased me most of all was the vigor of those farmers with their heavy brooding faces, and how easily they assumed the postures I desired. I like to paint with all my models about me, and since there was no large room available, I painted in the church below the high altar, with St. Lucy lying on the stone floor, the mourners and the gravediggers gathered around her. So every evening they would come to the church, and Father Gentile would offer prayers, and then I would paint late into the night.

"You keep them from their sleep," Father Gentile rebuked me gently. "Well, there's no harm done. Our Sicilians sleep too soundly —"

No one complained because he was being kept awake half the night. In their grave, calm way these Sicilians shared the father's love for St. Lucy, and they would have suffered more than sleeplessness if it would have helped the painting. They all hoped the painting would be ready in time for the feast of St. Lucy in December, and for my part I had no doubt that I would be able to finish it in three or four weeks. For some reason I found myself working hurriedly. I was working against time, but I could not have told myself why I was in such a hurry. One day at the beginning of November, when the painting was already nearly completed, I was sipping wine with Father Gentile in his garden when Anselmo di Guardi came hurrying up. He looked pale and dazed, and flung himself down beside Father Gentile.

"What has happened, my son?"

"It is beyond belief," Anselmo di Guardi said, and all the time he was gazing straight at me. "It is beyond belief that they should do or say such things."

I thought he was out of his mind.

"What is it, my son?"

"There is a galleon belonging to the Knights of Malta in the harbor. They are telling anyone who cares to listen that Michelangelo Merisi is a thief and a murderer and they are offering a thousand *scudi* as a reward to anyone who will surrender him to the Knights."

Father Gentile sprang up from the table. Soon the bells of the church of St. Lucy were ringing, and one by one and in small groups the parishioners came to the church from the fields. From the altar he addressed them, saying they must arm themselves to protect the painting, which God had given them. Guards were posted at the doors, while my models assumed their familiar positions. For the remainder of the afternoon and well into the evening I continued to paint, never knowing when the Knights would batter down the church doors. I worked as I had never worked before, and long before midnight the painting was completed. Then, in my presence, the painting was attached to ropes and hung above the altar.

"Give thanks to God who has given us this painting," Father Gentile said, and then the whole congregation sang psalms.

They were still singing when I slipped out into the night.

Father Gentile had given me a letter to a Genoese shipowner in Messina. He thought that if I could reach Messina in safety, then I would be sure of a ship to Genoa, and it was unlikely that the Knights would be able to stop me. The name of the shipowner was Giovanni Battista de Lazzari. He was a deeply religious man, and his great wealth was always at the service of the church.

All that week, and for many weeks, I wandered across Sicily. I avoided the towns, and slept in the open or in small villages in the mountains. Above Catania I found myself on the slopes of Mount Etna, peering at rivers of red lava and sheets of snow, walking barefoot on the heights. It was strange to be there, in that thin air, watching the blood-red lava flowing out of the volcanic wound, feeling the earth shaking beneath my feet. On moonless nights, when the stars were covered by clouds, I walked by the light of the red glow coming from the earth's fires. I had heard of the lava flow, but did not know it moved steadily and slowly, like a red snake slithering along the ground, or that one could bend over it and feel its heat against one's cheeks. And the shuddering earth stretched tight like a drum and one's footsteps echoing. I did not know one could walk on the rim of Hell without the necessity of dying, or that in my lifetime I would smell the sulphur stench of Hell.

I spent perhaps three days on the mountain, and sometimes I would find myself gazing at Catania below and watching the ships sailing out to sea. They were cloudy days, or perhaps I was wandering through the cloud which hovers permanently over Etna, for I saw only brief glimpses of the city and the sea. I was carrying little: my paints, a few rolled-up canvases, some food, and a water bottle given to me by the girl who posed for St. Lucy in Syracuse, saying she had dropped a few tears in it in order to sweeten my drinking, and God knows what she meant by this, for her tears were salty. She had filled the bottle with sweet water from the Pool of Arethusa, and on the first hot day I gulped down all her treasure of tears and sweet water. She haunted me during my wanderings.

Within a day, in Syracuse, I had found a safe anchorage. Now, though I had money in my belt, I was a footloose wanderer with no anchorage in sight until I came to Messina, for there are no great cities between Catania and the north of the island. I thought sometimes of settling down in some remote mountain village, but I knew I would be a stranger there; for who would buy me my paints and canvases? who would pay for my paintings? and what use is it to paint a picture for those poor farmers who know nothing of the art? I knew I belonged to the towns, and if God was kind I could hide as well in the towns as in the open countryside.

In all these mountain villages there is a priest, usually an old man with rheumy eyes who has forgotten his Latin and speaks only in harsh Sicilian; on Sundays he will mumble the Mass, and no one will know what language he is speaking. These priests saved my life, for I would tell them that I was a painter from Syracuse making my way to Rome, having been summoned by Cardinal del Monte, and though they scarcely knew what I was saying, and sometimes looked at me with incomprehension and indifference, they recognized that I was one of those wanderers who must be fed along the way. I never knew so much kindness as I received from these poor Sicilian priests. They would tell me the name of the priest in the next village, and whether he had a spare bed, and what humor he was in, and how much I could expect from him; and they would write letters for me, which served as passports. I never gave them my real name, and they knew me as Marcantonio degli Angeli.

Ever since leaving Malta I had developed the habits of conspiracy, and they did not fail me now that I became a wanderer in Sicily. I would never enter a village until nightfall, and I always slipped out of the priest's lodging before cockcrow. If it happened that the priest had been to Rome and could understand me, I took care never to tell the truth about myself, so that there came a time when I scarcely knew who I was, whether I was Michelangelo or Marcantonio or any one of the other names I gave myself. All the time I was deliberately delaying my entry into Messina. I was afraid of cities, especially big cities. I had felt the breath of the Knights of Malta, and I knew I would be in danger until I reached the safety of Rome.

One night in the middle of December I slipped into Messina and made my way to the house of the Genoese shipowner, praying that he would put me on board one of his ships that very night. I was weary of wandering from one abandoned village to another. I was afraid the shipowner might be away or that the Knights would find me even before I reached his house. But there were lights glowing in the windows, and I had scarcely reached the door when he rushed out to greet me.

He was a short, solid, well-built man with a square-cut red

beard, and the moment he caught sight of me he said: "Praise be to God you have come at last! We have waited for you all these weeks! Where have you been?"

I said I had been wandering in the mountains. He threw his arm round my shoulder.

"You should have come straight to me! Father Gentile has been here! He has told me all about you! You are under my protection! In my house no harm can ever touch you!"

Food was spread before me; servants waited on me; I was given new clothes, and one wing of the house was set aside for my use. Dazzled by so much luxury, I asked him why he should concern himself with my welfare to such an extent, since all I needed was a hole to hide in.

"God knows," he said, "it is not out of charity. It is because you are *valentuomo* and a painter blessed by God. If you had heard what Father Gentile has to say about your painting, you would blush with shame, for not even an angel could endure such praise."

He went on to declare that he possessed more ships than the Grand Master, and that if any ships belonging to the Knights put in at Messina, he would send boarding parties on them if they did not sail away with the first tide. He talked in short, clipped sentences with a heavy Genoese accent, and he seemed to be amused at the thought that anyone should take the Knights seriously.

"In Malta, no doubt, they regard themselves as the terror of the Turks, the champions of Christ against the infidels, but all the time they are trading with Barbary. You can buy a knight as readily as you can buy a dispensation from the Pope. It is absurd to be afraid of them."

During the following week he asked me whether I would paint for him a *Resurrection of Lazarus*, for it pleased him to believe that the de Lazzari family was in some way connected with Laza-

rus and he intended to give the painting to the Church of the Cro-
ciferi; and indeed he had long ago promised the gift of a painting,
but like Father Gentile he had failed to find a painter. I answered
that I wanted nothing better, and soon set to work on an immense
canvas. I found my models among the servants of his household. I
painted a towering and commanding Christ on the left of the canvas, and on the right Mary and Martha supporting the head of
Lazarus, who has emerged from the grave naked and faint with
the agony of waking into life. Around Christ's head a confusion of
heads: some demanding, some perplexed, some glancing fearfully
and timidly at Lazarus, whose body is touched with silver and
whose arm is outflung in a gesture of renunciation, which is also a
gesture of greeting to the Christ whose presence he dimly recog-
nizes. There was also a portrait of my benefactor among those in
the foreground, for I loved the man and could not resist painting
him with his small green eyes and red beard. He was pleased with
the painting, and asked me to paint a Nativity, and this too I
painted, but more hurriedly and with less enthusiasm, because I
felt in greater danger as the spring and summer came on.

It was something that I could not account for — that growing
sense of danger as the days grew longer. I painted a portrait of
him, and portraits of his wife and three sons. Sometimes, too, in
the midst of painting portraits, I would find myself looking at a
bowl of flowers and feel an overmastering need to paint them, as I
had painted them in my youth. He asked why I painted flowers,
when he could give me great commissions, and I answered that
they were my protection.

"You don't need protection! I am your protector, and no one
will ever dare to lay a finger on you."

I said I would not feel safe until I reached Rome, and I dared
not go to Rome because I had not received an amnesty from the
Pope. He shook his head, and added two men to my bodyguard.

On that same day, while I was walking through the streets of Messina with a bodyguard on each side of me and another in front of me, someone rushed out of the crowd and struck me with a dagger. Happily I was wearing the gold collar given to me by the Grand Master under my shirt, and the dagger glanced off the collar. The man who had attacked me disappeared into the crowd.

When I returned to the shipowner's house he affected not to believe that I had been assaulted, until I showed him the torn doublet. Then he grew serious, interrogated the bodyguard, and at last asked me where I would like to go, for his ships were at my disposal.

"To Naples," I answered, "for then I would be closer to Rome."

"Then you shall go to Naples," he said, "and I know the best place where you can stay. You can go to the oratory of the Holy Trinity and stay with Fra Bartolomeo, who was my confessor in the days when I thought God had intended me for the priesthood. He is a saint, and there is no greater safety than in the house of a saint."

The next day I sailed for Naples, and three days later I was received by Fra Bartolomeo and his servant Maddalena, and there I remained for many months waiting for the amnesty from the Pope.

Two days ago I decided I could bear my imprisonment no longer. I told myself that the Knights of St. John had surely forgotten my existence, and that if I took careful precautions I would survive a journey through the city. For more than seven months I had lived in seclusion, keeping to my own room, only rarely descending into the garden. I was well armed, and had never felt stronger or more sure of myself. I told Fra Bartolomeo of my intentions, saying that now at last I felt the fear lifting from me. He said that he too had the feeling that the danger was lifting, and he rejoiced with me that I had decided to venture abroad, and the news was especially welcome to him because he had heard that the amnesty would soon arrive.

"A new life is opening out before you, Michelangelo," he said. "You must prepare yourself for living again like an ordinary mortal. There is only one thing that I demand of you — you must let me ride with you, or at least within sight of you."

So it was arranged that he should ride some distance behind me, and that I should simply go to the center of the city and then make my way back to the oratory. It would be a journey of perhaps two hours.

It was one of those days when the sun seems to ride low in the sky, and all of Naples was scorching in the heat. Yet a wind was blowing, and there was a feeling of great freshness in the air. I rode at a quick canter on a small gray, which Fra Bartolomeo had borrowed from one of his parishioners, while he rode behind me on his own donkey. There was a crowd outside the Osteria del Ceriglio, where I had once spent many pleasant days, and the gray was forced to go at a walking pace. Suddenly, out of nowhere, three men sprang at me with drawn daggers. One slashed at my face, another toppled me to the ground, and soon they were all about me with their clubs and daggers. The crowd was screaming, and I knew that people were coming to my rescue, but the harm was already done. My face was cut to ribbons, and I was blinded by my own blood. Somehow I made my way to the steps of a nearby church. I collapsed at the head of the steps. At last, when I was able to wipe the blood from my eyes, I watched the blood streaming from my face, falling down the church steps with a sound like the falling of rain.

Now that I am recovering my strength, Illustrissimo, I have begun to paint again, and having no other model I have been painting myself, using only the bluish mirror which Maddalena gave me when I first came here. In this mirror I seem to be another person altogether, unrecognizable. I call it my magic mirror, for everything that appears in the mirror is strangely distorted and elongated. The surface of the mirror is not smooth, but has little bubbles and blisters, and it amuses me to see myself deformed.

Not that I am in any way presentable; on the contrary, the devil himself would flee from me in horror. I have grown old suddenly, and there is white in my straggling beard and heavy wrinkles under my eyes. I have lost some teeth. The wound in my forehead heals slowly, and Fra Bartolomeo despairs of seeing me whole again. For myself, as a painter, there is some satisfaction to be derived from a wound. I find myself admiring its colors — the hard yellow crust, the enflamed rednesses, the strange colors of the juices which are exuded from it. And gazing at this gold and crimson and purple wound, I find myself once more tempted to bright colors.

You would not recognize me if I came to your court, and your servants would spit at me and make the sign of the cross in the hope of averting the evil eye. They would say I was a leper, or worse, and it would be beyond their comprehension that this broken face concealed a painter whose paintings hang in the Palazzo Madama, St. Peter's, and in the palaces of princes, and will hang there for everlasting. They would say: "Who is this man who comes with bloodstained face to disturb our peace?" Sometimes it seems to me that I came on earth to disturb the peace of others, by seeing more clearly than others have seen.

When I look at myself in the bluish mirror, I see a wound exuding poison, and it is not beyond belief that my wounds will never heal. It may be — and this is something that I must ponder carefully — that for the rest of my life I must wear a mask like a leper. Yet even if I were a leper, I would still paint joyfully. The crusts of my flesh are unhealed, and I am accustoming myself to being a wound.

Every night Maddalena goes to the garden and collects the salving herbs which she pounds in a mortar and mixes into a potion and then smears on my face every morning, all the time muttering prayers. She says the herbs are most powerful when the dew is on them, but I suspect that she goes at night so that no one will observe her at work. Fra Bartolomeo consults the books in his library, pausing at every reference to the healing of wounds. It is a subject, he says, which is rarely treated by theologians.

Sometimes, my lord, a great weariness overcomes me, and I find myself gazing at my dagger enviously. My fingers run along the blade, and I tell myself that death will come more quickly than the time it takes to draw a breath. There will be little suffering, for I know exactly where to place the blade. And then it occurs to me that Maddalena will climb the stairs in the morning, and it is beyond my power to inflict any harm on her. I live for the sake of Maddalena and in the hope of once more painting for Your Highness.

I ask myself why I should die just at the moment when I am the master of my craft. Now at long last I know how to guide my brush across the canvas. It is in my power to paint as no one has ever painted before, giving so much life to the creatures of my imagination that the air around my paintings will echo their voices. On vast canvases I shall paint the entire cycle of the life of Christ. Give me but a year in Rome, and I shall show you such things as you have never dreamed of.

I wrote these words five weeks ago, and now at last the wounds are beginning to heal. I have decided to leave Naples and make my way to Rome. With the help of Fra Bartolomeo I shall be carried onto a ship in the dead of night, just before it leaves the harbor. Fra Bartolomeo says that I should wait for a few more weeks, because an amnesty from the Pope is certainly on its way, but it is my belief that I cannot place him in jeopardy any longer. For nearly nine months he has lived in a state of siege, never knowing from one moment to the next when the Knights of St. John will batter down his door. Though he pretends to great strength of character, he has suffered terribly from my presence. His hands tremble when he holds a candle, and his eyes are red with sleeplessness. Sometimes he looks at me broodingly, as though he were saying: "I have been long in your service, Michelangelo, and shall I never be released from bondage?" But he never says these words, never hints at them. Yesterday he said: "Stay with me a few weeks longer, Michelangelo. If any harm should come to you after all we have gone through together, how shall I forgive myself?"

Last night, to please him, I composed a prayer which I painted for him on canvas. It reads: "Oh Lord God, look down on your unworthy and unwashed servant, who has served Thee with his art as well as he could, being sinful and miserable above the average. Look down upon me, I pray Thee, and conjure new strength in me, for truly I have only desired to serve Thee. Deliver me out of bondage and darkness into the true sunlight of Thy glory, and let me be free to wander in my beloved Rome for Thy son's sake, and remember Fra Bartolomeo and Maddalena all the days of their lives, and be merciful to me in the hour of my distress."

"It is a good prayer," Fra Bartolomeo said, "but you have forgotten something which is very important. You forgot to ask forgiveness for those who have been pursuing and hounding you. In your prayers you must always ask God to forgive them, and perhaps that is the first thing you should ask."

"So I shall," I said, and he gave me his blessing.

During these last days I have felt like a prisoner about to be released from a long term of imprisonment. I have collected my paintings together, paid my few debts, repaired my clothes, cleaned out the small attic in which I painted so many pictures, and for the last time gazed out at the small garden below. I have only to shut my eyes, and I see myself walking across the Piazza Navona and making my way up the stairway of the Palazzo Madama. All the arrangements for the journey to the harbor have been made, the ship's captain has been paid, and I have had my last meal with Maddalena and Fra Bartolomeo, who have protected me for so long.

Tonight I shall leave Naples and sail for Rome with the first tide.

The manuscript of Michelangelo Merisi da
Caravaggio ends here.

A Letter from the Viceroy of Naples

To the most illustrious and most reverend Lord *Francesco Maria del Monte, Cardinal and Governor of the Congregation of Rites, residing at the Palazzo Madama in Rome, from Don Pedro Fernandez de Castro, Conde de Lemos, Viceroy of Naples, residing in the Presidencio at Naples, Greetings:*

MY Lord, when you asked me to relate to you the circumstances surrounding the unhappy death of the painter Michelangelo da Caravaggio, I must confess that my first thoughts were to wonder why Your Lordship should be concerned with anything so inconsequential as the life of a mere painter. I therefore made it my business to inquire whether any of his paintings were to be seen in Naples, and having seen many paintings reputed to have been painted by his hand, some in our churches and others in private possession, and a few in the possession of Fra Bartolomeo of the oratory of the Holy Trinity — to the number of some twelve or fifteen paintings altogether, I must confess to being ashamed of my previous ignorance. For truly he was a painter of some worth.

According to my inquiries, he had been hiding in Naples for

many months, saying, as Fra Bartolomeo has told me, that he was in deadly fear of the agents of the Knights of Malta, who had sworn to kill him for some offense committed when he was a painter in the court of the Grand Master. He said he was thrown into the prison of Sant' Angelo, escaped, and sailed in a fishing boat to Syracuse, and so to Messina and Palermo, whence he came to Naples. Whether indeed he had any reason to fear the vengeance of the Knights of Malta is a matter still undetermined. What is known is that he came penniless and barefoot to the house of Fra Bartolomeo, and sought sanctuary, which was given to him. For my part I believe he was deranged, and his stories about the Knights of Malta were fictions.

What is certain is that quite recently he was robbed and atrociously manhandled by some blackguards in the Osteria del Ceriglio, which is a place of ill repute. A man who attends such places may expect to be attacked for his worldly goods. From a report written at the time by a constable who observed the assault, the robbers were all cutthroats from the dregs of Naples. One who was later arrested confessed that he attacked Michelangelo da Caravaggio only because he suspected that he was in possession of a purse full of gold.

I have been to some pains to establish whether he had made any friends or enemies in Naples, but Fra Bartolomeo assures me that he had neither friends nor enemies, for he never left the house except for that single visit to the Osteria del Ceriglio. He was by nature a recluse, content to work in a small upstairs room, no larger than a prison cell, which the good father had set aside for him.

He had no sooner recovered from his wounds when — and here once more I depend on the words of Fra Bartolomeo, who alone knew him well — he decided to journey to Rome, having learned that the Pope was of a mind to grant him an amnesty for some crime committed formerly in Rome. He was in a state of great excitement, and kept saying: "The time has come! The time has come!" Fra Bartolomeo attempted to reason with him, explaining that it would be altogether better to wait until the amnesty arrived before he set sail. But he could not be reasoned with. He said that the most illustrious and most reverend Cardinal del Monte would protect him, and that he could no longer paint for obscure and unknown persons in Naples. "I have now mastered my craft," he said, "and for such masters there can be no other place but Rome." He also said: "Rome is calling to me. The walls of the Roman churches are calling to me."

Accordingly he set out for Rome in a felucca, and we heard later that he quarreled violently with the shipmaster and everyone else in the ship, and seemed distraught and ill. When the felucca reached the port of Ostia he hid in the hold and refused to come out, saying the Knights of Malta were waiting for him on shore. The shipmaster therefore decided to humor him and permitted him to remain on board until the next port of call at Porto Ercole, which is under the Spanish dominion. The shipmaster asked him whether he saw any Knights of Malta on the shore, and he replied: "Your Excellency, there are no Knights of Malta in sight." He then disembarked, and his belongings were taken to the customhouse.

I must confess that although the officials attached to the customhouse at Porto Ercole are loyal servants of the Spanish King, they are not notable for their veneration for painters. Michelangelo da Caravaggio's appearance did not inspire them with confidence. He was ill dressed and abusive, and when asked his name, the particulars of his birth and upbringing, and all the other questions which are asked of foreigners entering a Spanish dominion, he answered rudely, saying that such questions should not be addressed to great painters. Since he did not resemble a great painter, and indeed behaved like a madman, he was then asked to demonstrate his skill by showing examples of his art. I must stress that the officials showed admirable patience and good humor, and behaved throughout their examination with forbearance. Unfortunately, when Michelangelo da Caravaggio suggested that they had only to look in his luggage to see that he was a master of his art, his luggage could not be found. Since he could not prove that he had any means of support, or was master of any craft, he was thrown into prison. It was observed that he behaved quietly, and spent most of the time in an attitude of prayer, kneeling on the bare ground.

On the second day it was decided to release him, for he now answered all inquiries in a civil manner, saying that he was sorry for all the trouble he had caused and he went up to the officials one by one demanding their pardon, urging them only to return his luggage. A search was immediately made for the luggage, but since it could not be found, it was assumed that it was still on the felucca, which had sailed in the direction of Genoa earlier that morning.

When this information was conveyed to him, he showed no emotion, but asked how long it was since the felucca left Porto Ercole. He was told that it had left only an hour before. He then ran out of the customhouse and made his way to the shore. The felucca could be seen on the horizon, and he therefore began to run along the shore, hoping in some way to attract the attention of the shipmaster or to come up with the felucca at the next port of call. It was a very hot day, and our officials made no effort to follow him, although they knew the dangers of the enterprise. They say they heard him shouting even when he was out of sight.

That night Michelangelo da Caravaggio came to a small village along the shore. The villagers have told my officials that his clothes hung threadbare, his feet were swollen, there was blood on his face, and he was unable to talk. He was put to bed with a malignant fever. Although the kindly villagers watched over him, there was nothing they could do for him. He died a few days later.

It was said that he carried with him a leather bag containing three gold *scudi*, but no trace of it was found.

On the following day it was learned that his luggage was not in the felucca, but reposed safely in the customhouse. It consisted of some clothes, a rapier, a short Sicilian dagger, a prayer book, a knife, a coil of rope, four paintings, and some sheets of paper sewn together in which he appears to have recounted some of the incidents of his wasted life. He also left a box containing some rags and some old paintbrushes. All these are now in my possession, and I have not yet decided how I shall dispose of them. The paintings would appear to be of some value.

I have attempted to describe this unfortunate affair in as much detail as possible in accordance with your request. I find I have little sympathy for the poor man, who evidently suffered from delusions and an exalted estimate of his own grandeur. Such delusions and exaltations are now more common among the lower orders, and it is necessary that they should be prevented. I feel that he brought these disasters upon himself. I feel, too, that he would have been well advised if he had spoken with more respect about those whom it has pleased God to place above him.

In particular I find in his writings references to Your Highness which are most objectionable. In the very first words he addresses you as "formerly my bedfellow," and these words, even if true, are wholly unpardonable. He speaks at length of Your Highness's magnanimity and he rejoices in the affection which you lavished on him. He describes on many occasions how you visited his cellar at the Palazzo Madama and consorted with thieves and prostitutes, his friends and sometime models. I assure Your Highness that the customs of the cardinals of the Spanish dominion are such that they would find these practices intolerable.

I can see nothing in the art or habits of this young painter, who died at the age of thirty-six, to warrant so great an affection on your part. I fear that you must have misunderstood him. Arrogant, insatiable in his avarice, feckless, given to violence, he was one of those useless creatures who are to be found more often in Rome than in Naples. He was nothing but a swashbuckler.

Across the first page of this letter from Don Pedro Fernandez de Castro, Viceroy of Naples, there was written in purple ink in the handwriting of Cardinal del Monte the word: Bestia (*Beast*).

The Paintings

IN his brief lifetime Caravaggio painted perhaps a hundred and twenty paintings, and of these rather less than sixty have survived, so that they are almost as rare as Vermeers and almost as precious.

The lion's share, amounting to some twenty paintings, may be seen in the churches and art galleries of Rome. Two galleries — the Borghese and the Pamphili-Doria — share ten paintings between them. The wanderer in search of Caravaggio's paintings will find three in the Uffizi in Florence, three in the Louvre, two in Milan, two in Naples, two in Messina, two in Malta, while Palermo, Syracuse, Montserrat, New York, Kansas City, London and Leningrad have one each. I have seen most of them, and it seems to me that the very greatest of all is *The Raising of Lazarus* in Messina, cracked, broken and faded, but still fearfully alive.

This portfolio can only hint at the splendor of the coloring of his early works and the luminous darkness, which flashes like Beethoven, in the works of his maturity. I have chosen the paintings described in the novel, and placed them in the order of development. Sometimes the exact dates are unknown, and I suspect that there are often no exact dates, because he may have taken three or four years to complete a painting.

Fifty years ago his paintings were scarcely known. His fuse burned slowly and exploded only in our own time. So he speaks to us as a contemporary, belonging to our age and the ages to come.

UNA MUSICA

1594

New York, Metropolitan Museum of Art

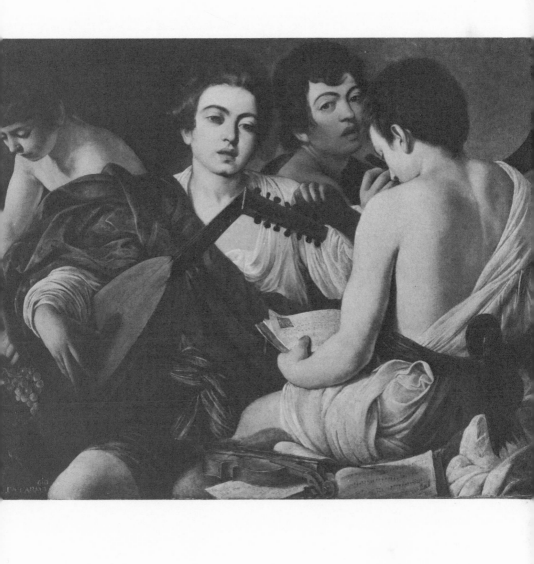

THE CALL OF ST. MATTHEW
1598-1601
Rome, San Luigi de'Francesi

THE DECOLLATION OF JOHN THE BAPTIST
1608
Valetta, Cathedral of St. John

PORTRAIT OF ALOF DE WIGNACOURT
1608
Paris, Musée de Louvre

THE RAISING OF LAZARUS
1609
Messina, Museo Nazionale

Manlius Public Library
Manlius, New York